EMER... DO...

In St Augustine's Hospital passions are about to ignite!

Medical Romance™

Six brand-new titles each month

...medical drama on the pulse

Available at most branches of WH Smith, Tesco, Martins, Borders, Eason, Sainsbury's, and all good paperback bookshops.

GEN/03/RTL6

EMERGENCY DOCTORS

We're proud to bring back this sensational trilogy by Medical Romance™ author

JOSIE METCALFE

FIRST THINGS FIRST

SECOND CHANCE

THIRD TIME LUCKY

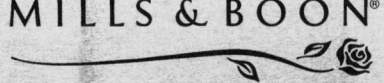

DID YOU PURCHASE THIS BOOK WITHOUT A COVER?
If you did, you should be aware it is **stolen property** as it was reported *unsold and destroyed* by a retailer. Neither the author nor the publisher has received any payment for this book.

All the characters in this book have no existence outside the imagination of the author, and have no relation whatsoever to anyone bearing the same name or names. They are not even distantly inspired by any individual known or unknown to the author, and all the incidents are pure invention.

All Rights Reserved including the right of reproduction in whole or in part in any form. This edition is published by arrangement with Harlequin Enterprises II B.V. The text of this publication or any part thereof may not be reproduced or transmitted in any form or by any means, electronic or mechanical, including photocopying, recording, storage in an information retrieval system, or otherwise, without the written permission of the publisher.

This book is sold subject to the condition that it shall not, by way of trade or otherwise, be lent, resold, hired out or otherwise circulated without the prior consent of the publisher in any form of binding or cover other than that in which it is published and without a similar condition including this condition being imposed on the subsequent purchaser.

MILLS & BOON and MILLS & BOON with the Rose Device are registered trademarks of the publisher.
Harlequin Mills & Boon Limited,
Eton House, 18-24 Paradise Road, Richmond, Surrey, TW9 1SR

EMERGENCY DOCTORS
© by Harlequin Enterprises II B.V., 2002

First Things First, Second Chance and *Third Time Lucky*
were first published in Great Britain by Harlequin Mills & Boon Limited
in separate, single volumes.

First Things First © Josie Metcalfe 1997
Second Chance © Josie Metcalfe 1997
Third Time Lucky © Josie Metcalfe 1998

ISBN 0 263 83160 4

05-0902

Printed and bound in Spain
by Litografia Rosés S.A., Barcelona

Josie Metcalfe now lives in Cornwall with her long suffering husband, four children and two horses; but as an army brat frequently on the move, books became the only things that came with her wherever she went. Now that she writes them herself she is making new friends, and hates saying goodbye at the end of a book – but there are always more characters in her head clamouring for attention until she can't wait to tell their stories.

Look out for Josie Metcalfe's brand-new linked duet, part of her popular
Denison Memorial Hospital **series.**
Coming soon, in Medical Romance™

MORE THAN CARING – October 2002
MORE THAN A GIFT – December 2002

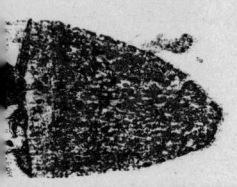

FIRST THINGS FIRST
by
Josie Metcalfe

CHAPTER ONE

HE SAT up in the pre-dawn chill and swung his legs over the side of the bed, bracing his elbows on his naked thighs. His shoulders slumped, his head dropping forward into his hands as his long fingers speared tiredly through the thick blond strands to massage the tension in his aching neck.

'So tired...' His deep voice was a husky rasp in the echoing darkness of the spartan room. 'So damn tired...'

Was he ever going to be able to sleep soundly again?

Would he ever be able to forget the events of that night, one year, eleven months and three weeks ago?

Forget...? Across the darkness of the room his eyes sought the pale shape, not needing to see the photograph clearly to know what it represented.

How could he forget when he had survived and she...*they* had died?

It was *that* guilt which wouldn't let him rest; which returned to torment him each time he closed his eyes and tried to lose himself in the oblivion of sleep.

In the meantime, all he could do was fill every waking hour with work and more work—anything to keep his brain occupied; anything to stop him dreading what would happen when he came home and tried to sleep.

'Well, *he's* certainly no Prince Charming!' somebody muttered into the uncomfortable silence after Nicholas Prince swept out of the room.

Polly knew she shouldn't but, in spite of her burning cheeks, she couldn't help herself from joining in the quiet gust of laughter which swept the scattering of people gathered in the small staffroom. At least it broke the tension which the irate consultant had left behind him.

Unfortunately, she thought as she turned to go back to work, such scenes had been happening more and more frequently over the last week. This latest episode had been the worst of the lot, and she wondered if it was time she spoke to someone about it.

It was a good sign that the rest of the staff could still crack a joke and laugh about the situation, but in the high-pressure world of St Augustine's Accident and Emergency Department it could be dangerous if one member of staff was endangering the working relationship of the team—especially such a senior member.

'Are you all right, Polly?' Hannah Nicholls demanded quietly. 'Old Nick's tongue can flay the skin off you at twenty paces.'

Polly had thought she'd been alone and had allowed her slender shoulders to droop, grateful for a few moments to regain her composure. Before Hannah had spoken she'd begun to check off the fresh stock needed to replenish the supplies they'd used in stabilising and patching up the first influx of accident victims on this rainy autumn Friday evening.

With a brief sigh she straightened determinedly as she turned to face her colleague with a smile of reassurance in her dark eyes.

'I'm fine, Hannah,' she said evenly and took the bull by the horns. 'Dr Prince had every right to criticise the state of readiness of the department and, in the absence of Sister MacDonald, it was my job to make sure that. . .'

'Rubbish!' Hannah interrupted loyally, the dark blue of her eyes almost spitting sparks as she leapt to Polly's defence. 'This place has been bedlam for the last hour. Oh, I grant you, there wasn't anything major, but it still wasn't reasonable for him to expect it to look like a showcase.'

'Except that the next batch of patients will expect the unit to be functioning at peak efficiency, and they'd be right,' Polly pointed out fairly, in spite of the fact that, inside, she was still burning with mortification.

'Even so, he had no right to take you to task in front of everyone like that,' Hannah complained, her short dark curls bouncing as she shook her head indignantly. 'He *knew* how busy you'd been with that elderly mugging victim going into shock.'

'It's all part of the job,' Polly returned calmly as she smoothed a stray wisp of her own shiny bob away from her eyes. She knew that if she so much as hinted that she agreed with Hannah it could only make a bad situation worse. The last thing the department needed in the existing uneasy atmosphere was for people to take sides in an unofficial war, no matter how much she'd like to tell Prince Charming what she thought of him. . .

'Well, *I* think you ought to tell him that you won't stand for it. . .' she began heatedly.

For the first time in a long time Polly actually blessed the interruption of the telephone as Hannah was forced to subside in mid-flow. She appreciated her friend's unstinting support, but just at the moment. . .

'A and E,' she said, and raised a hand to still Hannah in her tracks, then beckoned her back when she heard the hurried message. 'When can we expect them to arrive?' she demanded as she glanced down at the watch pinned to the front of her dark blue uniform, then pulled a face when the voice on the other end embarked on a lengthy explanation.

'Can you patch me through?' she interrupted. 'One of the paramedics could give me an update...' She covered the mouthpiece to speak rapidly to Hannah. 'Tell Dr Prince we've got another lot coming in across country. Multiple pile-up. ETA ten minutes. They're connecting me up with the emergency units so I can find out more details, but if you could let him know so he can decide whether to authorise a call-in for extra staff...'

Her attention was drawn back to the phone again, her hand automatically reaching for the pen in her top pocket as the information began pouring down the line. Out of the corner of her eye she saw the newly installed computer link chatter into activity as it began to display the vital signs of the first badly injured patient in transit.

'What have you got?' a husky baritone demanded abruptly from a point just behind her left ear. Polly glanced towards the familiar sound, and when she found his tall figure looming over her sidestepped to allow him to read her notes as she reached out to replace the phone.

'Multiple pile-up almost exactly halfway between here and St Mary's,' she clarified, mentioning the much smaller hospital to the north of St Augustine's. 'Obviously they're not equipped to deal with anything this big...'

'So they're dumping them onto us,' he finished for her, tight-lipped, his grey eyes as cold as winter.

'Of course,' she agreed, outwardly calm in spite of the way she had begun to seethe inside. He knew as well as she did that it was policy to send all the victims to the same hospital—the nearest one equipped to handle a large influx of injuries. 'We're newer and better equipped, while St Mary's isn't much bigger than a cottage hospital. They certainly haven't got the intensive care facilities that we have or the staff to call on.'

For a second there was silence, almost as if her sharp reply had surprised him. She could feel him radiating disapproval, but she didn't dare look up at him and kept her eyes fixed on the series of forms she was lining up.

'Well, I hope we can put up a more polished show than we did earlier on or, inadequate as it is, they'd be better off at St Mary's,' he finally growled as he responded to the approaching sound of sirens and turned to stride away.

Robbed of speech by his abrupt rudeness, she stared daggers at the breadth of his departing back, only managing to mutter a deep-felt, 'Bloody man,' before she was inundated with people demanding her attention.

Polly led her team of nurses into action with practised ease, pleased with their smooth efficiency.

As each ambulance disgorged its load of victims the current status of their injuries was checked against the paramedics' reports and they were swiftly dispersed.

In the case of the more seriously wounded, the advance information they'd received over the computer link meant that they could be sent immediately up to a theatre which was ready and waiting for their arrival.

The less seriously injured disappeared straight into one or other of the designated treatment rooms for attention, while those who had been lucky enough to have received more minor injuries were directed to seats in the reception area to wait patiently for attention.

'There are so many of them,' Hannah muttered in an

aside to Polly as their paths crossed yet again as they dodged through a mêlée of junior doctors and extra nursing staff, ending up entering the same treatment room together. 'Does anyone know what happened?' she asked under the all too familiar hubbub of questions and orders, all overlaid by the wails and groans of injured humanity.

'Apparently, the brakes failed on a coach as it was coming down a steep hill towards a junction, and it ploughed into the back of a second coach waiting at traffic lights,' Polly replied.

'Well, why are there so many hip and knee injuries?' Tina Wadland questioned, still slightly overawed by her first day in A and E as she finished cutting a pair of jeans off a patient. The paramedics had already split them up to mid-thigh at the scene of the crash to enable them to tape a dressing over the patient's badly lacerated knee, but now she had the task of removing the rest of his clothing.

'At a guess, that's because when one coach hit the other, pushed the rows of seats forward so the passengers' legs were trapped against the seats in front,' Polly hazarded as she and the waiting porter loaded her patient and his newly developed X-rays for transfer up to Orthopaedics and the start of a lengthy acquaintanceship with a bulky plaster cast.

Still, she thought as she stripped off her gloves and disposed of them, from the discussion she'd overheard in front of the X-ray viewbox between Nicholas Prince and the orthopaedic consultant, Alex Marshall, the coach driver had been lucky to escape a trip to Theatre for the surgical realignment of his broken bones.

'You'll probably find that there are quite a few whiplash injuries, too,' she continued in a quiet aside to

Tina as she snapped a fresh pair of gloves in position. 'Especially the people who didn't have their heads resting back against the seat at the time of impact, or didn't have time to brace themselves.'

A swift glance up at the clock told her that she should have gone off duty nearly an hour ago, but she mentally shrugged her resignation as she reached for the next set of forms and departed to collect her next patient, momentarily feeling rather as if she were working on a factory production line.

For a second she stood to one side of the waiting area and cast her eyes over the remaining group of people and belongings. As she mentally thanked whatever stroke of luck had enabled the majority of the patients to escape serious injury, one hand surreptitiously massaged the tight muscles in the small of her back before she drew in a deep breath and prepared to enter the fray once more.

'Standing and looking at the job doesn't get it done, Sister Lang,' growled a harsh voice. 'Every second you spend standing idly by means that someone else has to work harder and longer.'

Without so much as a glance in his direction, she knew whose acid words they were and her shoulders stiffened defensively before she could hide her reaction, her shock at the unwarranted attack drawing her eyes up to clash with the turbulent grey of Nicholas Prince's angry gaze.

'Well?' he prompted in an abrupt undertone. 'Are you waiting for a personal invitation to treat another patient? In which case, consider yourself invited. There are several people still waiting for lacerations to be stitched, and the longer they're left the less chance there is of making a good job of it.'

Overriding the stab of hurt at the injustice of his attack, Polly was suddenly struck by the awful desire to salute him as if he were some despotic sergeant major. Luckily, before she had a chance to follow through he was striding across the room towards his beckoning registrar, and she buried the insane urge under another hour of frantic activity.

'Well, in spite of what Old Nick says, I reckon we did well with that little lot,' Hannah mumbled round a mouthful of sandwich as she watched Polly gather up her belongings. 'Mind you, I don't think we'd have managed quite so well if you hadn't stayed on to help out.'

'Rubbish,' Polly muttered, bending forward to change her shoes in an attempt to hide the rising colour in her cheeks. 'There were quite a few people who responded to the call-in. I'm only another pair of hands.'

'Only another pair of hands? Hah!' scoffed her friend. 'You're only the best qualified member of nursing staff in the department, and that includes Big Mac,' she added, irreverently referring to Senior Sister Celia MacDonald. '*And* you were the most senior one here this evening who was in at the beginning of Old Nick's reorganisation. You'd think he'd be more appreciative.'

Polly clenched her teeth. She wasn't going to touch *that* topic with a bargepole.

'Why do you call him Old Nick?' she demanded in a rather blatant attempt at sidetracking Hannah. 'He might have the start of grey hair among the blond, but he's not that much older than we are—what is he, mid to late thirties?'

'It's got nothing to do with his age, although he certainly acts as bad-tempered as if he were middle-aged,' Hannah replied with a scowl. 'It's more to do with the fact that he breathes fire and brimstone like the devil himself—you ought to know about that. You've been in the firing line several times today.'

Since she'd first started her hospital training Polly had made a point of largely ignoring the gossip passed around on the hospital grapevine, and was going to let the comment pass unremarked as she straightened up with her bag in her hand—only to find herself tempted to probe.

'Hannah. . . God knows he's always been a bit of a perfectionist, but this is something else. Something. . .' She shrugged, at a loss for words. 'Have *you* any idea what's been setting him off the last couple of days?'

'You mean, apart from you?' Hannah gibed wryly.

'Seriously,' Polly said with a grimace. 'I know he's had a lot on his plate in the last year with the reorganisation of the department, and we know from the moans and groans that it's meant a return to shiftwork for the consultants to provide the twenty-four-hour supervisory cover. . .' She paused briefly to organise her thoughts.

'I thought the new rota had been in operation long enough for most of the kinks to be ironed out and lift the pressure off him a bit, but he seems. . .exhausted,' she finished with a shrug.

'You're right on all counts,' Hannah agreed as she folded the empty sandwich wrapper into an aeroplane and aimed it successfully at the bin, before glancing up at Polly. 'In theory, the new system should be spreading the load but lately it seems as if the daft man doesn't know when to stop. For example, today he was supposed to go home when Leo came on duty.'

'You mean he's been here for. . .' she paused for some mental arithmetic '. . .eighteen hours?'

'At least—especially if he turned up early this

morning,' Hannah confirmed. 'It makes you wonder if he's got a home to go to.'

Polly had enough to think about without speculating as to Nicholas Prince's living arrangements, and she wished Hannah a quiet end to her shift before she made a quick detour into the staff cloakroom.

Polly wasn't aware of having opened the door particularly quietly, but the only other occupant of the hushed surroundings must have been totally unaware that she had company as she continued to weep with quiet intensity.

'Tina?' Polly said softly, as she abandoned her bags on the corner of the vanity shelf surrounding the hand-basins and wrapped a consoling arm around the shuddering shoulders. 'What's the matter? Is it anything I can help with?'

'Oh, Sister!' she wailed, trying to stifle the sound with a large handful of tissues. 'It's no use...*I'm* no use! I'll *never* get it right!'

'Get what right?' Polly prompted as she grabbed a couple of paper towels from the dispenser and wet them under the cold tap, before offering them to Tina to cool her blotchy face.

Polly soon pieced together Tina's tale of woe and her anger rose again when she realised that once more Dr Nicholas Prince was the cause of the upset.

'Don't let it get you down, Tina,' she advised while the youngster blew her nose and tidied herself. 'We were all new to the department once. You'll learn soon enough.'

Polly was proud of the calm way she was able to deliver the encouraging speech, knowing that her inner anger was hidden behind her smile as she sent the young nurse back to work. It was a different matter when the door swung shut and she was alone in the cloakroom, and it was several minutes before she felt sufficiently composed to go out and look for the consultant.

'Enough is enough,' she muttered belligerently as she retrieved her bags and elbowed her way out into the corridor. 'It's time someone told him where to get off. . . Ah! Leo!' she called, catching sight of the registrar just as he was disappearing round a corner, and his head reappeared briefly.

'Hello, Polly, my love. I thought you'd gone home,' he said with his trademark killer smile as he approached her, his hair gleaming gold under the bright lights of the corridor. 'Can't stay away from me, eh? I knew you'd fall for my charms if I waited long enough!'

'In your dreams!' Polly retorted, the answering smile drawn out of her by his usual light-hearted nonsense.

'You wound me, heartless wench,' he complained, covering his heart dramatically with both hands. 'Your scorn will send me home tonight to weep into my pillow.'

'Hah!' she scoffed, but his teasing words had reminded her of the reason she'd called him. 'Speaking of crying,' she began determinedly, all trace of humour wiped from her face, 'can you tell me where your boss is hiding? I need to have a word with him.'

'Anything I can help with?' Leo offered, the levity gone from his voice, too, with the return of his professional persona.

'Not this time,' she said briefly, deliberately withholding an explanation. *This* was something which she needed to do face to face.

'I see,' Leo said thoughtfully, his tawny gaze scanning her face with quiet intensity before she caught a strange hint of approval. 'Only Nick will do?'

Polly was very conscious of his assessing look and nearly protested his choice of words, but in essence Leo was right. Dr Prince's behaviour over the last couple of days was becoming unacceptable and, while anyone could be excused for having a bad day, he was rapidly approaching the point where he could be reported to the 'three wise men' for a warning of disciplinary action.

'It's important that I speak with him personally,' she agreed, only her conviction that she was doing the right thing keeping her voice even.

'In that case...' Leo fished through an overladen pocket and pulled out a notepad, emblazoned with a drugs company logo. 'Here.' He held out a swiftly scribbled note. 'He went home about fifteen minutes ago, but that's the address.'

'Oh, but...' Polly was taken aback. It was one thing to confront the A and E consultant about a problem at work, but another thing entirely to carry the complaint to his own home.

'It's only a stone's throw away...unless you'd rather I dealt with it?'

There was a strange tone to Leo's voice, almost as if he was taunting her—or daring her to carry through with her intention.

'Thank you for the offer, but it won't be necesssary,' Polly said with a glance at the hieroglyphic scrawl and a conscious lift of her chin. 'I have to go in that direction on my way home. I'm sure I'll be able to find him.'

'I'm sure you shall,' Leo murmured blandly as she turned away, and she was conscious that he watched her retreating back all the way to the next corner in the corridor.

A squadron of butterflies had begun to hatch out inside her and were warming up for a spectacular aerobatic display by the time she'd walked half way to her destination, and it was only the memory of Tina's tearful face that stiffened her resolve.

If Nicholas Prince's venom had only been directed towards herself it wouldn't have mattered so much—she was an experienced nurse who'd learned to put up with the abuse hurled at her from the less amiable sections of society, and her own personal life had taught her how to turn the other cheek.

'But when he starts in on a newcomer as green as Tina it's time someone told him the facts of life.'

Her pulse rate skipped as she realised the temerity of her actions. It was all too possible that she might be making a big mistake; might even make a bad situation worse, but. . .

'Here we go,' she muttered as she paused in the gathering dusk to peer at the number Leo had written down for her, and climbed the shallow steps of the solid Georgian house.

The sound of the chimes had long faded away into the depths of the house and she shivered in the autumn chill as she impatiently pressed the button a second time. Almost immediately light streamed out into the encroaching darkness from the fanlight window over the heavy panelled wooden door.

'All right, all right, I'm coming,' growled a deep voice, as she heard the sound of heavy bolts being drawn.

'Ah, the familiar dulcet tones,' she whispered to herself in an attempt at stiffening her suddenly shaky resolve.

The door swung open and she was almost blinded by the sudden flood of light, her nemesis appearing as a large black silhouette as he stepped into the bright opening.

'What the. . .? Sister Lang?' Surprise robbed his voice of bite. 'What are you. . .? Do you need to see me? What's the matter? Has something gone wrong since I left? Is my pager on the blink?' He fired the questions at her one after the other, without allowing her time to think—let alone answer.

'Yes. . . No. . .I mean, as far as I know, there's nothing wrong with your pager, but I do need to see you.' She was almost squinting up at him as the light poured into her face, trying vainly to decipher his hidden expression.

There were several seconds of silence before he stepped back from the doorway and, pulling the door wide, gestured for her to enter.

As the door swung shut behind her she turned to face him, and suddenly realised that he was less than fully dressed. As her eyes were filled with the unexpected sight of his naked chest a flood of embarrassment heated her cheeks.

'I'm sorry, I didn't realise that you were getting ready for b-bed. Perhaps I'd better speak to you tomorrow. . .' She inwardly cursed the juvenile stammer as she turned towards the door and reached up to release

A lean-fingered hand covered hers briefly and she froze, the electricity of the light contact preventing her from turning the knob as effectively as if he'd used brute force, before he snatched it away and continued speaking. 'If your mission was important enough to have you tracking me down then I'd better find out what it's all about, hadn't I? Can I offer you a drink?'

His voice receded and she turned towards him, her

eyes reluctantly following his silent steps as he walked away from her down the empty hallway.

'But...'

She realised that there was no point in objecting to his high-handedness when he continued to stride away from her through an open doorway and disappeared from view, completely ignoring her attempt at speech.

'Coffee?' he prompted when she hesitantly followed him into the stark newness of a recently refurbished kitchen. 'Or can I offer you something stronger if you're off duty for the day...?' He reached for the solitary glass residing on the otherwise pristine work-surface and toasted her with the inch and a half of amber-coloured liquid in the bottom.

'No. Thank you for the offer but...' She felt quite uncomfortable with the thought of accepting a drink from him when she had come to tell him what she thought of his rotten temper.

'Oh, for heaven's sake!' He slapped the glass down but hardly seemed to notice that the contents splashed up the sides and over his hand. 'It would hardly constitute a gross impropriety if you were to accept a drink from me. What do you think I'm going to do—publicise the fact on a noticeboard? Everyone in A and E already knows you well enough to realise there'd be no*personal* in your acceptance!'

Polly was shocked into silence, her feelings at the unexpected attack widening her eyes as she stared at him, but even so she was still aware of a deep underlying bitterness in his voice.

Before she had a chance to do any more than register the twist of distaste which marred his face he swung away from her, his fingers spearing through the thick blond strands of his hair as he sighed heavily and dropped his head forward to massage the back of his neck.

'God, I'm sorry,' he said, rubbing both hands roughly over his face as he turned to face her again. 'That was totally uncalled-for.'

Polly agreed silently, suddenly aware of just how tired he looked. If it had only been the result of a self-inflicted long day's work she could have understood it, but this was something more—this was something bone-deep and it looked as if he wasn't coping with it.

'I'd better go,' Polly murmured, uncomfortably aware of the fact that his vulnerability was pulling at her, persuading her to drop her own animosity towards him. 'I can speak to you when you come on duty tomorrow.'

She turned to leave the kitchen.

'*If* I go on duty...'

She almost missed the words he murmured under his breath, but something make her turn back in time to see the flash of empty desolation in his eyes.

'I thought you were on early tomorrow?' she queried, and saw the way the corners of his mouth tightened before he turned away from her gaze to pick up his glass again.

'Yes,' he confirmed with a weary sigh, and flung the remaining liquid to the back of his throat with a well-practised flick of his wrist. The half-melted ice cubes hardly had time to settle in the bottom of the glass before he was reaching for the bottle. 'Are you sure I can't offer you one for the road? It's supposed to help you sleep.' He raised a questioning eyebrow and waved the bottle at her before he twisted the cap off and poured a generous amount over the tinkling ice.

Something in his tone made Polly pause before she spoke, her eyes running over him more analytically than before.

This time, instead of shying away from the fact that the all-too-attractive A and E consultant in front of her was clad only in a pair of hip-hugging jeans with his broad naked chest on view, she made herself take note of the fact that he didn't look as if he weighed as much as he should.

In fact, now that she thought about it, he seemed to have lost quite a bit of weight over the last couple of weeks, his face having take on a lean, fine-drawn edge, with hollows under his cheek-bones and shadows under his enigmatic eyes.

More convinced than ever that his sour temper around the department had a serious cause, and her heart softening irrevocably towards him, she finally took her courage in both hands.

'Do you have any "unleaded" coffee?' she asked as casually as she could manage, and had the pleasure of seeing that she had stopped him in his tracks, his lean hand holding the glass suspended in mid-air on its way to his mouth.

'I don't know,' he said, obviously bemused as he turned back towards her. 'Do you want me to look?'

'Either that, or tea,' she confirmed with a tentative smile. 'I find that ordinary coffee keeps me awake if I drink it too late in the evening.' She eyed the newly filled glass in his hand and chanced an explosion. 'Will you be joining me?'

There was a pause while his gaze homed in sharply on her face and then, just as she felt the heat beginning to rise in her cheeks, one corner of his mouth lifted in a wry grin.

'It wasn't subtle, but you made your point,' he said gruffly as he reached out his hand and tipped the contents of the glass into the sink, the ice-cubes clattering loudly as they landed on the stainless steel. He slid the bottle to the back corner of the work surface and turned towards the kettle. 'But, if I'm joining you, it will have to be a coffee. I can't make tea at this time of night. . .'

He paused, a strange expression crossing his face as he pressed his lips together in a grim line.

'Oh, God,' he muttered and closed his eyes as if in defeat.

'If it's a problem. . .' Polly began, not understanding the last few seconds at all. For a moment it had looked as if it was going to be all right, but suddenly. . .

'No. . . It's not a problem. At least. . .' He shook his head as he continued, the words emerging almost as if they were being dragged out of him. 'The smell of tea makes. . .made Dee feel sick so I stopped drinking it in the evening.'

'Dee?' Polly questioned faintly, shocked to feel a sharp twist of disappointment when she heard him say the woman's name.

'Deanne. . .' he elaborated. 'My wife.'

CHAPTER TWO

'YOUR wife?' Polly repeated in consternation, her eyes flicking around the pristine room for some sign of a woman's touch. 'I'm sorry, I didn't know. . . Leo didn't tell me that you're married or I'd never have disturbed you at home. . .at this time of night. . .'

She was scrambling for words to express her apologies, once more avoiding looking directly at the expanse of naked flesh Nicholas was displaying. Now that she knew he had a wife she felt even more awkward about being in the same room with him while he was wearing so little.

Had he been getting ready to go to bed with her? Had he had to pull some clothes on to cover his nakedness to answer the bell?

She started edging uncomfortably towards the door.

For the first time in several years she found herself fighting the mental image of a naked man and, what was worse, it was St Augustine's A and E consultant— and a married man—whose body she was imagining.

Her cheeks flamed as she studiously avoided looking at him and reached for the latch.

'I'm not,' he said abruptly, bringing her up short as her eyes darted up to meet his in confusion. 'Not any more,' he clarified, his voice a harsh rasp in the silence.

'Not?' Polly blinked, questions whirling around so fast inside her head that she couldn't catch hold of any of them for long enough to formulate them into an intelligible sentence, let alone dare to ask them.

Were he and his wife separated? Divorced?

'She died,' he said bluntly, as though that was the only way he could bring himself to say it. 'A year and. . .two years ago in a car crash.'

The words hovered in the air between them, the hollow sound of his voice seeming to echo endlessly inside her head.

'Oh, God, I'm sorry,' she said helplessly, her heart going out to him. She knew only too well how it felt to suffer such a devastating loss. 'I had no idea. . .'

'Very few people do.' His voice sounded rough, as though it still hurt to talk about it. 'I moved to St Augustine's after I. . .shortly after it happened so. . .' He shrugged dismissively. 'There was no need for anyone to know.'

Polly's mind was churning furiously now as she started to collect the snippets of information he was giving her, and the picture which she was building was beginning to sound very familiar.

'What time of year did it happen?' she asked, deciding on an oblique approach.

'Autumn,' he said, the slight frown indicating his puzzlement at the apparently random question, and when she remained silent he elaborated. 'The first weekend in October. We were on our way to visit her parents to tell them about the baby. . .' His voice trailed away. She knew he'd heard her involuntary gasp but she hadn't been able to help it when she'd realised that he'd lost a baby too. . .

'What?' he demanded.

'Nothing,' she began, but she could see from his expression that he wasn't going to believe her denial. 'It's just that. . .'

At the last moment she couldn't face exposing her

own pain and settled for voicing her second thought.

'It's almost *exactly* two years ago, isn't it?' she asked softly, knowing from her own experience that she could be touching open wounds.

'Tomorrow,' he admitted after an interminable pause, his eyes dark and empty. 'It will be two years tomorrow evening.'

'Oh, I'm so sorry,' she breathed as all her suspicions were confirmed, and she reached out to lay one gentle hand over his clenched fist in an involuntary expression of kinship. 'It's bad enough that it happened, but I know it's even harder when you get to the anniversaries...'

He stiffened in automatic rejection of her sympathetic touch, his eyes meeting hers in a stormy grey glare which denied pity. It was difficult but she bit her lip and managed to hold his gaze steadily, her own memories bringing the warning burn that tears weren't far away.

'You're not just taking pot-shots in the dark, are you?' he said finally, his voice sounding almost resigned as he recognised a fellow sufferer. 'How long has it been for you?'

'Nearly five years,' she confirmed. 'And, before you ask, no, it never goes away but, yes, it does eventually get easier to live with.'

There was little amusement in his brief laugh.

'Sometimes I think a lifetime won't be long enough,' he admitted in that awful hollow tone, and Polly felt a shiver travel up her spine as his words echoed inside her head.

Somewhere, in one of the rooms along the hallway, a clock chimed and the strangely uneasy silence was broken, but he spoke before Polly could find the words to make her excuses and go.

'I'm sorry, I still haven't made you that drink,' he

said apologetically as he reached out to switch on the kettle. 'By the way, why *did* you come after me this evening?'

Polly's heart sank. What could she say now that wouldn't seem like kicking a man when he was already down?

On the other hand, she argued silently, didn't she have a responsibility towards the younger members of staff—the ones who weren't in any position to remonstrate with an obstreperous consultant without making the complaint official?

'Ah!' Her silence had obviously gone on just too long and his intelligent brain was sifting unspoken information at lightning speed. 'In the absence of Sister MacDonald, were you nominated to beard the lion in his den? What is it that they want me to do—reorganise the duty roster or represent the department at one of those interminable fund-raising events? It's not something to do with the Autumn Ball?'

'No...not exactly,' Polly hedged while she cast about frantically for inspiration and came up empty-handed. 'It's not quite... It's rather... Oh, damn,' she muttered, wishing that she'd never had the bright idea of confronting him—and especially not this evening. Why hadn't she left it until next week?

After tomorrow night he would probably revert to being his usual serious, unflappable self and they'd all wonder what the fuss had been about—but, then, until a few minutes ago she hadn't known the reason why he'd been so...

'Spit it out,' he advised. 'Whatever it is, it's now considered illegal to kill the bearers of bad news so you're relatively safe.'

'Thanks!' She grimaced wryly as she clenched her

hands into fists inside the pockets of her down-filled jacket, feeling more uncomfortable with every passing minute. 'Except that it's not quite that easy to...'

'Oh, for heaven's sake!' he exploded, his meagre store of patience obviously exhausted. 'I know you haven't come here to proposition me and you've already told me I didn't leave any problems behind at St Augustine's so...'

'Actually, sir, that's not strictly true,' Polly broke in nervously, peripherally aware that she still wasn't certain what to call him in an off-duty situation, especially as her task was work-related.

'But when you arrived you told me that there wasn't a problem back at St Augustine's,' he objected harshly.

'That's not exactly...' she began, then froze when he took a swift step towards her, his six feet of lean masculine height making him loom almost menacingly over her much shorter five feet four.

'Then what *exactly* is it about?' He mimicked her choice of words cruelly. 'These days I haven't got a great deal of patience with people who won't come to the point.'

His words were just enough to stiffen her resolve, and her chin lifted belligerently as she glared at him out of dark brown eyes.

'Actually, *that's* what I came to see you about, sir,' she found herself announcing with barely a quiver in her voice. 'There have been several complaints from some of the younger nurses, as well as the other staff in the department, that lately you have been unnecessarily...' she hunted around frantically for an acceptible word '...harsh...with your criticisms.'

'Good God!' His astonishment sounded loud and clear. 'You mean to tell me you followed me home because some wet-behind-the-ears junior had a fit of the vapours when I told them off for falling down on the job?'

'Hardly,' she denied shortly. 'It was more a case of wanting to have a word with you to find out whether you had a valid reason for your unreasonable behaviour and,' she continued, determined to finish what she'd started in spite of his attempt at interruption, 'to warn you that if it went on much longer you were going to find yourself paying a visit to the "three wise men" in the near future.'

She thought it was her reference to the the hospital disciplinary committee which stopped him in his tracks because he'd looked ready to explode right up until she used their slightly tongue-in-cheek nickname.

There was nearly a minute of utter silence, except for the frantic beating of her heart which seemed to fill the room.

'Oh, hell,' he finally muttered as he dragged the fingers of both hands through his thick blond hair.

Polly released the breath she hadn't been aware of holding, her nerves still wound tight enough to send her into orbit when the kettle suddenly shrieked.

'Look, I won't stay for a drink now.' A late attack of cowardice had her hurrying into speech as she saw him turn to switch the noise off and open the honey-coloured wooden cupboard door to reach for two mugs. 'If you're on early tomorrow you'll want to go to sleep fairly soon...'

'Chance would be a fine thing,' he muttered bitterly as he braced his hands on the counter and hung his head forward, the broad nakedness of his shoulders rounding almost defensively. 'Please,' he murmured, his husky voice barely louder than a whisper, 'keep me company—just for the time it takes to drink a cup of coffee?'

Polly had the feeling that Dr Nicholas Prince didn't ask for favours easily and her heart melted.

She knew what it felt like to dread coming home to the lonely silence of an empty house; knew how hard it was to keep busy enough to stop your mind going over and over the same desperate series of events. She knew what it was like to lie awake, staring into the darkness and wishing that somehow you could go back in time and alter the course of your own personal history—to have the chance to change the single event that would switch it from tragedy back to happiness.

Wordlessly she pulled out a chair and sat at the table, one corner of her mind registering the simplicity of the design of the furniture and the soft patina of the freshly finished wood, while the rest of her senses were tuned to the man standing silently on the other side of the room.

When he didn't move she realised that he hadn't seen what she had done.

'A splash of milk and half a sugar,' she prompted and saw him stiffen with shock before he whirled towards her, disbelief clear on his face.

'What?' He was obviously bemused.

'In my coffee,' she elaborated patiently. 'I like it with a splash of milk and half a sugar, but don't make it too strong.'

He gazed at her a second longer before he turned away silently and reached up again for the two mugs.

While he was busy she gave herself permission to admire the smooth movement of the broad sheets of muscles across his back and the tension in his shoulder and arm as he lifted the kettle to pour water onto the spoonful of granules he'd deposited in each.

Without a word he carried both mugs over in one hand, juggling the sugar bowl, spoon and milk in the other as he deposited them on the table in front of her and pulled out a chair for himself on the other side.

After a quiet, 'Thanks,' Polly concentrated on adding the milk and sugar to her cup and stirred as if her life depended on it, all the while excruciatingly aware that they were separated by just the width of the table.

'Thank *you*.'

His husky voice drew her eyes up from their preoccupation with the ripples on the top of her coffee and she hesitantly met the pewter-coloured depths of his.

'What for?' she said, uncomfortably aware of the intensity of his gaze. '*You* provided the coffee.'

He shook his head.

'I don't know how but you know damn well that it wasn't just the cup of coffee,' he said with low vehemence and sipped at his own jet-black mugful.

Polly *did* know what he meant, and because her own heart still clenched in her chest at the memories she made herself voice some of her thoughts.

'It. . . It's the simple fact that someone else is in the house,' she said huskily, flicking a quick glance up at him and seeing his knuckles tighten around the mug as she continued softly, 'Someone else moving, making noise, breathing. . .'

His murmur of agreement was a low rumble in the depths of his chest and she watched him draw in a deep breath and release it slowly.

'Have I really been bad?' he asked quietly, all the fire gone.

'Awful,' Polly said. 'And the worst of it was the fact that none of us knew why and no one dared to ask.'

'And I can't even guarantee that the situation is going

to get any better,' he added despondently. 'God knows what I was like last year—no one said anything—so I don't know whether I'm still getting worse or gradually improving.'

'If this is an improvement I'm glad I didn't see you last time!' she dared, and was pleased to see the lightening of his expression, no matter how reluctant it was.

'All I've got to do now is get through tomorrow,' he said sombrely. 'It would be a crime to wish for back-to-back casualties, but I've seriously been thinking about sending the rest of the team home and doing twenty-four hours straight through myself.'

'Just like the good old days?' Polly questioned with a raised eyebrow. 'A and E staff risking serious misdiagnoses because they're dead on their feet?'

'God forbid! That's what the new regime is supposed to replace.'

'Well, then, there isn't a lot of sense in going back to it, is there?' she pointed out. 'Wouldn't it be better if you worked your assigned shift, then planned to do something else to occupy the rest of the day? Perhaps that way you won't get quite so tired and you won't be chewing pounds and spitting pennies. . .'

This time the chuckle came a little more easily and Polly was able to leave shortly afterwards with the memory of the husky sound still echoing in her ears.

'He might not have wished for it, but it looks as if he got it anyway,' Polly muttered to herself the next morning when it looked as if the A and E reception area was going to overflow. 'It looks as if the world and his wife are here.'

She held her hand out for the next batch of case

notes and followed the wheelchair through to the treatment room.

'Good morning, Mr Chandralal. I'm Sister Lang. What have you done to yourself?'

While the elderly man began to explain in great detail how he had come to stab a garden fork through his foot Polly helped him up onto the examination couch, wincing at the bloody mess he had made.

'Tina, Mr Chandralal's injury needs careful irrigation. I'll just get Dr Prince to check him over to see whether he's going to need to go upstairs or if we can deal with him down here. In the meantime, he's going to need a tetanus shot.'

She paused briefly at the door to make certain that Tina had recovered from her emotional outburst of the previous evening. In no time at all the young woman had confidently collected the supplies she would need and when she began explaining carefully to the elderly gentleman exactly what she was going to do Polly knew it was time to go in search of Nicholas Prince.

In spite of the fact that she had been on duty for over an hour, so far the consultant had been just a distant white-coated figure *en route* between examining rooms. Now she was going to see him face to face and she found herself strangely nervous.

'Idiot!' she muttered under her breath. 'He can't eat you, in spite of the fact you tried to call him to book last night.' She chuckled inwardly at the idea of a lowly junior sister having the temerity to tell a consultant off, but the humour of the situation faded as she remembered the empty vulnerability she had glimpsed when he'd told her of the reason behind his uneven temper.

'Busy enough?' she taunted softly when she caught up with him just as he dispatched an elderly stroke victim up towards the wards, the patient's tearful wife clutching his blue-veined hand as she accompanied his trolley towards the bank of lifts.

'Getting there.' He tilted his head towards her in wry acknowledgement, his grey eyes shadowed by bone-deep tiredness even at this early hour of his shift. 'Next time I open my big mouth remind me of the old saying—"Be careful what you wish for. . ."!'

'Well, I've got another one waiting for your expert assessment—a gentleman who stuck a garden fork through his foot.'

'Ouch,' he winced and turned to follow her while she continued talking.

'Because he was walking on it he's been bleeding like a stuck pig, but I don't think he hit anything major—unless he's done any nerve or tendon damage.'

'OK. Let's take a quick look. . .'

By the time they entered the treatment room Mr Chandralal was sitting forlornly on the examining couch, clutching his ruined shoe. Tina had obviously finished irrigating the injury to his foot and had covered it with a dry sterile dressing.

'Good girl,' Polly murmured quietly as the young woman stepped aside to allow the consultant to take her place.

'Well, Mr Chandralal,' Dr Prince said when he finally straightened up from his systematic examination of the elderly man's reflexes and functional responses, 'as far as I can tell, you haven't damaged any nerves or tendons in your foot, but the nature of the injury and the actual position means that you're going to be in quite a bit of pain while you're healing.'

'Thank you, Doctor,' he said fervently, tears of relief

making his dark eyes gleam. 'I am so sorry to have caused so much trouble.'

The consultant smiled briefly and Polly saw the fugitive creases at the corner of his eyes before he grew serious again.

'Well, if you don't mind me offering a word of advice, I think you would be wiser to wear something a little more substantial when you're gardening next time—maybe something with metal toecaps to give you some protection.'

Suddenly there was the harsh sound of an approaching siren and their heads all swivelled towards the sound.

Within seconds directions for the completion of Mr Chandralal's treatment had been given and hasty farewells had been made.

Polly's eyes followed the tall figure through the swing doors, then she dragged them back to the task in hand, quietly supervising Tina's careful work.

'You're doing well,' she encouraged when they were clearing the debris away, ready for the next patient.

'I'm just glad Dr Prince had to leave,' Tina said in a fervent aside. 'I was certain he'd end up shouting at me if he stayed to watch. I could feel myself beginning to shake, and I'm sure I'd have dropped everything on the floor.'

'I didn't know you were so badly affected by his good looks,' Polly deadpanned.

'His looks!' Tina squeaked, then realised that she was having her leg pulled. 'Sister! That's the *last* thing I think about when he's anywhere near me—although I suppose he isn't bad-looking for an older man.'

'Damned with faint praise!' Polly commented, then

grew serious again. 'You haven't had any further set-tos with him, have you?'

'Not since last night,' the young nurse confirmed. 'Mind you, I've been making certain that I keep well out of his way—he scares me!'

'He's only a man,' Polly said calmly, squashing down the memory of the semi-naked body she'd seen last night. 'He has to put his trousers on one leg at a time, the same as the rest of us!'

Tina giggled infectiously at the thought. 'Now I'll have to try to keep a straight face when he speaks to me.'

'That's better than quaking in your boots. Just make certain you're doing your job right and ask questions when you aren't certain.'

'Yes, Sister.'

'Sister Lang. . .?' a voice called from the other side of the swing doors, and Hannah Nicholls's dark head appeared. 'Big Mac wants to know if you're free to help Leo,' she murmured when Polly joined her by the door, quietly referring to the senior sister by her nickname. 'He's got a problem in room four with an OD.'

An overdose. . . Polly gave a little shudder of dread.

'I'll be right there, Hannah. . .'

She had no time to say any more before the head disappeared and the doors swung open smartly to admit a wheelchair, closely followed by a staff nurse and a rather green-looking junior doctor.

'I'll stay, shall I?' Tina volunteered gamely when she saw the blood-soaked cloth wrapped around the hand of the middle-aged man in the wheelchair.

'Good idea,' Polly agreed after a careful look at her determined expression, and swiftly left the room.

She just had time to signal her arrival to the diminutive martinet who was affectionately called Big Mac, and reached the doors of room four just as her nemesis approached them from the other direction.

'After you, sir,' she offered, flattening her palm against one door to push it open for him.

With a sharp glance and a brief murmur of thanks he strode into the room ahead of her.

'What's the problem, Leo?'

In the sudden silence that greeted his crisp voice Polly could have echoed his words, her eyes skimming over the disaster which seemed to have befallen the orderliness of the room. It was obvious from the spread of containers and equipment strewn around the floor that their patient had been strenuously resisting all offers of medical assistance. Finally her gaze came to rest on the unaccustomed expression of bemusement on Leo Stirling's handsome face.

'Problem?' a belligerent female voice answered, and they all found themselves following the shrill sound to the bedraggled figure on the examining table. 'There wouldn't *be* a problem if *he'd* only leave me alone. I don't *want* him to help me!'

The young woman glared fiercely at them, the expression in her reddened eyes reminding Polly of a cornered animal—or perhaps an injured one, afraid to believe that their assistance was kindly meant.

'But, Mrs Bishop... Sharron...' Leo obviously hadn't given up trying. 'If you won't let us help you you might die...'

'That's the whole bloody idea,' she swore, her voice slightly unsteady as it rose higher and higher. 'I *want* to die...I might just as well be dead...I'm no use as I am...'

The angry phrases degenerated into hopeless, helpless sobbing and Polly took the opportunity to hurry to the woman's side, one arm going around the heaving shoulders while the other reached for a handful of paper tissues.

'Here,' she offered gently, tightening her grip slightly to immobilise one arm when she felt the young woman stiffen and pressing the rustling white handful into her free hand.

For a second there was silence, as if everyone was holding their breath, before, with an unexpected, 'Thanks,' she used both hands to blow her running nose and scrub the streams of tears from her pale cheeks.

With no more than the lift of an eyebrow Nicholas Prince signalled to Polly, and when she nodded briefly in reply he silently gestured for the rest of the team to leave the room. Equally silently he crossed the room to position himself beside the swing doors so that he, too, was out of sight of their suicidal patient.

Polly breathed an inner sigh of relief that he was close enough to come to her help if necessary, and turned her attention back to her charge.

'Why can't they understand?'

The words were plaintive and sounded quite a bit more slurred than before.

'What don't they understand, Sharron?' Polly asked, knowing that the young woman's mental state wouldn't bear too much pushing but horribly conscious that time was ticking away.

'Why I don't want to be alive... No one understands... No one knows what it's like...inside...to know you're just a failure...'

As Polly tried to formulate another question two fat

tears spilled over and trickled down Sharron's pale cheeks.

'Man trouble?' she ventured.

'What else?' she slurred bitterly. 'They only l-love you when you give them what they w-want, and if you can't. . .' She rolled her head against Polly's shoulder and looked up at her, defeat obvious in her expression. 'I. . .I can't give him a b-baby and he s-said. . .he said. . .'

The poor woman was unable to continue but Polly didn't need to hear the words to recognise her agony.

It didn't matter that in her own case it had been Tim's self-righteous condemnation and his impatience with her crippling guilt and fear which had destroyed their relationship and locked her emotions away inside.

'Shh. . . He's not worth it, Sharron,' Polly soothed, hoping against hope that she could find some common ground with the woman before the effect of drugs she'd taken became irreversible.

'How would you know?' Sharron challenged with a feeble burst of energy. 'You've got a good j-job. . . You've pro-probably got your own f-family.'

'No.' Polly shook her head sadly, fixing the young woman's gaze with her own and allowing the pain of all the memories to show. 'I'm divorced and he's remarried and starting a family.'

'Bastards. . .' Sharron hissed. 'They're all b-bastards. . .'

'But *I* decided I wasn't going to let the bastard win.' Polly repeated the epithet and shifted her grip so that she was holding Sharron by the shoulders. 'Don't *you* let him win, either,' she commanded fiercely. 'If he only wants you as a brood mare then he's ignorant and selfish and he's not worth killing yourself for. You're worth more than that.'

Sharron blinked at her owlishly, her thought processes slowing visibly as she tried to reason it all out.

''s right...' She nodded ponderously. 'Sh-selfish bastard...' Then she drew in a shuddering breath and gave a little whimper. 'I don't want to die... Please... Don't let me...die...' She closed her eyes and sagged forward against Polly's slender shoulder.

Instantly strong arms reached around her and relieved Polly of the weight as the swing doors flew open to admit the rest of the team.

'Airway,' Dr Prince's voice rapped as the limp body was stretched out and he wielded the first syringe. 'She needs a cuffed endotracheal tube before we can start to wash her out. Let's get that oxygen going...'

His words were almost superfluous as the team swung into its horribly familiar routine, the nasogastric tube swiftly positioned to allow the stomach to be lavaged.

'IV lifeline in,' Polly reported, relieved that she wasn't dealing with the collapsed veins of an habitual drugs user. 'Five per cent glucose going in.'

'Pinpoint pupils and respiratory depression,' Leo reported. 'Cardiac rhythm settling since you got the naloxone into her.'

'Do we know how much codeine she took?' Polly demanded when she saw the number of half-dissolved tablets being flushed up out of the young woman's stomach.

'Half a pharmacy, by the look of it. She certainly wasn't playing at it like some of them. It was sheer chance that her neighbour called round. This wasn't a cry for help, hoping to be found in time,' Dr Prince's voice broke in, his tone strangely flat.

'You're telling me,' Leo said with feeling as he sent blood samples up to the lab to check for drug concentration levels and flicked a glance across at Polly. 'She wouldn't let any of *us* touch her—fought like a wildcat. How did you do it?'

Polly felt the wash of heat over her cheek-bones as attention focused briefly on her, more conscious of a certain pair of wintry grey eyes than any others.

'Sometimes you just click,' she said dismissively. 'Some patients can relate better when they aren't surrounded by a crowd.' She made the mistake of allowing her gaze to travel across the trolley, but it wasn't until she was caught by the darkly knowing expression in Dr Prince's eyes that she remembered that he had been in the room when she'd been talking to Sharron and had heard everything she'd said.

Suddenly she couldn't remember exactly what she *had* said. How much had she told the young woman in her attempt at gaining her co-operation? How much had she said and how much had he gleaned of what she *hadn't* said?

'Sh-shall I find out if there's a side-ward bed she can go into?' Polly volunteered unsteadily when the first set of encouraging results came down from the lab, grabbing the first opportunity to put a little distance between the two of them to get her thoughts in order.

His agreement gave her the perfect excuse to leave the room and she contrived to take her first chance for a break immediately after the errand.

'He's being ever so quiet today,' Hannah commented under her breath as she offered the packet of biscuits.

'Who?'

'*Him*,' she said with a meaningful tilt of her head towards the door leading out into the department where, even as they spoke, they could hear the familiar deep tones of Nicholas Prince's voice.

'Oh. Good,' Polly said, deliberately taking a bite to excuse her lack of conversation on the subject. She usually shared her thoughts with Hannah and felt slightly guilty that she hadn't even mentioned the fact that she'd spoken to the consultant last night, much less that she'd visited him in his own home. In some strange way the whole episode had felt too personal to talk about, even to Hannah.

'I don't know if it is a good thing,' Hannah mused, pursing her lips thoughtfully. 'He's almost *too* quiet. You know—like a volcano just before it erupts. Well,' she continued with her usual good humour, 'if he does let's hope we get enough warning to evacuate the troops!'

Polly smiled at the joke, but she knew exactly what Hannah meant. So far today he *had* been strangely subdued and she had a bad feeling that it wasn't a good sign.

CHAPTER THREE

'HAVE you seen the notice?' Tina demanded eagerly as she slid the strap of her bag over her shoulder in preparation for going home.

'Notice?' Polly returned vaguely as she changed her shoes, preoccupied with the fact that not only had Dr Prince grown quieter and more withdrawn as the day had gone on but he had also left the hospital immediately his shift had ended. Although she had no right to be concerned, she was worried about him and wondered if she dared make a brief detour past his house now that she knew where he lived, to see if he. . .

'About the hospital fund-raiser.' Tina's voice intruded again.

Polly sighed silently and forced herself to concentrate, knowing that she would have to respond.

'Fund-raiser? When?' She glanced across at the cork noticeboard on the other side of the room and tried to see which one of the various brightly coloured posters had attracted Tina's attention.

'It's the Autumn Ball to raise money for the new whole-body scanner,' she elaborated, her young face alive with enthusiasm. 'This year, to help boost the funds, the committee have decided to combine the usual Ball with an Auction of Promises.'

'A what?' Finally Polly's attention was caught and she walked across to read the notice for herself.

'They want people to volunteer prizes for the auction,' Tina pointed out.

'Ohh,' Polly groaned. 'It'll end up being like some dreadful car boot sale, with everyone's worst Christmas presents up for sale.'

'Hardly, with prizes like a day's sailing in a twenty-five-foot yacht on offer,' Tina gloated.

'What?' Polly squeaked in amazement and looked more closely at the handwritten list below the announcement. 'Look! Someone's put up a week's accommodation in a holiday cottage in Brittany. . .and dancing lessons. . .'

'And a massage!' Tina giggled. 'I wonder if we get a choice of masseur—there's a really dishy bloke over in Physio that I wouldn't mind getting to grips with!'

'Tina!' Polly nearly choked. Was this the same tearful person she'd almost had to wring out last night? It was good to see how resilient she was—a quality much needed if she was determined to specialise in A and E.

They were both still laughing when they left the locker room to go home, but before they reached the exit doors Polly heard her name called with the clear precision of a Highland Scots accent.

'Yes, Sister,' she replied immediately and turned to answer the summons with a quiet, 'See you tomorrow,' for Tina.

'Dr Stirling tells me that your journey home takes you past Dr Prince's house,' Sister MacDonald announced in her usual no-nonsense manner. 'Unfortunately, after he left I found his wallet beside the chair in my office, and I would hate for him to think it was permanently lost. Would you be kind enough to drop it off for me?'

'Certainly, Sister. I'll take it straight away,' Polly agreed willingly, and tucked the well-worn leather folder into her own bag with a smile that barely hid her elation. She'd been wondering how she could possibly justify turning up on his doorstep again, without having to admit that she was worried about his mental state.

Now, out of the blue, she'd been handed a cast-iron reason for going to his house again. It might only take a few seconds for her to deliver his wallet, but she would be able to see him and set her mind at rest.

There were no lights on when Polly approached the house, in spite of the fact that the October evening was rapidly drawing in and the streetlights had started coming on. Anyway, she told herself, it didn't really signify anything—he could be in one of the rooms at the back of the house. . .

As she stepped forward to press the bell two things caught her attention almost simultaneously.

The fact that the heavy wooden front door hadn't been closed properly struck her as very strange, especially as she remembered the sound of the bolts he had drawn on her last visit, but it was the slight movement she caught out of the corner of her eye which made her blood run cold.

'Oh, God!' she breathed as her horrified gaze took in the sight visible around the edge of the open curtain.

There, in the sparsely furnished lounge, sat Nicholas Prince with a low wooden coffee-table in front of his chair and an array of guns spread out on the top of it. As she watched with her breath frozen in her throat he reached out a white-shirted arm to pick up a pistol and fit his finger around the trigger.

Suddenly it was as if her feet had grown wings and she whirled towards the front door and, without a thought for the social niceties, flung it open and raced inside.

'No! Nick. . .don't!' she called frantically as she found the right door and pushed her way into the shadowy room where he was sitting. 'You can't. . .! You mustn't. . .!' she protested as she stumbled to a halt just inside the door.

He swung towards the intrusion and, in the stunned silence which followed her outburst, Polly was sure that the sound of her wild heartbeat must be reverberating off the walls as his startled grey eyes stared at her over the dully gleaming metal, the empty circle of the barrel pointing straight at her like a malevolent eye.

'Please, Nick,' she pleaded in a shaky voice when his aim remained unfalteringly on her. 'Please put it down and think about it. . .talk about it.'

'It?' he echoed, seeming almost puzzled by her words.

'The gun,' she whispered, as fear for him caused her nails to score deeply into her palms, hardly daring to take her eyes off him to look at the ugly thing. 'Will you put it down while we talk about this?'

'The gun?' She saw him glance down at it almost dismissively, then she saw his expression change to utter disbelief as his eyes swung back up to hers. 'My God! You didn't think I was going to. . .? Dammit, you did!'

His incredulous tone brought her up sharply, its bite more convincing than any words he could have used as he thumped the weapon down on the table and straightened up to his full height.

Polly stood staring mutely up at him, the effects of the adrenaline which had flooded through her system leaving her with a sick trembling sensation deep inside, her skin clammy enough to make her shudder in spite of the warmth of her down-filled jacket.

'I'm sorry...' she mumbled when the uncomfortable silence seemed as if it would stretch into eternity, and she dragged her eyes away to gaze at the wall—at the furniture—anywhere except at him. 'I shouldn't...I didn't mean to...' She shrugged and fixed her eyes on the fringed edge of the slightly faded Indian carpet square centred on the polished parquet flooring just inches away from his naked feet.

'What's going on here?' he finally demanded, his harsh voice seeming too loud for her overstrained nerves. 'Why are you here? What gives you the right to come in here and insinuate that I...? How *did* you get in here in the first place?' He changed his angle of attack suddenly. 'I certainly didn't hear the bell.'

'The door wasn't shut.' Polly opted to answer the easiest question first, her voice thin and reedy-sounding after his powerful anger. 'I was just going to ring the bell when I saw that you must have left it open when you came in.'

'So you decided that gave you the right to march right in and throw accusations around?'

'No...'

She might as well have saved her breath because he wasn't listening.

'Well, I'm sorry I didn't realise that I had to be so careful about shutting doors,' he continued sarcastically, his hands clenching spasmodically as he raked her with eyes like honed steel. 'I obviously didn't know that it was an invitation to any passerby to invade my home and...'

'No... Please... It wasn't like that...' she burst out.

'Wasn't it?' he snapped. 'It seems to me that it was *exactly* like...'

'No, it's not! Here...' Before he could work up a

good head of steam Polly scrabbled in her bag, suddenly remembering the official reason why she had been standing on his doorstep in the first place. 'Sister MacDonald found this on the floor in her office but you'd already gone home.' She held up the well-worn leather object. 'She asked me to drop it in on my way home.'

In the ensuing silence Polly felt the guilt of half-truths heating her cheeks, and was grateful for the deepening gloom in the room when she remembered how delighted she'd been with the legitimate excuse to visit.

'My wallet,' he murmured after his hand reached back automatically for his trouser pocket and found it empty. 'I hadn't even realised it was gone...'

Silently Polly reached out to hand it to him but, instead of accepting it, he stepped forward and took the hand holding it between his own.

'I'm sorry,' he murmured contritely, but all Polly could concentrate on was the huskiness of his voice and the electric heat which travelled through her body like lightning from the contact between their hands.

'Will you forgive me for jumping to conclusions?' The huskiness in his deep voice affected her nerve endings like the insistent caress of a cat's tongue, and she had to drag her gaze away from its preoccupation with the way her own small pale hand was almost swallowed up in the lean strength of his.

'Pardon?' She blinked up at him, only managing to focus on what he was saying when she broke the contact between them by pulling her hand away. For several seconds all she'd been able to concentrate on was exactly how *much* she had cared that he might have been thinking of killing himself.

'Apologising to you seems to be becoming a regular

habit these days,' he said wryly as he slid both hands into his pockets. 'It's happening on a daily basis now.'

'Well, this time I need to apologise too,' she admitted as her eyes strayed towards the small array of weapons. 'It's just...I know from what you told me yesterday that you were dreading today, and at the hospital you seemed...withdrawn...' She let the words die away as she shrugged.

'So you added two and two?'

'Well, what would *you* have thought if you'd glanced towards a window and seen someone pick up a gun and point it at himself?' Polly demanded. 'I didn't even know that you kept guns, or I'd have...' She stopped speaking and bit her tongue, suddenly aware that the words hovering on its tip would have revealed just how worried she had been about him—just how much she had started to care for this taciturn man.

'They were my father's,' he volunteered and turned towards the table again, scooping up the small case lying on the floor beside it. 'When he died several years ago I transferred them to my name—nostalgia, I suppose—and locked them securely away. I'd all but forgotten I had them until I heard something on the radio earlier on...I was just cleaning them one last time before I surrender them at the local police station.'

As he was speaking he paused with his hand over the switch on the small table lamp, then glanced towards the open curtains. When he left the room in near darkness Polly guessed that he had realised that it was safer to finish what he was doing without giving any passerby the chance to see into the room.

Moving with his customary swift efficiency, he slotted each weapon into its own recessed slot in the case and then did the same with a small steel box and several anonymous lumps of metal.

'What are they?' Polly was intrigued in spite of herself and took a step closer.

'The firing mechanisms for each of those.' He nodded towards the guns. 'Each is useless without the other so I take them apart and secure them separately so that even if I'm burgled it's unlikely that both parts will be taken.'

'And you'd already taken them apart before I arrived?' Polly guessed, feeling more stupid with every passing minute.

'That's right,' he confirmed and she thought she saw the brief gleam of his smile as he glanced up at her. 'So, when you saw me, not only was I holding a gun without a firing mechanism but I don't even possess any ammunition.'

'Well, at least when I make a fool of myself I do a good job of it,' Polly said in a strangled voice, knowing that he was laughing at her—knowing that he thought she was a fool. 'But now that I've delivered your wallet I'd better be on my way home.'

'Polly. . .' His voice halted her at the door. 'You know, you didn't make a fool of yourself. It was actually a very brave thing to do.'

'Brave?' The word surprised her. She hadn't thought of it like that. . .hadn't expected him to think like that. All she'd been conscious of at the time was the fact that she hadn't wanted him to do something so destructive while he was depressed. She had the feeling that real bravery was what she would be needing a large measure of when she had to face him in the morning when she went on duty.

'Yes. Brave,' he insisted, as if he could hear the

argument going on inside her head. 'What if the gun *had* been loaded? I could easily have killed you too.'

She considered the idea briefly and shook her head.

'No. You couldn't,' she said with utter conviction. 'You're too good a doctor to waste a life like that.'

There was a long silence before he gave a short bark of laughter.

'At least, not intentionally,' he agreed with a depressingly swift return to bitterness. 'It doesn't mean that people don't end up just as dead.'

Polly had an idea that she knew only too well what he meant, but she knew that she daren't comment as she listened to the sounds as he picked up the case. She could only dimly perceive his movements in the light that seeped into the room from the streetlamps, and suddenly realised just how dark it had grown since she had pushed her way into his house.

'I'm sorry,' she murmured, not knowing what else she could say, and reached for the door. 'Well, I. . .I'll see you tomorrow, then.'

'Stay. . .'

The word was hardly more than a husky whisper but she heard it as clearly as if he had shouted it, and her breath stopped in her throat. What exactly was he asking?

'Please. . .'

They were both standing still in the darkened room, his face nothing more than a paler shadow among shadows, but she could remember all too clearly the desolation in his expression when he'd told her that his wife was dead.

'But. . . Dr Prince. . .'

'Nick,' he prompted softly.

'Pardon?'

'You called me Nick when you thought I was going to blow my brains out,' he reminded her, and she felt the heat rise in her cheeks. She'd used his name unconsciously and had hoped that he hadn't noticed the slip.

'Yes, well, that was...it was...'

'Please. I need someone to talk to—someone who'll understand.'

How did he know the one argument which she couldn't refuse, much as she knew she should?

'But I...'

'Just for a little while?'

Polly closed her eyes tightly as she fought to ignore the little voice inside her head which was telling her to leave. She knew that it was the sensible thing to do, but when had she ever been able to make her head rule her soft heart?

'All right,' she agreed. 'Just for a little while.'

For several seconds he was silent, as if he couldn't believe what she'd said, then she heard him release a deep sigh.

'I need to lock these away.' He lifted the case of guns. 'Would you like to go through to the kitchen, or...'

'The kitchen's fine,' she interrupted hastily. 'I could put the kettle on, if you like.' She pulled the door open and stepped out into the hallway, then came to a full stop.

The fanlight window over the front door allowed a small band of streetlight into the hallway, but it didn't reach far enough to show her the way to the kitchen door.

'Light switch on the wall to your left,' he murmured, and she squeaked as his voice sounded right beside her ear.

'You made me jump,' she complained as she fumbled

across the cool expanse of freshly painted wall in search of the elusive switch. 'I didn't hear you move.'

There was a sharp click as she found it, and the hallway was flooded with brightness.

'Sorry to startle you,' he apologised, 'but it's a bit difficult to make a lot of noise with bare feet.'

Polly could hear the hint of laughter in his voice and refused to look, hurrying towards the door at the end of the hallway as if her life depended on it.

She had made a pot of tea and was just about to pour it out into two mugs when she suddenly remembered his reaction to the beverage last night. Swiftly she took the teapot over to the sink, but before she could pour it away and substitute coffee he was there.

'Ah, good. Did you find everything you needed?'

He scooped the two mugs up off the table and brought them towards her, a quick glance inside showing him that she'd already put milk in each.

'No. . . Yes. . . I. . .I'm sorry, Doctor. . .'

'Nick,' he reminded her. 'You were going to call me Nick, remember?'

'Nick,' she echoed, then dragged in a shaky breath and forced herself to face him. 'I'm sorry. . . Nick. . .but I forgot about. . .I forgot that you can't. . .I made tea,' she finished lamely. 'It won't take a minute for the kettle to boil again for coffee. . .'

'No,' he said sharply and pressed his lips tightly together and started again in a calmer tone. 'No. It's quite all right, Polly. It's time I started consciously putting it behind me, and the first step might as well be a cup of tea.'

He deposited the mugs on the draining-board and waited while she poured in the tea, then took charge of them again as he led the way back into the sitting-room, drawing the curtains and switching on the table lamp in the corner before inviting her to sit.

When he settled himself down in the other corner of the enormous squashy settee and angled his long legs towards her own she suddenly became aware that the two of them were closer now than they'd ever been before—closer and totally alone, without the possibility of interruption from other members of staff.

Nervously she directed her eyes away from him, determined to make a minute inspection of her surroundings rather than allow herself to notice the way the soft light highlighted the golden gleam of his rumpled hair or outlined the angles and planes of his face.

In the mellow lamplight the room no longer looked stark and bare—in fact, now that she looked more closely, she could see that everything looked freshly decorated.

'You've been having a lot of work done in the house,' she commented brightly, trying to fill the suffocating silence which seemed to have fallen between them like a thick grey mist. 'Is it nearly finished?'

'It'll be a while yet—the downstairs rooms are all but finished, but I've only just begun upstairs.'

'You?' Polly's eyes widened. 'You mean you've been doing the work yourself?'

'As much as I can,' he admitted. 'I decided for safety's sake to leave things like wiring and plastering to the professionals, but as for the rest...' he shrugged '...I quite enjoy the challenge.'

'The kitchen, too?' Polly demanded, her admiration making her forget that she'd been determined not to look at him. She'd taken a real delight in exploring the design and finish of the beautiful fitted cupboards while she'd made their tea. 'All those fantastic cabinets?'

'Made them and installed them,' he confirmed, with more than a touch of justified pride in his voice.

Polly was quite speechless at the scope of his talent and patience. Knowing how many hours he had been spending at the hospital and seeing the result of many hours of labour here, it was no wonder that he was short-tempered and exhausted. He could hardly have been sleeping at all...

'I'm impressed,' she said finally, with massive understatement. 'And you're working your way right through the house?'

'Room by room—do you want to see how far I've got?'

He straightened up eagerly out of his corner and held out his hand to pull her up out of the comfortable embrace of the deep upholstery.

The contact between them was brief, but Polly was conscious of a strange residual tingling in her hand after he'd effortlessly set her on her feet, and she was careful to keep enough distance between them to avoid any accidental contact as he led the way through the quiet elegance of the ground-floor rooms.

'I love the mixture of furniture you've chosen,' she commented as they ended up in the hallway again. 'The pieces you've made yourself complement the older ones very well.' She smiled up at him, marvelling at how easy the atmosphere had become between them.

'It's not the same up here,' he warned as he padded his way up the freshly polished bare treads in his equally bare feet. 'The house was owned by an elderly man and he'd been unable to go upstairs for several years before he finally had to sell.'

'I see what you mean,' she said, screwing up her

nose at the grim dinginess of the upstairs hallway. It seemed so much worse after the beauty they'd just left downstairs.

'And that's *after* I've scrubbed everything down,' he pointed out ruefully as he pushed open the first door at the top of the stairs and flicked the switch to light the bare bulb hanging in the centre of the room. 'There are two more like this.'

'What had you planned doing with them?'

Once she got over the appalling state of decoration she could see that the proportions of the room were good and her imagination started working.

'Probably pretty much the same as down there.' He tilted his head towards the stairs. 'The floors aren't in the same good condition up here because the original timber wasn't of the same quality so I'll probably have to carpet them, but apart from that. . .'

After seeing what he had achieved downstairs she could easily picture what the doors and windows would look like once he'd stripped the chipped paint, finished the wood underneath to a soft golden shine and painted the freshly plastered walls.

'I've nearly finished in here. . .' He pushed open the next door to reveal a partially tiled bathroom, the pile of boxes in the corner proving that eventually the rest of the walls would be covered with the same creamy onyx tiles that surrounded the bath and shower.

'Is that as far as you've gone?' she said, almost disappointed to have come to the end of the tour. She'd thoroughly enjoyed being shown round his home and seeing the work he'd put into its restoration. It had given her an insight into a totally unexpected side of the reserved man she thought she'd known.

She didn't know whether it was her imagination, but

he seemed to hesitate briefly before he indicated the last door.

'Only this one,' he said as he pushed the door wide with sudden determination and flicked the switch. 'My room.'

Polly hung back for a second, her cheeks flushing as the significance struck her, but overwhelming curiosity forced her to step forward.

It was a very masculine room, full of natural wood and earth tones from pale oatmeal to the rich depth of terracotta and bitter chocolate, the furniture scaled to fit his height.

'It's lovely,' she said honestly and smiled at him—anything to keep her eyes away from the smooth expanse of the magnificent polished wood double bed. Then he returned her smile, and with an instantaneous leap in her pulse she realised that she could see behind the withdrawn façade to the person walled up inside the pain.

Suddenly it wasn't just the bed she couldn't look at—it was the man standing beside her. What on earth was she doing in his bedroom, for heaven's sake?

In their busy quest for something to look at her eyes alighted on a small silver frame on top of the tallboy beside her, and before she could stop herself she'd reached out and turned it towards her.

'Oh...!' she breathed when she saw the image of a much younger, happier Nick Prince, laughing as he tried to shield his beautiful new wife from a shower of confetti.

Polly shut her eyes tightly, horrified by what she had done—and today of all days.

The silence went on and on and she wished that the

floor would simply open up and swallow her. How could she possibly apologise?

'Our wedding day,' he confirmed needlessly, his voice sounding as painful as if it were travelling over rough gravel, and he reached out to touch the photo gently with the tip of one lean finger before he clenched his hand and pulled it away again. 'We met when Dee was in her final year of nursing training.'

'Please. . .' Polly turned and reached a tentative hand out towards him. It was tearing her apart inside, just hearing him talk about it—hearing the pain in his voice. What must it be doing to him? What must it be like for him to drag all the memories out? 'Nick, you don't have to tell me.'

'Yes, I do,' he said, suddenly fierce as he gripped her hand. 'Please, Polly, I need to talk about it—to tell you. . .'

She gazed up into his face and saw the pain bracketing his mouth and shadowing his eyes and nodded.

'We'd been married for four years before we were ready to start a family, and couldn't believe it when we were successful on our first attempt.' His smile was almost bashful and she saw a hint of colour wash along his cheek-bones.

'For safety's sake, we waited until she'd got past the twelve-week stage and was just beginning to show before we went to visit her parents to break the news— only we never got there. Some drunk tried to beat the traffic lights and ploughed right into her side of the car.'

'Oh, God,' Polly breathed, longing to comfort him— longing to wrap her arms around him to let him know that he wasn't alone—but she had a feeling that this was the first time that he had allowed himself to talk about it, and knew from the tension in his body that there was more to come so she didn't dare move.

'She was trapped,' he whispered, his wintry grey eyes so desolate as he gazed down at her that she knew he wasn't seeing her but the memories which haunted him. 'The two cars were so tangled together that they had to cut them apart to get to her, and all the time the drunk was cursing and swearing about his no-claims bonus while she was bleeding to death.'

He closed his eyes and a solitary tear spilled over and ran down his cheek.

'Oh, Nick. . .'

Finally she dared to reach up and wrap her arms around him, one hand cupping the back of his bent head. For just a second he resisted, then his own arms wrapped convulsively around her and the sobs shook his broad shoulders.

The storm was brief but fierce, and when he would have turned away in embarrassment at having let down the barriers so comprehensively Polly calmly handed him the man-sized handkerchief from her pocket and suggested that a cold flannel would soothe his eyes.

She avoided looking at him, hoping to allow him enough time to regain control, and when she heard the soft whisper of his bare feet leaving the room she busied herself by folding back the covers on his bed.

For a moment she contemplated going back down to the kitchen to heat some milk, but before she could carry the idea out she heard him returning.

'I'd better be going. . .'
'I'm sorry. . .'

They both began to speak together and broke off in confusion.

'There's nothing to apologise for,' she said firmly, saddened when she saw the way he was avoiding her eyes. 'I expect you'd have done the same thing for me if the positions had been reversed. I'm just glad that I was here for you. Perhaps it would be a good idea if you tried to catch up on some sleep?'

He glanced at the prepared bed and chuckled wryly. 'Not something I can do a lot of these days,' he commented tellingly. 'I've been here for nearly a year and the house has never seemed so big and empty as it has the last few weeks.'

'I can remember that feeling,' Polly said. 'I even resorted to leaving music playing.'

'Did it work?'

She shook her head. 'The only thing that helped was when a friend's marriage was going through a sticky patch. She came to stay while she thought things through, and just the presence of another person. . .'

'Will you stay for me?'

The sudden request shocked her so much that she thought she must have misheard him, her eyes widening in disbelief.

'Stay?' she whispered, while her heart stumbled and her breath caught in her throat.

'Just to talk. . .just so there's someone there,' he pleaded softly. 'If I don't get some sleep soon. . .' He closed his eyes tiredly and sighed.

She looked at the lines of exhaustion marking his face and all her sensible objections flew out of the window.

'I could stay for a while,' she conceded, 'but I'll need to get some sleep myself if I'm going to be any use tomorrow. If you like, I could make you some hot chocolate while you get yourself settled.'

As soon as he agreed she made her way swiftly down the stairs, firmly squashing the nervous skip in her pulse when she had a mental image of his powerful body sliding between the crisp cotton covers.

For safety's sake, she gave him nearly ten minutes before she made her careful way back up the stairs with a steaming mug in each hand.

He'd piled the pillows against the polished wood of the headboard and the bedside light was gilding the curve of one shoulder when she approached him, her eyes carefully focused on the unsteady surface of the liquid rather than on the broad expanse of naked chest in front of her.

'Thank you, Sister,' he said with a self-mocking grimace as he accepted her offering. 'I can't remember how many years it's been since I had a hot milky drink at bedtime, but at this point I'm willing to try almost anything.'

He screwed up his nose like a sulky little boy as he took the first sip, and Polly chuckled at the startled expression which came over him.

'Now *that's* what I call a milky drink,' he said with a smile as he took a second larger mouthful. 'I take it you found the brandy bottle.'

'And lowered the level in it,' she agreed with an answering smile as she sipped her own drink.

'Did you put some in yours too?'

'No way! I'd fall asleep standing up if I was to drink any,' she joked as she transferred her weight uneasily from one foot to the other while her gaze flickered from his bed to the chair full of clothes which stood almost at the edge of the circle of light.

'Well, then, the least you can do is take the weight off your feet and get yourself comfortable.' He patted the bedclothes beside him in invitation. 'There's plenty of room.'

'Oh, but. . .'

'Tell me,' he continued, completely overriding her attempted objection, 'what do you think of the way the new system's working in A and E? What sort of feedback are you getting from the rest of the staff?'

Polly was so startled by the abrupt change in pace of the conversation that before she realised it she was sharing the pile of pillows and was in the middle of a heated discussion about staffing levels and emergency recall procedures in the event of a large-scale disaster.

It must have been nearly an hour later that she realised that Nick's pause for thought had turned into genuine sleep when his head came to rest heavily against her shoulder.

'Nick?' she whispered, loath to disturb him but she needed to go home.

Over the space of the last hour the two of them had gradually slid down so that it should have been a simple matter for her to extricate herself from his trusting weight. Unfortunately, as soon as she tried to move away he muttered something unintelligible and rolled over to face her, one muscular arm draping across her to pin her more firmly in position than ever.

CHAPTER FOUR

POLLY had no idea what time it was when she woke up. All she knew was that it was still dark outside.

For several seconds she hadn't even been able to work out where she was but when she tried to turn over and found herself held firmly against a solid, naked body she remembered.

'Nick?' she whispered as she tried to lift his arm off her ribs, but all he did was tighten his grip so that her back was plastered against his chest, his face burrowing into the curve beneath her ear with a husky murmur.

'Nick?' She tried again, accompanying the word with a wriggle as she tried to slide out from under his hold, but when his hand closed convulsively around the softness of one breast she froze.

For more than a minute she lay absolutely still, her mind refusing to find a solution to her predicament as it took delight in cataloguing her every reaction to his touch.

Her breathing had grown rapid and her pulse jumped as her sleep-warmed flesh revelled in the touch of his hand, tinglingly aware of each long finger as they cupped her swelling roundness.

He lay motionless behind her, his even breathing teasing the back of her neck, but just when she thought he must have returned to deep sleep his hand moved again, his fingers flexing against the revealing hardness of her nipple so that she nearly moaned aloud.

'Mmm,' he murmured huskily, moving restlessly

behind her, and suddenly, as his thighs brushed against the backs of her legs, she was shocked to realise that she was no longer lying on top of the bedclothes. At some time while she'd been asleep she had ended up sharing his covers.

'Nick!' she whispered again, her scurrying heartbeat lending an edge of panic to her voice as his fingers probed the opening between the buttons on her blouse and discovered the silky heat of her naked breast.

'Beautiful,' he whispered, his voice deep and husky with sleep as he teased and taunted her aroused flesh with knowing fingers. 'Ah, sweetheart, come here...' And he rolled her towards him and took possession of her mouth.

For several seconds shock robbed her of the instinct to fight but by that time his tongue had insinuated itself inside her mouth, and when her own greeted the intruder with a sinuous dance of welcome she knew she was lost.

Somewhere in the back of her mind a small voice was trying to tell her that this was wrong, but when he lifted his head briefly to gaze down at her all she could see was that he needed her, desperately, and when he found the swollen slick evidence of her own blatant desire all she wanted to do was wrap her arms around him and welcome him into her body.

'Thank goodness for half-days,' Polly murmured as she changed out of her uniform the next day.

'And quiet shifts,' agreed Hannah as she prepared to go back on duty. 'Although why I'm pleased that it was quiet for you, I don't know. The second half of my shift will probably be bedlam! Still, at least I've got a late start tomorrow so think of me when you have to get up in the morning. . .' She waved a cheeky goodbye and left Polly to her thoughts.

She'd been lucky so far today. The second time she'd woken up she'd only just had time to dash home and dive under the shower before it had been time to go to work. Lucky, too, that Nick hadn't had to go to work until later, and that he'd still been sleeping so heavily that she hadn't disturbed him when she'd slid out of the wildly rumpled bed.

She hadn't been able to resist pausing at the door of his room for one last look at him, storing up in her mind the magnificent picture of the powerful symmetry of his body sprawled bonelessly across the bed, his modesty unnecessarily protected by one corner of the sheet.

Her cheeks burnt as she realised where her eyes were fixed and she dragged them away to look at his face.

The thick old-gold strands of his hair were tousled boyishly across his forehead, all the lines of stress and tension smoothed out so that he looked years younger. His thick, much darker lashes threw fan-like shadows onto his cheeks, temporarily hiding the darker shadows which insomnia had caused to grow there over the last few weeks.

His jaw was heavily darkened by his early-morning beard, and her breasts tingled as she remembered the sensuous rasp of it over her tender flesh while he'd explored them.

One arm was flung up over his head, displaying the strangely vulnerable tuft of darker hair, and the other lay across the space she had so recently vacated, the fingers loosely curled as though he had been reaching out for her in his sleep.

Part of her longed to join him there—to wake him

up and lose herself once more in the glory of his love-making—but the saner half knew that it wasn't possible.

She knew that, in spite of the fact that he'd been blameless, even after two years he was still racked by grief over the death of his wife and unborn child and wasn't ready to welcome anyone else into his life.

Anyway, she reminded herself, she knew how much it hurt to cry for the moon, and she'd promised herself that she wouldn't put herself through that again.

She shivered in the early morning autumn chill, dreading their first encounter. He probably wouldn't even need to say anything to make her blush from head to toe. Just one look from those molten steel eyes would be enough to turn her bones to jelly, especially when she remembered the way he had looked at her when he'd taken possession of her body...

'It's no good thinking about it when you know it's safer all round if the two of us put the whole episode behind us,' she muttered as she picked up her bag and started walking along the hospital corridor, scowling at the thought that before she could catch up on her sleep she'd got the shopping to do on the way home then the laundry and...

'Polly.'

One husky word stopped her in her tracks and her heart felt as if it was going to leap right out of her chest.

She turned to face him, her eyes flicking nervously from side to side to see who might be watching.

'Dr Prince,' she greeted him, her eyes firmly fixed on the broad burgundy stripe in his tie. She didn't dare look up into his face—even thinking about it was flooding her face with heat.

'It's Nick, remember,' he said in the same slightly roughened tone he'd used last night when he'd finally caught his breath enough to cradle her against his side and murmur endearments.

He took a step closer, and when she tried to retreat she found herself neatly backed against the wall. 'You should have woken me before you left,' he complained, his intonation making every nerve ending tingle as if he were stroking her with velvet.

'I had to go home to change for work.' She tried to be prosaic in an attempt at controlling her reaction to him. She was uncomfortable talking about the episode at all, never mind that the conversation was taking place in a busy corridor.

'I would still have liked. . .'

'Anyway, you needed your sleep,' she butted in, desperately wishing that she'd left the hospital just two minutes earlier. Then this conversation would never have taken place. 'There was no point in waking you up just to say goodbye.'

'It would have been more than just goodbye, Polly.' He leant towards her and she felt surrounded by him, drawing in the indefinable mixture of soap and skin which could only be Nicholas Prince.

'But. . .'

She was totally flustered. Ever since she'd first met him he'd always been slightly withdrawn, and she'd always thought it was a result of the responsibilities heaped on his shoulders.

This Nicholas Prince was a stranger and she had no idea why he was behaving like this towards her—and in such a public place. Although this area was officially out of bounds to members of the public, staff could appear at any time and heaven only knew what they'd have made of the scene that confronted them. Had he lost all respect for her after she'd fallen into his arms so easily?

When her thoughts finally spiralled to a halt she realised that he'd been staring down at her in silence for some time and heat washed up her throat again.

'We need to talk, Polly.'

He straightened away from the wall and took a step back, and she nearly made a run for it, her heart starting to thump like a startled rabbit's again.

'T-talk?'

She'd only stayed to talk last night, and look what had happened...

'I should be finished by eight tonight. Can I take you out for a meal?'

It had been phrased as a question, but inside she quivered when she recognised the steely determination behind it.

Before she could dig an answer out of her paralysed brain the corridor was filled with the shrill sound of his pager.

'Dammit...' He silenced it with a frustrated stab of one finger and then leant towards her again, for the first time touching her as he raised her chin with the tip of the same finger.

Polly couldn't resist. Her gaze slid inexorably up over the neatly tied knot in his tie and the tanned column of his throat, pausing briefly as she fought to subdue the memories of what that mouth had felt like when it had possessed her own with such fervour, until at last she met the burning intensity of his eyes.

How could she ever have thought that grey eyes were cold when his seared her like molten steel with a single glance?

'Polly.' His deep voice was huskier than ever and

the sound sent a shiver right up her spine. 'We *do* need to talk—the sooner the better,' he continued, dragging her thoughts back from their heated wanderings. 'I'll see you as close to eight as I can make it.'

As he straightened up again, allowing a few more inches between their bodies, Polly began to draw in a silent breath of relief that the encounter was over, but she'd relaxed too soon. Before she'd realised what he intended to do he'd swooped down again and kissed her, the warmth of his lips lingering just long enough to brand her with his touch.

Before she could even think about whether she should reject the contact or respond to it he was gone, his long legs eating up the distance as he hurried towards the nearest phone.

Reaction still had Polly's legs quivering like jelly, and she had to lean weakly against the wall for several minutes while she gathered her thoughts enough to make for the nearest exit.

'Ah, Polly. . . Light of my life!' Leo called after her, and Polly groaned as she turned to face him. Was she never going to escape?

'Hello, Leo. What do *you* want?' she said, softening the exasperation in her question with a smile.

'Don't be like that.' He feigned hurt. 'You know I only have eyes for you.'

'And the rest!' Her grin was starting to feel more natural, his nonsense managing to bring her feet back to the ground far faster than a fight with a trolley in the local supermarket. 'What is it this time?'

'Well, it's about the Autumn Ball or, to be more accurate, the Auction part.'

Polly frowned. 'I don't see how I can help. I'm not quite in the same league as the consultants who are offering holidays in Brittany or sailing on a yacht.'

'Actually, that's why I needed to talk to you. Have you got a minute?'

'So much for getting all my chores done and catching up on some sleep,' she moaned, pulling a wry face. 'All right. But only on condition that we find somewhere to sit outside. I'm late going off duty as it is, and I refuse to stay inside this building one minute longer.'

'And I bet you haven't eaten either. Hang on, then. Let's make a quick detour.' He grabbed her elbow and directed her towards the coffee-shop, plying a steady trade in one corner of the enormous ultramodern foyer.

Within minutes a blushing matronly volunteer had succumbed to his good looks and cheerful charm and he was paying for a selection of freshly cut sandwiches and fruit and two lidded containers of orange juice.

'Any preferences for the venue?' he demanded as they jogged out of the way of an ambulance which was turning towards the nearby outpatients block.

'How about the grassy area behind the special care baby unit? There's a wooden bench under the trees.'

'Your every wish is my command, fair lady,' he declared, and led the way.

'So, Leo, what's the problem?' Polly prompted when she'd finished tucking all the empty wrappings into one paper bag and turned to face him, one arm resting along the back of the wooden bench. 'If you're looking for me to provide you with a star prize you're out of luck. It's all a bit out of my league, I'm afraid.'

'That's the problem in a nutshell,' he admitted in a worried tone. 'I was absolutely delighted at first when people were so generous but it wasn't long before the murmurs started.'

'Murmurs?'

'That there wasn't going to be anything of interest for the majority.'

'You mean the rest of the plebs, like me, who would never dare to bid on tickets to a West End show when they know they're up against the financial muscle power of a consultant?'

'Exactly! And now that I've backed myself into a corner I can't see how to get myself out of it.' He ran the fingers of one hand distractedly through his thick tawny hair.

'Embarrassing, especially as, by all accounts, the whole thing was your idea in the first place.'

'Don't remind me!' he groaned as he straightened up and sat back against the bench, mirroring her own position.

The sullen grey light of an autumn afternoon struggled its way through the almost leafless branches of the tree behind them to play over his lean body as he glowered in the direction of the massive new wing of the hospital.

Polly was silent for a moment, thinking, but nothing immediately came to mind.

'Have you got a list of the promises so far? Perhaps that will give us an idea?'

'Here you are. . .' Leo leant towards her as he fished in his pocket to pull out several sheets of paper folded together. 'The list so far. I've read it so often I'm beginning to have nightmares about it!'

Polly skimmed her way down it with an appreciative whistle. 'Wow! What a fantastic haul! You should be able to raise quite a bit towards the scanner with this little lot.'

'But only if there are enough people with deep enough pockets to bid for them,' he complained in despair. 'If everything goes too cheaply it'll seem like an insult to the people who have made such generous donations, but the majority of the people at the Ball won't get a look-in if the prices are too high.'

The offer of a massage caught Polly's eye and she smiled as she remembered the way Tina Wadland had coveted it—especially if she had her choice of masseur.

Suddenly she had a glimmer of an idea and she straightened up sharply, leaning forward to rest her elbows on her knees as she scanned the list again.

'Have you got a pen?' she demanded, her eyes fixed on the paper propped on her knees as she started reading from the top again.

'Here.' Leo handed her one then leant over her to see what she was doing. 'What have you got?' he queried hopefully as he rested one arm around her shoulders.

'Just an idea. Give me a minute while I...' She concentrated fiercely, the pen swooping at intervals to add notations down the side of the page, before she straightened up again. 'Listen to this...'

She read out a partial list of the wonderful prizes people had promised and Leo's face grew longer.

'So?' he challenged. 'As I said, people have been very generous.'

'Now listen to these...' She began reading again, but this time, instead of the 'star' prizes, she listed such items as the massage—with Tina's comment about her preferences—and the offer of dancing lessons—with an aside about Fred Astaire's understudy being available if Patrick Swayze couldn't make it after all...

'Give me that!' There was a current of excitement in his voice as he reached out and snatched the list from her hand, his eyes skimming quickly down the items she'd marked and he whooped. 'You marvellous woman! I think you've cracked it!' He flung both arms around her and delivered a smacking kiss.

Polly laughed aloud at his boyish exuberance.

Out of the corner of her eye she saw an anonymous, tall, white-coated figure pause by one of the huge plate-glass windows in the overlooking corridor, and her heart leapt with the thought that it might be Nick.

Suddenly one small corner of her mind marvelled that a kiss and a hug from this gorgeous specimen of virile male did absolutely nothing for her, while all she had to do was *think* about the husky tone in the voice of a certain A and E consultant and her pulse went haywire.

She dragged her concentration back to the matter in hand.

'As far as I can see, Leo, all you need to do is make sure that you mix the fun items among the swanky ones and play the humour of the situation for all you're worth. You might need a few more of the light-hearted items...'

'*That* won't be a problem now I know what I'm looking for!' he exclaimed animatedly. 'In fact, it might even be an idea if we had one or two prizes that were outside the auction itself—perhaps a raffle prize or a draw of the Ball tickets...' His voice faded away and she could see that his mind was racing on at full speed, his tawny eyes getting a faraway look as he forgot that she was there.

'Well, sir.' Polly gathered up her belongings and got to her feet, wrapping her jacket around her as a chilly breeze caught her and made her shiver. 'Now that I've solved your problem, please may I go? There's a supermarket trolley just waiting to wrench my arms out of their sockets and a washing machine that can't wait to chew my clothes up and help all the colours to run together.'

'Oh, Polly, I'm sorry,' Leo apologised ruefully as he dragged himself away from his planning and straightened up to his full six feet, apparently unconcerned that the same breeze had tousled his hair and heightened the colour in his cheeks. 'You've been a wonderful help, sweetheart. I'd never have seen the solution if you hadn't pointed it out. I'll show you how far I've got when you have a break tomorrow.'

He leant forward to plant another swift kiss on her cheek and then loped away across the grass, turning to call over his shoulder, 'How about eleven o'clock, and you can make the coffee. . .?'

'OK. It's a date,' she agreed laughingly, then watched as he paused long enough to offer a gentlemanly elbow to an elderly lady struggling out of a taxi and steadied her on her feet.

Polly shook her head as she made her way towards the shops, stepping out briskly to minimise the effects of the dismal day. It was hard to realise that Leo and Nick were within a few years of each other in age. Oh, they were both excellent A and E doctors and had apparently known each other for some years, but Leo was such a live wire that he seemed far younger—as if life had yet to make its mark on him.

Whereas Nick. . . The excitement stirred inside her when she thought about his unexpected invitation, only slightly tempered by the quiver of apprehension she felt about his insistence that they needed to talk. He'd seemed so serious, as if. . .

She forced out an exasperated breath when she realised that she had just walked past the entrance to the supermarket, and resolved to make herself concentrate on the chores she still had to do before she could think about getting ready.

In spite of frequent stern reminders, she couldn't help her thoughts wandering as she tried to decide what to wear.

In the few seconds available in the corridor he'd given her no idea where he was going to take her, and she had an awful mental picture of opening her door dressed to the nines to find Nick on the step in jeans and a casual jumper.

Then she couldn't decide if it would be worse if the situation were reversed and she ended up sitting in a very smart restaurant with an escort in a three-piece suit and an expensive pure silk tie, while she wore leggings and a voluminous jumper.

By the time eight o'clock came round she was a nervous wreck. It seemed to have taken her hours of trying on and discarding before she'd settled on her favourite heavy silk pleated evening trousers and a wrap-over jade silk blouse, and it had taken her another age to put away the rest of her wardrobe so that the flat was tidy again before he was due to arrive.

One part of her was insisting piously that it didn't matter if she left the bedroom in a mess because Nick was only coming to take her out so that they could talk and would therefore not see if the room was tidy.

The other, more hopeful part was alive with the possibility that if the evening went well Nick might very well see the inside of her bedroom when he returned her home later tonight...

She glanced around the room to feverishly check one last time that everything was neat and tidy, her eyes skimming over the African violet just coming into flower on the window-sill and the ticket to the Autumn

Ball which she had propped up on the mantelpiece just behind the photo...

Her eyes, her thoughts, her breathing, *everything* slammed to a halt when she focused on the precious oblong, framed in silver, which gleamed softly in the subdued lighting.

She took a step towards it, her hand shaking slightly as she reached out a finger to stroke the image tenderly.

In the stillness of the room she clearly heard the clock chime the hour as a car drew up outside the building, and she dragged her eyes away from the photo to look out of the window, smiling at Nick's punctuality...only it wasn't Nick who got out of the car which had parked under the streetlight outside. The man was a stranger who waved and called a greeting as one of the other tenants in the subdivided house went out to join him.

Knowing what life could be like in an accident and emergency department, Polly wasn't unduly worried when the time crept round to quarter past and then half past eight, but when nine o'clock came and went without so much as a phone call she didn't know what to think.

Could she have mistaken the day?

In the confusion of her surprise at the invitation and his pager distracting the two of them, had he actually said eight o'clock—and had it been tonight or tomorrow?

Polly went over it carefully in her mind and was certain that he'd said he hoped to finish at eight tonight. That meant that he must have been delayed by some medical emergency.

Should she phone the hospital...? She toyed with the idea briefly, thinking that she could ask if there had been any major problems this evening—but how could she ask without drawing attention to the fact that it was Nick's whereabouts she was interested in? Wouldn't the hospital grapevine have a field day with that item of gossip? Sister Polly Lang chasing after Nicholas Prince!

She kicked off her smart court shoes and curled her legs under her in the big squashy chair in the corner by the window, resting her chin on her fist so that she could watch the comings and goings in the street with a steadily sinking heart.

For just a little while she had been ready to abandon her self-imposed restriction on getting involved. For just a little while she had almost let herself believe that something good could grow from the meeting of wounded souls which she'd believed had happened last night.

'Ha!' she laughed, a brief, bitter sound in the silence of the room. How could she have been so stupid as to allow herself to be fooled again? She knew only too well that men couldn't be trusted to keep their word, and she only had herself to blame for letting her guard down.

Even so, it was after eleven o'clock before Polly finally gave up her vigil.

She scooped up her discarded shoes in one hand and forced herself to walk calmly into her bedroom and push the door to, before stripping off her finery.

Force of habit made her hang her clothes up neatly but she found herself putting them away at the very back of the wardrobe. In spite of the fact that it was one of her favourites, she doubted that she would be wearing *that* outfit again in a hurry. . .

It was hard to remove her careful make-up without meeting her own eyes in the mirror but somehow she managed it, afraid of what she might see if she looked too closely.

Finally she was curled up under the covers, shivering slightly in spite of the warmth and comfort of her duvet and refusing to remember her half-formed expectation that by now she might have been sharing her bed with Nick. It took a long time, but eventually she fell asleep and was able to block out the leaden emptiness that filled the aching space around her heart.

As Polly approached the entrance portico of St Augustine's the next morning she was aware that, in spite of the drizzly rain, there was more than a touch of eagerness in her step and she cursed herself silently.

Although she would never admit the fact to a living soul, she'd been badly hurt by the fact that yesterday had been the first time since her divorce that she'd taken a chance and agreed to go out for a meal—and Nick had stood her up without so much as an explanation.

Still, she couldn't help hoping that there was a simple reason why he hadn't arrived last night, and as soon as she reached the department her eyes were scanning the various white-coated members of staff, hoping to see a familiar set of broad shoulders.

Unfortunately, the first time she saw him he was moving too quickly to notice anything around him, dashing across the corridor to disappear through a set of double doors into one of the major trauma rooms.

She peered briefly through the wired glass safety window as she hurried past on her own errand, but the bright lights were shining down on a badly injured patient, surrounded by a forest of equipment, and at least five or six frantically busy medical staff. The only way she could tell which of them was Nick was by the colour of his hair, the blond strands shining like platinum under the lights.

Within minutes an ambulance arrived from one of the large farms in the area where hunter trials were in progress, and Polly dived in at the deep end with no chance to think about anything but the job in hand.

'This is Olivia Harper,' began Ted Larrabee, his face shining with sweat induced by the combination of the warmth of the hospital, hard physical exertion and having to wear the waterproof layer of his paramedic's uniform. 'She's eighteen, and her horse hit a jump and fell on her. It was several minutes before we could get her out from underneath. Her pelvis is very painful.'

'Lord...' Polly murmured, her eyes taking in the slender blonde's pale sweaty face under the clear plastic of the Entonox mask as she reached automatically for the girl's wrist.

As she'd expected, the pulse rate was too fast and Olivia's rapid breathing wasn't just the result of agitation. 'What have you done so far?'

'One of the local GPs was on duty and, between us, we managed to get two large-bore IVs up and running with saline. She's had a small dose of ketamine to help her cope with the journey, but we only waited long enough to put a collar on her and strap her on the full-length backboard before we rushed her here. She's tachycardic but her blood pressure's still normal.'

He handed Polly his notations of their patient's vital signs and she added it to the clipboard which was the start of her casenotes. She noted mentally that the combination of readings Ted had given her meant that so far Olivia was unlikely to have lost much more than ten per cent of her blood volume.

There was no room for complacency, though, because apart from minor abrasions there was no obvious sign of a bleeding wound, and she'd seen similar situations change for the worse in the blink of an eye, especially if, as she suspected, the patient was haemorrhaging internally.

'Olivia? Can you hear me?' Staying well out of the way of the member of staff who was cutting away a very expensive-looking set of riding clothes, Polly leant over and carefully tucked two fingers into one pale, cold hand. 'Can you squeeze my fingers?' There was a weak but definite increase in pressure on her fingers and Polly smiled.

'Good girl,' she praised, relieved that the youngster was aware enough to follow directions. 'My name is Polly and I'm a nurse, Olivia. You've had an accident and in a minute we're going to move you off the stretcher and onto a bed. I want you to let us do all the work. Do you understand?'

There was another squeeze but when Polly received the signal from Leo that they were ready for the transfer and tried to take her fingers away she met with resistance, and glanced down to find a pair of hazel eyes looking up at her pleadingly.

'Please. . .' The whisper was so weak that Polly almost had to lip-read it.

'What is it?' She leant closer and lifted the edge of the mask slightly. 'What's the matter?'

'My horse. . . Jessie. . . Is she. . .?' The hazel eyes filled with anguished tears.

'I don't know, sweetheart, but I'll try to find out,' she promised with a sympathetic smile and an extra gentle squeeze of the pale fingers.

For several minutes there was very little conversation, other than brief orders and requests from Leo, while the various items of mobile life-support and monitoring equipment were disconnected and Olivia was hooked up to the hospital system.

Polly had her back to the door when the ambulance crew called out their farewells so she wasn't aware that the set of footsteps behind her had any special significance.

'Have the bloods gone up?' a deep voice demanded and her heart leapt alarmingly as she realised that Nick had just entered the room.

'Yes, and she's gone on O negative while we're waiting for group and cross-match,' Leo confirmed. 'We've got plenty of plasma and expander ready to go in case her pressure starts dropping. I've also sent a message to Alex Marshall on Orthopaedics. By the time he gets here we'll have the X-ray plates developed. Apart from anything else, she's badly bruised.'

Nick nodded briefly, his face expressionless as he looked straight past Polly to ask one of the other nurses to pass him Olivia's notes.

Polly knew that an emergency room was hardly the time or place for personal conversations, but over the next few minutes she gradually became aware that, far from being carefully discreet about their new intimacy while they were surrounded by colleagues, Nick was actually looking straight through her as if he'd never seen her before, his grey eyes as cold as permafrost.

CHAPTER FIVE

'I DON'T like the look of this,' Polly heard Leo mutter in an aside to Nick. 'Just the slightest pressure on her pelvic bones causes pain, and they look uneven enough *without* an X-ray for confirmation of at least one break.'

'I agree,' Nick said decisively. 'We can't do any more down here without the X-rays because we don't know if we're dealing with spinal injuries or not and, meanwhile, she could be bleeding out. Let's get her ready to go straight up to Theatre. Her pictures can join her there, rather than doing a detour down here. Get hold of Alex and tell him about the change of plan. . .'

'Her blood pressure's dropping,' Polly broke in hurriedly. 'Not very much yet but she's losing ground, and in spite of everything we're pumping into her she's not responding to—'

'Right, that's it! Move it, people. . . We don't want to lose her,' Nick said sharply, cutting right across Polly's words, and the team was galvanised into furious activity.

Within seconds Olivia had been switched from the piped oxygen supply to a mobile unit, and the portable monitoring equipment was stacked across the end of the trolley for the rapid transition up to Theatre.

'Doors,' Leo called as the side rails clanged up into position and the wheels were unlocked. With the minimum of effort the bed began to glide swiftly across the room. 'We don't know what damage has been done internally so we don't want to jar her any more than we can help.'

Polly was closest to the double doors and gave a practised flick so that first one and then the other slotted back onto their automatic catches.

'Ready,' she called as she preceded the entourage out into the corridor to make certain there were no obstructions on the way to the lift. She knew from long practice that it could make quite a difference to the transit time if she went ahead to press the call button so that those doors could be ready and waiting, too.

As soon as they were safely on their way up she returned towards the emergency room, suddenly realising that she might have a chance to speak to Nick now that his part in the drama was over.

She was so preoccupied with her thoughts as she turned the corner that it took several seconds for her to realise that it was Nick's figure she could see striding away from her towards the opposite end of the department.

'Nick!' Polly called as she hurried after him, almost having to run to catch up as his long legs ate up the distance. 'Dr Prince, wait. . .'

She rounded the next corner in his wake and nearly ran into him as he stood, facing her, in the middle of the corridor.

'Sorry. I didn't expect you to stop just there. . .' she began breathlessly, but the words congealed on her tongue when she saw the anger in his gaze and wondered if calling after him had been terribly indiscreet. She'd never contemplated having a liaison with a colleague—even a fledgling one such as the relationship between Nick and herself—and had no idea of the proprieties.

'Well?' he barked. 'What did you want?'

'N-Nick?' She was almost speechless with shock at his harsh tone. What on earth gave him the right to be so rude? It wasn't as if *she* was the one who had stood him up last night.

'Come on. I haven't got time to waste,' he prompted. 'Why did you come chasing after me?'

'Well, an apology wouldn't go amiss,' she retorted and closed her mouth tightly, her teeth almost grinding together as she seethed.

'Apology accepted,' he snapped coldly. 'Perhaps you'd do better to. . .'

'What do you mean, "apology accepted"?' she demanded, so utterly incensed that it was difficult to remember to keep her voice down. 'I'm waiting for an apology from *you*—or is a consultant above the normal rules of polite behaviour?'

She glared defiantly at him, so angry at his high-handed attitude that she barely noticed his startled reaction to her accusation.

'The last *I* heard,' she continued forcefully, denying him the chance to interrupt, 'good manners dictate that you turn up on time when you've made arrangements to meet someone, and if you're going to be late you do your best to send a message. And as for standing someone up. . .!'

She didn't bother finishing the sentence, letting the disgust in her voice carry the message.

'A lesson from Miss Manners?' he taunted bitterly as he folded his arms across his chest and stared down his nose at her. 'And where in those rules for good manners and polite behaviour does it tell you how to deal with someone who doesn't bother to tell you that she's not free to accept your invitation?'

'Not free?'

Polly didn't understand what he meant. It wasn't as if she was still a married woman... He knew she was divorced, so what was he talking about?

After the heartbreak of that time she'd made a decision not to get involved again, and since then she'd hardly even spoken to a man on a personal basis, let alone... But he couldn't know about that, nor could he know that just one night in his arms had even tempered her fear of being hurt—her fear of taking a chance and trying again.

'*Doesn't* she look puzzled and innocent?' he derided with a sneer on his face. 'Perhaps you should learn to be a little more discreet when you arrange your meetings. Your social calendar seems to be a little full at the moment.'

'What...?' Polly had no idea what he was talking about—she didn't *have* a social calendar because she didn't have a social life.

'Still,' he continued, ignoring her confusion, 'you can cross me off your list as a one-night stand.'

Polly gasped in shock, her face flaming at his cruelly unfeeling reference to their night together. Had the soul-searing magic she'd been so certain they'd shared been so unimportant to him that he could belittle it like that? Had *she* meant so little that he could deliberately hurt her like this?

Well, she thought, drawing in a steadying breath and straightening her shoulders, she'd be damned if she was going to let him know how deep the wounds went. A sudden bitter inspiration struck her and she stared straight into his wintry grey eyes to deliver her parting shot.

'Don't worry, Dr Prince, you can be certain that it

won't be happening again. Usually, you kiss a frog, hoping it will turn into a prince. Unfortunately, I had the bad luck to do it the other way round!'

She turned smartly on her heel and strode firmly away, determined that Nicholas Prince would *never* know how much he had hurt her.

For the rest of her shift Polly threw herself into her work with a vengeance, but even though her hands were seldom unoccupied she still found her thoughts circling back to the unanswered question. Like a pebble in a shoe or a thorn in a finger, it wouldn't let her forget it.

Why?

Why had he reacted like that when, just one short day ago, he had smiled at her and asked her out for a meal—even stolen a hasty kiss in the middle of the corridor?

Why had he said those hurtful things?

It was almost as if. . .as if he hated her or, at the very least, didn't have any respect for her.

Even through the difficulty of trying to calm a young woman in the pain and heartbreak of an ectopic pregnancy she found herself trying to work out what she had done to change his attitude towards her.

It wasn't until she was finally lying in bed, staring up at the pale nothingness of the ceiling, that she realised what she was doing to herself—realised how self-destructive she was being.

'Stop it!' she said aloud, her voice echoing back sharply from the pastel peach walls like a deliberate order.

'You've been through this scenario before,' she continued in a slightly quieter tone, mindful of the other tenants in the building but still determined that she wasn't going to travel down the same devastating road again. 'You keep making the same old mistakes—trying to take the blame for every situation on your own shoulders. This time break the mould and take another look—see whether it really *is* your fault.'

Systematically, step by step, she went over the events of the last few days.

The first significant step seemed to have been her decision to speak to Nicholas Prince about his overharsh criticism and erratic mood swings when he was on duty.

She'd been under no obligation to tell him that she wasn't going to stand by and watch him demoralise her nurses, she reminded herself, but her well-developed sense of fair play had prompted her to speak.

She had never dreamt that the self-contained man she thought she'd known would have told her such details about his private life, and her sympathetic heart had gone out to him when she'd found out about the traumatic loss of his wife and child and the impending anniversary of the event.

It had been the fault of that same compassionate heart that she had wanted to see him the next night, worried about how he was coping with the devastating memories and his own misplaced feelings of guilt, but when Sister MacDonald had specifically asked her to deliver his wallet—giving her a cast-iron reason for being there—the decision had been taken out of her hands.

If she hadn't looked in through his window and misinterpreted an innocent scene into a suicide attempt she liked to think that she would probably just have completed her errand and gone home. As it was, she'd spent the evening learning about a completely hidden side of the enigmatic man as he'd shown her around his house, and they'd ended up sharing his magnificent hand-made bed.

'But I don't understand,' she whispered into the darkness in a voice choked by suppressed tears. 'If he was so insistent that we needed to talk that he asked me to go out for a meal with him why didn't he turn up? And why does he seem to be blaming *me*?'

The lack of answers was frustrating, but at least she had now sorted through her memories and was certain that, as far as she knew, she wasn't to blame for his change of mind.

If only . . . the small voice in her head said wistfully, and she smiled up at the ceiling. Those two words had to be the saddest in the whole language and she seemed to have spent so much of her life saying them.

If only Andrew hadn't died. If only Tim had been more patient. If only. . . If only she'd stuck to her guns and stayed well clear of any entanglements.

Still, while there was no remedy for the events of the past she could certainly avoid similar pitfalls in the future. All she had to do now was contrive to stay out of Nick's way as much as possible and, with any luck, they would eventually be able to work together as if none of this had happened.

Perhaps, one day she might even know *what* had happened.

As she curled up on her side and clutched a spare pillow in her arms honesty forced her to admit that dispelling her own mistaken feelings of guilt wasn't making her feel any happier but at least, now that she'd put her thoughts in order, she would hopefully be able to relax enough to go to sleep.

She had another full shift to work in the morning, and she would need all the sleep she could get to make sure that she could cope with whatever the day—and Nicholas Prince—chose to throw at her.

Her only real consolation was the memory of his shocked expression when she'd all but called him a frog...

'Sister.' Leo's voice hailed her as she passed the door and Polly detoured immediately, a smile already on her face.

Over the last week or so the good-looking young registrar had obviously noticed the chilly atmosphere between Polly and Nick and seemed to have set himself up as her champion, deliberately asking her to work beside him on numerous occasions. It was just unfortunate that in a growing number of cases the patient's condition had necessitated calling in Nicholas Prince as well.

Polly stifled a resigned sigh when she saw that this time her nemesis was already in the room, his tall frame bent forward in concentration over a young patient who couldn't have been more than five years old.

'Fell into a cold-frame,' Leo muttered. 'Legs and arms cut to blazes—full of glass and bleeding like a stuck pig—but at least it didn't touch her face.'

The next half-hour was a torment as she fetched and carried to order, monitoring their small patient and responding as promptly to Leo's smiling requests as to Nick's growled orders as they battled to stop the poor child from bleeding to death.

Finally, they had little Emma stabilised well enough to transfer her up to Theatre.

'Did you put in that request for extra supplies of blood?' Nick demanded brusquely as he stripped his bloodstained gloves off with a snap and pulled his mask down to hang around his neck.

'Yes, sir.' Polly's reply was coolness itself. 'Mr MacFadden is scrubbed and waiting, and Dr Panagiotis is on his way to set up for the plastic surgery.'

He grunted a reply but Polly was already turning towards Leo as he came back from his trip upstairs, the porter following him with the trolley.

'Does he think he'll be able to save her leg? Will she be able to walk?' she demanded eagerly, still horrified by the depth and extent of the damage done by the enormous shards of glass embedded in the child's flesh.

'No guarantees—it'll depend how much of the muscle he has to take away. Some of that glass in there looks as if someone's emptied a sugar bowl into the wound and given it a stir so it could be hours before she's off the table.'

Polly winced at the graphic description but she knew what he meant and what a problem it was going to be for Ross MacFadden. He would have to continue the job they'd started of irrigating the wound to remove as much of the glass as he could and then excise what couldn't be washed away in case it worked its lethal way into other structures of the body.

She sighed silently and turned to finish putting a fresh disposable cover on the bed and checking the supplies they'd used. She knew that her part in the child's recovery was over. Now it would depend partly on the surgeon's skill and partly on luck exactly how much muscle had to be taken away.

That, and how much permanent damage had been done to the nerves and tendons, would decide whether little Emma would be able to run and play again, or even if she would be able to walk.

The next patient through the door almost seemed like light relief after Emma.

'Which one's the doctor?' said a hoarse voice as a burly man came to a halt in the doorway, his eyes flicking from one member of the group to another. Tina Wadland looked quite tiny beside him as she tried to usher him into the room, but he was refusing to move, one large hand padded in a fluorescent pink wadded-up towel and cradled gingerly in the other.

'If you'd like to take a seat on the edge of the bed, Mr Percheron,' Tina prompted, and Polly had to turn away to hide a smile. She caught sight of Leo's expression and nearly laughed aloud—the name was so wonderfully apt! His muscular body even seemed to resemble the big heavy horses...

'Not till I know who's the doctor,' he said warily, looking from Leo to Nick and back again.

'Both of us,' said Nick, taking charge of the situation in a voice as smooth as silk. 'Come and tell us exactly what's wrong. Are you in pain?'

Mr Percheron nodded, his face pale and sweaty. Polly had the feeling that the big man was probably feeling faint and didn't really want the task of trying to lift a young Goliath off the floor.

'Can I help you?' she offered with a calm smile. 'If you're in a lot of pain you'll probably want to sit down.' She was careful not to jar his hand, creating a comfort zone around him with an outstretched arm as she directed him onto the table.

Out of the corner of her eye she saw Nick approaching and had to concentrate on what she was doing.

'Do you want me to unwrap the towel or would you rather do it yourself?' Polly offered him the choice so that he would be forced to take the initiative, otherwise the stand-off could last for ever.

'I'll do it myself,' he said, hurriedly moving it out of her reach and treating her to the same suspicious glare as the rest of them. Slowly he unwound the bright pink cloth, drawing in a hissing breath through his gritted teeth when he accidentally jarred it.

There were several seconds of silence when his hand was revealed, one finger sticking up at a most peculiar angle.

Polly made the mistake of looking towards Leo. Just one glimpse of the sparkle in his golden eyes was enough to have her fighting a fit of the giggles again. From the big man's reaction, they had expected at least a partial amputation or a spectacular puncture wound. A simple dislocation seemed such an anticlimax.

'May I have a look, Mr Percheron?' Nick requested, as he approached their apprehensive patient.

'What are you going to do with it? Will you have to cut it off? Only I can't stand this pain, but. . .but I don't like needles neither.'

'Well, then.' Polly watched the consultant smile reassuringly at the big man and her stomach clenched. He'd smiled at her, too, before. . . She dragged her attention back as Nick continued speaking, his deep voice infinitely calm and reassuring. 'If I could just have a closer look at it to see what we need to do?'

Polly watched Nick pointedly fold his arms before he leant forward to look at the painful digit and wondered why—until she saw the way Mr Percheron relaxed when he realised that no one was going to be touching it. Yet.

Nick made quite a pantomime of looking all round

the finger from every possible angle, then frowned thoughtfully.

'I'm going to need to touch your finger to see how badly you've damaged it,' he said, fixing Mr Percheron with a serious look. 'I'll be as quick and gentle as I can, but I'll need to squeeze your finger and I need to feel the back of your hand.'

Mr Percheron went a shade paler at the thought.

'And if I let you do that you'll be able to tell me what's wrong with my finger?'

'I promise.'

It seemed as if all of them were holding their breaths while they waited for the answer.

'OK,' the big man agreed hoarsely, and presented his hand on the outstretched palm of the other—like some delicacy being offered to a diner in a restaurant.

It was only then that Nick unfolded his arms and took a step closer. In a smooth action, which showed exactly how many dozens of times he'd had to perform the same manoeuvre, he gripped the meaty hand in one of his, the upraised digit in the other and gave a steady pull.

'Ouch! Dammit. . .!'

Mr Percheron's outraged shout coincided with the audible click as his dislocated finger slid back into position.

Nick released his hold and stepped back swiftly— almost as if he was taking the precaution of removing himself from the range of those meaty-looking fists.

'How does that feel?' he queried. 'Can you move it?'

His attention having been instantly distracted from glowering threateningly at the man who'd caused him pain to his precious finger, the big man concentrated on gingerly bending the finger and straightening it again.

'Hey! It's working again!' he exclaimed in disbelief. 'I thought I'd broken it right off.'

'No. You'd only dislocated it, and the quicker we got it back in the right place the less the likelihood of permanent damage,' Nick explained, then gestured towards Polly. 'Sister will tape it for you to give it some support. . .'

She tuned out the rest of his explanations, knowing that they were only for the benefit of the patient. She'd taken care of so many like it that she could almost do the work blindfolded. The thing she couldn't cope with was the fact that Nick hadn't so much as looked at her when he'd consigned the patient to her care, and he'd left the room immediately after.

'It always surprises me,' Polly commented when Mr Percheron had disappeared out of the room far faster than he'd come in. 'He's such a big man, but he was almost shaking in his shoes at the thought of what was going to happen in here.'

'That's the point, though, isn't it?' Leo said pensively. 'It was the *thought* of what we might do that was terrifying, and that makes him no different from the rest of us. We've all got things which frighten us— some real and some imagined.'

'In his case, pain and needles,' she agreed.

'And in yours?' Leo questioned for the first time, his voice quiet and his eyes full of concern. 'You haven't been looking very happy lately.'

'Perhaps I'm just afraid of having doors slammed in my face,' she said cryptically.

'Perhaps overcoming your fear depends on how badly you want what's on the other side of the door,' he suggested, all traces of the facile charmer gone. 'It would be a shame if you let something precious slip away because you're afraid of opening a door...'

Polly stared at him in the growing silence and saw the serious side which he usually kept so well hidden, and for the first time she realised that perhaps he hadn't just skated easily through life on a joke and a smile.

'I'm sorry.' The teasing expression was back in force as he raised his hands in a gesture of surrender. 'I'll stop practising psychology until I'm qualified.'

'I think you probably *are* qualified, but you make certain nobody knows you've taken the practical route,' she said quietly, feeling her way instinctively. 'The only way you could speak like that is if you've been through something like it yourself.'

'Who, me?' he started to scoff, then closed his lips tightly and drew in a deep breath. '*Touché*,' he murmured, and saluted her with one finger in imitation of a fencer's gesture.

'Bad?' she questioned sympathetically.

'Bad enough.' He closed his eyes briefly, but she'd already seen the pain.

She gave him the second he needed to push it aside, knowing that he wasn't one to talk about the shadows in his life either.

'Still, what can't be cured must be endured,' he said in a resigned tone. 'Unlike you,' he continued with a touch of determination. 'Up until a couple of weeks ago you seemed to be perfectly happy in your work and well able to keep the likes of us rabble in line if we tried to step too close.'

He raised one eyebrow like a question mark but she just shrugged, not knowing what to say. She hadn't told anyone at St Augustine's about the circumstances which had resulted in her return to full-time nursing and her application for the job in A and E, and now was not the time to start. After the pain of her brutal rejection by Nicholas Prince her emotions were far too close to the surface.

'Well,' he conceded gracefully, 'my shoulders are broad if you ever feel you want to use them, or,' he added as if he'd just thought of it, 'if I seem a little too callow and lightweight you could always talk to Nick. He's good at—'

'No!' She was aghast at the thought of confiding her troubles to the man who now seemed to be at the centre of them. 'I couldn't! He. . .he doesn't even *like* me. . .'

'*That* can't be true,' Leo declared instantly, seeming quite taken aback. 'He thinks you're a damned good nurse.'

A swift glow of pleasure suffused her face but she fought to ignore it, knowing that Leo's eyes were mercilessly sharp.

'You wouldn't know it, the way he snaps and growls at me,' she pointed out, trying to hide her hurt.

'You can't tell me he frightens you,' Leo said dismissively. 'I didn't think *anything* frightened you—and, anyway, I thought you knew his bark is worse than his bite.'

The heat in Polly's cheeks increased as she remembered Nick biting her, and just how gently he had done so. . .

'No,' she said, her voice slightly breathless as she tried to banish the memory, while remembering the thread of the conversation they were having. 'It's not so much people that frighten me as— Hey! What about you?' she demanded suddenly, needing to turn the tables on him before her distracted state had her spilling her every thought. 'I've been hearing rumours.'

'Rumours about what?' he demanded warily. 'Anyway, I thought you didn't listen to rumours.'

'Ah, but this was such a juicy one...about you and Sexy Samantha up on Obs and Gobs?' Polly taunted, having heard about that young woman's determined pursuit of Leo Stirling.

'That's not a rumour, that's a *nightmare*,' he retorted with a theatrical shudder. 'That barracuda scares the living daylights out of me. Have you seen the upholstery on her? If I bumped into her in the corridor I could suffocate before anyone rescued me!'

Polly burst out laughing.

'You don't mean to tell me that you won't be taking her to the Ball? I would have thought a playboy like you would have jumped at the chance.'

'No way!' He looked over his shoulder with a haunted expression. 'Can you remember how much of her overflowed that skimpy strapless thing last year? I'm just glad I've got a cast-iron excuse not to take *anyone* this year. I'll be fully occupied with the Auction.'

'Speaking of which,' Polly said, finally letting him off the hook as they both began to make their way back towards the reception area, 'how's the new idea working? Did the people who made the promises go for the comedy idea? I've hardly had a chance to speak to you since you wined me and dined me in such style under the trees the other day so I haven't heard the latest update.'

Before Leo had a chance to answer a sudden noise in the doorway they were just passing drew their attention and they came face to face with Nicholas Prince, an arrested expression on his face.

'Problem, Nick?' Leo said. 'Anything I can help you with?'

'No.' He sounded preoccupied, and Polly noticed the way his eyes were going from Leo to herself. 'No problem,' he confirmed, and turned away from them.

Polly didn't have the heart to restart the conversation with Leo. She didn't think she would have been able to concentrate on anything he said.

All she could think about was the strange expression on Nick's face when he'd looked from Leo to herself, and when she recalled that they'd been talking about their meeting on the lawn to discuss the auction she had a sudden mental image of the white-coated figure she'd seen through the window.

Could it have been Nick, watching them? Was that why he'd made the comments about her busy social life—or was she clutching at straws in an effort to find a reason for his anger towards her?

Her heart ached when she remembered how tired Nick had looked—so grey and drawn.

She had hoped that once the anniversary of his wife's death had passed he would have returned to his previously inscrutable self, and had looked forward to some sort of respite—at least until the rawness of his accusations had subsided.

Unfortunately, he seemed to be working longer hours than ever and, in spite of the fact that she had tried to harden her heart towards him, she was now seriously worried that he was headed for some sort of breakdown.

'Does he *ever* go home?' she demanded in a fierce undertone as she swung to face Leo. 'He's absolutely exhausted and it's not good.'

Leo took her by the elbow and ushered her into the nearby staffroom, glancing around to check that their conversation couldn't be overheard before he turned to face her.

'Not good for the department, or not good for Nick?' he challenged perceptively.

'For...for both, of course,' she hedged, unable to meet his eyes as she felt the blood rush to her cheeks. 'That's why the new rota system was put into operation—so that there was always a senior person on duty, not so that the same person was on duty all the time!'

'You obviously care about him, and you know better than most that an experienced nurse like you can do an awful lot to lighten the load... Yet you seem to be doing everything you can to stay out of his way.'

'I *have* been working with him,' Polly protested heatedly, stung by the suggestion that she hadn't been pulling her weight and only just remembering in time to keep her voice down. 'Sometimes it feels as if the two of us spend the whole day joined at the hip...!'

She bit her tongue to stop the flood of words but from the expression in Leo's eyes she could see that it was already too late. She'd already revealed how difficult it was for her to work so closely with Nick.

'Ah, Polly,' he murmured and shook his head.

She hated the glimpse of pity in the dark gold of his eyes, and suddenly she couldn't bear the thought that he might have guessed what had happened between Nick and herself; couldn't bear that he might have guessed how much she had come to care for their irascible boss and how little it mattered to Nick; couldn't bear that Leo might be feeling sorry for her because her feelings weren't returned.

'Don't you worry about me, Leo Stirling,' she

declared huskily, her chin coming up and her shoulders straightening with determination. 'I'm a survivor, and I've got the scars to prove it.'

CHAPTER SIX

'Dammit, Leo! Don't you dare do this to me again!' Polly snarled. 'You've been pushing me into Nick's pocket for days and it's...it's utterly childish!'

She didn't dare mention the fact that Leo's campaign to keep Nick and herself in close proximity was the most excruciating mixture of pleasure and pain that she'd ever experienced. He would probably see that as some sort of success and redouble his efforts to effect some sort of understanding between the two of them.

She might as well have saved her breath because all she got in return for her objections was a shrug from a broad pair of shoulders and a wave as Leo disappeared into the lift with the patient he'd volunteered to take up to Theatre.

It wouldn't have been so bad if she hadn't caught the broad smile which crept over his face just before the doors slid shut.

'I've been set up—again!' she muttered, as she turned back towards the emergency room and her next stint as the other half of Siamese twins. 'Can't he see that it isn't doing either of us any good?'

She glanced across at Nick but he seemed supremely indifferent to Leo's manoeuvres. It was Hannah's puzzled frown she encountered as she turned to the task of setting the room to rights.

All she could do now was hope that the rest of the day was particularly quiet so that she could spend as little time as possible in Nick's presence. Anything else didn't bear thinking about.

Unfortunately, it didn't look as if she was going to get her wish because within a matter of minutes she was answering a call from the ambulance control station.

'Priority. Major incident,' the voice said, and her heart sank as she recognised the code and reached for her pen.

Soon she was scribbling as fast as she could go, pausing only to beckon to Hannah as she underlined the words 'mobile medical team'.

Hannah nodded and took off at a fast walk, leaving Polly to take down the rest of the details—her hand flying towards the computer terminal in between to call up essential information onto the screen.

By the time she'd finished with the call there was already an extra buzz in the department, which told her that Hannah had passed on the message, and she grabbed the clipboard and went to join the fray.

She was looking down at her notes as she left the room or she'd have seen Nick coming in the other direction. As it was, they struck each other a glancing blow and she reeled back against the wall.

'Polly! I'm sorry. . .' He grabbed her flailing arm to steady her and she was suddenly aware of the warmth of his hand on the soft flesh of her arm. 'Are you all right? You should watch where you're going. . .'

'I'm sorry, sir.' She pulled away from his hand, angry with herself that she was reluctant to break the contact when he seemed totally unaware of it. 'I was checking my notes,' she continued, concentrating on the important matters in hand.

'Sister Nicholls said they need a mobile medical team so I've paged Leo. Now, what have you got?' He turned to follow her back into the office and perched one hip on the corner of the desk, the casual pose completely belied by the intensity in his face.

'A car apparently out of control in the town centre has mown down pedestrians. So far the estimates of the number of casualties reported range from several to dozens, but Ambulance Control will clarify as soon as possible. God only knows what the severity of the injuries will be or what type but, as you know from Hannah, they asked for a mobile team.'

Nick nodded, his brow furrowed with the intensity of his thoughts. 'I don't know who the other nurse on duty is, but Leo and Hannah are getting kitted up and John Preece is on his way down.' Polly recognised the name of the anaesthetist and could picture his lean wiry frame and quicksilver wit.

'We'll probably have the first of the walking wounded arriving in a few minutes so can you start clearing our department and Outpatients of all but the urgent cases?' Nick continued briskly. 'As soon as we get a more accurate picture of the numbers involved we can make decisions about whether convalescent patients will have to be discharged but, in the meantime, can you organise a quick audit of the hospital bed state?'

'The audit's already under way, via the computer...' Polly gestured over her shoulder towards the omnipresent electronic equipment '...and a message has gone out to the operating theatres that routine admissions have been cancelled and cold surgery deferred until further notice. They've been alerted to make ready for casualties, and so have Radiography and Blood Transfusion, and extra staff have been mobilised.'

'Good.' He blinked as if amazed by how much she had achieved already.

Polly pointed towards the computer again. 'The wonders of technology—all that phoning and running around achieved at the touch of a few buttons.'

'If only treating patients could be as easy,' she heard him mutter under his breath, then his head came up as he recognised the significance of the sudden increase in noise. 'That sounds like the first of them arriving. Let me know as soon as we get some figures so I can decide whether to call in any more staff. . .' As he was speaking, he'd straightened up from his desk and was striding out of the room.

For a while Polly was in charge of the control centre, with responsibility for the mobilisation of the various levels of personnel. When the number of reported casualties reached the twenties, with more arriving under their own steam—as well as those being ferried by ambulance—the department was beginning to groan under the sheer weight of numbers.

The sound of distressed humanity was becoming quite deafening, especially when the relatives and friends of the injured started arriving to demand information.

In spite of her experience with such situations, faint glimmers of panic were winding their way through Polly when a group of determined pressmen and -women tried to invade the department. She could have hugged Celia MacDonald when her superior bustled into view, every inch of her uniform immaculate in spite of the fact that she was supposed to be off duty today.

'Right, everybody,' she called, her Scottish accent cutting through the hubbub effortlessly. 'If the media personnel would kindly follow that gentleman there. . .' she pointed to one of the porters '. . .he will show you to the room where the consultant will give you a statement.'

She paused just long enough for the eager group to get out of the way before she continued in an aside to Polly, 'Though when the consultant will have time to speak to you lot is another matter altogether!'

Polly chuckled.

'I'm glad to see you, Sister. I was beginning to think they were after my blood.'

'No problem. It all comes with experience,' she said lightly. 'Now, I recognise these two.' She indicated two well-dressed ladies, walking briskly towards her. 'They're the counsellor and the lady who organises the volunteers. They'll need the two little interview rooms, but if you'd like to get yourself off to the busy end of the department I think you're needed there.'

Polly agreed with alacrity, glad to relinquish the reins into the senior sister's capable hands.

On the way towards the reception area Polly had time to reflect on the enormous amount of organisation inherent in her job—and the fact that it would get worse when she eventually made senior sister.

Still, she consoled herself, Big Mac had a few more years to go before she retired so that meant there was plenty of time for Polly to learn all the finer points and practise them until they became second nature to her. After all, she, too, was intending to stay in the profession long term. There was no chance that she would be leaving to become a housewife—not a second time.

There was only time for the thought to be accompanied by an emphatic shake of her head and then she was in the thick of it; close to the ambulance entry.

The noise was much greater here, with the cries of the injured mixing with the sobs of those in shock and more than a few terrified children.

Over all, though, was the determined attempt at organisation, with triage being repeated for every patient as they came into the accident and emergency department.

'Sister.' Nick's distinctive voice reached her clearly over the din and she made her way straight across to him, the colour of his hair standing out like a beacon to guide her.

'Will you take over here with me while Sister Ohlen helps in Outpatients with the walking casualties?'

Polly nodded, but her agreement wasn't necessary—she would work wherever he told her to.

They were starting to see some of the more seriously injured casualties now, those who had been too seriously injured to do anything but wait for medical assistance at the scene.

As each one arrived Nick checked them over, making his own judgement as to whether they should be classified as immediate, urgent or non-urgent, and colour-tagging them accordingly with special labels.

To the uninitiated it might look like a waste of time to repeat the examination and tests done at the scene of the accident, but she knew that out in the field it could be all too easy to miss tiny vital clues—such as the tell-tale area of bruising which could herald a massive internal bleed.

When Nick was satisfied with his decision the casualties requiring immediate care were sent to resuscitation areas, urgent casualties to the main treatment areas and the non-urgent cases were directed to the outpatient department where the minor treatment area had been set up.

Polly always found this one of the most frustrating

aspects of a major trauma. She knew that the triage work was essential so that the team could provide the greatest good for the greatest number, and she was as meticulous as ever in incorporating the information on the notes begun at the site of the accident into the hospital records. But she would rather have been working in either the resuscitation area or one of the main treatment areas where she would have been actively nursing.

'Hello, Polly,' a familiar voice greeted her, albeit in a subdued tone, and there was Leo. 'Last live casualty,' he reported formally, then continued in the familiar shorthand. 'Flail chest. Don't know if he'll make it—they had to cut him out of the car with the jaws—and he's high as a kite on something...'

Polly realised suddenly that this patient was the cause of all the misery she'd been seeing for the last hour but, although she knew that Nick would have made the same connection, it made no difference to his professionalism as he began to check him over, the two of them setting off at a brisk trot towards the resuscitation area with the trolley between them.

As this was the last live patient to leave the scene John Preece had travelled back in the same ambulance and followed close behind.

'No seat belt on,' Leo continued, while the monitoring and life-support systems were transferred over, 'so when he finally smacked the big concrete planter at the base of the tree his ribs didn't stand an earthly against the steering-wheel. Both femurs gone,' he detailed as he pointed out the injuries to the patient's legs. 'One of them's been pushed right up through the socket, by the looks of it, so his hip's probably a mess—to say nothing of probable internal injuries. And, on top of that, he hit his head on the door pillar and knocked himself out and there's a query on a neck injury.'

'Blood pressure's terrible,' Polly interrupted. 'He must be losing an awful lot of it somewhere, in spite of two large-bore IVs running in flat out.'

She glanced up in time to see Nick and Leo look at each other in concern.

'Lung?'

'Spleen?'

The suggestions were simultaneous but the result was the same, with John Preece ensconced behind his high-tech equipment to monitor the anaesthetic while the two of them began work on opposite sides of the body.

There was a brief pause while X-rays were taken and quiet relief when there was no evidence of a neck injury, but the rest was done with dogged determination as they found and stabilised one injury after another.

'It's still too low,' John said into the desperate silence. 'If we can't...'

He was interrupted by the shocking single tone which told them that their patient's heart had stopped beating.

'Dammit! No!' Nick shouted in frustration. 'Don't you dare...!'

They worked on him for the next ten minutes, first with chemical stimulants and finally—because they daren't put any pressure on his broken ribs in case they punctured his lungs—they tried open-heart massage and direct electrical stimulation.

'Nick?' Leo questioned, one eyebrow raised when there was still no viable response.

'OK,' he conceded, his voice weary as he straightened up and stepped back from the trolley, his hands dark with blood. His eyes flicked up towards the large clock-face on the wall. 'Note the time of death,' he added flatly, before he stripped off his gloves and apron and strode out through the doors without looking back.

Worried about the strangely dead expression she had seen in his eyes as he'd turned away from the body, Polly wished that she could go after him. She knew that he must be reliving the death of his wife and longed to comfort him, but there was work to be done.

She stepped forward to begin detaching the ECG leads but Leo's hand halted her.

'Go with him,' he murmured quietly. 'We can manage here.'

'But. . .' She looked up at him, for a moment thinking that this was just another episode when he tried to push the two of them together, but his expression told her that Leo knew about Deanne, too.

'What good can I do? He doesn't even *like* me,' she reminded him in a hoarse whisper, wishing that it wasn't true—wishing that she had the right to go and offer him comfort.

'But he *needs* you.' Leo's simple words were as solemn as his expression so she couldn't doubt him.

With a tentative half-smile she nodded and turned away to strip off her own disposables and hurry after Nick.

'Which way did Dr Prince go?' she demanded when she nearly cannoned into Tina in the corridor.

'Towards Reception,' the young woman said, then grinned cheekily. 'And he didn't even growl at me. . .!'

Her humour fell on deaf ears as Polly took off in the same direction, guessing what she would find.

'Sister MacDonald.' She greeted her superior with a smile. 'How is the staff rotation going? Have we got enough relief in for Dr Prince to take a break?'

The blue-grey eyes examined her intently for a

second. 'Lost him, did we?' she said astutely, and Polly knew that it wasn't really a question.

She nodded and her eyes were drawn across to the tall figure, speaking to the uniformed policeman—no doubt filling him in on the fate of their culprit.

'In which case, I think a break might be a good idea—for both of you. The rest of the "immediate" patients have all been dealt with and have left the department, and the "urgent" ones are well in hand. There's nothing here that can't wait an extra fifteen minutes while you both catch your breath.'

'Thank you, Sister.' Polly gave a rather wan smile. 'Now all I've got to do is persuade him to do it—what do you suggest? Shall I throw him over my shoulder?'

'Go on with you, lassie!' The usually stern face softened into a broad smile. 'He'll go if *I* tell him to!' Polly watched with bated breath as the diminutive woman bustled swiftly across the department and spoke to the burly policeman, before turning her attention on the tall man standing tensely beside him.

'What did you do?' Nick demanded with a tired display of aggression when he followed her into the room two short minutes later. 'Did you bribe her to make me take a break?'

Polly glanced up at him warily as he stood just inside the doorway with his clenched fists held rigidly against his sides and his jaw set, then she turned away just long enough to carefully put down the two empty mugs she was holding in case the temptation to throw them at him grew too much to bear.

'I thought about it,' she retorted as she turned to face him with all the calm she could muster. 'But in the end she didn't think she'd need danger money because she noticed that you weren't wearing your Superman outfit, and she has no trouble dealing with mere mortals.'

It was definitely a day for bad jokes, she thought as his grim expression remained unchanged, and she turned back to spoon coffee granules into the mugs and pour water over them from the steaming kettle. She had decided that she was going to stay calm and make allowances for his bad mood, especially after the way he had reacted to the loss of their patient, and the sheer domesticity of the commonplace actions was soothing.

'Here,' she offered as she carried the brimming mugs over and put them on the low table, proud of the steadiness of her hands. 'Black. No sugar.' She sank into one corner of the four-seater settee and leant her head back against the soft upholstery, grateful for the chance to sit down.

The silence stretched out between them but Polly was determined not to let it upset her. They had both needed a break and she'd made certain that they'd got one. That was all there was to it. . .

'Thank you. . .'

For a minute she didn't move, thinking that she'd imagined the husky words.

'Polly?'

Slowly she allowed her eyes to open, hardly daring to believe that he wasn't sniping at her.

In spite of his size she hadn't heard him move, but now he was sitting on the chair set at right angles to her own, his elbows planted on his knees and the coffee-mug clasped between his long-fingered hands like a lifeline while he stared down into its dark depths.

Slowly he raised his head, his stormy grey eyes lifting to meet hers, and as she watched he dropped an opaque veil over the emotions revealed there until once more she was seeing the calm enigmatic persona he presented to the world.

'I needed this,' he admitted quietly, gesturing with the mug before he took the first mouthful.

Polly found herself watching his every movement as though mesmerised, her eyes charting the way the harsh artificial light bleached the blondest streaks in his hair to silver and painted shadows in the tired hollows under his cheek-bones.

She already knew that his eyelashes were several shades darker than his hair, but she hadn't really noticed before quite how long and thick they were. On a less virile man they could have seemed almost feminine, but on Nick they just accentuated the. . .

'Polly?'

She blinked when his voice interrupted her self-indulgent train of thought, then leant forward swiftly to pick up her own steaming mug, hoping against hope that he hadn't noticed the way she'd been gazing at him.

'I'm sorry,' he murmured into the silence, the quiet words jerking her eyes up from their contemplation of her own mug to see him gesture towards the patient they had just lost. 'I didn't cope with that one very well and I had no right to take it out on you like that, especially when you were only using your common sense.'

'Well. . .' She paused for a minute, the unexpectedness of the admission leaving her almost speechless.

It was true that his reaction to the young man's death had been extreme but, even so, he should have known better than to carry on without a break—especially when he'd made certain that there were enough members of staff to cope.

There was no way she was going to mention the fact

that Leo had said that his boss *needed* Polly's company. But still. . .

'You'd certainly have torn Leo off a strip if he hadn't taken a break when it was time to,' she pointed out as gently as she could, and held her breath, not knowing if she had pushed too far.

'True,' he admitted with a heavy sigh. 'I don't know why this one hit me the way it did—God knows I've dealt with plenty of them since Dee. . .

He glanced up at her and, in spite of the fact that they hadn't even begun to talk about the rift between them, their gazes caught in wordless communication for several long seconds before he looked back down at his mug with a wry smile. 'Perhaps it's a good thing we've got our resident Scottish dragon breathing fire down our necks to keep us in line. . .'

Polly felt the smile creep over her face and chuckled as she visualised Celia MacDonald as a dragon—a very small dragon to face down Nicholas Prince in one of his towering tempers. . .!

'Sister? Do you know where. . .? Oh. . .!' Tina Wadland subsided in confusion when she came flying into the room and found the intimidating consultant, who had reduced her to tears, laughing aloud.

Polly saw the speculative look that crossed the junior nurse's face as her eyes went from Nick's smiling face to her own and she groaned silently.

For days Nick had been cold and cutting towards almost everyone in the department and now, within minutes of going off for a break in her company, he was apparently in high good humour. Just wait until the hospital grapevine got hold of *this*.

'Yes, Tina?' Polly prompted, with a mental shrug of resignation.

'Oh.' The young woman gulped audibly and Polly watched the tide of colour sweep over her cheeks as she met Nick's direct grey gaze, then dragged her eyes away hurriedly as she delivered her message. 'Sister MacDonald asked me to apologise for disturbing your break, Doctor, but could you go to her office as soon as you're free?'

'No peace for the wicked,' he groaned with a wry smile for Polly, and she had to swallow another chuckle when she saw the stunned expression still decorating Tina's face as she hurried out of the room.

'What?' Nick demanded, and she realised that she hadn't been as successful as she'd hoped at hiding her amusement.

'Nothing much.' She dismissed his question with an airy wave of her hand as she watched him drag himself unwillingly out of the depths of his chair and tug his white coat straight. 'Just that there's one young nurse who will never be quite as frightened of you again.'

'What?' he repeated, clearly at a loss.

'She's found out that Old Nick knows how to laugh,' Polly explained wickedly. 'Just wait until she spreads *that* rumour around!'

The sound of his groan of disgust stayed with her for hours as she went about her duties, her heart lighter than it had been for days.

Still, at the back of her mind was the unsolved puzzle as to why Nick had treated her the way he had. Why, after spending the night together in his magnificent bed and then arranging to take her out for a meal the following evening, he had apparently decided not to bother to turn up.

Worse still had been the way he had cut her dead the next time they'd met at the hospital, and the hurtful words he had used like weapons when she had tried to confront him.

She shrugged, wondering if she would ever find out what had happened to change his mind, but when she contemplated asking him for an explanation she found herself silently shaking her head. Much as she wanted to know the answers, they weren't as important as the fragile truce which seemed to be in force between them.

Luckily for her proccupied state of mind, the department was fairly quiet for several hours—almost uncannily quiet—so that the call that came through from Ambulance Control just half an hour before she was due to go off duty came almost as a shock.

'Triple car pile-up. Three injured on their way in. One with multiple injuries and smoke inhalation, one with a possible neck injury and one with thirty per cent burns and smoke inhalation.'

Polly swore silently, knowing how devastating such injuries could be, and hurried to pass on the information, but it wasn't until the first ambulance arrived that she realised that the burns victim was a young child who had been trapped in her safety seat when the car she'd been in had burst into flames after the crash.

'Gently!' she reproved sharply through her mask as their tiny patient was transferred as rapidly as possible onto the hospital's life-support and monitoring systems.

The injured little body was swathed in sterile water-gel dressings, but in spite of the fact that she was covered by a blanket to prevent systemic heat loss the poor child was shivering uncontrollably, her eyes tightly closed above the smallest size Entonox mask.

Swiftly checking the plasma and saline drips already set up and running, Polly completed the task of drawing off blood samples for cross-matching and testing for haemoglobin, electrolytes and urea and sent them straight up to the lab. Then she joined in the awful task of removing the rest of the poor mite's clothing.

'All right, Fiona,' she crooned softly as she worked. 'It's all right, my sweetheart. We're looking after you now...' She kept up her low-voiced litany, never certain just how much her little charge could hear or understand, but knowing instinctively that if she *was* listening she needed to hear something more than the usual impersonal medical conversation which surrounded such an injury.

For a brief moment, when the full extent of the little girl's injuries were uncovered, she met the wintry grey of Nick's eyes above his mask and she knew that they shared the same thoughts.

Each recognised that this amount of damage was going to mean months of hospital treatment while grafts were harvested from the uninjured regions of the child's body to cover the large areas of full-thickness burns. They could only guess at the amount of pain she was going to suffer while the treatment continued.

A little wordless moan from the child between them drew their eyes down again and, after a swift demand for a further dose of morphine, it was Nick who bent forward to speak gently to her.

Polly saw him administer the drug as soon as it was handed to him, then watched as one lean hand ventured up indecisively before he stroked the sweat-soaked hair behind a soot-blackened ear.

'Hang on, Fiona,' he murmured softly, his deep voice full of caring as he tried to calm her. 'The pain will soon be gone, sweetheart...'

In that second Polly knew that she had fallen in love, but not with the disguise Nicholas Prince hid behind—

the persona of a big, self-contained man who fought against allowing anyone to come too close although, heaven knew, even like *that* he drew her like a magnet.

No, the man she loved was the gentle, loving person who lived inside the mask—the man who recognised that a tiny child needed more from him than just his medical expertise and who didn't care who saw him comforting her.

CHAPTER SEVEN

IT WAS sheer will-power that helped Polly to keep her mind on the job as the team eventually managed to stabilise little Fiona enough for the journey to the specialist burns unit. The fact that she had just made such a momentous discovery about her feelings for Nick couldn't be allowed to detract from her care of the suffering child.

Unfortunately, she seemed to have used up her day's quota of self-control on the job because, when Nick threw her a quick smile of appreciation for team work well done, she couldn't help the way her eyes followed him when he finally left the room.

Even when the doors had swung closed behind him she continued to stare blankly in his wake, stunned by the changes which had come over her in such a short time. It had been years since her husband had let her down badly, and she'd sworn then that she would never let another man turn her life inside out. She hadn't even been tempted until...

'Aha,' came a gleeful murmur in her ear and she jumped, blinking as she turned to find Leo grinning down at her.

Her frantic hope that the preoccupied expression on her face hadn't betrayed her vanished when she saw the way his golden eyes were gleaming with unholy mirth.

Her heart sank as she fought the heat rising up in her cheeks.

'You've got it bad, haven't you, Polly, girl?' He

sounded as if he was taunting her, but underneath the glee there was an air of... Was it delight? Whatever it was, Polly was too flustered to care.

'I—I don't know what you mean,' she stammered weakly, feeling the heat envelop her neck and face in spite of her efforts as she turned quickly away from his knowing gaze.

Her eyes flicked rapidly around the room, partly because she was worried that his words might be overheard by the other members of staff still in the vicinity, but also because she didn't dare take a chance that he might guess the true nature of her recent discovery.

She drew in a steadying breath before she turned to face him again. It was bad enough that he thought she was attracted to their boss—she had listened to his brand of teasing often enough and dreaded being the butt of it—but if he realised that she'd fallen in love with Nick...

'Perfect!' Leo crowed under his breath as he rubbed his hands together. 'Just a few weeks ago the two of you hardly noticed each other, in spite of the fact that you've been working together practically joined at the hip, and now...!' His laughter was full of open delight, and several pairs of eyes turned their way.

'Leo... Please...' Polly implored when she saw the attention they were attracting.

'Come on, then,' he urged, grabbing her by the elbow and barely allowing her enough time to get rid of her disposables before he dragged her out into the corridor. 'Perhaps I could start a secondary career as a matchmaker. Wait till I catch up with Nick...'

'No!' Polly squeaked, the soles of her shoes protesting on the shiny surface of the corridor when she refused to move an inch further. 'Don't you dare!'

She was horrified by the turn of the conversation. Her brain was already whirling with the confirmation that Leo had been deliberately throwing her into Nick's path, but for him to make a joke about the fact that his tactics had resulted in her falling for Nick...

'If you dare to say *anything* to him I'll...' She cast about frantically for a threat terrible enough to guarantee his silence, then found the perfect one. 'I'll tell Sexy Samantha that you'd be delighted to escort her to the Autumn Ball!'

'Oh, no! Not that!' he protested, and Polly was amazed that he seemed genuinely alarmed by the prospect. 'Please, Poll, promise me you won't do that. I couldn't stand another evening of fending her off, especially as I'll have my hands full trying to organise the auction. You couldn't be so cruel!'

'What's he whinging about now?'

Hannah's question cut through the intense confrontation, and for the first time Polly witnessed the way Leo's naked discomfort was quickly hidden behind his usual thousand-watt smile and the teasing glint in his eyes.

'I was just offering to find him a partner for the Autumn Ball,' Polly said, responding to the silent appeal he threw her way. Well, in a way she was only telling the truth...

'Since when has *he* needed someone to drum up partners?' Hannah scoffed. 'The last time I looked they were taking numbers and standing in line.'

'How well organised! And which number are you?' Leo challenged flirtatiously.

'Oh, I'm far too discriminating for that,' Hannah retorted with a grin for Polly. 'I want to know that I'm the *only* one on the list before I'll agree to go out with a man!'

Polly glanced up at Leo and realised from the quick narrowing of his eyes that he, too, had seen the shadows hiding behind Hannah's cheeky bravado.

'Obviously not a match made in heaven, then,' she quipped lightly, breaking into the suddenly prickly silence. 'On the one hand we have a man reputed to have a host of followers, and on the other a lady who doesn't like to be one of the crowd. It seems as if the two of you are destined to be nothing more than friends.'

'If that!' Hannah retorted tartly and briefly flicked her eyes to the watch pinned to the front of her dark blue uniform. 'Still, at least we can rely on him to provide the entertainment for the Ball—either intentionally or accidentally—when his harem closes in for the kill!'

Polly watched as her friend swept off down the corridor with her head in the air, and she couldn't help the chuckle of approval which escaped her.

'Hey! Whose side are you on?' Leo demanded.

'I pride myself on not taking sides,' she retorted primly, trying vainly to subdue a smile, 'but, after your admission that you've been sticking your nose where it wasn't wanted, I'm thinking of making an exception...so watch your step!'

'All right! All right!' He backed away from her, both hands raised in submission. 'If you'll promise not to involve your pneumatic colleague, I promise not to try to push you and Nick together...in spite of the fact that I think the two of you would be—'

'Leo! Enough!' she cried in exasperation. 'Get back to work before I make that call up to Obstetrics!'

He subsided, grumbling under his breath about

ingratitude as he returned to Reception.

The rest of Polly's shift was relatively quiet, filled with a complete mixture of the sort of minor ills and ailments which should never have been brought to an accident and emergency department in the first place.

'When will they ever realise that they're supposed to go to their GP for this sort of thing?' Hannah muttered as she cleared away the debris from a session of syringing out an elderly gentleman's ears. '*And* he had the nerve to complain that he'd been kept waiting for twenty minutes.'

'He's lucky he came when we weren't rushed off our feet with a *real* emergency or he wouldn't have been seen at all—just told to make an appointment with his GP's practice nurse to have it done,' Polly commented as she removed the paper sheet covering the trolley and unrolled another length. 'Some days I reckon anything up to three-quarters of the people sitting out there, complaining about the amount of time they're kept waiting, shouldn't even be here at all.'

'*You* know it, and *I* know it, but how do we get *them* to realise that they're wasting everyone's time when they clog the system up unnecessarily. . .? Oh, what's the use of telling you?' Hannah pulled a face. 'You know it as well as I do.'

'I think everyone in the department has ridden *that* hobbyhorse at some time,' Polly agreed wryly. 'But until Mr and Mrs A. N. Other out there get the message we're wasting our energy getting cross about it.'

'True,' Hannah agreed as she reached for a fresh set of disposable gloves. 'At least Reception now tells them that if they're non-urgent cases there might be a long delay. The prospect of an indefinite wait does persuade a few of them to take their problems elsewhere.'

The room once more returned to pristine readiness, the two of them left to collect their next charges.

Although she wasn't working with him the whole time Polly had time to notice, during the rest of her shift, that Leo seemed unusually subdued.

He worked quietly beside her while they took care of stitching up a rather nasty gashed arm where a youngster had slipped while climbing between several rows of barbed wire, and he complimented her on her quiet proficiency as she calmed a young child and held him still while Leo retrieved the lentils the youngster had pushed up his nose.

On her way home Polly congratulated herself that her threat to deliver Leo into the hands of his nemesis seemed to have worked.

It wasn't until he wasn't doing it any more that she realised exactly how often in the last few days Leo had stepped aside with his thousand-watt grin to allow Nick to work beside her.

Not for anything would she admit, even to herself, that she was actually missing the chance to work so closely with Nick. She had the greatest respect for him as a doctor, which was only increased by the depth of her emotional attachment to him, and although she hadn't realised at first that it had been a deliberate ploy on Leo's behalf she had enjoyed the chance to spend so much of her time at Nick's side.

Still, she sighed as she finally stretched her tired muscles and curled up under the puffy duvet, she would be seeing him again tomorrow and the day after that, and her empty soul would have to be satisfied with that.

After the heartbreak she had suffered five years ago she had made a decision to avoid any permanent relationships, and she knew from what he had told her about the tragic end of his own marriage that Nick's past had left him too raw to be looking for anything more than friendship. . .

As she drifted into exhausted slumber she tried to ignore the numb grey ache that surrounded her heart but, for the first time, she couldn't subdue an unaccustomed feeling of regret which followed her into her dreams.

'Polly. . .I need you,' Leo called cheerfully, and beckoned to her just before he disappeared around the corner.

'Oh, but. . .' Polly closed her eyes in exasperation at yet another summons, then turned back to make her apologies to Nick—again. 'Excuse me. I'd better see what he wants.'

As she turned away she saw the swift scowl which drew Nick's brows together over his steely grey eyes and realised just how often she'd seen it happen over the last few days.

Mind you, she thought as she set off in pursuit, it was hardly surprising that Nick should be getting more than a little annoyed with the way Leo was carrying on.

The trouble was that it seemed as if it was all her own fault.

Ever since she'd told Leo to stop matchmaking and had threatened him with a fate worse than death—the prospect of an evening in the company of Sexy Samantha—he'd turned the tables on her completely. Instead of engineering situations so that she and Nick were almost constantly working together, whenever he saw her anywhere in Nick's vicinity now he seemed to find another task which needed her urgent attention.

Unfortunately, several other members of staff had

seen what was going on and, although they didn't know *why* he was doing it, they thought it hilarious, especially when he began peppering his conversation with flowery words and phrases and fulsome praise.

Her blood came close to boiling point when she thought about how many times he'd called her *sweetheart* and *darling*, and the way he put his arm around her waist and squeezed as he gazed down at her with his big golden eyes.

Why? she railed silently. Why was it that she was the only one who could see the laughter hidden there as she was powerless to curb his nonsense? And why was it that when he did it she was never quick enough to retaliate—to tread on his toes or jab him in the ribs with an elbow?

It hadn't taken her long to realise that Leo's changed tactics were an attempt at making Nick jealous. She might even have been able to see the humour in the situation if it wasn't for the fact that the truce between Nick and herself was so new and frail that instead of drawing them together Leo's activities were driving them further apart.

Unfortunately, the realisation of just how much Nick had come to mean to her was still fresh and untried. She'd barely had time to wonder if, in spite of her fears, there might be a chance of some sort of relationship between them when Leo had begun his campaign of disruption.

There was no chance of that now, with Nick glaring at whichever one of them happened to be nearest— his temper slowly fraying at the edges as the whole department began to join in.

It didn't matter that Polly had tried several times to have a quiet word with him to explain what was really going on. Somehow, each time she made a move Leo seemed to guess what she intended to do and managed to head her off with another over-the-top display of flattery and appreciation until Nick was well out of the way.

She'd even tried to corner Leo to plead with him to stop his nonsense, but he'd only taken advantage of the situation when Nick chose to walk past at the same time.

'Nick! Help!' he called in mock fear as he wove his fingers firmly between Polly's and raised their joined hands to the wall above his head. 'Get this woman away from me!'

Too startled by his antics to think about struggling against his hold, Polly's horrified eyes watched as Nick approached. His stride barely altered as his eyes flicked coldly over the two of them before he continued wordlessly on his way.

'Leo!' Polly implored under her breath, her cheeks flaming as she realised what their little tableau must have looked like to the disdainful consultant passing by. To anyone who hadn't seen the way her fingers were trapped between Leo's it must have seemed as though it was *Polly* who had him pinned helplessly in position. 'Let me go, you idiot!' she demanded. 'This isn't funny.'

There was an audible catch in her voice and the pressure behind her eyes warned that she was close to tears so when he finally released her she whirled away and fled to the nearest bathroom to lock herself in. Too bad if someone else needed the toilets—they would just have to go to the other end of the unit.

She leant her head back against the door and drew in several deep, slow breaths while she fought for control.

In the plain oblong mirror she could see the way her

hands were curled into white-knuckled fists and the tension in her face was evidence of the way her teeth were clenched tightly.

Fixing her eyes on the image in the mirror, she concentrated on relaxing her jaw and allowing the muscles in her hands to release their tight grip.

Gradually, she realised that it was not despair that was tying her up in knots but a deep, complex anger.

There was anger towards Leo for playing his silly games, however well-meant; anger towards Nick for taking Leo's play acting at face value and judging her accordingly, but most of all anger at herself for allowing the situation to get to her as badly as it had without either calling a halt to it or retaliating.

Not that she would ever do anything which would jeopardise the work of the department—God forbid that the patients should suffer—but the more she thought about it the more she realised that it was time Leo swallowed a little of his own medicine.

'Polly? Are you all right?'

The tentative words were accompanied by a quiet tapping on the door behind her head, and she smiled wryly. Since she'd moved to St Augustine's Hannah had become the best friend she'd ever had. It created a warm glow in the cold corners of her heart to know that there was someone who genuinely cared about her and wouldn't hesitate to come to her defence.

'I'm fine, Hannah,' she murmured just loud enough to carry to her friend. 'I'll be out in a minute.'

She straightened up and walked towards the hand basins, determination squaring her shoulders as she went.

'Are you really all right? What happened?'

Polly smiled easily when she found Hannah waiting

for her as she emerged from the bathroom.

'I'm fine. Really,' she insisted, and knew that she meant it. Those few minutes had been enough to get her feet firmly on the ground again.

'But what happened? Tina said there was some sort of a fight in the corridor.'

Polly chuckled aloud. Trust the hospital grapevine to get the whole story mixed up!

'Nothing happened, Hannah,' she reassured her friend, giving her arm a squeeze. 'I just needed a quick breather and the only place to be alone in this place is the loo!'

'Are you certain? Only I know Leo has been a pain in the backside the last couple of days and Old Nick has started breathing fire and brimstone again so it could have been either of them—'

'Hannah, I'm OK. Honestly. In fact, I'm better than OK so let's get our sleeves up and get on with the job.'

Polly led the way towards Reception with a fresh spring in her step. Just let Leo try any of his silly tricks and he'd find out what Polly Lang was like when she went on the warpath!

'Polly, sweetheart, could you lend me a hand?' Leo said in his most cajoling tones, and Polly smiled to herself before she turned round. She hadn't thought that he would chance his arm quite so soon, but Nick had just walked into the room and it was obvious that Leo's campaign was still running.

What a shame he didn't know that the rules had changed... Still, he'd soon learn...

'Of course, Leo,' she said sweetly, pointedly rolling her eyes for the other people in the room.

Nick's face remained impassive, but Tina had to stifle

a giggle. Like the rest of the staff, she'd been following the byplay all day and fairly goggled as she watched Polly join Leo by the small kitchenette area where he was boiling the kettle to make some coffee.

'What can't you manage? Can't you find the sugar, or are the mugs too heavy for you?' she mocked, and was delighted to see the deep flush which swept over his face when he realised that she'd finally called his bluff.

John Preece had arrived a little early for his shift and had taken advantage of the time to relax bonelessly in one corner of the settee. He'd already made himself a mug of coffee and nearly drowned himself with it when he saw Leo's reaction.

'Uh, no,' Leo said uncertainly as he glanced over his shoulder towards the sight of Tina, thumping John's back while he fought for breath. 'I...er...wondered if you could help me pass the mugs round.'

'No problem,' Polly agreed easily as she reached for the two mugs already filled. 'I'll take these two for Nick and myself, shall I?'

Before Leo could comment she'd turned away with her hands full, delivering the first one to the coffee-table in front of a darkly frowning Nick.

'Shh!' she signalled with a finger to her lips and another exaggerated roll of her eyes towards Leo, hoping Nick would appreciate the way she had finally spiked Leo's guns.

For a second she was afraid that he wouldn't respond, but then she had the pleasure of seeing comprehension of her tactics dawn on Nick's face. Suddenly the eyes which had frozen her with their wintry chill had a sparkle like moonlight over rippling water, and one corner of his lips tilted briefly into a smile.

As she stepped away to find a chair he nodded

towards the empty seat beside him and raised one eyebrow.

'Thank you,' she murmured, feeling an unaccustomed shyness as she took up his silent invitation to join him.

She tried to leave a careful space between them but managed to nudge his shoulder as she subsided, and even when she murmured an apology and shuffled away to break the contact she could still feel the heat emanating from the long lean length of his thigh.

'Oh.' Leo's voice broke into their wordless communication and the two of them turned to gaze up at him silently as he stood there with his mug of coffee, neither of them making any effort to make room for him to join them.

'I'll. . .er. . .find another seat, then,' he mumbled, seeming unexpectedly uncomfortable with the situation, and Polly was hard pressed to fight down a giggle.

'One of these days you'll have to tell me what all that was about,' Nick murmured under cover of the renewed conversation in the room.

'When I work it all out myself I promise you'll be the first to know,' she retorted, hardly able to believe that all it had taken was one determined stand, in front of witnesses, to stop Leo in his tracks. And she'd wasted so much time trying to get him alone to talk some sense into him. . .

'So you and Leo aren't what they call an item?' Nick asked. His tone was apparently idle but his intent grey eyes weren't when he turned to meet her startled gaze.

'Hardly!' Polly scoffed and her heart began to thump unevenly when she realised that they had finally started talking to each other. Perhaps now she would have the chance to explain all his misconceptions, and ask for a few explanations herself.

She managed to keep her voice steady as she tried to decipher Nick's impassive face. 'He's not my cup of tea—or coffee!'

'I thought he was every nurse's ideal?' he prompted lightly. 'He's certainly never lacked for company ever since I've known him.'

Polly looked across at Leo and smiled to herself at the very idea that Leo could be her ideal.

She'd seen him watching Nick and herself for several seconds after he'd moved away from them, as though contemplating whether to make another attempt at joining them, but his attention had been caught by one of the other staff members and he'd soon ignored the two of them to perch himself on the arm of one of the chairs on the other side of the room.

Now he was apparently busy teasing Tina and making her blush.

'Oh, he's ideal if you don't mind taking a number and waiting in line,' she said, borrowing Hannah's assessment of the situation. 'I don't doubt that, one-to-one, he's a lot of fun to date, and he's intelligent and hard-working and I could write him a wonderful testimonial, but. . .' She shrugged, not bothering to finish.

Her frankness seemed to startle Nick but his laughter was overshadowed by the strident sound of the telephone. Leo was closest and he was still joking with Tina as he stretched across the back of her chair to grab the receiver.

As soon as he answered the call Polly knew from the way his expression changed that they weren't going to like what was coming in.

'RTA,' he announced in the familiar shorthand

almost before he'd put the phone down. 'We've got two policemen arriving in less than ten minutes. Someone rammed their patrol car and nearly came through the windscreen at them.'

There was a wordless murmur of anger in the room as they all reacted to the thought of yet another injury to vulnerable public servants. Polly had noticed, in the limited time of her own involvement in the specialty, how many more such injuries were turning up in Accident and Emergency departments.

It didn't seem so long ago that policemen, doctors and teachers were treated with the same respect and care as the elderly and the very young. Now it seemed as if no one was safe any more...

It wasn't until the two victims arrived that the team found out that one of them was a young female, only recently transferred to the area.

'Oh, God,' Tina whispered in horror when the young woman, wearing a neck brace and strapped to a backboard, was wheeled in under the unforgiving brightness of the lights. 'Her poor face...'

It wasn't the first time that Polly had seen the effects of a face full of windscreen glass, in spite of the fact that the wearing of seat belts was law.

This time, though, the victim *had* been belted in safely. The problem was that the driver of the stolen car they had boxed in had decided to reverse into them at high speed in an attempt to push the patrol car out of their way, and had actually mounted the bonnet and pushed the windscreen in at the two occupants.

'First things first,' Polly reminded her young colleague, consciously quoting one of Nick's favourite phrases to steady her. 'Her face looks bad, but we have to find out what other injuries she has before that can be dealt with.'

'I know, Sister,' Tina agreed quickly. 'ABC—airway, breathing and circulation, but I'm glad Dr Prince can send for the plastic surgeon to have a look at her. I'd hate to think that she was going to have to live with... Oh, Lord,' she squeaked, her eyes riveted on the second trolley being wheeled into the other side of the room. 'What's happened to *him?*'

Polly glanced across quickly at the second officer and for a moment all she could see was the frantic activity as he was stripped of his remaining clothes by one set of hands, while others worked over and around them to attach monitors, IVs and breathing apparatus.

Suddenly one of the team moved aside and she saw the man's face for the first time.

He, too, was covered with dozens of cuts, but the most startling aspect of his injuries was the way that one of his eyes was nearly bulging out of its socket.

'It could be several things,' she said, keeping her voice down as she turned her attention back to their own charge. 'Can you think of any?'

Tina thought for a moment, then suggested, 'Could it be the result of a blow to the eye socket? If the cheek-bone was shattered, it could be forcing the eye out like that.'

'Could be. Anything else?'

'Fractured skull?' she offered as she automatically fetched and carried to order.

'Is that a likely cause? Think about it—what would be causing the bulging?' Polly prompted, her own hands working independently of her conversation as she helped to prepare the young WPC for the attention of the plastic surgeon. The X-rays of her neck and back had been cleared and she would soon be ready for transport up to Theatre for the long job of piecing her face back together.

'No, I suppose it's not very likely,' Tina conceded. 'The fractured skull wouldn't cause the eye to bulge out like that unless there was bleeding behind the eye socket. Then the pressure could force the eye forward.'

Polly caught Nick's eye across the width of the room and she could tell that he was amused by the way the younger woman was verbally sorting through the options, but there was also a gleam of approval for the way Polly had used the event as a teaching situation.

For Tina's sake she was glad that her own mask hid her smile as they listened to the quick-witted young woman sorting through the possibilities. It was one of the best ways Polly knew for taking the newer recruits' minds off some of the uglier sights they saw in an accident and emergency department, and it was amazing how much they learnt this way.

'What about bleeding going directly into the eye socket?' Tina suggested, with a quick glance towards the other side of the room to check on events over there 'Or if the blood supply to the eye itself has been damaged, or. . .? Oh, God!' she breathed and Polly heard her swallow convulsively when she finally saw the reason for the prominent eye. 'His eye socket is full of *glass*. . .!'

The final count, at the end of a backbreaking stint as Nick painstakingly retrieved every tiny sliver, was seventeen pieces of glass—some of them nearly half an inch across—which had been forced into the eye socket by the force of the collision.

'Will his eye be all right or is he going to lose the sight in it?' Tina asked when Nick finally straightened up and groaned in relief, his fingers digging into the muscles in his lower back.

'As far as I can tell, there's no major damage to the eye itself,' he said as he pulled his mask down to hang around his neck, then added on a cautionary note, 'We'll have to wait for the swelling to go down before we know for certain, but it looks good so far.'

He glanced up at the clock on the wall and groaned again. 'Thank God for that—it's time to go home.'

He stripped off his disposables and dumped them in the bin as the patient was wheeled out through the swing doors and towards the lifts. He rotated his shoulders as if he needed to work the stiffness out of them, too.

Polly was seized with the mad urge to offer to massage the kinks out, but she knew that the whole department would hear about it in a nanosecond and she'd never be allowed to live it down.

As it was, she just had to imagine what it would be like to be granted permission to touch his body and bring him comfort, the way she had once before. . .

The trouble was that the more she thought about it the less likely she was to be able to sleep tonight.

CHAPTER EIGHT

'Hey, Polly! Hang on a minute!'

It was only because she recognised Hannah's voice that Polly bothered to slow down, her umbrella trying to turn itself inside out as the wind tugged at it.

'Hurry up, then, or we'll both be soaked! Get underneath this thing with me—it might keep a little bit of the rain off you!'

The two of them scurried towards the main entrance, their feet splashing through the rivulets of water which coursed between the fancy paving slabs in front of the big glass automatic doors.

'Ugh! I'm wringing wet right up to my knees,' Hannah complained bitterly as they made their way along the corridor towards the staff cloakroom. 'Good job I've got a towel and a spare pair of tights in my locker.'

'Still, it's always warm enough inside the hospital to dry off fairly quickly—too hot sometimes, especially when you come inside on a winter's day. I've got a feeling that's why everyone seems to get so many colds these days—going from freezing cold to too warm and back again.'

'You could be right,' Hannah returned in a muffled voice as she nearly disappeared inside her locker, trying to unearth the elusive packet of tights. 'This place is better than my first job after I qualified, though. I swear the boiler there was so old it had to have coal shovelled into it all day just to keep the radiators lukewarm!'

She gave a crow of victory and backed out of the locker with the missing packet held aloft. A pale blue envelope floated to the rain-spotted floor like the last of the autumn leaves.

'What on earth. . .?' she muttered as she stooped to retrieve it. 'Ah! I'd wondered where that had got to. . .' Ignoring the state of her clothes, she ripped the flap open and fished inside to withdraw several sheets of closely written paper.

Not wanting to appear nosy, Polly turned back to her own locker.

Quickly retrieving several pages of yesterday's newspaper which she'd never had time to read, she crumpled them up and stuffed them into the toes of her shoes. If she was lucky, it would absorb some of the moisture before she needed to put them back on at the end of her shift.

'Fantastic!'

Hannah's jubilant cry quite startled Polly and she turned to find her friend waving her letter and dancing a damp-footed jig.

'I take it that's good news,' she commented wryly when Hannah finally stood still.

'The best!' Hannah promised. 'Do you remember me talking about one of the nurses I trained with—Laura Kirkland?'

'Didn't you both start off specialising in paediatric nursing together?' Polly said with a frown of concentration, her memory jogged by the fact that they had both started off on the same career track as she had done.

'That's right. Then I decided to change to A and E, and when I got the job here it looked as if we were going to drift away from each other.'

'It happens a lot when you move from one hospital to another,' Polly agreed. 'You get so wrapped up in the new job and a different set of colleagues that you don't seem to have time to keep up the old friendships.'

'And it doesn't help if you lose letters before you've even opened them,' Hannah added with a flick at the pale blue sheets. 'Laura wrote this nearly a month ago to tell me that she changed direction shortly after I did and she's now working in A and E, too.'

'What a coincidence!' Polly smiled at Hannah's pleasure, conscious of a twinge of regret that she hadn't kept in touch with any of the group she'd trained with. She'd still maintained contact when she'd married, in spite of the fact that her priorities had changed, but after she'd lost. . .

'Ah, but you haven't heard the best of it,' Hannah gloated, breaking into Polly's painful introspection, then glanced briefly at the letter again as if to check her facts. 'She's coming here—to St Augustine's.'

'To visit you?'

'No! To work!' she clarified, then added with a flourish, 'Laura's the new member of staff we've been waiting for!'

There wasn't time for much more conversation if the two of them were going to be on time, but Hannah was almost bouncing with pleasure at the idea that her old friend was going to be joining the team.

'Hey! She'll be here in time for the fund-raiser!' Hannah exclaimed a little while later. 'I'll have to put her name down for a ticket to the Ball. Do you think I should get an escort lined up for her? After all, she won't know anybody. Do you think Leo would be willing?'

'He said he was probably going to be too busy with

the organisation on the night to take anyone, and he *has* got Sexy Samantha waiting in the wings if he changes his mind!' Polly informed her, and they both had to stifle their laughter. It seemed to be common knowledge that Leo turned pale and hid whenever the busty barracuda appeared.

'Speaking of the Ball,' Hannah continued later on when they met up for a cup of coffee, 'have you heard any more about the Auction? Someone told me there's a rumour going round that there's going to be a surprise draw of some sort.'

'In which case, you know more than I do,' Polly admitted. 'I know Leo had some problems with the fact that the prizes were much more lavish than he'd expected and he was afraid it would put people off bidding, but he solved that one some time ago.'

'Well, if this draw is going to billed as some sort of surprise, he probably won't tell us, but if he's trying to drum up interest...'

'Unfortunately, if he drums up too much interest it's going to be hell trying to sort out off-duty for everyone who wants to go,' Polly said glumly. 'There'll always be someone who gets the short end of the stick, no matter how hard we try.'

'And you can't always operate a first come, first served system either,' Hannah elaborated, 'or the same people would always put their names down for every do, and the ones who have to hold off until they've found a partner or a babysitter would miss out every time.'

'Then, of course, there's always the possibility that there'll be some sort of major accident that evening and that the people who get the chance to go will end up dashing in to work in their evening clothes.'

Hannah chuckled. 'Wouldn't the inevitable press photos look good! I can see the headlines now—*The Best-Dressed A and E in the country*!'

'It wouldn't do much good for the fund-raising part of the evening if Leo lost all his potential bidders.'

'Well, there's not a lot of point in worrying about it until or unless it happens. I've bought my ticket and I found a gorgeous dress in that nearly new shop in the little road just past the library. All I've got to do now is find a pair of shoes and a man!'

They returned to the department and the next stream of patients, but Polly's brain was working overtime as she realised that her own situation had changed.

She had decided that as she didn't have an escort she wouldn't bother buying a ticket to the Ball. She had quite resigned herself to feeling very magnanimous about letting someone else have the evening off to attend.

Now she realised that everything was different.

Since she and Nick were talking again she couldn't help the fact that a little shoot of hope had started growing. Perhaps, as Nick was going to the Ball, he might decide to ask her to accompany him.

Her musings were abruptly shattered as a young woman staggered into the department, carrying two young children.

'Please, Nurse, help me. . . My babies are sick. . .!'

Polly reached her side just in time to catch one child as he slid out of her grasp.

As Polly took his weight she could feel how hot and feverish he was, his skin strangely red and dry.

'Can you manage to carry your little girl? We just need to bring them through here and the doctor will see them.'

'Yes...but please hurry. I think they've been poisoned!'

Out of the corner of her eye Polly saw one of the junior nurses hurrying to help, and she shook her head.

'I can manage here for a minute. Get Dr Prince—as quick as you can!'

She continued on her way into one of the emergency rooms with the young boy in her arms and laid him on a trolley, quickly raising the sides into position in case he rolled over, then she turned and held out her hands for the little girl.

'What makes you think they've been poisoned?' she questioned as she laid the second child on the same trolley. It wasn't until she saw how alike they were that she realised that the two of them were probably fraternal twins, but there wasn't time to comment on the fact. She had important information to elicit before Nick arrived. 'Did you see them eating something? Did they get hold of some tablets?'

'No. It's this...' The mother reached into her pocket and drew out a handful of greenery just as Nick swept into the room.

'Hello. I'm Dr Prince. What have you got there?'

'I'm not sure, but I think it's deadly nightshade. The children found it in the garden and they were eating the berries.'

The poor woman was shaking from head to foot, as pale and sweaty as her children were hot and dry. She was obviously terrified as she watched Nick bend over first one and then the other little one. 'I didn't know it was there—we only moved into the house two days ago and the kids have never had a garden before...'

'Well, they've certainly got all the classic symptoms of belladonna poisoning, including dilated pupils and tachycardia. Sister, let's get IVs running.'

While Polly collected the equipment and set up one IV Nick combined questioning the mother with setting up the second one, and soon he was ready to begin infusing the antidote to belladonna.

'I'm going to begin with a quarter of the dose over five minutes for each of them, and repeat until we see a change. Have some atropine ready in case we have to reverse any side-effects.'

Polly found she was almost holding her breath as the first dose went into the IV for each of them and then, five minutes later, a second one.

She shared the mother's delight when, just as Nick was administering the third dose, the two children started visibly responding to the antidote.

'Oh, thank God!' she breathed faintly, seeming to grow even paler as relief struck her, and Polly had to catch her and deposit her on a chair before she fell over.

By the time the final dose had been slowly infused it was obvious that the two little ones were well on the way to recovery.

Nick straightened up after his final examination and smiled.

'I think they're going to be all right now, but I'd like to admit them to the children's ward overnight for observation.'

'Oh, Doctor, you don't think they'll go unconscious again, do you?' Their mother had just started regaining some colour, but at the mention of admitting her precious babies she went as white as a sheet again.

'Not for a minute,' he soothed. 'But I would like them to stay on the drip for the time being, and the antidote can have some side-effects of its own so we like to monitor it.'

'But. . .'

'We do have facilities for parents to stay with their children so you could stay with them if you want to,' Polly prompted, and received a shaky smile of gratitude.

'Oh, yes, please. I couldn't bear to go home to an empty house without them. My husband had to leave this morning to start his next shift on an oil platform. He'll be away for several weeks but I told him I could cope as long as he was here for the day we moved house.'

She covered her quivering mouth with equally shaky hands.

'Oh, God,' she breathed tearfully. 'He's hardly been gone for a day and I nearly let our babies die. . .!'

'Hey! None of that!' Polly scolded gently. 'They're perfectly normal, mischievous youngsters who thought they'd found something nice to eat. It happens!'

'But. . .'

'But as soon as you realised what had happened,' Polly continued, not allowing her to interrupt, 'you did everything right. You got them here as fast as possible, and you remembered to bring a sample of the berries they'd eaten so we could identify it and administer the right antidote first time.'

'It's very kind of you to say so, but I still shouldn't have let them. . .'

'She's right, you know.' It was Nick who interrupted her this time. 'You did everything you should, and I'm willing to bet that the first thing you do when you get home is scour the garden for anything else they might want to experiment on, and tell them in no uncertain terms that they mustn't eat anything without asking first.'

'You're not kidding!' she said with feeling,

responding to Nick's gentle humour and his confidence in her as much as the reassurance he was giving her. 'Could you put a padlock on their mouths while we've got them here so I won't have to worry about this happening again?'

'I don't think you'll have this problem again,' Nick said wryly. 'All you'll have to do is remind them what happened when they ate the berries—there aren't many children who'd want a second dose!'

He'd finally managed to coax a chuckle out of the poor woman, and Polly had a feeling that she would be able to cope with the rest of the episode more than adequately—after all, she'd had the courage to move house with two inquisitive youngsters under school age, and with the minimum amount of help. She and her children were obviously survivors...

If only she could say the same for herself, she thought wryly as she took the first opportunity to hide herself in the tiny kitchenette round the corner from the consultant's office.

The room was too small for a chair so she had to lean back against the work surface, but it wasn't until she cradled both hands around the steaming mug that she realised that they were still trembling in the aftermath of the tension of the last hour and she was grateful that she had the room to herself.

When she remembered how close those two precious children had come to death she felt physically sick— the same way she had for the last five years ever since the tragedy which had turned her own life inside out.

Oh, it wasn't bad enough that she couldn't do what had to be done—if anything, the tension inside her seemed to make her hypersensitive to her little patients' needs. But afterwards, even when the outcome was as good as this one had been, she always felt totally wrung out...

'Polly? Are you feeling all right?'

Nick's deep voice broke into her gloomy introspection and she looked up from her contemplation of the rapidly cooling contents of her mug to meet the concern in his grey eyes.

'No. Yes. I'm fine,' she assured him, plastering a smile on her face.

'I don't think so,' he said quietly as he stepped into the little room and propped himself against the front of the tiny sink. 'I've started to know when something's not right. What is it? A headache, or are you going to be the first flu victim in the department this year?'

The light touch of his humour was just what she needed to release the tension inside her, and she felt the knots in her shoulders begin to unwind.

'Yes and no,' she said with a wry smile. 'It's not a headache in the accepted sense, but it is for me.'

'Explain.'

Eyes which could be as icy as an arctic wind seemed softer and warmer as he encouraged her to speak.

'It's the children,' she began, then pressed her lips together as she tried to find the words which would allow her to explain, without laying bare her soul. She wasn't ready for that, even though it had happened five years ago, and some days she didn't think she would *ever* be ready...

'Those twin imps?' he questioned with a frown, referring to their most recent case. 'What's the problem? They're going to make a total recovery and are probably already starting to cause a riot up—'

'No. Not just them,' Polly interrupted. 'It's all the children, especially the babies. That's why I changed from Paediatrics. I couldn't stand it any more...the reminders of what could happen...what did happen...'

'A bad experience?'

She nodded wordlessly, trying desperately to stop the tears from gathering, but her memories—coupled with his gentleness—were stretching her control to the limit.

'Do you want to talk about it?' he offered softly as he leant towards her, one hand stretched out in invitation. 'We could go into my office if you don't want to be interrupted.'

She squeezed her eyes tight and shook her head, drawing in a deep breath before she chanced using her voice.

'No... I—I don't want to talk about it. Thank you for offering but I'll be all right.'

'You're sure?' He reached out and placed one warm hand over hers as it curved around the forgotten mug in her hand.

The contact seemed to reach deep inside her, the warmth travelling all the way into the cold dark corners around her heart, and she found herself struggling for control again.

'I...I'm sure,' she whispered as her eyes travelled from the lean dark fingers, cradling her own slender paler ones, up to the intent expression of concern on his face.

Suddenly the love she had been trying to hide from him escaped her shaky control and she dragged her gaze away from the lean planes of his face, afraid that if she wasn't careful it would blaze up at him like light from a beacon.

She remembered the day when he had told her about his wife. His anguish had made it very clear to her that he had loved Dee and wouldn't be interested in an affair, permanent or otherwise. Honesty made her admit that, in spite of the physical attraction which had flared between them, she had no reason to suppose that he'd changed his mind. There'd been nothing private between them since his stolen kiss in the corridor—not even a chance to talk.

At least now he knew that there was nothing between Leo and herself, but what would he do if he realised how much she had come to love *him*? He was a fair-minded man. Would he feel that he was being unfair to her that he couldn't return the emotion?

She was burningly conscious of the fact that his hand still rested over hers, and she could feel his eyes skimming her face as clearly as a physical caress.

Was it just wishful thinking on her part that there was a new closeness beginning between them? A sensitivity to each other's thoughts and feelings?

Not so long ago she had been firm in her decision not to allow anyone to touch her heart. Now everything had changed.

But had it only changed for her? When they finally had their talk would Nick insist that they kept to a purely professional association? If he couldn't return her love might he even hint that it would be more comfortable for both of them if she were to look for a job elsewhere?

How would she bear it—to go away, knowing that she would never see him again?

She couldn't. Not after the searing heartbreak she'd suffered when her marriage had shattered around her. . .

The only solution was to make certain that he never found out how much her feelings had changed towards him, and the best way was to make certain that they spent as little time as possible together.

Nervously clearing her throat, she hunted for a way to put some distance between them and turned slightly so that when she pulled her hand away from the contact with his it would look casual.

'I'll be fine,' she repeated, and straightened her shoulders, lifting her chin a notch without meeting his gaze. 'I'll be out as soon as I've finished my coffee.' She turned away, knowing that she wasn't ready to face him yet.

She held her breath for a moment but he didn't comment on her rather obvious ploy, and the next thing she heard was the sound of his footsteps, leaving the cramped room and receding along the corridor.

Polly was worried that her clumsy attempt at dismissing his attention might have soured her working relationship with Nick. As it was, he seemed a little preoccupied and several times she had felt as if he was watching her.

Elsewhere in the department a child was rushed in by her parents with suspected meningitis, but when it proved to be a minor unexpected food allergy Polly allowed herself to relax again.

It was frustrating to react to children's emergencies like this, but she consoled herself that it was usually only this bad immediately after a close call. Within a few hours and after a dozen or more other patients she would be coping as well as ever.

Until the next time, a little voice inside her head reminded her, and she grimaced, knowing she couldn't deny it.

The next person she had to take through to a cubicle was an elderly man who was complaining that his leg felt 'all wriggly'.

'Would you like me to help you to slip your trousers

off so we can have a look?' Polly suggested, breathing shallowly as a defence against the rather rank odour of his grubby clothes.

'I'm not taking my clothes off for a slip of a girl to see my privates!' he exclaimed in horrified tones. 'It's not proper!'

'It's all right, sir. I'm a nurse and it's part of my job,' Polly explained gently.

'Well, you shouldn't be doing a job that gets you looking at men's privates,' he retorted belligerently. 'You should be at home, looking after babies and keeping things nice for your husband.'

Tim had thought the same thing, although she hadn't known that when they'd married, and her insistence on returning to nursing had been the reason why he had been able to crucify her with guilt when disaster struck. . .

'But I'm not married,' she explained calmly, forcing herself to concentrate on the confrontation in front of her rather than the one she'd never been able to win.

'There you are, then,' he said, inexplicably triumphant. 'I never showed my privates to my wife in forty years of marriage, and I'm certainly not going to show them to a slip of a girl who can't even catch a man of her own.'

Halfway through his tirade Polly was conscious that they weren't alone in the cubicle any more and she turned to find Nick, standing impassively behind her.

'Right, Sister, what seems to be the problem here?' he said. His voice was imperturbable but she could see a fugitive gleam of humour in his eyes and knew that he had overheard at least part of the old man's complaint.

'Mr Ferguson is complaining that his leg feels all wriggly, and I was just asking him if he needed any help to take his trousers off,' she said, keeping her face straight with difficulty.

'Fine,' Nick said, obviously taking the initiative before their elderly patient could get started again. 'In that case, Mr Ferguson, perhaps you can answer a few questions for me while I just slip your things down. Sister, could you get a clipboard to write the answers down?'

'Certainly, Doctor.'

She smiled as she slipped out of the cubicle and grabbed the nearest clipboard, knowing that it was just a ploy to enable the old man to save face. She and Nick both knew that she'd already taken the clipboard with the start of his case notes into the cubicle with Mr Ferguson.

By the time she returned the elderly man was sitting bolt upright on the examining couch, his body covered from his waist to his grey knobbly knees with a plain blue cotton blanket.

When he heard her draw the curtain closed behind her he glared at her, looking as if he wished he could pull the blanket down to cover the rest of his legs, too.

It wasn't his angry expression or the fact that his lower legs were naked that caught her eye so much as the gaping wound down the front of one shin.

Compassion for the pain he must have suffered when the injury happened and concern that such a large wound covered by such unsanitary clothing might have become dangerously infected—even gangrenous— made her take a step forward.

It wasn't until she caught the bemused expression on Nick's face that she took a closer look, and realised that the wound was teeming with maggots.

'*That's* why your leg feels wriggly, Mr Ferguson,'

Nick said with admirable aplomb, for all the world as if it were a sight he saw every day. 'Now, we'll just get Sister to clean you off and put a dressing over the wound, and you can get dressed again.'

'But what about the wriggling?' he demanded querulously as he squinted short-sightedly down at his leg, obviously unable to understand what was causing his discomfort. 'Will the wriggling go away?'

'Sister will get rid of the wriggling for you as soon as she uses some special stuff on your leg,' Nick promised, evidently giving up all idea of explaining what had happened in favour of solving the problem as swiftly as possible.

Before the cantankerous old man could remember that he'd objected to her presence Polly was carefully irrigating the gash, catching the stream of water and its various water-borne inhabitants in a strategically placed bowl.

'The wound is beautifully clean,' she commented in a brief aside to Nick.

'Good. That means the maggots had just about finished their work. Without them, he'd probably have lost his lower leg to gangrene.'

'What are you two mumbling about? What's happening to my leg?' The fretful voice held a touch of fear this time.

'Nothing at all,' Nick reassured him with a smile. 'You've given it a bad knock at some stage, and it's been trying to heal itself. We'll just give it a bit of a helping hand with a dressing and it'll soon be good as new.'

'Still don't see why I had to take my trousers off. You could have just hiked them up a bit to look at a scratch.'

Nick silently rolled his eyes and Polly had to stifle a chuckle, her fingers working quickly and deftly as she covered the wound to protect it from further knocks while it finished healing.

'You'll need to go to your doctor's surgery to have the dressing changed, Mr Ferguson...'

'Haven't got a doctor any more,' he interrupted her. 'He died several years ago, and the new one's too young to know what he's doing.'

Polly didn't dare look at Nick for fear she'd start laughing. Luckily, he took charge of the conversation.

'In which case, you'd better come back here for someone to change the dressing and keep an eye on it.'

'I won't have to take my trousers off again, will I?' he demanded suspiciously, looking from one to the other.

'No. Next time you can tell the nurse that you only need to roll your trouser-leg up,' Nick confirmed.

As Polly escorted the elderly man across to Reception to arrange another appointment she wasn't certain whether it was a good idea—after all, some poor nurse was going to have to work uncomfortably close to those awful trousers. But at least they wouldn't have to fight the elderly man to get him to take them off so perhaps the one outweighed the other.

She turned away from the appointments desk and glanced down at her fob watch, surprised to see that it was only a couple of minutes to the end of her shift.

Suddenly she realised how tired and hungry she felt, and she sighed at the thought of the shopping she would have to do on her way home if she was going to have anything to eat.

She was just passing the emergency reception area when a pair of headlights stabbed through the gloom beyond the automatic doors as an ambulance sped into view and reversed swiftly up to the emergency entrance.

In spite of the fact that it was the end of her shift, there was no way she could ignore the urgency of the vehicle's arrival.

As she began to hurry towards it her instincts told her that something terrible was happening inside, and she was almost running by the time the back doors flew open.

CHAPTER NINE

THE first person to emerge from the back of the ambulance was Ted Larrabee and he didn't bother with the steps to the vehicle, gaining the entrance ramp with a leap which continued into a run straight towards Polly.

For a second Polly's step faltered when she saw the tiny bundle cradled in the paramedic's arms, but her training kicked in instantaneously.

'This way.' She indicated the closest emergency room. 'What's happened?'

'SIDS.' The hated acronym almost disappeared in the sound of the mobile respirator he was squeezing, and Polly was glad she was holding the door for him or the sudden shock would have had her on her knees.

No! Not today! she screamed inside her head. *It's too soon . . .*

Outwardly, apart from the stark whiteness of her knuckles as she clutched the door, she was totally in control, releasing her grip to hurry across as he deposited his tiny burden and restarted heart massage alternately with oxygenation.

'He's four months old and he didn't wake for his feed. Slightly snuffly earlier in the day but otherwise perfectly healthy,' Ted continued, reciting the stark facts.

Without a second's hesitation Polly began to check the child, firing questions about how long it was since the parents had last seen the child and whether resuscitation had been initiated as soon as the ambulance was called.

One part of her mind was registering the facts—that the child had been put down for a sleep and hadn't woken for his next feed; that he was already cold when the horrified mother had discovered what had happened; that the parents had started CPR themselves while they'd waited for the ambulance to arrive, then had followed the vehicle in their own car while the paramedics had taken over the attempt at resuscitation.

The other part of her mind was screaming out in denial at the fact that it had already been too late when the baby had been found.

Somehow it always seemed to be too late, she thought as her heart tore apart inside her.

It wasn't fair!

He was a beautiful, healthy little boy. There was absolutely nothing wrong with him except a touch of the snuffles. She'd been caring for him properly. She was a good mother.

It wasn't right!

He hadn't deserved to die. He'd deserved a long, happy life and she'd loved him so much. . .so very much. . .

'Polly. . .? Sister!'

It wasn't Ted's voice which brought her out of the living nightmare, but Nick's. *His* arm which circled her shaking shoulders and offered her a handful of paper handkerchiefs to mop up the tears which streamed down her cheeks to fall on the pale, still body.

'Ross MacFadden's on his way down, Polly,' he said quietly, using the familiar paediatric consultant's name to help to steady her.

She suddenly realised that Ted had gone and she was

alone in the room with Nick and the tiny still figure on the bed beside them, and she had no recollection of anything that had happened after she'd realised that the little boy was dead and there was nothing she could do about it.

Memory had taken over and she'd been totally immersed in her own personal nightmare.

'Ross will take over here and speak to the parents,' Nick continued, his soothing voice reassuring her by telling her all the things she already knew. 'He'll tell them what's happened and see if they want to spend some time with their little boy to say their goodbyes.'

'But. . .'

Somehow, in spite of the fact that she knew that there was absolutely nothing either of them could do for him, she couldn't bring herself to leave. It didn't seem right that the little boy should be left all alone—as if he'd been abandoned.

'Hannah's waiting to come in and sit with him. We won't leave him by himself,' Nick said, as if he'd understood what she was thinking without her having to say anything.

'Come on, Polly,' he prompted softly when she paused by the door and looked back one last time. 'It's time to go home.'

Polly looked up at him, at the compassion in his eyes, and realised that somehow he knew what she was going through; knew why she had reacted this way to someone else's tragedy, and she knew that she could trust him to take care of her.

'I need to get my things,' she mumbled as her mind began to function again. 'My clothes and my bag from my locker. And my shoes. . . They were wet this morning. . .'

Was it really just this morning that she and Hannah had sheltered under her umbrella? It seemed as if a decade had passed and she felt as if she'd aged a century.

'We'll detour past your locker and then I'm driving you home,' he said decisively, as he pushed the door open and nodded to Hannah.

'Oh, but you can't just leave the hospital without. . .'

'Polly, I'm off duty too,' he said, giving her shoulder a little shake and indicating with his free hand the fact that he'd already exchanged his white coat for his suit jacket. 'I was handing over just as the ambulance arrived so I'm free to play chauffeur.'

'Oh.' She subsided, suddenly conscious that, although he wasn't tempting the hospital grapevine by walking along the corridor with his arm still wrapped around her shoulders, he was still holding her arm.

The warmth of Nick's fingers penetrated the fabric of her sleeve as he held her, his grasp as gentle as if he thought she was as fragile as a Dresden figurine.

He waited for her to retrieve her belongings, and when she rejoined him in the corridor he wove his fingers between hers and led her out to his car.

Polly sank into the luxurious upholstery and as soon as she'd fastened the seat belt she closed her eyes wearily and leant back.

As if in a dream, she listened to Nick sliding into the car beside her and heard the smooth thrum of the engine as he turned the key and set off through the darkness.

Time didn't seem to have any meaning as she sat trapped in an endless replay of the nightmare scenes in her mind.

She was vaguely aware that she had started crying

again but it was Nick's gentle ministrations as he used his own handkerchief to dry her tears that finally made her open her eyes, and she realised that the car had stopped.

She drew in a deep shuddering breath and reached for the seat belt release so that she didn't have to meet his eyes.

'Thank you for bringing me home,' she whispered as she reached for her bag, which had slipped off her lap and onto the floor by her feet. 'I—I'll see you tomorrow.'

She went to open the door but paused when she heard Nick's soft chuckle.

'Polly. . .look out of the window.'

Puzzled, she did as he said and felt a slow wash of heat scorch her cheeks when she saw where they were.

'I'm sorry, I didn't realise we'd come to your house. Did. . .? Do you want me to walk the rest of the. . .?'

'Don't be silly,' he chided gently, not waiting for her to finish her question. 'I've brought you here because I don't think you should be on your own just yet. If you'll accept my hospitality I can promise you a reasonably good cup of tea.'

She summoned up a watery smile and nodded, grateful for the fact that she wouldn't be going into an empty flat just yet, then sat limply and watched as he came round to her side of the car to help her out.

'What do you want first—the tea or the bathroom?' he offered when he'd closed the front door behind her and she found herself once more in the welcoming warmth of his hallway.

Suddenly she had a mental image of what she must look like. Her uniform was rumpled after a day's work and she had never managed to look pretty when she cried so could just imagine how red and blotchy her eyes were.

'The bathroom, please,' she said wryly, and turned towards the little ground-floor cloakroom.

'How about a long hot shower and a change of clothes?' he suggested, one dark blond eyebrow raised questioningly.

Polly's initial reaction was to refuse the offer, but the thought of standing under steaming hot water and washing all the stress and tension down the drain was too enticing.

'That would be wonderful, but are you sure...?'

'I'm sure.' He smiled his approval and gestured for her to go up. 'Do you remember the way? There are clean towels on the rail and more in the airing cupboard if you need them. Take your time.'

She was conscious that he was watching her as she made her way up the still-uncarpeted stairs, and knew that he didn't start walking towards the kitchen until she reached the top and turned towards the bathroom door.

Just that small demonstration of concern was enough to start her crying again, and she hurried to strip off her clothes and climb under the pelting spray to disguise the sounds of her distress.

Polly didn't really know how long it was before she finally climbed out of the shower, and she felt a twinge of guilt for the amount of hot water she must have used. Then she wrapped herself in one of Nick's enormous towels and realised that she felt too exhausted to care about anything other than the fact that she wasn't alone.

'Polly?' The deep voice was accompanied by tapping on the door. 'How are you doing in there? Are you nearly ready for something to eat?'

Now that she was out of the shower she realised that

the room was full of the tantalising aromas of cooking, drifting up from the kitchen below, and Polly gave a rusty chuckle when her stomach gave a loud rumble of appreciation.

'Suddenly I'm starving and I'm nowhere near ready to come down. My hair's still soaking,' she called.

'Well, why not wrap it in a hand-towel and borrow the robe on the back of the door?' he suggested after a pause, his voice sounding strangely rough. 'It'll be miles too long but you can always roll the sleeves up.'

'Oh, but. . .' Polly began, the very idea of sharing a meal with Nick while dressed in nothing more than his robe sending sharp shivers of awareness up the back of her neck.

'The food will spoil if you leave it until your hair's dry,' he prompted. 'Mushroom omelette and crusty bread rolls,' he added, tempting her beyond bearing.

'All right! All right! I'm coming down!' she surrendered swiftly. 'Don't you start on mine before I get there!'

She felt self-conscious when she padded down in her bare feet, with his towelling robe wrapped nearly twice around her, but when he teasingly hovered his fork over a plump button mushroom on her plate she rushed to protect her food and the discomfort was gone.

When they'd finished eating, Nick insisted that she left the plates stacked on the drainer and carried the tea-tray through to the lounge.

He must have lit the fire while she was under the shower because it was now burning brightly in the refurbished fireplace, adding a cheery warmth to the room.

'I can't remember the last time I sat in front of an open fire,' Polly mused as she gazed vacantly at the patterns made by the flames, her feet tucked up beside her on the settee with the hem of Nick's robe pulled down to enclose them.

'I read somewhere that it's a tribal comfort symbol,' Nick said in a relaxed voice, and she looked across at him to watch the way the flickers of the flames glimmered along the thick blond strands of his hair and gleamed in his half-closed eyes. 'Apparently, it's supposed to be some sort of universal memory from our long-ago cave-dwelling ancestors... Just sitting in front of it is supposed to make us feel more secure.'

Silence fell and stretched out as Polly thought about what he'd said, and she found herself agreeing.

'I can see what you mean,' she murmured, looking back at the fire before he caught her gazing at him. 'It's as if you know that the fire can protect you from all the nasty predators, lurking out there in the darkness.'

'And the nightmares?' he suggested softly, and she felt his eyes on her. This time she felt compelled to meet his gaze.

'Maybe,' she conceded equally softly, in spite of the nervous way her pulse had begun to race.

She had known, subconsciously, when she'd accepted his invitation to take her home that they would eventually talk about the cause of her ignominious collapse in the presence of the dead child.

Part of her had been afraid of it—she had been trying to cope with that particular nightmare alone for five years—but now that the time had finally come she felt almost at peace with herself.

Drawing in a deep shuddering breath, she leant back into her corner of the settee and closed her eyes while she searched for the courage to begin.

The sudden warmth of his hand as it covered hers startled her into opening her eyes again, and she turned her head to face him, strengthened by the caring gesture.

'I suppose you've guessed that I lost a baby to SIDS—a little boy almost the same age as that one today,' she began in a husky voice, her eyes stinging with the renewed threat of tears.

He murmured a wordless agreement and the compassion she saw in his eyes helped her to continue.

'I'd just returned to work part time after my maternity leave. Tim didn't want me to. He thought I ought to stay at home full time and devote myself to being a wife and mother. We argued about it, and I said we needed the money—and we did, if we wanted to have a decent holiday and replace the car—but really I wanted to go back because I enjoyed my job.'

She paused, having to fight a little harder for control as she drew closer to the nightmare, until she felt the slight squeeze he gave her fingers. It was all the encouragement she needed to grit her teeth and go on.

'I was lucky to get a place in the crèche provided by the hospital and, apart from the fact that Tim picked a fight every time I was late or the house wasn't tidy, I had started to get into a routine and I thought it was all working out.'

She had to stop to swallow hard, her throat nearly closed by the lump of misery put there by the memories she was dredging up. Then she began again, her words coming faster and faster as she was bombarded by details.

'Andrew had been a bit snuffly the day before, but I thought perhaps he'd picked a bit of a cold up from one of the other children in the crèche. I strapped his carrycot in the safety harness on the back seat of the car to drive him to the hospital, and he was just dozing off to sleep as I set off.

'I had the local radio station on and there was a newsflash about an accident, blocking the road I wanted to take and warning drivers to take an alternative route. It was a bit longer, but at least I wouldn't get stuck in a big snarl-up and be late for work.

'It must have taken me about half an hour altogether, and I was just s-signalling to turn into the hospital car park when I caught sight of Andrew in the mirror and I just *knew* that there was something wrong.'

She was shaking all over, in spite of the fact that somewhere during her recitation Nick had put his arm around her shoulders and pulled her close to his side.

'I...I drove straight to the emergency department entrance with my hand on the hooter and...and they w-worked on him for half an hour, but it was already too l-late. The coroner said he must have d-died shortly after I set off.'

'Ah, sweetheart, hush,' Nick murmured into the silky strands of her towel-dried hair as she fought for breath.

'He... He blamed me,' she said in a voice full of misery. 'Tim said it was *my* fault Andrew died. He said if I'd stayed at home the way he'd wanted I'd have been taking care of him properly instead of taking care of other peoples' children. He said...he said...'

She couldn't go on, the memory of Tim's rejection and condemnation fuelling her sobs until they obliterated any coherent speech as she wept her heart out on Nick's broad shoulder.

When Polly's grief finally subsided into hiccups and copious nose-blowing she discovered that at some time Nick had pulled her onto his lap and she was totally surrounded by the warmth and security of his arms. Even so, she was embarrassed to have poured everything out like that.

'I'm sorry,' she whispered. 'I've never...never made a fool of myself like that before.'

'Then it was time you did,' he said firmly, squashing her attempts at sliding off his knees by the simple expedient of tightening his hold on her. 'Wasn't there anyone you could talk to? Didn't the hospital put you in touch with a counsellor?'

She shook her head. 'They offered, but I couldn't...couldn't bear to talk about it.'

'So you locked it all inside.'

His knowing tone drew her eyes up to meet his and the expression there confirmed what she'd suspected.

'You did the same thing,' she said softly. 'Locked all the pain away and cut yourself off.'

She felt his chest expand as he sighed. 'At the time it was the only way I could cope.'

Polly nodded and murmured, almost under her breath, 'If I didn't let anyone get close then it wouldn't hurt when I lost them...' Her voice trailed away and as the silence lengthened she became aware of a new tension in the strong arms that surrounded her.

'I...I ought to be getting back home,' she said, trying to find some way out of an increasingly awkward situation.

Out of the kindness of his heart Nick had given her a lift home after she'd come apart at the seams. He'd even thrown in a shower and a hot meal, and she'd repaid him by weeping and wailing on his shoulder. He must be heartily sick of the sight of her and wishing her gone by now. It was just politeness which was stopping him from...

'You're not going anywhere, Polly...except upstairs to bed.'

Shock had her eyes flying up to meet his, the echoes

of his husky words still whirling round inside her head.

'*What. . .!*' she whispered, and felt her eyes widening.

She was incapable of anything else, robbed of breath by the mental images of their night together which had joined the words already short-circuiting her brain. His warmth and strength when he'd held her cradled in his arms; the leashed power in his body as he'd braced himself over her before he'd joined their two bodies, and the expression on his face when ecstasy held him in thrall; his naked body stretched out on his beautiful bed in the abandon of sleep, and her last view of him after they'd spent the night together.

'Polly. . .you'll catch flies,' he teased as he touched her chin with the tip of one finger, and she flushed as she snapped her mouth shut.

'Well, you said. . .you said. . .'

'I said you were going upstairs to bed,' Nick repeated, his voice very serious now. 'You're tired and upset and I don't think you need the hassle of getting dressed to go home, then spending the night alone in your flat.'

He paused and Polly's heart sank at the prosaic reasoning, no matter how caring the sentiments were.

'Of course,' he continued, his voice taking on a slight roughness, 'if you were to tell me that you'd rather not spend the night in my house, or if you were to tell me that you'd rather spend the night in your own bed, I'd willingly take you home.'

'But. . .?' Polly challenged softly, a little frisson of excitement causing her pulse rate to pick up, and she marvelled at the recovery rate of the human body.

'What?'

'I heard a "but" at the end of that sentence,' she said as she gazed at him, and even in the subdued lighting of the room, she saw the betraying hint of colour shade his cheekbones.

'But. . .if you want to stay here. . .with me. . . If. . .' He paused and she felt his chest expand sharply as he drew in a swift breath before he continued speaking; felt the tension in the body which curved protectively around her and the arms which still surrounded her. 'If you want to share my bed so that I can be there for you and take care of you the way you took care of me when I fell apart. . .'

'If?' she repeated, and felt the smile creep over her face. 'I can't think of anything I want more. . .*need* more than to have you hold me and keep the nightmares away.'

The small voice inside her head was screaming out a warning, telling her that she was risking heartbreak and misery if she offered herself so openly, but for the first time in five years she didn't care.

Subconsciously she realised that there had been no mention of love on either side, but suddenly she could see a glimmer of light in the darkness and if there was any chance that it would turn into the warmth of full sun she was willing to take the chance.

Perhaps Nick wouldn't ever be able to let go of his grief over Deanne and their unborn child and perhaps she would never find the courage to have another child but, in the meantime, they could find comfort in each other and, perhaps, in time. . .

It was almost as if Nick had been paralysed by secret voices of his own because it was several seconds before he reacted to her acceptance with a release of the tension which had gripped him in a long exhaled breath.

'I'll keep you safe,' he promised as he slid one arm

under her legs as if he was going to lift her into his arms and carry her upstairs.

'Nick! I can walk!' Polly objected, and wriggled round on his lap to put her feet on the floor. She ignored the involuntary groan he quickly stifled, in spite of the fact that she was only too aware of the reason for his discomfort and inordinately pleased that she'd had such an effect on him.

'In fact,' she continued briskly as she reached for the tea-tray, 'I'm going to take these cups through into the kitchen and do that washing up while you go and have your shower—if there's any hot water left.'

'You don't have to do that,' he objected with a frown as he straightened to his full six feet. 'It's not one of the conditions of you staying here, you know.'

'I know,' she said with an impish grin, then lowered her voice to continue. 'But you did promise to take care of me the way I took care of you last time and, if my memory serves me right, you started off with a shower that time.'

She turned away and walked out of the room, almost laughing aloud at the stunned expression in his eyes.

As she began to deal with the few items they'd used she was conscious of several minutes' silence before Nick's footsteps sounded in the hallway.

She heard him turn the key in the front door to lock the rest of the world out, then followed his hollow tread on the bare wood as he went up the stairs. As she squeezed washing-up liquid into the water she wondered what he had been thinking about as he'd stood in the sitting-room so silently.

Then she heard the sound of the shower running in the bathroom up above and her imagination ran riot. She visualised the way his body would gleam as the water poured over each curve and hollow and the way his hands would spread the soap over his chest, rubbing it into the curly hair which spread across the width of his chest and down towards. . .

Stop it! she ordered herself as she nearly dropped the plate she'd been polishing for what seemed like the last week. Get the job finished and then you can go upstairs and see for yourself, if that's what he wants you to do.

There was no doubt in her mind that he wanted her in his bed—the powerful reaction of his body when he'd cradled her on his lap told her that. But she knew that Nick was an honourable man, and if he had decided that all he was going to do was hold her in his arms to keep the nightmares away. . .

She chuckled silently at the irony of the situation.

Here she was, a divorcee of five years who had decided unequivocably that she was never going to allow another man to get close enough to hurt her, and what was she contemplating? Only the best way to persuade the man she'd fallen in love with to take her into his bed and make love to her until he fell as deeply in love with her as she was with him. . . Only the best way to show him exactly how much he meant to her and how much she wanted to spend the rest of her life with him.

Not much. . .really!

Polly reached out one shaking hand to turn off the light and padded her way almost silently along the hall. She realised how nervous she was when she tried to climb the stairs and her knees refused to comply.

'Idiot!' she muttered under her breath as she grabbed hold of the bannister rail and heaved herself upwards, nearly tripping over the hem of his voluminous robe.

'You can't show him anything if you're down here and he's up there!'

She reached the top of the stairs and hovered uncertainly, not knowing where Nick was. Had he already gone into the bedroom? Was he sitting up and waiting for her to join him in the polished wooden splendour of his bed?

For just one second she contemplated racing back down the stairs and curling up in front of the fire for the night, but then the bathroom door opened and Nick came out, wearing nothing but a towel wrapped round his hips, and she was lost.

For timeless moments her besotted eyes roamed greedily over him, charting the actuality of the memories which had been tormenting her, and he looked even better than she remembered—taller, broader, more perfectly symmetrical, more virile and infinitely more. . .

'Polly,' he whispered huskily, interrupting the increasingly lascivious train of her thoughts, 'if you keep looking at me like that we're not only going to set the towel alight but probably the whole house!'

'Nick!' She covered her flaming cheeks with her hands, horrified that he'd seen her ogling him like that and tempted once again to flee.

'Come here, sweetheart,' he ordered softly and spread his arms wide in invitation. 'Come to me, Polly.' And his eyes gleamed like softly polished silver in the half-light as she flew into them.

CHAPTER TEN

NICK came awake slowly, surprised to find that the bedside light was still on. He usually turned it off before he lay in the darkness, trying to ignore his demons long enough to snatch a few hours of fitful sleep.

He turned his head to look at the clock on the bedside cabinet to see how many hours he'd managed this time, and suddenly realised that he wasn't alone in the bed. There was a tousled dark head sharing the pillow with him.

Moving carefully so that he didn't disturb her, he rolled over and propped himself up on one elbow, then he allowed himself the luxury of gazing down at her.

'*Polly*,' he whispered soundlessly, just for the pleasure of using her name as he charted the perfection of her features relaxed in sleep.

Not that either of them had had much time for sleep, he thought ruefully as he remembered their hunger for each other. He snorted softly as his body stirred again. How could he have thought he had sated himself with her last night when, just hours later, he needed to bury himself in her again so badly that he could hardly wait for her to wake?

Was it just lust? The overwhelming result of his self-enforced celibacy?

He shook his head.

No. This feeling didn't have anything to do with rampant hormones—well, maybe a little, he admitted as his lower anatomy reacted to his perusal of the pink-tipped perfection of her breast, peeping over the edge of the bedclothes.

This was *more* than just hormones, he corrected himself as he contemplated the new peace which filled his hungry soul.

He'd been in love before, and if Deanne had lived he would probably still be happy with her and the child they'd made between them. But she was gone and, whether he wanted it to or not, life had moved on.

He drew in a shaky breath as he felt the tight bands loosen around his heart.

The word 'love' seemed too small to encompass the enormity of the emotion he felt as he realised that it was Polly who had filled the empty spaces inside him, Polly who had taken him by the scruff of the neck and made him face his shortcomings, Polly who had understood the pain and the guilt and whose resilience in the face of her own tragedy had finally taught him to look towards the future.

He couldn't resist the temptation to look at her again and carefully lifted the edge of the bedclothes away from her body so that the soft light could touch her, spilling over the pale curves and hollows as if she were a statue in palest pink living marble.

The cooler air reached her breasts and he watched with pleasure as her nipples tightened in reaction, the flesh darkening into tempting berries that he longed to take into his mouth.

Greatly daring, he pursed his lips and blew a soft stream of air towards them and was rewarded when not only did they grow more prominent, more enticing, but Polly shifted in her sleep, arching her back as though offering her breasts for him to taste.

Nick licked his lips in anticipation and smiled lazily.

Polly didn't have to go to the hospital until later today and he'd been accustomed to functioning on too little sleep for years so what difference would it make if he lost a little more because he'd seduced Polly into waking up for another session of the most mind-blowing love-making he'd ever known?

He licked the tip of one finger and was just reaching out to dampen one tightly furled rosy bud when the realisation hit him full force and he froze.

That was the difference. That was what made everything different with Polly. The word 'love-making' said it all.

Nick drew in a deep breath as certainty poured through him and he smiled again.

He loved her, right to the depths of his soul, and as soon as she was awake he would tell her so and ask her to marry him.

His smile dimmed slightly when he remembered the way she had sobbed her heart out in his arms when she'd told him about the loss of her child. He had felt a measure of that same grief and could well understand why she had cut herself off from any further hurt.

Last night had changed all that.

Last night she had been ready to consciously and willingly share his bed, and that meant that she must love him, too.

As he gazed down at her a flood of certainty overtook him as he looked towards a future filled with the presence of Polly and the children they would one day create.

He had a sudden image of a tiny mouth, greedily suckling at her, and desire to do the same twisted deep inside him.

He licked his finger again and reached out towards the tip of her breast, circling her nipple with moisture before he blew on it very softly.

As he'd hoped, the cool breeze caused the delicate flesh to darken and tighten still further and Polly stirred again, the pattern of her breathing changing with her unconscious excitement. This time she shifted her legs restlessly, tilting her hips so that her thighs parted—as if in anticipation of the pleasures he wanted to give her.

He'd been amazed how sensitive her breasts had been when he'd stroked and suckled them last night—so sensitive that, as he was doing now, he could bring her to full arousal without touching the rest of her body at all.

He settled his head more comfortably on his hand, and prepared to be as patient and as thorough as he knew how. He would enjoy seeing if he could bring her the same pleasure while she was still asleep—he couldn't imagine a more erotic way of waking her up to ask her to marry him. . .

'Damn!' His hand froze again when he heard a distant sound and realised that it was his pager. He must have left it in the bathroom when he'd had his shower last night—the first time he'd ever forgotten to bring it into the bedroom with him.

But, then, he *had* been rather distracted last night, wondering if he was going to lie in agony all night while Polly slept in his arms—or whether he really had seen the gleam in her eyes which meant that she was looking forward to sharing a bed with him as much as he was with her.

With a last regretful look at the ripe perfection of her engorged breasts he softly lowered the bedclothes over them and slid out of bed to pad, naked, towards the bathroom. If he didn't get to that pager soon and turn it off it might wake Polly, and he wanted that pleasure for himself.

He was smiling as he passed the mirror in the bathroom and saw the wolfish glint in his eyes when he remembered just how little sleep he'd allowed her to have before exhaustion had claimed them both, then he swatted the infernal gadget to silence the noise.

Five minutes later he was glumly padding back up the stairs to retrieve his clothes.

John Preece had taken over from him at the end of his shift, and Nick had noticed that he didn't look quite up to par. Since then he'd gone down with a monumental migraine and wasn't fit to work so, in line with the rota drawn up for A and E cover, Nick was going to have to turn out to take John's place.

He held his breath as the wardrobe door creaked when he opened it, then reached inside for a clean shirt and looped a tie around his neck. His shoes were in the bathroom and his keys. . .

He paused in the doorway for one last look.

God! She looked so beautiful lying there, her dark hair and dark lashes such a stunning contrast to her pale skin and her lips still slightly swollen and rosy after the tumultuous kisses they'd shared.

He glanced at the clock, wondering what the chances were that she'd still be asleep when he returned. If she was then perhaps he could still enact his fantasy of arousing her to wakefulness and a heartfelt proposal of marriage.

He shook his head.

No chance of that now, and he didn't want to break her sleep just to tell her that he'd been called in to the hospital. He'd have to write a note to make certain that she knew that he'd be thinking of her...

Polly stretched as she woke and winced at the unaccustomed ache in muscles she'd all but forgotten she had, then smiled like the cat that had got the cream when she remembered what she'd done to make them ache like that.

'Mmm... Nick?' she murmured, feeling too lazy even to open her eyes, and reached out a hand to stroke him—but he wasn't there.

She surged up from the covers, her eyes wide open now as she gazed anxiously around the room. There wasn't a sound to be heard—nothing from the bathroom and nothing from the ground floor of the house to tell her where he was.

She sat there for a moment, listening and shivering slightly as the air touched the warmth of her naked back, and she knew that the house was empty.

It didn't take her long to decide that she was just wasting her time, sitting there, and she slid to the edge of the bed before dashing, barefoot and stark naked, across the partially renovated hallway and into the bathroom.

Wherever Nick was she would probably have to wait until she got to the hospital to find out what had...

Glancing towards the mirror over the sink to see what sort of tangled mess the night had made of her hair, she was startled into laughter.

All over the mirror, written in soap, was a message from Nick.

'Called in. John sick. See you soon. Don't use all the hot water!'

There was a smear at the bottom which could have

been more writing, or his name, but she couldn't read it.

She laughed again as she stepped into the shower, hugging the thought to herself that he'd cared enough about her to leave a message to tell her why he'd had to leave.

As she turned her face up to the spray she couldn't help the smile which grew at the thought that perhaps he was closer to loving her than she'd realised. He'd certainly been very loving when she'd bared her soul last night and told him about Andrew and then, when he'd taken her to his bed. . .

She reached for the soap and began to spread the lather over her shoulders, remembering the way he had pushed his robe off them and kissed his way down her neck and then further down over the slopes of her breasts. . .

As she remembered the way he'd explored her curves her hands were retracing his path until she was cupping them in her palms. She marvelled at the way they felt so heavy, so sensitive, when all she was doing was remembering the way he'd taken them in his much larger hands and finessed her nipples until she'd been moaning with desire.

Even now they were so engorged that it was almost painful to touch them, and she wondered for a moment if it was a result of his attention to them.

She remembered the obvious pleasure he'd taken in finding out what pleased her most, and the delight he'd taken in suckling her until she couldn't bear the suspense any longer and had taken matters into her own hands.

As she stood under the spray to rinse the lather away she marvelled at the fact that just the play of the water droplets over her breasts made the tingling spread deep down inside her as her body prepared itself for him.

She didn't think her body had ever been this responsive before. The last time she'd felt anything like it was when she was...was when she was pregnant...

The shocking thought came to her so suddenly that her knees refused to bear her weight and she nearly collapsed in a heap, just barely managing to hang onto the tap while she turned the water off and staggered out onto the mat.

Pregnant?

Polly shivered convulsively and reached for a towel to wrap it tightly around herself.

She couldn't be pregnant. It was impossible. She didn't want to be pregnant ever again... She couldn't stand the anguish of waiting for something terrible to happen to her baby. She'd only just survived the loss of Andrew. She couldn't—wouldn't—put herself through that again. She was too frightened.

In spite of the fact that she'd just climbed out of a hot shower, she was icy cold through and through. As she mentally added up the days which had passed since the first time they'd made love the weight of dread wiped her silly smile away. How could she not have realised sooner?

Even when Nick had taken pains to protect her last night she hadn't remembered that their first time together had been too explosive for either of them to think of their responsibilities.

And it wasn't just herself she had to think of—there was Nick, too.

She'd known right from the first that he was still in love with his wife, and the guilt that he was still alive had stopped him from even contemplating a commitment to anyone else.

They'd each known the pain of losing a child and, while she knew how well he related to their smaller patients in the department, he'd never said anything about wanting a family—and she could hardly expect him to change his life just because she was expecting a baby.

Yet even if she were willing to have the child without his support—without anyone's support—there was no way that she would be able to cope alone...

Polly drew in a shuddering breath, conscious that her thoughts were chasing each other round and round. At the moment she was too shocked at the mere idea that she was pregnant to be able to think clearly.

The only logical idea in her head was that she had to get dressed and go back to her flat to change. Then, on the way to work, she would make a detour into the local chemist for a kit to test herself.

When she had the result she would know that it was time to start making decisions.

Positive.

It felt as if the word must be engraved across her forehead she kept thinking about it so often.

When she'd done the test she'd fixed her eyes on the sweep hand of her watch while she waited for the chemical reaction to take place. Right up to the second she looked up from her watch and focused on the telltale colour change she had hoped that she was wrong, but she wasn't that lucky.

Now she just had to try to keep her mind on her job until the end of her shift. Then she would have to decide what she was going to do and when she was going to do it.

Her mind shied away from the narrow range of

options open to her, and she concentrated on taping a young man's fingers together to support the one he'd injured.

'How did you say you cracked the bone?' she asked, longing to hear anything but the sound of her own thoughts.

'I. . .er. . .I had an argument with a door,' he said sheepishly.

'You argued with a door?' Polly knew from his expression that there was more to the story and she flicked him a grin. 'And the door won?'

'Well, it was locked.'

'Wouldn't a key have helped?' she suggested, surprised to feel a bubble of laughter rising at the mental image. It was a relief to find out that her sense of the ridiculous was still intact, in spite of the problems weighing her down.

'Yeah, except my girlfriend had the key and she was on the other side of the door—just because I stayed late at my mate's and forgot to pick her up from work!'

'And it always looks so easy on the television when the hero smacks the door and it just bursts open, doesn't it? You never see them going round with a broken finger in the next scene.'

'No. And if my girlfriend sees these little bits of tape around my fingers she's not going to believe that I broke it either. Couldn't you put something. . .bigger. . .on it?'

'Ah.' Polly nodded her understanding. 'Trying for the sympathy vote? Will it help if I tell you that you'll need to rest it in a sling for the first day or two?'

'Really?' The young man's eyes brightened. 'And if I get some cotton wool for padding—just so it doesn't get knocked or anything.'

'And if you take her some flowers to apologise for

losing your temper and some chocolates to apologise for forgetting to pick her up?' Polly suggested. 'And while you're playing the wounded soldier don't forget to move your fingers every so often to keep the circulation going. You want the finger to mend while you're getting all that sympathy.'

She was still smiling when he disappeared in the direction of the reception area, but the sound of Nick's voice in a nearby room soon wiped it off her face.

As she hurried towards the next waiting patient she thought wryly that it was all too easy to give advice to others but it was far harder to organise her own life.

Ever since she'd come on duty she'd been avoiding Nick, knowing that she daren't risk talking to him until she'd had time to think. But that didn't mean that she hadn't found herself watching him when he was working nearby, her eyes searching out his mannerisms for her heart to store away.

She knew that he'd been watching her too. She had felt his eyes like a caress as she'd gone about her own work and, in spite of the fact that he was operating on less sleep than usual, there was a noticeable spring to his step and a hint of a smile in his eyes.

Thank goodness he would be going off duty soon. At least she could relax for the second half of her shift without worrying about staying out of his way. Somehow today it seemed that every time she turned around he was there. . .

'Sister Lang?'

As if her thoughts had conjured him up out of thin air, he was right behind her.

'Yes, Doctor?' she replied formally, ever conscious that any number of people could eavesdrop on their conversation. All it would take was a hint of intimacy between them and the hospital grapevine would blow it out of all proportion in no time.

'Any chance of having a word with you when you go for your break?' he asked, and Polly was powerless to stop her pulse responding to his ruffled hair and the sleepy, sexy look in his eyes. But she had to start pulling away—had to learn how to resist the attraction before it destroyed her.

'I'm sorry, but I've already had my break,' she lied, squashing the impulse to cross her fingers while her heart continued to beat a rapid tattoo. 'Was it anything important?'

He was silent for a moment, a frown pleating his forehead as his silvery eyes searched her face. He had obviously recognised the new coolness in her tone and he was already trying to analyse the reason.

'It can wait till later,' he conceded. 'I'm off home now to catch up on some sleep.'

Polly must have said something before she turned away but all she could think was that she would have loved to share a secret smile with him when he'd mentioned needing sleep; would have loved to see the gleam in his eyes which meant that he, too, was remembering the reason *why* he'd missed so much sleep last night.

As it was, all she could allow herself to feel as she heard his footsteps receding along the corridor was relief that he was leaving her in peace for a while.

Peace? With the decisions she would have to make in the next few days and weeks? She didn't know whether to laugh or cry, and felt horribly close to both.

*   *   *

Polly stepped out into the chilly night and shivered as she drew in a lungful of fresh air while she wrapped her thick padded jacket around her.

'Polly?'

The deep voice reached her before she saw him, waiting by his car.

'Get in. The car's warm.'

Her heart sank.

She wasn't ready to speak to him yet. She hadn't had time to make any of the decisions that needed to be made. She'd barely come to terms with the fact that the test had been positive, and with the majority of the accident and emergency staff in an uproar of anticipation over the imminent Autumn Ball it felt as though her thoughts had been through a mincer.

'Come on. You're getting cold.'

Her feet started to take her towards him while her heart wished that she didn't have to see him again; didn't have to have the conversation which was going to rob her of his friendship, and so much more, and leave her nursing a broken heart.

'I've cooked us a meal,' he announced as she fastened her seat belt and she had to blink back tears.

Don't be so nice to me, the little voice pleaded inside her head. It will make it so much harder to lose you.

The journey was over too soon, and in no time he was ushering her inside the familiar hallway and taking her jacket.

'Right,' he began purposefully as he showed her into the sitting-room, his voice so calm that it raised all the hairs on the back of her neck. 'The casserole is in the oven and won't hurt if it isn't eaten straight away so it's your choice—do you want to eat first or do you want to tell me what the hell's going on?'

Polly took a reflexive step backwards when she finally caught sight of the anger in his face. She hadn't seen his eyes looking that cold and wintry for a long time, and hated the fact that she had put the expression there again.

'I...' She gestured helplessly, not knowing what to say. She would rather put this discussion off for ever, but if she suggested eating first she knew she wouldn't be able to swallow a mouthful.

'For God's sake, what's the matter with you?' he stormed. 'Yesterday you were understandably upset but I thought, after last night, that at least you knew you could talk to me. Am I wrong?'

It was the hurt she saw in his eyes that put the first crack in the wall she was hiding behind.

'No, Nick. It's not you, it's me. I... I've made a mess of everything and I don't know how...' She shook her head.

'Do you regret it...going to bed with me?' he demanded in a raw voice. 'Is that why you've been avoiding me all day?'

'No! Oh, Nick, how could I regret it? It was the most...most wonderful...' Her throat closed completely.

'Then why?' he exploded. 'What's gone wrong between last night and this morning? What did I do? What did I say? Please, Polly, tell me. Don't you know how much I lo—'

'I'm pregnant,' she blurted out baldly, then covered her mouth with both hands as if she wished the words had never escaped.

There was a profound silence in the room and she couldn't bear it.

'It happened that first time,' she explained, driven to

fill the void with sound. 'The time I stayed with you and fell asleep. And then we woke up and I forgot that I wasn't protected, but I didn't even think about it until this morning in the shower when my breasts were tender and then I realised that I'd missed my period and...and...'

She ran out of words and drew in a shuddering breath, waiting for him to speak but too afraid to look at him.

'Did you hear what I said?' he murmured softly, and she heard the soft tread of his feet as he came towards her.

What *had* he said? She'd been so busy trying to find the words to explain...

The touch of his hand on her cheek was the shock which drew her eyes up to meet his, and this time they gleamed gently at her like polished silver.

'I said I love you, Polly Lang, and if John Preece hadn't had the appallingly bad timing to go sick in the middle of his shift I had every intention of asking you to marry me this morning.'

Now Polly knew what it was like to travel from hell to heaven and back again in the space of a few minutes, and the tears slipped silently down her cheeks as she shook her head convulsively.

'I can't,' she cried, feeling as if her heart were being torn out by the roots. 'Didn't you hear what *I* said? I'm pregnant.'

'So we'll have a "slightly premature" baby,' Nick said airily, a smile beginning to curl the corners of his mouth. 'We won't be the first—or the last.'

'But I *can't* have the baby,' she sobbed. 'I couldn't bear it. What would happen if it died too?'

'Oh, sweetheart, don't,' he murmured as he wrapped both arms around her and cradled her head on his shoulder with one comforting palm. 'It doesn't have to be like that. The chances are that this baby will only have to worry about being murdered when it becomes a teenager and drives us insane. Anyway, if you were worried we could always get a monitor...'

'*If?*' she howled, and tried to fight her way out of his embrace. '*If* I'm worried? You don't know how many nights I've cried for Andrew, how many days I've sat and wondered what he would have been doing by now if he'd lived.'

'Yes, I have,' he reminded her quietly, and the very softness of his voice acted as a rebuke. 'I've gone through exactly the same thing, wondering about my own child—whether it was a girl or a boy, whether it took after me or Deanne. *You* actually got to welcome Andrew into the world and to hold him. You had time with him to build some memories...'

'But...' The tears were falling faster as Polly heard the sadness in his voice and saw it in his eyes. Surely he could understand that she daren't risk it again.

'Don't you see, Polly?' He held her shoulders and caught her gaze with his. 'There aren't any guarantees in this life. Some of us lose a wife and child, some of us lose a child and some of us get to keep it all—and there's no way of knowing which it's going to be.'

'But I don't think I could face it again,' she wailed, wishing there was an easy answer.

'*You* won't have to. *We* will—together.'

'But...'

'*I'm not Tim.*' This time there was steel in his voice to match the glitter in his eyes, and Polly realised that below his calm exterior was a seething cauldron of emotions.

She went to speak again but he covered her lips with

his fingers and wrapped his other arm tightly around her so that she was held closely against him, breast to chest and thigh to thigh, as he gazed intently into her eyes.

'I know we've never discussed it, and I know we're both carrying too many bad memories around with us, but you have to believe that I would never blame you if this baby suffered the same fate as Andrew. Surely you *know* that I would always stand by you?'

'Yes, of course,' she answered without hesitation. 'But, Nick...'

'Hush,' he soothed as he cradled her cheeks in his palms and stroked his thumbs tenderly over her cheekbones. 'First things first. Do you love me?' he demanded huskily, and in spite of all her fears there was only one answer.

'Yes. Oh, yes, Nick, I love you so much,' she replied, and his fingertips moved against her lips like a caress.

'And will you marry me and let me share all your worries and happiness?'

Suddenly she realised that it *was* that simple.

'Oh, Nick... You're right,' she whispered happily as she gazed up at him. 'It *is* a case of first things first, and the most important thing is that we love each other. Everything else comes second and we'll take it as it comes...together.'

'Was that a yes?' he demanded huskily, his mouth hovering close to hers as he slid his fingers through the silky strands of her tousled dark hair to cradle her head possessively in his palms.

'Oh, yes, Nick, I'll marry you. I love you too much to do anything else.'

*   *   *

'Nick?' Polly murmured as she caught him signalling to Leo across the room. 'What are you doing?'

The Autumn Ball was in full swing and while he would rather have stayed at home with Polly she had pointed out that, as one of the consultants, he was duty bound to make an appearance.

The week since Nick had proposed had passed in a flash, and there had been so much to do that she'd all but forgotten about the hospital fund-raiser until Hannah had reminded her this morning.

'Leo's in fine form,' Nick commented without answering Polly's question. 'I never realised that he was hiding a talent as an auctioneer.'

'He's certainly managing to raise a lot of money for the scanner,' she agreed as she looked around at the shimmering array of evening dresses, complemented beautifully by the stark black and white worn by the majority of the men.

Her own dress was in rich burgundy velvet, which showed her pale skin and dark hair off to perfection, and she was certain that no one in the room wore their formal evening dress as well as Nick did.

The auction was turning out to be a rousing success, the mixture of serious, big-money offerings cleverly balanced by the more light-hearted contributions, with much teasing and laughter to leaven the proceedings.

'The trouble is that the bidding goes so fast on some items that I don't have time to see who's after what. Where has he got to now?'

She ran one carefully painted nail down the list of prizes on offer and had just reached the line detailing the holiday cottage in Brittany when she heard Leo's voice rise to signal another successful conclusion.

'Sold. To Dr Prince,' he announced gleefully. 'And,

although it's not a castle, I hope you have a wonderful honey- , er, holiday!'

Polly gasped. 'Nick! Did you really bid for the week in Brittany?'

'And got it, my love!' he gloated, then bent closer to murmur in her ear, 'Leo only just stopped himself spilling the beans just then, but how *do* you fancy going there for our honeymoon?'

'Oh, could we?' Polly knew that her eyes were shining with pleasure as she gazed up at Nick.

To avoid any hullabaloo, they'd tried to keep the fact of their impending marriage very quiet, but suddenly she didn't care *who* saw that she was in love. The hospital grapevine would find out soon enough that they were getting married.

'We can leave right after the ceremony tomorrow,' he said, his eyes full of fervent promises.

Polly thought about the simple ivory-coloured suit hanging ready in the wardrobe next to his deep charcoal one, and smiled.

Neither of them had wanted any ostentation—it would be enough for them to satisfy the legal requirements by exchanging their vows in front of Leo and Hannah. As far as the two of them were concerned, they had already made their committment to each other.

'But what about work?' Her sense of responsibility reared its head at the last minute.

'It's all arranged,' he soothed. 'That new nurse, Hannah's friend, started today.'

'Laura,' Polly supplied.

'That's the one. And I've been in contact with the man who was supposed to join us in a couple of weeks. He's one of Leo's contemporaries—another one I had a hand in training at my last hospital—and I asked him if he could start this week so we could get away.'

Just then Leo began his wind-up for the next item on the agenda, and there was a sudden buzz of interest.

'Now we come to one of tonight's star prizes so will all you lovely ladies take out your tickets and keep an eye on the number because *this* is what you could be winning!'

The lights in the room dimmed and a spotlight lit up the stage area as a man stepped into view. He, too, was dressed in an impeccable evening suit, but his hair was just a little too long and the narrow black domino mask which hid part of his face lent him an air of danger.

Even so, he was the epitome of tall, dark and handsome as he stood there with his shoulders proudly squared and his fists braced on his hips.

'Can we go home now?' Polly prompted as she turned away from the man being greeted by the female contingent with a chorus of wolf whistles.

'Don't you want to wait for the draw?' Nick teased. 'You might be lucky enough to win.'

'I'm not interested,' Polly declared confidently. 'You've helped me to get my priorities in order and I'm a firm believer in first things first.' She looked up at him, knowing that her love was shining in her eyes. 'I've got the man I love and that's enough for me.'

Second Chance is the next story in this wonderfully exciting trilogy.

Turn the page for Laura's story, in which she encounters the charming, irresistible Wolff Bergen — has Laura found her very own Mr Right…?

SECOND CHANCE
by
Josie Metcalfe

CHAPTER ONE

'No way!' The deep husky voice was outraged. 'I won't do it, Leo. . .not even for you!'

'But, Wolff. . .' Leo began in his most persuasive tone.

'No!' his old friend reiterated firmly. 'This is the sort of stunt we might have pulled when we were students, but now. . .!'

'Please, Wolff. I'm desperate.' Leo ran the fingers of both hands through his hair as he paced agitatedly backwards and forwards, leaving the thick blond strands standing up in tufts all over his head while he navigated through the scattered piles of Wolff's belongings. 'The bloke I hired to do it had his appendix out this morning and I only got the message an hour ago.'

'So?' He fixed Leo with an impassive stare, knowing that his ice-blue eyes could intimidate most people with their laser-like intensity.

'So the Autumn Ball starts in less than three hours and I've lost my star prize!'

'There are plenty of other prizes,' Wolff rebutted calmly as he finally allowed himself to relax against the high-backed leather comfort of Leo's favourite fireside chair, stretching his long legs out and frowning absently at the rumpled state of the elderly jeans he'd managed to unearth from the muddle.

He folded his arms across the lean plane of his stomach, the rolled-up sleeves of his shirt very white against the deep tan of his skin as he subsided into quiescence.

Wolff's very stillness was in striking contrast to the anxious activity of his long-time friend as he returned to his objections. 'You've just spent most of the afternoon telling me that you've had some fabulous prizes donated, and the way you're going to be presenting even the lesser ones sounds as if there'll be plenty of prizes to go round.'

'Not like *this* one!' Leo protested urgently. '*This* prize is the one that's sold the tickets. . .'

'Oh, come on. . .!' Wolff shook his head chidingly and when he felt the drag of his over-long dark hair against the butter-soft upholstery he remembered with a twist of distaste that, apart from a shower and change of clothes, he still hadn't had time to do anything about his unkempt appearance.

The unexpected change in plans meant that this was just one more thing to think about before he was due to start work tomorrow. He really needed the rest of today to get himself organised. It was good of Leo to put him up until he could find his own place, but. . .

'No, really! I'm serious!' Leo pushed a pile of journals aside and perched himself on the edge of his sturdy coffee-table, then leant forward to press his case.

'I'll admit that there was the usual loyal interest in the Autumn Ball from the senior members of staff, but even with the added attraction of the auction they can't come up with the sort of money we need to finance the scanner appeal without help. To make a success of it, we needed to get the *whole* of the hospital interested.'

Wolff nodded his understanding. He'd just spent endless months trying to work out how to make pennies stretch as far as pounds, and had then watched the tragic results when it didn't—*couldn't*—work.

Openly encouraged by his friend's apparent attention, Leo continued.

'It was Polly's idea to make the whole proceedings more light-hearted—she suggested having the ticket draw—and as soon as the word got out we could hardly sell tickets fast enough! Against all expectations, we've actually got a chance of making our target by the end of the night. We should have the scanner months ahead of schedule!'

'That's fantastic,' Wolff said sincerely. 'But what I don't understand is why you ever thought of *that*!' He gestured with one lean hand towards the costume, hanging behind the door. 'Where's the *rest* of it, for heaven's sake?'

Leo's golden eyes gleamed wickedly. 'The costume was delivered just before I got the message about the appendectomy, and I can only presume that the dancer supplies the rest of it—his body!'

'But. . .' Wolf began faintly when he realised exactly how few garments the hanger contained. Even if he'd been tempted to take the job on for bravado, the thought of exposing *that* much of himself to public gaze was enough to paralyse him with stage fright. It was a good job he had no intention of. . .

'Oh, come on, Wolff! You're the only one I know who could pull it off. I'd do it myself if I wasn't going to be fully occupied as auctioneer. Anyway, you've always been a far better dancer than I am, and the rest of your equipment isn't bad. . .!'

Wolff felt a wash of heat travel along his cheek-bones at the assessing glance his friend threw his outstretched body, and thanked his lucky stars that the deep tan he'd developed—in spite of his avoidance of the fierce sun—would hide the fact from his irreverent friend. He'd never hear the last of it if Leo realised how easily embarrassed he still was...

'Leo, I *can't*,' he began, marshalling his thoughts to kill the idea off once and for all. 'I'm absolutely shattered after all that travelling—I was supposed to have nearly ten days to get myself together before I started here, remember?'

'Your part will only take half an hour, and then you can come back here and crash out,' Leo wheedled. 'And the short notice is hardly *my* fault, anyway. How was I to know that Nick would take it into his head to ask you to start early so that he and Polly could get married straight away?'

'Huh!' Wolff scoffed. 'By your own admission, you've been scheming to push the two of them together for weeks.'

'Yes, but...'

'Anyway,' Wolff continued, determined to finish his objections with the final clincher, 'I'm supposed to be covering the department for Nick while he's away. What sort of authority will I be able to wield if the whole hospital knows I've taken part in this sort of stunt? You haven't even got any control over who I'd have to dance with—it could be anyone from one of the most junior nurses to the wife of one of the senior consultants!'

Leo was silent for a moment, then a crafty expression crept over his face.

'Not necessarily,' he murmured, half under his breath, as he gazed almost absent-mindedly across the room. 'In fact, that's the beauty of this outfit, old friend,' Leo crowed triumphantly as he leapt to his feet again and clambered exuberantly across his cluttered living room to reach for the despised costume.

'Look!' He held up a black satin domino mask. 'Your hair's still all long and shaggy and you'll have this on your face. By the time you come on duty tomorrow you'll have had a shave and a haircut, and no one will ever know that it was you!'

'*I'll* know,' Wolff muttered darkly, but he had a nasty feeling that he might just as well give in now as prolong the agony. He'd known Leo since they'd met during their training rotation under Nick Prince, and knew that he was as tenacious as a terrier when he got his teeth into an idea.

'But you'll do it,' Leo said hopefully, obviously scenting victory.

'Under duress,' he conceded, a sinking sensation taking up residence in his gut as he became more and more certain that he was making a monumental mistake.

'But I'll tell you now that I'm going to be wearing more than half a handkerchief to cover my essentials and, while I'm up there making a complete ass of myself, I'm going to be concentrating on the fact that you'll owe me—big time! Now, tell me what I've got to do before I come to my senses...'

'Oh-h, let me sit down,' Laura groaned as she flopped onto the seat beside Hannah. 'My feet are killing me!'

'And we're hardly halfway through the shift,' her friend pointed out.

'Don't remind me.' Laura scowled as she leaned her head back against the upholstery. 'The whole morning has been filled with a succession of my least favourite cases— they seem to be the same whichever hospital you work at.'

'You mean the patients who should have made an appointment to see their doctors, but decided to come here instead because they thought they'd be seen faster?'

'And then they create hell because triage means that the more urgent cases are taken through ahead of them and they're going to be late for work?'

'Exactly! How many have you had today?'

'So far, only one—a businessman who was certain he had an ulcer, and wanted some medicine to take straight away so that he could enjoy his usual boozy power-lunch at twelve o'clock.'

'Was that the one who thought he was more important than the little boy who'd cut his leg open on broken glass?'

Laura nodded. 'That's the one—a real sweetheart he was.'

'I bet he was delighted when Leo told him to go back to his doctor if he wanted to be referred to a specialist,' Hannah commented with an almost gleeful expression, knowing that the hospital was committed to educating the patients as to the *real* purpose of an accident and emergency department.

'Especially when he suggested that the man could do with losing at least fifty pounds in weight and drinking milk instead of martinis!'

They both laughed wryly.

'Well, as far as I can see, the patients are turning up in droves today on purpose,' Hannah said, returning to her original complaint. 'They must know we're going to the Ball tonight and want us to be too tired to enjoy ourselves.'

'We?' Laura demanded, picking out the one word which jarred on her sensitive antennae. 'Which "we" are you talking about?'

'You and me, of course,' Hannah elaborated as she finally gave in and copied Laura, sliding her feet out of her shoes and wriggling her toes blissfully.

'Me? I'm not going,' Laura said in surprise. 'I've got the rest of my unpacking to do. And, anyway, I haven't got a ticket.'

'Oh, yes, you have,' Hannah contradicted smugly. 'As soon as I knew you were coming to St Augustine's I bought you one. You can pay me back later!'

'Hannah!' Laura sighed. 'I won't be able to afford to pay you back until my wages come in and I can't afford the time to go.'

'Oh, phooey!' Hannah said rudely and screwed up her nose. 'It'll be a whole year until the next shindig, apart from a few boozy parties at Christmas. Can't you look on it as a way of celebrating the fact that we're working together again?'

Laura pulled an answering face. She'd never been much of a one for parties and formal Balls, and the last couple of years had been worse than ever. There honestly didn't seem to be much point in going through all the rituals of dating when there was no chance of anything coming of it.

'Please?' Hannah coaxed. 'You can keep me company.'

'What do you mean, keep you company? You hardly need me to hold your hand—you'll be swept off your feet all evening. Who's your escort for the evening? Leo Stirling?'

'Leo? Hardly!' Hannah hooted. 'If the word hadn't been hijacked by a certain section of the community, he'd be a prime example of your typical bachelor gay. A different woman every night, and every one a stunner.'

'Well, you're no wallflower! Is the man blind?'

'Far from it!' Hannah laughed. 'Thank you for the vote of confidence, but I've got my feet firmly planted on the ground. I've got far too much sense to think of taking him on—I'd only get trampled in the crush! Anyway, he's decided to go stag as he'll be fully occupied with running the auction part of the evening.'

'Even so,' Laura continued, 'I haven't been here long enough to find a suitable escort of my own. Perhaps, by next year...'

'If that's your excuse you've just lost the argument,' Hannah said smugly. 'At St Augustine's it's always been perfectly acceptable for groups of people to go to the Autumn Ball without being paired off in the traditional way. Some sensible person, years ago, decided it was more important for people to enjoy themselves while they help to raise money for good causes than to limit the numbers by imposing restrictions.'

Laura sighed, cursing silently as she realised that Hannah was slowly but surely demolishing every objection she voiced.

What made the whole situation worse was that the Laura whom Hannah had known would have given in with a smile. She didn't really have the heart to tell Hannah bluntly that things had changed since those days—that nowadays she just couldn't see the point of going to such gatherings.

While Laura tried to marshall her thoughts she glanced down at the watch pinned to the front of her mid-blue uniform and realised with a sense of relief that her break was all but over.

'Well, it's time to go back to the bedlam,' she said as she slipped her shoes back on and slid forward on the seat.

'Wait.' Hannah grabbed her by the elbow to stop her from standing up. 'Please, Laura,' she said earnestly, 'I would like you to come to the Ball with me. I think you'd enjoy it.'

Laura felt the frown pleating her forehead as she found herself fighting her natural inclinations in favour of giving in to Hannah's pleading. They'd been friends for so long and it was wonderful that they were back working together again. . .

'At least promise me that you'll think about it,' Hannah begged. 'It's just—you don't seem to be the same as you were when we last worked together. It's as if. . .as if it's an effort for you to laugh. . .as if you *need* to be taken out of yourself.'

'Neither of us are the same people we were when we first met,' Laura agreed, unsurprised by how observant her friend was but inwardly saddened by how accurate her words were.

As far as the rest of the world was concerned, she seemed to have learned how to cover up her feelings but Hannah had known her long enough to learn how to see below the surface, and evidently she hadn't lost the knack.

'You always were too sharp for your own good,' she grumbled good-naturedly. 'But you're right about the laughing. Sometimes it *is* hard to find things funny any more.'

'Well, you know you can always talk to me if you want to,' Hannah offered, all teasing put aside. 'I might have changed in some ways, but my ears still work just as well. Anyway, that's all the more reason to join me tonight,' she declared, her voice taking on an encouraging tone. 'Apart from anything else, it'll give you a chance to meet some of the other people you'll be working with in a more social atmosphere.'

'Enough! Enough!' Laura laughed as she finally made her escape. 'All I'm promising for now is that I'll think about it. . .OK?'

'OK,' Hannah conceded. 'But don't imagine that I won't be increasing the pressure the closer we get to the end of our shift. . .!'

It hadn't been an idle threat, either, Laura thought as she turned the hairdryer onto her freshly washed hair. All afternoon Hannah had been enlisting her friends to add their voices to the chorus of invitations.

Leo had been the funniest.

'Laura,' he'd said with an unaccustomed seriousness to his expression, 'I realise that you're a friend of Hannah's, and I freely admit that the thought of what she would do to me if I misbehaved is enough to strike terror into my manly heart, but. . .' he drew in an ostentatious breath '. . .if you come to the Ball, I hereby promise faithfully *not* to dance with you!'

She chuckled at the memory of the waggling eyebrows which had accompanied the declaration, then pulled a face at herself in the mirror.

Once again she was forced into the realisation that, in spite of her efforts at sophistication and her careful application of cosmetics, with her diminutive height and colouring and the short feathery style of her haircut she still looked rather like a slightly flustered elf.

She tugged at the top of her dress, but the boned bodice fitted her slender waist too well to allow her to pull it up any higher over the soft swell of her breasts. The forest-green shantung almost exactly matched her eyes, but the dark colour had the unfortunate effect of making her skin look almost as pale as milk—especially as there was so much of it on show. If only she had some of Hannah's natural colour.

'Are you ready yet?' Hannah's voice demanded from the other side of the door, and Laura reached for her small evening bag with a sigh.

'As ready as I'll ever be,' she admitted when she opened the door.

'Wow! I love the dress,' Hannah said, gesturing with one hand for Laura to turn around for her. 'Is it new?'

'Several years old, but this is the first time I've worn it. Yours is very sophisticated. The halter neck is so flattering and I love that shade of blue on you.' She deliberately turned Hannah's attention away, shutting her mind to the memory of the excitement she'd felt when she'd bought her own dress—the anticipation of the momentous occasion which had never happened...

Afraid that her thoughts would show on her face, she turned and reached for the lacy black shawl she'd put ready on the back of the chair.

'Well, our coach is ready and waiting,' Hannah began, then giggled when she realised what she'd said. 'Sounds like something out of a fairy story, doesn't it? Unfortunately this one's powered by diesel, not six white horses, and there's no guarantee that Prince Charming is going to appear tonight!'

'Actually, Hannah, I've decided to go in my car.'

'Laura!' her friend wailed. 'That means you're already planning on ducking out part way through the evening!'

'I'll have to, or I'll probably fall flat on my face,' Laura pointed out. 'I've still got half my unpacking to do and I've hardly had time to catch my breath at work before you've browbeaten me into going out for the evening.'

'Oh, well,' Hannah said with a resigned shrug as she stepped back out into the corridor and waited for her to lock the door. 'At least you're going to the Ball with me so I suppose I should be grateful.'

'Grateful enough to share the car with me to show me where this extravaganza is taking place?' Laura suggested.

'OK. We can let the rest know not to wait for us on our way out.' Hannah's good humour seemed to have reasserted itself as they made their way down the stairs of the nurses' accommodation, and she kept up a stream of cheerful chatter right through the journey.

Laura was glad she didn't have to do much more than supply the odd word. Between her concentration on navigating her way through the still-unfamiliar streets and her nerves at the prospect of walking into a room full of strangers, she couldn't spare any brain cells for following a conversation.

'It's a shame you had to park quite so far away from the entrance, but at least we found you a space under a light,' Hannah commented as they made their way into the spacious foyer of the country-house-styled hotel on the outskirts of town.

In seconds they were surrounded by the bright lights and cheerful hubbub of the gathering throng.

'Hannah?' Laura called, attracting her friend's attention as she made her way back from the cloakroom over two hours later. The meal was over, and she had no real interest in the auction part of the evening.

'Hi, Laura,' Hannah panted, still winded from her latest foray onto the dance floor. 'You can't be cold.' She gestured towards the shawl Laura had draped over one arm.

'No. It's warmed up a lot since everyone started dancing. Actually, I was thinking about leaving in a minute. I've already stayed much longer than I...'

'Laura...!' Hannah wailed. 'I thought you were enjoying yourself?'

'I was,' Laura hastened to reassure her. 'I have enjoyed myself—far more than I expected to—but...'

'You can't leave yet,' Hannah begged, her manner almost agitated.

As Laura watched Hannah glanced uneasily towards the easily recognisable gleam of Leo's head as he approached the rostrum. Although she had no idea why, Laura had the feeling that her friend was worried about something.

'The auction is about to start and there's still the draw to come. Can't you at least wait until then?' Hannah coaxed.

'Hannah...'

'Please? Pretty please?' Hannah said with her hands together as if she was pleading. 'In fact, if you stay until after the draw I'll be quite happy to travel back with you.'

'Don't be silly. You don't have to cut your own evening short just because I want to leave early.' Laura began to feel guilty. Was she really such a wet blanket?

'But you will stay until after the draw?'

Laura gave in gracefully, just as the loudspeaker burst to life.

'And now...' Leo began, and within seconds he had the room rocking with laughter as he teased and cajoled them out of their money as item after item came up for auction.

'He's so good at this,' Laura said as she wiped tears of mirth from her cheeks after Tina Wadland had successfully bid for the coveted free massage with the masseur of her choice.

'At least Leo now knows what he can do to earn a living if he decides he doesn't like being a doctor,' Hannah quipped, her own eyes bright with laughter.

Laura was fascinated by the byplay as Nicholas Prince began bidding hotly for the pledge of a week's holiday in a cottage in Brittany, and when Leo finally knocked it down to the A and E consultant she was even more fascinated to see the reaction of Sister Polly Lang, standing at his side.

'Hannah?' she said, careful to pitch her voice just for her friend's ears. 'Is there something going on between Dr Prince and Polly Lang?'

'Not much,' Hannah said cryptically, and glanced around cagily before she leant closer. 'Just that they're getting married tomorrow. The cottage is probably where he's taking her for their honeymoon.'

'Really?' Laura exclaimed and turned to look over her shoulder again at the couple, standing near the back of the room. She'd hardly had time to get to know them as new colleagues, but a warm feeling of pleasure filled her when she saw the way they were looking at each other—pleasure mixed with just a little touch of envy, perhaps.

'No one said anything about it today,' she commented with a frown. 'You'd think I'd have heard something on the grapevine...'

'Shh!' Hannah nudged her in warning. 'I'll tell you more later—it's all a bit secret.' Her eyes were bright with suppressed glee. 'Aren't you glad you stayed now?'

'All right. All right. I've thoroughly enjoyed myself so

I give you permission to say it,' Laura said with a smile, resignation in her voice.

'What? You don't mean, "I told you so", do you? As if I would!'

They were both laughing when a drumroll silenced the hubbub of conversation which had followed the last of the auctioned pledges.

'Oh, good. It's time for the draw.' Laura watched as Hannah anticipated the next announcement and rummaged in her evening bag to withdraw the tickets, comparing the serial numbers on both of them before handing one to her.

'Here. This one's yours,' she announced, with another strange glance towards Leo.

Laura just had time to register that her friend seemed almost furtive when Leo began his patter.

'Now we come to the last of tonight's star prizes so will all you lovely ladies take out your tickets and keep an eye on the numbers because *this* is what you could be winning!'

As Laura craned to see between the heads and shoulders of the people who had suddenly clustered in front of her, she cursed the fact that, even in her highest heels, she still felt as if she must be one of the shortest people in the room.

The women around her had erupted into a chorus of shouts and wolf-whistles of approval, but she still couldn't see what they were looking at.

'Hey! Hannah!' She tugged her friend's elbow, having to shout to be heard over all the noise. 'What's going on?'

Hannah glanced back at her and suddenly seemed to realise her problem, stepping to one side to allow Laura her first clear view of the front of the room.

The lights had been dimmed, a single spotlight now

illuminating the stage area where a solitary man stood in silence.

At first glance he seemed to be dressed in an impeccable evening suit like the rest of the men in the room but, unlike them, his hair was just a little too long, the dark silky tendrils almost brushing his broad shoulders.

The final touch was a jet-black domino mask which partially obscured his face and lent him an almost sinister air of danger.

As Laura gazed at him, almost mesmerised by his strange stillness in the face of the bedlam in the room, her heartbeat gave the first skip of awareness in several long years. She tried to drag her eyes away but she couldn't stop them running over him as he stood there with the arrogance of a superb wild animal.

In the stark black of his traditional evening suit he was the epitome of tall, dark and handsome as he stood there with his fists braced on his lean hips with an almost insolent swagger.

'Ladies! Ladies!' Leo called, and Laura saw the white gleam of his teeth as he smiled. 'You'll make the rest of us men jealous if you continue like that!'

The chorus turned to cat-calls until he held up a dark fabric bag and, with all the aplomb of a fairground showman, delved one hand inside and pulled out a square of white paper with a flourish.

'And the winner is. . .number two hundred and nineteen,' he declared.

The announcement was greeted with a chorus of moans and groans as each of the women eagerly checked their tickets. When there was no triumphant cry everyone started looking around at their neighbour.

'Don't be shy, now,' Leo said in a coaxing tone. 'He'll only bite if you ask him to.'

'Well, he won't be nibbling on me—my number is miles out,' Hannah declared as she turned towards Laura, her eyes almost feverishly bright. 'What number were you?'

Laura had been too busy watching the events around her to bother checking her own ticket. She'd never won at any game of chance and had given up trying long ago, but just out of interest she turned her ticket over and tilted it towards the brightly lit stage to decipher the numbers stamped in the corner.

'It's you!' Hannah squealed when she saw the number over her shoulder. 'It's your ticket!'

Her voice was loud enough to travel right through the murmuring throng and before Laura could follow her inclination to thrust the offending evidence into her friend's hand a path had magically opened up in front of her and hands were reaching out to touch her, guiding her reluctant feet towards the front of the room.

'Hello!' Leo greeted her, his voice as hearty as ever, although he seemed slightly puzzled by her presence, his eyes glancing over the top of her head and into the crowd behind her.

'Who is this lucky lady?' he demanded jovially as he reached for the ticket she was still clutching tightly in her hand, and she emerged from her horrified trance just long enough to hand it to him.

'Lucky?' she echoed faintly, hating the feeling that she was the focus of so many eyes, then realised that she hadn't given him an answer. 'I. . .I'm Laura,' she stammered.

'Well, Lucky Laura, are you ready to claim your prize?' Leo stepped aside and Laura's senses were assailed by her first close-up view of the man standing in the spotlight.

For just a few seconds she had actually thought of asking Leo to draw again, but the words 'No, thank you,' remained for ever frozen in her throat as she met the stranger's eyes for the first time.

They were a pale icy blue and were fixed unerringly on her own, sending a shiver of atavistic awareness up the back of her neck.

Somewhere music started playing and she saw him blink, as though the sound had taken him by surprise, before he straightened up, his chin going up a notch as he held out one lean hand towards her.

For several long seconds she found herself looking from his hand to his eyes and back again while the music played on.

She hadn't bothered to find out any of the details of this part of the evening—hadn't expected to stay long enough to find out.

What was supposed to happen now?

What did he want her to do?

Leo's helping hand under her elbow drew her into the bright circle of light before he disappeared into the surrounding darkness.

From the moment she'd met the masked man's eyes for the first time he hadn't allowed her to look away, the intensity of his icy blue gaze holding her prisoner so that she felt as if they were somehow connected within the encircling prison of the spotlight.

The music changed and slowly he started to move with the new rhythm. Not dancing, exactly. More a matter of shifting his weight, swaying and twisting his torso as if he was testing his muscles. One shoulder rotated forward and shrugged, followed by the other and then the stark black of his jacket was sliding backwards and down.

She'd assumed that he was dressed in the same impeccable way as the other men but as soon as the jacket fell away from the width of his shoulders she realised that, apart from the black bow at his throat, the only clothing remaining on the upper half of his body was a waistcoat shot through with gleaming metallic threads.

The roar of approval which greeted this manoeuvre broke the spell he'd woven around her.

Suddenly Laura remembered that they *weren't* alone and she felt the heat of embarrassment surge up into her face.

'Laura. . .?'

She saw his mouth form the word as he held out his hand towards her again. This time he took the single step which brought her within reach, and she found herself placing her hand in his.

He tightened his fingers around hers and pulled gently, and she gave in to the pressure as he drew her into his arms.

'Relax,' he whispered, his mouth close to her ear as he captured her other hand and lifted both of them up to his shoulders.

'How?' she whispered back as her hands clenched nervously on the glimmering fabric. She thought she heard him suppress a snort of laughter but, with the sound of the music and the cat-calls and wolf-whistles of the audience surrounding them, she couldn't be sure.

'Link your hands behind my neck and follow my lead,' he whispered and, grateful for the suggestion, she did, sliding her fingers tentatively under the silky strands of his long dark hair to clasp them together.

As soon as he released her hands he stroked the backs

of his fingers down her arms, his hands cupping her shoulders as he drew her against his body so that she couldn't help following the same hypnotic rhythm.

She'd once seen a couple dancing the lambada and she remembered thinking that it was one of the most blatantly sexual dances she'd ever watched—but this was something else...

As he'd drawn her against his body he'd widened his stance so that they were now moving together with one of his thighs pressed firmly into the cradle of her body and one of hers trapped firmly between his.

She felt almost surrounded by him—his size, his strength, his heat—and she looked up into his face, helpless to resist his powerful physical magnetism.

Even though he was wearing the mysterious mask she could see enough of his face to know that he was a handsome man, his eyes very pale for such tanned skin and his eyelashes sinfully long and dark.

'You're good,' he murmured in her ear, and his arms tightened around her until there wasn't a breath of space between their bodies.

Laura was stunned to realise how easily she'd been following his lead, moving to the insistent beat of the music as if they'd rehearsed it all before, even though it had been several years since she'd danced at all—and she'd *never* danced like this before.

Without realising that she'd done it, her head had come to rest in the curve of his shoulder, and a deep shudder of awareness had her tightening her own hold on him when he nuzzled the soft flesh of her exposed throat.

'Hold tight,' he warned as the music finally drew to a close, and she just had time to draw in a sharp gasp of breath as one of his hands slid down intimately to the curve of her bottom and the other angled across her back to clasp her shoulder.

Before she realised what he was going to do he'd tilted her backwards over his arm into a classic pose, and his mouth had swooped down to cover hers in a brief but utterly electric kiss.

CHAPTER TWO

'WAIT!'

In spite of the command, Laura's pace hardly faltered as she hurried across the car park towards her car, shivering as the chill of the November night struck her over-heated flesh.

She'd never heard his voice properly—just whispers and murmurs in her ear, almost drowned out by the surrounding din. Even so, she knew the identity of the husky voice, calling out to her through the darkness, and she didn't want to have anything further to do with him...didn't dare.

As she slid the key into the lock she blessed the fact that she'd had them ready in her hand. After what had just happened between them on the stage she'd been half expecting this to happen, especially as she'd had to tear herself out of his arms, but she'd thought that at least she'd have a little more time than this to make her escape.

Her stomach clenched when she thought of her undignified flight across the crowded room. Her face still felt as if it must be lit up like a neon sign, but she forced herself to block the thought out of her mind.

If she didn't concentrate on getting her crabby old Mini started he would catch up with her before she could get away.

Once she got back to her room there would be plenty of time to replay the shocking events of the evening...when she wasn't worried about coming face to face with *him* again.

'Thank you, thank you,' she said fervently, sighing with relief when the engine coughed into action. Even so, she couldn't help casting one last look over her shoulder before she turned out onto the road—just as the tall figure reached the empty space where her car had stood.

This time it was a streetlight which illuminated the taut muscles in his naked shoulders and arms, highlighting the ghostly halo that the cold night air made of his rapid breathing and drawing metallic gleams from the exotic fabric of his waistcoat as he threw his jacket down in disgust.

That must be why he'd been able to reach the car park so quickly—he'd done little more than grab his discarded jacket from the stage before he'd followed her. He was even still wearing that stupid mask, for heaven's sake.

The silence inside the tiny car was broken by the semi-hysterical giggle which escaped from her as she accelerated away. Who did he think he was? The Lone Ranger?

Laura groaned when her alarm went off the next morning. She felt as if she hadn't slept at all, what with the endless mental replays of the events of last night and her guilty denial of her reaction to it...to *him*.

What a way to get to know her new colleagues—to be dragged up on a stage to dance with a half-naked man and then make an utter fool of herself when he kissed her for a finale.

Everything would have been all right if only she hadn't responded so fervently and then, when she'd realised that he'd become every bit as aroused as she had, she'd lost her nerve and run like a scared rabbit.

Her face flamed again as she remembered the chorus of whistles and applause which had filled the room when he'd held her all-too-willing body against the stark masculine power of his.

When the noise surrounding them had brought her to her senses all she'd been interested in was grabbing her shawl and bag from Hannah and getting out of there.

Now all she had to do was turn up for her shift in the accident and emergency department and pretend that the whole thing had never happened. . .and keep her fingers crossed that something else cropped up quickly to keep the hospital grapevine busy.

Perhaps the new doctor due to start in A and E today to cover for Nicholas Prince's absence would occupy everyone's wagging tongues—and keep her own mind off the fact that the hormones which she'd thought had ceased to function seemed to have been kick-started into a full-throttled roar.

At least she wouldn't have to face Hannah's inquisition until later. She and Leo had both managed to arrange to have the morning off in order to act as witnesses at Polly's marriage to Nick Prince. Neither of them would be on duty until the afternoon.

The brisk walk through the crisp chill of the morning from her room in the nurses' accommodation to the A and E department was just long enough for her to get herself under control. She was guiltily glad that her arrival coincided with the banshee wail of two ambulances so that she was pitchforked straight into activity.

Her own charge was a little girl of six, the paramedic all but running beside her as she was wheeled into the emergency room.

He had one hand pressing firmly on the child's femoral artery, high up on the skinny little leg, compressing it against her pelvis in an attempt to control the massive blood loss.

'Severe trauma to right leg about four inches below the knee—pretty close to complete amputation,' reported Ted Larrabee as he handed over. 'She's bleeding profusely and very shocked so we had to put a tourniquet on as well, and we've managed to get three IVs into her and they're running wide open.'

'Oh, God...' Laura breathed as she swiftly completed the task of connecting up the dainty child to the hospital monitoring systems and got her first look at the extent of the injuries.

Whatever had happened, it had chopped through skin, muscle and bone until the lower part of her leg looked as if it was hanging on by little more than a narrow band of flesh.

There was a warning call and all those without the heavy protective aprons stood back while the first X-ray was taken, then stepped forward again in an elaborately choreographed dance to continue their own tasks while the next plate was positioned.

'How the hell did *this* happen?' a deep husky voice demanded, and all the hairs went up on the back of Laura's neck.

There wasn't time to do more than flick a swift glance over the man beside her and determine the fact that she hadn't met him before, then she blocked her strange reaction to him out of her mind and concentrated on the task in hand.

'She was being dropped off at school and started to get

out of the wrong side of the car,' Ted detailed succinctly. 'An oncoming car couldn't help ploughing into the open door and shut it on her leg.'

Laura wasn't the only one to gasp as the graphic image flashed across her mind, but there wasn't time to dwell on it.

There were blood samples to be cross-matched and supplies to be confirmed for the duration of the child's extensive trip to Theatre. Time was of the essence now, with every wasted minute compromising the healthy survival of the leg tissues deprived of blood and lessening the chances that the limb could be reattached successfully.

Out of the corner of her eye she saw a second dark-haired man arrive on the scene, and the two of them conferred briefly in front of the X-ray view-box.

'Good,' muttered Celia MacDonald beside her. 'If the poor wee thing's got Alex Marshall working on her she stands a better than average chance—he's a damn good orthopod.'

Laura blinked. She knew from what Hannah had already told her about their superior that Big Mac rarely said two words where one would do so this was praise indeed.

It wasn't long before the youngster had been stabilised enough to be taken out of their hands and on her way to Theatre, where the team was waiting to begin the long task of piecing her together again.

As Laura had guessed, Alex had confirmed that although it would be a three-dimensional jigsaw to put together the time-consuming plating and screwing together of her shattered leg would be the simplest part of the task.

He'd been the first to admit that it was the hours of microsurgery the six-year-old would require to rejoin her crushed and mangled nerves and veins which would determine whether her leg could be saved—and how much use it would be to her.

Laura had finished her clearing-up duties and had just turned to leave the room when she cannoned straight into a large, dark-haired immovable obstruction and began to lose her balance.

'I—I'm sorry!' she stammered as she tried to find her feet, but when she went to take a step back her elbows were firmly held in the hands which had saved her from disaster.

Startled, she looked up over a smoothly shaven chin and slightly lopsided grin into a pair of strangely familiar pale blue eyes. When she saw that they were surrounded by sinfully long black lashes her breath caught in her throat.

Her eyes flew over the neatly barbered dark hair, then took in the pristine shirt and tie, framed by his conservative dark suit, and for a second she almost doubted the evidence of her own eyes.

Then she gazed up again and a newly familiar shiver of awareness skated right up the length of her spine to raise all the hairs on the back of her neck as she realised that she *did* recognise those unforgettable eyes.

'The Lone Ranger, I presume,' she murmured, and was surprised to see him flinch.

Suddenly she realised what she'd done, and she could have bitten her tongue off. She closed her eyes briefly as a flush of embarrassment filled her face, and she knew that those few words had ruined her chance of ever denying that she'd recognised him.

Her gaze meshed with his, and she was helpless to drag her eyes away until she caught sight of an answering heat washing over the leanly sculpted cheek-bones she hadn't seen under the domino mask last night.

'For God's sake, keep your voice down,' he muttered, his dark eyebrows drawing down into a deep V. He suddenly seemed to realise that he was still holding her elbows and released them hastily to swing a haunted glance around the room. 'I hope you haven't told anybody? Leo promised you could be trusted.'

'How could I tell anyone?' she murmured, grateful that he'd finally broken the physical connection between them. She was stung by the accusation in his tone and more than a little puzzled by his reference to Leo. 'I've only just recognised you...and what's Leo got to do with it?'

'He's the one who picked you...supposedly because you were trustworthy,' he repeated, visibly agitated. 'He must have told you how important it was to keep it quiet?'

'No. Why would he tell me that?'

'Because of my position here, of course,' he snapped as if the answer should have been obvious.

'Well, if you were that worried about people's reaction to your little sideline perhaps you shouldn't have offered to do it,' she snapped back, hard pushed to keep her voice down.

'I didn't,' he snarled, and ran one agitated hand over his newly shorn hair, visibly startled when he realised how short it now was. 'It isn't a sideline. I was badgered into it—by Leo!'

'But...'

'Look...'

Laura saw him draw in a steadying breath and when she realised just how worked up he was she decided to hold her tongue and give him first shot at explaining.

'Apparently, the chap he had lined up to do that dance thing had his appendix taken out yesterday—here in St Augustine's—and that meant Leo was stuck for someone to do his finale.'

'And he twisted your arm?' she ventured as she began to understand the sequence of events.

'With the promise that no one would be able to recognise me, and that he'd try to find some way of fixing it so that the person chosen was someone utterly trustworthy.'

'And, instead, you got me,' she said softly, and saw him grow visibly paler.

'You mean, you *aren't* the person he asked?' he said with more than a touch of panic in his voice. 'Then how did you know who I was?'

'I recognised your eyes,' she replied, grateful that he would never know about the strange awareness she seemed to have developed about his presence. When he'd joined her beside their little patient the hairs had gone up on the back of her neck before she'd even caught sight of his icy blue eyes. 'They're an unusual colour against your tanned skin and dark hair.'

'But I was wearing that stupid mask last night,' he pointed out agitatedly. 'Leo said that would stop anyone recognising me afterwards.'

Words seemed to fail him as she shook her head, and for a moment she thought about drawing out the agony but relented.

'Don't forget, apart from Leo, I was the only one to get close to you,' she reminded him gently. 'And you won't have to worry about me talking because I've got just as much reason to want the whole thing kept quiet as you have.'

He gazed down at her for a moment before he answered, as if he was gauging her sincerity, 'So, perhaps we should make a pact to watch each other's backs?' he suggested with the hint of a smile.

'Sounds good enough for me,' Laura said with an answering smile, and offered her hand. 'Laura Kirkland. Newly appointed Staff Nurse, A and E, St Augustine's Hospital. Second day here.'

'Well, you're one day up on me, Laura Kirkland,' he said as he enveloped her small hand in the warmth of his and held it just a little longer than necessary. 'Wolff Bergen, at your service.'

'Wolff?' She couldn't help the way the thread of laughter gave a lilt to her voice.

'Yes, Wolff. And I've already heard all the jokes,' he said wearily as he turned towards the door. 'Unfortunately, it's a family name on my father's side and I got landed with it.'

'I like it,' Laura decided as she walked out through the door he held open for her, her head tilted on one side as she looked up at him. 'I think it suits you, especially since you've had your hair cut—or was that a wig last night?'

'Hush,' he cautioned softly with a quick glance both ways down the corridor. 'I think *that* had better be a topic of conversation we agree to limit to discussion outside the hospital.'

In other words, topic closed, Laura said to herself as she followed him along the corridor, his long legs carrying him further and further ahead.

Ah, well, it was probably for the best. She wasn't in a position to start any relationships and even if the reciprocal attraction she'd seen in his eyes persuaded him to begin pursuing her he was far too good-looking to hang around waiting for long once she showed him she wasn't interested.

She tamped down the unhappy ache into the shadowy corner inside her heart which it had occupied for so long now, and straightened her shoulders with new determination. This was the second day of her new post at St Augustine's, and if Hannah's recommendations were anything to go on she could look forward to a long and happy career here.

She would just have to be satisfied with what she could have, rather than what she wanted.

The trouble was that she couldn't switch her mind off, and by the time Hannah came in to work she had a whole list of pointed questions to ask her about the events of the previous evening.

Unfortunately, before she had time to corner her friend Hannah was surrounded by half the staff in the department.

'Is it true?' Tina demanded eagerly. 'Is Polly getting married to Old Nick?'

For a second Hannah looked almost taken aback, as if this was the last question she had expected, but then she smiled broadly when she realised that somehow the secret was out.

'Yes!' she confirmed with glee. 'Polly married her Prince at eleven-thirty this morning.'

'And they asked you to be a witness?' demanded another voice.

'Leo and me, and then we joined them for a celebratory meal afterwards,' she elaborated.

'Oh, I think it's so romantic, especially the way they managed to keep it all a secret.'

'From *some* of us,' Hannah pointed out with a grin.

She was being so unbearably smug about the fact that she'd been in on the secret that Laura longed to take her down a peg or two with a few sharp words of her own about trustworthiness, but she'd have to wait until she could get her alone.

There was no way she was going to have her own private concerns turned into grist for the rumour mill.

But later, when there were no other ears around. . .

She turned away from the chattering group and went back to the reception area. If nothing else, she could always find work to occupy her hands, even if it was the nauseating job of soaking off a pair of toxic socks which had all but welded themselves to the feet of the elderly lady she took through to the cubicle.

'Oh, Maggie, what have you done to yourself?' she chided the elderly bag lady gently. First, she'd soaked the malodorous feet in a povidone-iodine solution and now she was patiently picking the remaining rotting threads of a pair of disintegrated socks out of her heavily infected flesh.

'Me boots got wet, missy, and I didn't have any dry ones to put on.'

Laura glanced wryly at the sodden wrecks, lying abandoned under the edge of the trolley. She'd actually had to cut one of them apart to get it off so Maggie wouldn't be wearing *them* any more. When she'd finished this part of the job and applied antibiotic dressings she'd have to make some quick enquiries about St Augustine's connections with local charity shops—or perhaps they had a cupboard somewhere with oddments of clothing donated or left behind.

'Where have you been staying, Maggie?' she asked

gently when she noticed that her A and E form was incomplete. 'Is there someone we can contact to tell them you'll be staying in hospital for a few days?'

'No point cos I'm not staying,' the elderly woman replied aggressively. 'Anyway, why d'you want to know where I live, missy? Going to come and visit me, then?'

'I was just hoping it wasn't too far away for you to come back to have your feet dressed,' Laura said calmly. 'You're going to need to have them attended to regularly for a while or they might turn really nasty.'

'It's not that far away,' she said stoically. 'I'll get here one way or 'nother. Got to be able to walk, see. Else I can't get me soup from the kitchen by the station.'

'Right. Well, if you'd like to keep your feet up there for a minute I'll just see if there's a spare cup of tea going begging. Do you want sugar in yours?'

''Ow much?' she challenged with a scowl, one hand covering the bulging carrier bag she'd held clutched to her side throughout.

'This one'll be free, Maggie, my love, but you'll have to smile at me if you want another one,' Laura quipped.

'Depends what it tastes like whether I'll *want* another one, missy...and I take three sugars.'

'Three it is.' Laura nodded and drew the curtain across behind her as she marvelled at the old lady's amazing resilience. Her feet must have been causing her agony for ages before she'd finally given in and asked for help.

She went back with the tea quite quickly, but it took a little longer to sort out the problem of new footwear.

In the end, she turned to Sister MacDonald and explained the circumstances, telling her that she hadn't tried too hard to persuade Maggie to allow herself to be admitted.

'You're quite right,' the senior sister agreed. 'We know Maggie of old and there's little chance that you'll get her to agree to stay in here, even though she'd be in comfort while her feet heal. She's too independent. As for the problem of replacement footwear...' She reached for the telephone, paused in thought for a second and started dialling.

'Now, then, Maggie,' Laura said when she finally returned to the cubicle with the new footwear tucked out of sight under one arm. 'I've got a bit of a problem and I need you to help me out.'

'Me, missy?' she questioned warily, one hand still wrapped tightly round the empty mug while the other clutched her precious bag of belongings on her lap. 'What d'you want?'

'Well, I had such trouble getting your boots off that I ruined one of them.' She picked up the offending article and showed it to the old lady, holding her breath so that she didn't have to breathe in the awful smell emanating from it.

'You made a proper old mess of that and no mistake,' Maggie grumbled.

'I'm sorry,' Laura said as she deposited it again as far away as possible. 'I'm hoping you'll accept these in exchange—so that I won't get into trouble for spoiling yours.'

She saw the flash of acquisitiveness in the old lady's faded blue eyes when she caught sight of the footwear Laura was offering. They weren't new but they'd been well looked after and were sound and watertight, and Big Mac had even scrounged up a couple of pairs of socks to go with them.

'Well, I s'pose I can take 'em if it stops you from getting

a flea in your ear—mind, you'd better not ruin these ones when I come back to get the dressings changed,' she warned as she gingerly pulled the socks over the fresh white dressings, then posted her feet into the new boots and laced them up.

'If you'll promise to come back for every appointment I'll promise not to spoil your boots,' Laura bargained.

'I bet you'll forget 'ow many sugars I take in me tea,' she challenged with a wicked grin.

'Three, stirred clockwise, you terrible woman. Now let me get you out of here so I can have a bit of peace.'

She offered a helping hand as Maggie slid over the edge of the bed and found her feet, then drew the curtain back while she gathered up her meagre belongings.

'Missy?' The old lady had paused to look back. 'Thanks. You've got a good heart...lousy tea, mind, but a good heart.'

Laura was still laughing when she came out of the cubicle with a tightly tied plastic bag.

'Maggie's boots?' Wolff grinned as he nodded towards the burden she was holding at arm's length, his eyes gleaming down at her.

'How did you guess?' Laura asked with a grimace. 'I thought I'd captured all the smell inside the bag.'

'I heard the whole saga from next door.' He tilted his dark head towards the next cubicle. 'It helped to take my client's mind off the fact that I was having to stitch the back of his hand together after his girlfriend's cat's claws had ripped it open.'

'Glad to have provided some entertainment, but now it's time for my break—and I won't be having tea!'

'I'm due to put my feet up, too,' he said as he began

walking beside her. 'Speaking of entertainment,' he continued, lowering his voice, 'has anyone said anything to you?'

Laura knew immediately that he was talking about last night's events and she felt the beginnings of a blush work its way up her throat.

'Nothing so far. Everyone seems far more interested in talking about Nick's and Polly's marriage. Anyway, Hannah's been kept busy since she started her shift.'

'Interesting, the way you said her name through gritted teeth,' he said musingly, one dark eyebrow arching up towards his hair as he folded his arms across his chest and leant back against the work surface in the kitchenette. 'I take it that she's the one who *should* have joined me up on the stage last night.'

'Yes. And I'm almost certain that the switch was deliberate,' she added heatedly as she checked the water level in the kettle and switched it on. 'Just wait till I give her a piece of my mind.'

'Was my dancing that bad?' he challenged softly, his voice just that bit deeper and huskier as he leant towards her in the confined space. 'I got the distinct impression that you had really entered into the spirit of the thing—especially by the time we got to the finale...'

'Don't...' Laura covered her face with her hands, mortified that he had realised how much she had been affected by him.

'Hey! I was there too, remember? It was pretty explosive stuff!'

'But I don't *do* that sort of thing!' Laura exclaimed, rounding on him.

'What sort of thing? Dance? Enjoy yourself—?'

'Make an exhibition of myself,' she butted in, hoping to stop him speaking, but his eyes were gleaming with unholy glee as he completed his list of suggestions with one which robbed her of breath.

'Respond sexually to a complete stranger?'

'Oh, God,' she breathed, her eyes wide with horror as she gazed up into an icy blue that seared her like a laser with the knowledge they contained.

She'd hoped that he hadn't realised exactly how much her body had responded to his—after all, a woman's arousal wasn't as blatantly obvious as a man's...as *his* had been. But no such luck.

'If you were a gentleman you wouldn't have said that,' she enunciated through stiff lips as she dragged her eyes away and closed them in mortification. She could almost feel the colour draining out of her face.

'Ah,' he said silkily, 'whatever gave you the idea that I was a gentleman? In fact, I don't think I *want* to be a gentleman if it means I have to pretend that I didn't enjoy the sensation of having you in my arms and...'

'Don't... Please!' she begged. 'I don't...I'm not...'

An arrested expression crossed his face.

'You're not married, are you?' he demanded. 'Or engaged?'

'No,' she wailed. 'It's nothing like that.'

'Then where's the problem?' he said, suddenly far too cheerful for her liking. 'I'm single, you're single and we're both normal, healthy human beings.'

'Speak for yourself,' she retorted bitterly, then whirled away from him as several years of suppressed emotions threatened to overflow. 'I'm sorry. I've got to go,' she muttered and hurried out of the room just as the kettle began to scream.

'Laura?' he called after her as the door swung shut behind her, and she nearly laughed. That was the second time she'd ended up running away from him, for all the good it would do her.

'Hey, Laura! Got time for a coffee?' Hannah asked with a breezy smile when they all but collided in the corridor.

'Not just at the moment,' Laura replied tightly, hardly glancing towards her startled friend as she continued rapidly on her way.

One part of her wanted to let fly at Hannah for dumping her into such an embarrassing situation without any warning, but she was so upset at the moment that she didn't trust herself not to explode.

It had been bad enough last night when she had thought it was just her bad luck to have her number pulled out of the bag, but now that she knew that Hannah had done it on purpose she felt as if she'd been betrayed.

There hadn't been time since she'd moved to St Augustine's to talk to Hannah about all the reasons which had made her change her speciality from Paediatrics to A and E, or the circumstances which had made her decide to move to another hospital.

Even so, she had thought that Hannah had been a good enough friend not to risk hurting her like that.

She'd almost reached the entrance to the reception area when raised voices dragged her out of her thoughts. Through the glass-paned door she caught sight of the flash of light on what must surely be a seven- or eight-inch blade and she froze, all her own problems instantly forgotten.

CHAPTER THREE

'COME on, now, son. Put it down,' said a voice just out of Laura's sight in the L-shaped area. 'We don't want anyone getting hurt.'

'Speak for yourself, old man,' retorted a strident male voice. 'You can't tell me what to do.'

'It's my job to make certain people don't get hurt in here,' said the first voice, his words admirably calm and measured amid the furore, and Laura suddenly realised that he must be the member of the hospital security force who was on duty in the accident and emergency department.

'Well, it doesn't look as if you're doing much of a job today,' taunted the youngster, whose strutting progress around one end of the waiting area had just brought him back into Laura's view.

He could hardly have been more than twenty-two or -three—possibly much younger—and although Laura had never seen him before his uniform was becoming increasingly familiar, with his scruffy drab clothing and his matted hair hanging in stringy disarray across feverishly bright eyes in an unhealthily pale face.

The thing which drew most of her attention, though, was the wicked-looking knife he held in one hand, the gleaming blade the only well-cared-for item he seemed to possess.

Out of the corner of her eye Laura caught sight of a movement and turned her head slowly to see Sister MacDonald, signalling surreptitiously for her to get help.

Laura nodded once, careful not to draw attention to herself, and waited just long enough for the young man's next shambling journey to take him out of sight before she spun round and sprinted silently away.

She assumed that the security guard followed the same practice as the staff at her last hospital, and that he was carrying an alarm to call for assistance. Unfortunately, she realised that if he'd been taken unawares when this thug had pulled out his knife he might not have had time to activate it.

The same was true of any panic button situated by the admissions desk. She'd known other incidents where the staff had been so concerned for the safety of those closest to the threat of danger that they'd delayed just too long before they thought to activate it.

'*I'm* the one with the knife and I know how to use it, too,' shouted the increasingly agitated youngster, his chilling words echoing along the corridor towards Laura, just before she smacked the next set of fire doors open with both hands and barrelled into the staffroom.

'Hannah,' she gasped, relieved to see that her friend hadn't disappeared. 'How can I find out whether the silent panic button has been activated for the reception area? There's a nutter out there, threatening people with a knife!'

The welcoming smile on Hannah's face changed instantly to one of concern as she leapt to her feet and reached for the internal phone.

A second figure straightened up equally quickly from a comfortable sprawl, and Laura realised that Wolff must have stayed to drink his cup of coffee after all.

'Has anyone been hurt?' he demanded as he strode towards her.

'Not as far as I could see, but I wasn't actually in the room,' she explained as she led the way rapidly out of the room.

Hannah was now speaking to someone on the other end of the phone, and Laura blessed the fact that at least one of them had been at the hospital long enough to know the system.

Once again Wolff's longer stride enabled him to draw ahead of Laura, and she had to sprint to catch up with him and grab his arm before he got too close to the reinforced glass panels in the door.

'Wait a minute,' she breathed, suddenly stupidly aware of the strength in the leanly muscular forearm she was holding. 'Can you see what's going on in there now?'

Peering round his shoulder, she could see that everyone was still frozen in the same places as when she'd left. Celia MacDonald nodded briefly to let them know that she knew they were there and was ready to react when needed.

They listened for a moment and, to Laura's relief, little seemed to have changed since she'd fled for help, except the excitability of the young tough and the increasingly incoherent violence of his language.

As far as they could tell, he was still marching erratically about and still brandishing the lethal blade in people's faces, obviously relishing the way they cringed away as he brought the razor edge closer and closer.

'I've got to find some way of distracting him or he's going to take it too far,' Wolff muttered, his voice a husky rumble next to her ear and his dark brows drawn tightly into a frown of concentration.

'Well, you can't just walk in there,' Laura objected. 'In your white coat you're just another authority figure and you could tip him right over the edge.'

Wolff froze for a moment in deep thought, then threw her an unexpectedly wicked grin and sent her pulse rate into overdrive.

'Clever girl! That's the answer!' he whispered jubilantly as he began stripping off the tell-tale white coat.

'What on earth. . .?' Laura began, but he didn't even pause to explain as he continued to pull his burgundy patterned tie askew and undid several buttons on his pristine white shirt.

'Quick,' he directed. 'Help me to look dishevelled—as if I've been in a fight or something. . .'

Laura wasn't certain what was going on but she grabbed one side of his shirt and yanked it out of the waistband of his trousers before she undid the cuff of one sleeve and left it flapping.

'Like that?' she asked softly, overwhelmingly aware of the scent of soap and man which surrounded her. 'What a shame you got rid of that wild hair of yours. . .'

'Enough about the hair,' he said with a swift flash of white teeth, and she suddenly realised that he was almost enjoying himself.

'Now listen,' he continued as he kept one eye on the events on the other side of the door. 'When he comes up this end again where there are fewer people I'm going to burst through the doors as if I'm being chased. I want you to come flying in after me, shouting the odds, and with any luck the little toad will be distracted long enough for the security man to take him down.'

'OK.' Laura nodded and drew in a quick breath to calm her roiling stomach. 'But, please, be careful,' she whispered.

She didn't know where the words had come from but suddenly realised that she didn't want him to be injured.

'Why, Laura, I didn't know you cared!' he teased with a quick heart-stopping grin, then his eyes lost their glint as he faced the door again, waiting for their quarry to come into view.

Laura watched as he held one hand up with three fingers extended for Celia MacDonald to see. When she calmly nodded and surreptitiously copied his signal Laura realised that she was actually relaying the message on to the beleaguered security man.

She drew in a deep breath to calm herself as Wolff removed first one digit then another in a silent countdown before he slammed both hands forcefully against the doors and hit the room at a run.

Afterwards, Laura couldn't remember what she'd shouted during the bedlam of the ensuing five seconds. All she knew was that it felt like a thousand years as she watched the courageous security guard seize the opportunity to run up behind the distracted thug and attempt to bind his arms harmlessly at his sides.

Even then his wiry opponent was struggling and screaming obscenities, and before Wolff could get close enough to lend assistance he made one final desperate lunge with his pinioned arms to try to force his captor to release him.

'Oh, my God!' shrieked the woman closest to the heart of the action. 'He's stabbed himself!'

For several seconds there was an almost deathly silence as everyone stared in awful fascination at the spreading tide of red which began to pour down the young man's legs.

'Trolley. . .quick!' Wolff snapped, his voice overriding the wailing curse of disbelief and pain that the young thug let out when he realised what he had done to himself.

'He's losing his viscera,' Laura warned when she saw the dark shiny protrusion of the young man's intestines through the slash in his disreputable clothing, and she dashed towards him.

'Get him horizontal—now!'

The command in Wolff's voice was totally at odds with his dishevelled appearance and brought instant results.

Within seconds the bully boy was surrounded by the very people he had been threatening, but instead of meting out retribution they were working as fast as they could to save his life.

As soon as he'd been whisked into the emergency room he was pounced on from all sides, his clothes efficiently stripped away and a wet dressing applied to cover and protect the protruding contents of his abdomen while several IV lines were inserted and some O-negative blood started.

A quick telephone call warned Theatre what to expect, and he was on his way.

'Well done, everyone,' Wolff said as he finally stripped off his blood-spattered disposables and dumped them. 'Now, I think I'd better go back out there and let them know that the crazies haven't completely taken over here.'

There was a round of laughter as the team realised that some of the poor people who had been terrorised by their erstwhile patient might not have realised what had been going on earlier when Wolff had burst in amongst them.

'Well, you were a very *convincing* escaped patient when you dashed into the reception area like that,' Celia MacDonald commented with a broad smile of her own. 'In fact, I think it might be an idea if you were to tidy yourself up a wee bit before you go back out there or they might wonder about the calibre of the staff working at St Augustine's these days.'

Wolff glanced down at his clothes and blinked, and they all noticed for the first time since the youngster had almost disembowelled himself just how disordered he was still looking, with his tie at half-mast and his shirt-tail still hanging out of the waistband of his dark trousers.

'It's not my fault,' he said as he looked around the room, his expression as innocent as a choirboy's until he flicked a quick glance in Laura's direction.

She had a sudden sinking feeling that she wasn't going to like what was coming next.

'You should have seen Sister Kirkland!' he continued in tones of bitter complaint. 'She was like a wild woman, wrenching at my clothes as if she couldn't wait to get me out of them!'

For one horrible moment Laura thought she was going to die of embarrassment and then she was afraid she wasn't, but in the end she decided that retaliation would be far more satisfying than either option.

'Well, you *are* the newest doctor in the department and we haven't had any fresh meat for a while,' she commented, her own brand of apparently accidental innuendo garnering another round of laughter which finally dispelled the air of tension which had been hanging over the department.

'So you're after fresh meat, are you?' Wolff murmured in her ear as he followed her out of the room, and Laura cursed the fact that she hadn't moved faster to avoid the possibility that he would continue to make her the focus of his wicked taunts.

'Not personally,' she said, pleased to note that her voice was calmly dismissive.

He was silent for a moment as he paced along beside her and, while she was all too conscious of the fact that he kept glancing towards her, she could almost hear his brain working.

'Do you mind if I ask you a question?' he ventured at last, and the very hesitancy of his tone made her pause to look all the way up at his puzzled expression.

She shrugged, giving him tacit permission.

'Are you a lesbian?'

He asked the question very softly but, as far as Laura was concerned, it felt almost like a shouted accusation.

'No!' she gasped, her shock at the unexpectedness of it robbing her of further speech.

'So why the strange "blow hot, blow cold" attitude towards men? Do you brush us all off the same way?'

For several seconds Laura felt quite sick that somehow she had apparently betrayed the raw hurt she carried inside. She'd always thought that she managed to keep her emotions under fairly good control, but Wolff Bergen seemed to have picked up instantly on the distance she preferred to keep between herself and any man.

There was one brief moment when she thought she was going to be overwhelmed by the memories of her betrayal and for just an instant she imagined what it might be like to pour all the agony out, but then anger roared in to rebuild her shattered defences and she turned on him.

'Oh, I'm so sorry,' she said in a voice positively dripping with sweetness, 'I didn't realise that it might hurt your ego not to have *all* the nurses at your feet.'

He didn't reply, but she witnessed the way the muscles

in his jaw tightened when he clenched his teeth.

The silence began to feel as if it were stretching into infinity when he finally broke it.

'A bad relationship?' he suggested, almost too gently, and Laura felt the sudden pressure of scalding tears behind her eyes at the accuracy of his insight.

'Dr Bergen...?'

Before Laura could confirm or deny his theory there was an imperative call in a clipped Scottish accent.

'Yes, Sister?' he replied, without breaking eye contact with Laura.

'There's a child arriving in just a matter of minutes. He fell out of a window onto a garden cane and impaled himself.'

'Warn Theatre and get the blood bank to stand by,' Wolff directed, his mind instantly firing on all cylinders. 'Which room is clear?'

'Two, and John Preece is calling Alex Marshall so they'll be on standby,' Celia informed him before she turned away smartly.

With those words, Laura realised that to save time her superior had already contacted the duty anaesthetist and her favourite orthopaedic surgeon.

For just a moment she was overwhelmed by the sheer volume of knowledge and experience she would need to amass before she was ready to take on a post as senior as Sister MacDonald's and then she, too, switched onto automatic pilot and hurried towards emergency room two.

By the time the banshee wail of the ambulance was heard outside the doors she'd double-checked all the supplies they might need and the room was ready for action.

'Vital signs all apparently normal,' were the first words

she heard as Ted Larrabee's opposite number, Mike Wilson, wheeled the trolley through. 'This is Simon. He's seven.'

'Hello, Simon. I'm Laura,' she said in a soothing voice as she leant towards him, trying to reassure him with a gentle squeeze when she held his limp hand.

Huge blue eyes looked up at her in open terror over the clear plastic Entonox mask, tears sliding silently out of the corners and into the soft spikes of his tough-kid haircut.

'You'll have to stay very still until we find out where you hurt yourself, OK?'

He tried to nod, but was prevented by the collar protecting his neck until he could be checked for fractures.

The radiographer called a warning and Laura released his hand to step back while the first shot was taken, her eyes riveted by the sight of the blood-stained stick angled up through the centre of his chest.

The injury was so near so many vital organs—his heart and lungs, as well as the major arteries supplying them and the rest of his body. And this was totally separate from the fact that the fall alone could have caused terrible skeletal damage.

As the minutes passed Laura's awful feeling of dread gradually began to lift as test after test proved negative.

'No broken neck,' Wolff confirmed when the plates went up on the view-box, 'and it looks as if the stick has passed right through, without causing any real damage to any of his vital organs.'

Laura drew in a deep breath and reached for Simon's hand again as the next round of tests began, hoping that this time a miracle had happened.

'Good boy,' she murmured as she smiled down at

him again. 'You're staying nice and still for us.'

She'd been holding his little grubby paw for comfort and, when she had to move out of the way to allow Wolff to move closer, released her hold on his hand and gave his foot a little squeeze instead before she moved aside.

Knowing how ticklish children tended to be, she was surprised when he didn't react to the pressure, and a nasty bell began to ring at the back of her mind.

Before she could voice her concern Wolff had begun his neurological screening test by drawing the pointed handle of his reflex hammer along the sole of Simon's foot.

There was no reaction and, suddenly, instead of the light sound of relief in the talk around the table there was an ominous silence.

Laura met Wolff's shadowed eyes as he straightened up briefly beside Simon on the other side of the trolley, and without a word being spoken she knew that he shared her fears.

'Simon? I'm Dr Bergen,' he said as he leant towards the young lad with a gentle smile. 'Can you help me do some tests?'

'Yes,' he whispered, and Laura's heart went out to him. He was trying to be so brave and, if her suspicious were correct, he was going to need every ounce of courage he possessed.

'What I'm going to do is touch your skin in different places,' Wolff explained. 'I want you to tell me when you can feel my touch so I know which bits you've hurt. OK?'

'OK,' he whispered.

He'd stopped crying now, but the silvery tracks were still visible on his pale skin.

Systematically Wolff moved his hands backwards and

forwards and up and down the child's limbs, and while Laura heard Simon whisper a quiet 'Yes' whenever his arms and chest were touched there was a heart-rending silence when the contact moved below mid-chest level.

'That's all for now, Simon. Thank you for helping me.' Wolff smiled again as he reached out a hand to ruffle the silky hedgehog strands of blond hair.

'Doctor?' The youngster paused and swallowed, his chin wobbling as he gathered his words. 'Do. . .do my mum and dad know where I am?'

'Yes, Simon, they know. They're waiting outside.'

'Can. . .can I see them?' he asked hesitantly. 'Is. . .is Mum really mad at me?'

'Of course you can see them, Simon, but it will only be for a few minutes because then we'll be putting you to sleep so we can take the stick away.'

'Oh. . .OK. . . But before they come in. . .' he glanced pleadingly from Laura to Wolff and back again '. . .will you tell her I'm sorry for opening the window?'

'I'll tell her,' Wolff promised with a smile, but Laura realised that it didn't quite reach his eyes.

As he stripped off his disposables and left the room she began to coil the various IVs and monitor leads neatly around Simon's still form as she began to prepare him for transfer up to Theatre.

She knew that the desolate expression she had witnessed in Wolff's eyes meant that he was already trying to find the words to tell Simon's parents the bad news—that it looked as if the stick that their son had fallen on had missed all his internal organs, only to sever his spinal cord.

* * *

It was nearly half an hour before she saw Wolff again, and he looked as if he'd aged ten years in the interim.

'Have you got time for a coffee?' Laura offered, beckoning him towards the kitchenette. She'd heard the kettle whistle not long ago and it seemed like hours since she'd last had time for a drink.

Wolff probably hadn't stopped for one either and, by the look of him, he needed it more than she did.

He propped himself silently into the corner formed by the two work-surfaces and watched silently while she spooned granules into two mugs and topped them up.

Laura handed him one of them and waited while he took his first couple of sips before she spoke.

'How is he?' she asked, knowing that she wouldn't have to say who she was talking about.

He closed his eyes and shook his head.

'Apparently there's an outside chance that the damage to his spinal cord isn't total, or might be temporary, but...' He shook his head again, sighing deeply before he raised sombre eyes to meet hers. 'That's what I had to tell his parents so I didn't take away all hope but, if I'm honest with myself, I'd have to say that it's pretty certain that he'll be paralysed from mid-chest downwards.'

'And if that happens he'll lose control of all bodily functions below that point, too,' Laura said, confirming what they both knew to be the almost inevitable outcome, and she dragged her eyes away to stare silently down into the steam wafting up from the mug.

'It just seems so bloody unfair,' Wolff suddenly muttered, his delivery of the words almost vicious. 'He's only seven years old, for heaven's sake!'

Laura knew what he meant.

Her thoughts had been running along similar lines ever since she'd realised the probable extent of young Simon's injuries. It didn't matter that she was seeing the results of accidents and illness all day long—it was the children who touched her heart.

She'd watched Simon's mother when she'd seen her son lying helpless on the trolley, the garden cane still sticking up grotesquely out of his chest, and had marvelled at her control.

How had the poor woman managed to stay so calm and brave while she'd stroked his forehead and reassured him that she wasn't really cross with him for opening his bedroom window?

How had she managed to stop herself from screaming aloud at the devastation that one bout of childish disobedience had made of his life?

How would *she* have coped if it had been *her* precious child lying on that trolley instead. . .?

But it wasn't her child because she didn't have a child, and it was about time she resigned herself to the fact that it was unlikely that she ever would. . .

'Thanks,' Wolff murmured, breaking into the misery of her wandering thoughts. 'I needed that. . .and the company.'

'You're welcome,' she said, realising that he seemed to have lowered some sort of defensive screen. For the first time she felt as if she was seeing the real man rather than the ever-alert, tightly controlled doctor she usually saw.

In spite of the coffee, he still looked far too weary and there were several hours yet before he could sign off and go home.

'Any idea what's waiting for us out there?' he said as

he reached across and rinsed out his mug under the tap.

'Last time I looked there were three assorted chest complaints, two lacerations waiting for stitches...'

'And a partridge in a pear tree,' he finished with a sigh and an attempt at a smile. 'Well, let's get going and see how fast we can get rid of them before the next few verses arrive!'

They were doing well until they came to the first of the lacerations and found an elderly military gentleman cradling a blood-soaked dressing round one hand.

Even then, it wasn't his injury that caused the problem.

He began by describing how he'd gashed his hand when he'd tried to prise the top off a tin of paint with a screwdriver which had slipped.

After that, his sole topic of conversation had been the earlier disturbance with the young knife-wielding thug.

'They all know their rights, you know,' he pontificated, wincing as Wolff injected around the edges of the wound to deaden feeling, ready for cleaning and stitching. 'They all know what they're entitled to from the rest of society, but how many of them bother fulfilling their responsibilities towards that same society?'

Wolff flicked a glance towards Laura and raised one eyebrow. For the sake of their verbose patient he made a noncommittal noise as he concentrated on trimming the ragged edges of the gash, but as a response it was obviously enough to persuade his patient that he had a willing audience.

'They've had it too easy all their lives, that's what's wrong with them—free medicine, free schooling, cash handouts so they can spend it on drugs and trail round the countryside like rent-a-mob to cause the maximum disruption to other law-abiding people.

'Ah, but,' he continued, barely taking the time to draw a breath, 'just look what happens when you suggest that they get off their lazy backsides and look for a job to *earn* their living! They lift their hands up in horror and say you're encroaching on their precious rights! Pah!'

He fixed Laura with a baleful gaze.

'Do you know, sometimes I think it would be a damn good idea to flood the whole country with a batch of bad drugs and wipe the whole lot of them out. Bloody parasites. . . Ow!'

'I'm sorry, sir, did I hurt you?' Wolff asked, obviously surprised because he'd already got halfway through the job of stitching the gash up without any problem.

'No, no, Doctor. You carry on. I'll be all right,' the dapper gentleman assured him, studiously avoiding looking at his injured hand.

'I can put some more local anaesthetic in if you need it,' Wolff offered, reaching out one gloved hand for the syringe on the tray beside him. 'There's no need for you to suffer.'

'No, thank you, Doctor,' he said courteously, and Laura saw a slight hint of heightened colour in his leathery cheeks. 'Actually, I hate to have to admit it but I can't stand injections of any kind so if you can put up with me sounding off while I take my own mind off what you're doing. . .?'

Wolff nodded his understanding. 'Feel free, if it helps you to cope with it,' he invited. 'From what I can gather, there are a fair number of people who would agree with every word you've said.'

'And they're probably the ones who do a fair day's work for a fair day's pay and can't stand the injustice of those who milk the system without ever having contributed towards it,' their patient replied, back in full flow again.

'I hope I'm not on duty when he needs those taking out again,' Laura joked as she rubbed her ears. 'I now know what the expression "an ear-bashing" means—I wonder if that's how he copes with all the problems in his life?'

'I thought it was women who were supposed to talk their problems to death?' Wolff said, poker-faced, as he completed his notes.

'Some doctors think that's why women live longer than men—because they take the edge off their problems by talking about them,' Laura pointed out. 'And no jokes about it just *seeming* longer,' she added hurriedly when she saw the start of a sly smile on his face.

'As if I would!' he countered, then grew serious again. 'I sometimes wonder...' He shook his head.

'Wonder what?' Laura prompted, an intuitive feeling telling her that it was important to get him to complete the thought.

'Whether talking about a problem really *would* make things more bearable or whether it would just keep dragging it up again, like picking the scab off a wound instead of letting it heal in peace.'

Laura was surprised at the depth of thought Wolff had obviously given the idea. Perhaps he, too, had had bad experiences he was trying to cope with. She was still trying to decide what to say when Leo's voice intruded on them.

'Hey, how's it going?' he demanded jovially as he

almost bounced into the tiny room and slapped his old friend on the back. 'Is everyone taking good care of the new boy or have you started as you mean to go on and terrorised the lot of them straight away?'

CHAPTER FOUR

LAURA could have cursed when Leo interrupted her quiet conversation with Wolff. Then, when Hannah arrived almost on his heels, she had to resign herself to the fact that the opportunity to find out more about this intriguing man was gone—at least for the time being.

'Hey! What's this I've been hearing about the two of you rescuing the hospital from sabre-wielding terrorists?' Hannah demanded. 'I turn my back for a minute and you turn into heroes!'

'Rubbish!' Laura muttered. 'You know better than most how everything gets exaggerated in a hospital.'

She was looking at Hannah as she turned towards Wolff and saw the way her eyes widened in appreciation. She'd watched him on the stage last night—as had everyone else at the Ball—but this was obviously the first time she'd seen him in his freshly barbered doctor persona.

'Well, I can understand why you two are such good friends,' Hannah said with a grin Laura knew of old as she waved a hand towards Leo and Wolff, standing side by side. 'It's because you look so pretty beside each other!'

There were several seconds of startled silence before Leo objected heatedly.

'Pretty? Pretty?' he demanded, his strange golden eyes shooting sparks. 'I'll have you know. . .'

'Thank you kindly for the compliment,' Wolff interrupted, his slightly husky voice filled with laughter as he sketched a bow in Hannah's direction. 'It certainly scores highly for novelty value!'

Laura found it hard to agree with Hannah's description. It was true that the the two of them complemented each other, Leo's golden good looks and ready smile a perfect foil for Wolff's lean, dark and dangerous handsomeness, but she'd never have chosen such an insipid word as pretty.

Her eyes went thoughtfully from one to the other and she realised that she could imagine a good friendship developing between herself and Leo, but with Wolff. . .

She looked back at him and their eyes met, the icy blue of his cool and analytical.

There was a questioning expression in them, as if he knew that she was thinking about him and wondered what conclusions she had reached.

It was strangely difficult to drag her eyes away, as if she was forming some sort of elemental bond with him—a strange awareness that she'd never felt until she'd met his eyes for the first time last night—and she found herself shivering slightly in spite of the more than adequate heating.

Then, as if something equally elemental had told him of her new vulnerability, she saw his expression change. There was an intensity in his gaze that hadn't been there before, and she realised with a fresh shiver that the wolf he'd been named for had woken and that he was hungry and ready to prowl.

'Well,' Leo's hearty voice broke in on the strange intensity of their connection and Laura found herself dragging in a shaky breath, almost as if she'd forgotten to breathe while her gaze was held by his.

'You two weren't there to hear the announcement, but

we did it!' Leo continued triumphantly. 'We reached the target last night!'

For a second Laura wasn't certain what he was talking about until she remembered the whole purpose of the fund-raising event.

'Well done,' she congratulated him distractedly, managing to drag a polite smile up from somewhere.

How could she concentrate on the figures he was quoting, good as they were, when she was still trembling inside from the unexpected intensity of her feelings towards his friend, standing so silent and motionless beside him.

She'd never felt like this before, not even two years ago when she had been preparing to announce her engagement to the man she'd wanted to marry...

Suddenly, with a sickening jolt, she remembered the reason why the engagement hadn't gone ahead...why she wasn't married...why she'd moved to St Augustine's...and why she'd realised that it was pointless for her even to think about taking part in the timeless mating rituals of advance and retreat.

There would be no mate for her, no happy-ever-after of marriage and family.

Two years ago she had realised that there was nothing for her to look forward to but her career, and she'd turned her attention on it with single-minded intensity.

Oh, she'd made a few adjustments, such as the change from Paediatrics to A and E, but as far as the rest was concerned everything was going well, with the next step up to Sister due soon and then...

'Laura?' Hannah's voice reached her, her tone making it clear that it wasn't the first time she'd spoken. 'Are you all right? You seem a bit distracted.'

'Sorry, Hannah,' she apologised, belatedly aware that Leo and Wolff must have left the room while she'd been lost in her memories. 'It's been a bit busy this morning and I'm still tired after the late night last night.' She stopped, silently cursing herself for bringing the topic up then sternly berating herself for wanting to avoid it. It was Hannah who had dumped her into the situation without warning, Hannah who had some explaining to do.

'Speaking of last night,' she began with a militant tone in her voice.

'Do you know, when I got my first look at Wolff I almost regretted giving you first go,' Hannah began in a teasing rush, carefully keeping her voice down to a confidential level.

'Especially now I've had a better look at him in daylight! Leo told me he was an old colleague so I expected someone just like him—you know, light and harmless, the typical carefree bachelor having far too much fun with far too many women to think about settling down—but *he's* rather delicious, isn't he?'

Laura couldn't help agreeing, but she was startled by a sharp twist of jealousy when she realised that Hannah would have no reason to rebuff Wolff's advances when he decided that Laura's unwillingness wasn't worth the effort to break down.

'That's neither here nor there,' Laura said as she banished the familiar little grey cloud to the darkest corner of her heart.

Determination lifted her chin as she fixed Hannah with a stern gaze. 'You persuaded me to go the Ball on the pretext that it would be a good way to meet my new colleagues, and then you pull a stunt like that! What on earth possessed you to set me up like that? Was it deliberate? Was that why you wanted me to go?'

Hannah obviously heard the hurt in her voice, which she'd tried so hard to hide, and she reacted instantly.

'No, Laura!' She sounded stricken, one hand reaching out to cover Laura's clenched fist. 'It wasn't like that, I promise you.'

'Well, then, what *was* it like? Why *did* you do it?'

'Because I thought it would be a harmless bit of fun, and I thought you would enjoy it,' Hannah said earnestly, her dark blue eyes utterly guileless. 'I know you've never been much of a one for making an exhibition of yourself but you've seemed so. . .so subdued since you arrived and I thought it might cheer you up.'

'Cheer me up?' Laura questioned heatedly, finding it difficult to remember to keep her voice down. 'You thought it would cheer me up to make a spectacle of myself in front of everyone? I rather thought that when you started a new job the idea was to make a good impression!'

'In your work, yes,' Hannah agreed. 'And, if what I've been hearing over the last couple of days is anything to go by, you've already *made* a good impression.'

She held her hand up when Laura tried to interrupt, obviously determined to have her say.

'Look, Laura, I don't know what happened to you after I moved away, and I won't pry. You can tell me as much or as little as you want to in your own time. But you *must* know that I wouldn't willingly do anything to jeopardise your career.'

'But. . .' Laura began.

'Anyway,' her friend continued as if she hadn't even noticed the attempted interruption, 'it was St Augustine's staff at that do last night, and you know as well as I do what a closed shop the medical world is.

'We have to behave according to the perceptions of the outside world when we go outside our milieu, but when we're among our colleagues we actually get the chance to let our hair down without worrying that someone is going to turn round and say, "But you're a *nurse*!" in a scandalised tone if we get a bit tipsy or tell a risqué joke.'

Laura subsided. She had to admit that, within certain boundaries, Hannah was right. It was just that *she* had never been in that position before and it had left her feeling strangely vulnerable—especially when she was overwhelmed by the memory of her reaction to Wolff's kiss and realised that it had been watched by several hundred pairs of eyes!

'I wish you'd warned me,' she murmured as she fought the heat rising in her cheeks. 'It was such a shock. One minute I was getting ready to come back here and collapse into bed and the next I'd been manhandled up onto that stage and...'

'And looked as if you were ready to come back here and collapse into bed...with him!' Hannah completed. 'Wow! What a kiss! Was it as good as it looked?'

Laura glanced down at her watch in an attempt at buying time, but her brain was whirling. She had to find something to say to defuse Hannah's interest or she'd never hear the end of it.

'Oh, good,' she said calmly as she forced herself to meet her friend's eyes as if her heart weren't galloping out of control just at the memory of that kiss. 'Wolff and I hoped that the audience would feel that they'd had their money's worth when we planned it.'

The way Hannah's face fell was so comical that Laura almost apologised for spoiling her illusions.

'You planned it?' she squeaked in disbelief. 'When? You only met him when Leo helped you up onto the stage.'

'While we were dancing,' Laura elaborated, making sure she kept the story simple. 'You must have seen us talking?'

'Well, yes...but I thought he must have been saying something...' She shrugged, obviously disappointed.

'As far as I remember, it was something like, "Here we go," or "Hold tight," before he did the deed,' Laura said, keeping her crossed fingers out of sight. 'And, considering the fact that we were both dragooned into it, I think you and Leo got a better deal than you deserved.'

'But I only...'

'Now—' Laura continued quickly with an ostentatious look at her watch '—I've stood chatting quite long enough so I'm going back to work.' She swished past her friend and out into the corridor, making her escape before Hannah could get her second wind.

The last part of her shift was relatively uneventful, especially when compared to the turmoil of the earlier half.

She was surprised not to see Wolff about—according to the board his spell of duty was due to end at the same time as hers—and then silently scolded herself for even noticing.

Her last port of call at the end of her shift was the staffroom, where she intended to collapse in a heap with a cup of coffee before she went out into the cold and dark of the night for the walk back to her room.

Unless Hannah called in before she went home to her tiny flatlet, or one of her new neighbours knocked on her door to speak to her while she finally forced herself to finish her unpacking, this would be her last chance for a bit of company before she came back on duty tomorrow.

She pushed open the door and paused, surprised to find the room deserted and most of the lights turned off.

Mildly disappointed, she'd just decided that she might as well grab her belongings and go back to her room for the longed-for coffee while she started the dreaded chore when a strange sound drew her attention towards the furthest shadowy corner of the room.

There was someone there, slumped in the corner of a two-seater settee with his head twisted at such an awkward angle that he must have fallen asleep unexpectedly.

As she watched his whole body twitched—almost as if he were trying to fight an invisible enemy—and he made the same strangled moaning sound deep in his throat which had first attracted her attention.

She hovered in the doorway, not quite certain what to do.

If it was a junior doctor, taking advantage of a lull in his duties to grab a few minutes of sleep, he wouldn't be very pleased if she woke him up to ask if he was all right.

On the other hand, if it was someone in pain, or. . .

Her train of thought was completely derailed when the shadowy figure moved again and the meagre light caught the newly familier shape of Wolff's face.

Involuntarily she found herself walking towards him, a frown pleating her forehead as she tried to see what was the matter with him. Was he unwell or. . .?

'No. . . Don't. . . Please. . .'

His husky voice was roughened still further by sleep and now that she was closer she could see that he was in the throes of an awful dream.

'Please. . .don't die. . .'

There was such an awful emptiness in his voice that Laura couldn't help reaching out towards him in sympathy. His cheek felt so hot against her cool hand that it almost seared her, and as he moved convulsively in the throes of the nightmare his jaw rasped audibly against the soft skin of her palm.

'Wolff?' she murmured, bending forward to call him out of the nightmare. 'Wolff, can you hear me?'

She could tell when he woke up as his whole body seemed to grow tense from the electric point of contact with her hand, as though he was prepared for some kind of blow. Then the dark crescents of his lashes rose and she was captured in the stunning clarity of his blue eyes.

He blinked up at her, clearly disorientated, and she snatched her hand away, feeling almost guilty for invading his privacy.

'Laura?' His voice was a deep rumble and seemed to reverberate inside her chest long after it had left his. 'What. . .what's the matter? Am I needed on duty?'

He started to struggle upright on the seat, the effort clearly a major effort, and she stepped back to allow him more space.

'No. It's all right. You're off duty now, but you'd fallen asleep and. . .' She paused, not quite knowing what to say.

'Oh. . .'

It seemed that she didn't need to say any more as he rubbed the palms of both hands over his face.

'Was I shouting?' he asked quietly as he took his hands away and looked up at her. 'Sometimes. . .'

'No,' she hastened to reassure him. 'More of a mutter, and I wouldn't have heard that much except for the fact that I came in for a cup of coffee.'

He sighed deeply and rested his head back against the nubbly upholstery.

'I suppose I should be grateful for small mercies,' he said quietly. 'Poor Leo hasn't been quite so lucky. I think he's beginning to regret letting me stay.'

'Why?'

'Because he's hardly had any sleep since I arrived.'

Laura nodded her understanding. Her eyes had grown used to the low level of lighting and when she saw the shadows like bruises under his eyes and the tension around his jaw she chanced a question.

'I take it this is a relatively new problem?'

For nearly a minute she thought that he wasn't going to answer, and was beginning to feel embarrassed at her temerity in asking something so personal.

They might have 'met' on the stage last night but, in actual fact, their acquaintance was far too new for him to. . .

'Three months,' he said baldly, staring down at the linked hands hanging between his knees. He'd propped his elbows on his thighs, as though he needed them to help him remain upright, but now the slump of his shoulders just looked defeated. 'Nearly four, all told.'

Laura was silent, trying to work out the significance of the timing without having to ask.

He looked up at her and obviously saw the puzzlement on her face.

'I volunteered for a stint in a refugee camp—just a month, initially, to give one of the other medics a break.'

He mentioned the country, and Laura's eyes widened.

There had been so much in the news over the last couple of years about the atrocities committed in that region, including horrific attempts at wholesale genocide. She had never realised that people like Wolff were on the ground there, trying to take care of the people.

'It's a living nightmare,' he said hoarsely, as if the words were forcing their way out of him whether he wanted them to or not. 'During the summer it was so hot and dry that people were dropping like flies because of dehydration, dysentery. . .you name it and we had it. It's so overcrowded that there's no way of regulating sanitation and hygiene successfully.'

He drew in a shuddering breath, as though he were drawing in strength to continue.

'It felt as if we were starting to get things a bit better organised, and I volunteered to stay on to see the job through.' His laugh was short and harsh and directed at himself.

'Then the autumn rains came, and when the temperature began to drop and the winds started blowing it wasn't long before they started dying of hypothermia. . . Then the bastards started shooting at them. . .men, women, little children. . .they didn't care. . .'

He shook his head, an expression of utter desperation on his face as he looked up at her with eyes full of unspeakable memories before he looked away—his gaze once more fixed on his knotted fingers.

She longed to be able to step forward and take him in her arms to give him some measure of comfort, but she didn't have the right.

All she could do was offer him some space while he gathered his composure so she turned towards the kettle in the corner.

'I was just going to make myself a coffee before I went

back to my room. Decaffeinated. Would you like one?'

'Ah, Laura, I think I've got beyond that.' He laughed wryly. 'I've tried staying awake to stop me dreaming about it and I've tried various ways of knocking myself out, starting with hot milky drinks right up through alcohol and drugs.'

'Not together!' Laura exclaimed in horror, wondering just how terrible his memories were that he would think of taking such chances.

'I might be desperate for a good night's sleep but I'm not terminally stupid,' he replied shortly.

'I'm sorry. I didn't mean to suggest. . .'

'No,' he interrupted with a grimace as he straightened up out of his seat, '*I'm* sorry for jumping down your throat. It was probably a reasonable question, given the way I look at the moment. Can we blame exhaustion for my lack of equanimity?'

The kettle began to hiss and Laura turned away from the all-too-attractive sight of a sleepily rumpled Wolff Bergen to reach for two mugs.

'Black?' she asked as she twisted the lid off the coffee granules.

'Actually, I think I'll go back to Leo's place, if you don't mind. Perhaps I'll be able to get some sleep before he finishes his shift, then it won't matter so much if I have to stay awake to give him a chance to sleep.'

'Good idea.' Laura smiled as she screwed the lid back on the jar again, deliberately ignoring the swift stab of disappointment that their time together was over so quickly.

She watched silently as he patted his pockets until he heard the jingle of keys and smiled in answer to his tired grin of victory.

'Well, we'll probably see each other at some stage tomorrow,' he said as he reached the door, then he paused and turned back to her, the lean planes of his face highlighted by the brighter light streaming in over him from the corridor.

He gazed at her wordlessly for a moment, as if he was trying to find words, then smiled at her, his teeth impossibly white against the dark tan of his face and his expression impossibly gentle.

'Laura...thanks for listening. You'll never know how much talking about it has helped.' He drew in a slow breath and straightened his shoulders. 'You never know, I might even be able to get some sleep.'

'I hope so,' Laura said, her voice a little shaky with her reaction to the events of the last few minutes. 'Goodnight, Wolff.'

She watched him pull the door open wider and answered his brief salute as he left the room.

'Sleep well,' she whispered as she heard his footsteps recede along the corridor.

She finally slid down under the covers about an hour later with a glow of satisfaction at a job well done.

As she reached up to turn off the bedside light she cast one last look around the room and saw the few knick-knacks she'd collected, displayed on the dresser and window-sill, and knew that she'd done all she could to make her temporary abode welcoming.

At least now she wouldn't feel as if she was living out of a suitcase, and she could take her time about looking for accommodation further away from the hospital when she was ready. Hannah had promised to keep her ears open but there was no rush, especially when she was intending to stay at St Augustine's for the forseeable future.

With a soft click the room was plunged into darkness and she closed her eyes with a grateful sigh, welcoming the oblivion which was never long in coming...only this time, her brain didn't seem to want to switch off.

Hardly surprising, she snorted softly, when she thought about all the things that had happened since she arrived.

But even as she began to make a mental list of all the events which had bombarded her it was the face of one man which filled her mental vision.

Dr Wolff Bergen.

What was it about the man that she felt such a sense of connection?

For two years she'd had no difficulty keeping men at arm's length because she'd been all but unaware of them as anything other than colleagues at work. But there was something about Wolff Bergen...something special which had enabled him to break effortlessly through the wall she'd built around her emotions.

For two years she'd been able to live and work without letting anything touch her too deeply, but when she'd listened to his brief account of the last three months of his life she'd been unable to prevent herself from feeling the pain she heard in his voice.

And it wasn't just Wolff Bergen, the caring doctor, who affected her, nor the fact that he had the lean grace and power of the wild animal he was named for... It wasn't even the fact that he danced better than Patrick Swayze...

Her cheeks grew warm in the darkness when she remembered how it had felt to be held so close to his body that they had seemed to become part of each other, swaying in complete harmony as if the dance had been a vertical prelude to a more ancient horizontal dance...

Shocked by the suddenly explicit pictures flooding her brain, she opened her eyes wide and stared up at the plain white ceiling above her bed. She was horribly conscious of the fact that her pulse was galloping at the base of her throat and her ragged breathing was causing an exquisite friction between her tightly furled nipples and the soft knitted fabric of the oversized T-shirt she wore to bed.

That was just a sample of the chaos which Wolff was causing in her life.

It was a long time since she'd allowed herself to think and feel like a woman, and in the space of twenty-four hours the man had managed to make her all too aware of her feminine side.

She flounced over in the bed and thumped her pillow, wondering if he was having any more luck than she was at falling asleep, before she determinedly banished him from her thoughts.

Tomorrow was soon enough to let the dratted man into her head again. Tonight she needed to sleep or she'd never be able do do her job properly.

A quick glance at the board when she scooted past on her way to get rid of her damp parka gave Laura the unwelcome news that Wolff was starting his shift at the same time as she was, and she groaned silently to herself.

If she hadn't known that the rotas were worked out in advance she would almost have suspected Hannah of engineering the amount of time she and Wolff seemed to have spent together since he'd arrived.

She'd be glad when Nick Prince and his bride returned

from their honeymoon. At least it would mean that there was one less chance that she'd be rostered at the same time as Wolff.

It wasn't that he was a bad doctor, she mused as she tried to calm a hysterical woman. On the contrary, the way he was dealing with the severe asthma attack from which the woman's four-year-old son was suffering was ample evidence that he was very good.

Almost as soon as the mother had run into the department with the youngster in her arms Wolff had recognised the symptoms, grabbed an oxygen mask and slipped the elastic over the back of the child's head to hold it in position.

'Nebuliser,' he rapped out urgently while he was checking the child's abnormally slow pulse and his almost non-existent breathing.

Laura was already reaching for the unit, knowing that he was going to need it to administer the life-saving drugs directly into the child's lungs like an aerosol. Only then would the dangerous spasms be released so that the boy could draw in the air he needed.

'Connect the unit to oxygen rather than compressed air,' Wolff directed as he added the correct quantity of bronchodilator to the normal saline in the compact machine and set the delivery rate.

While he was busy with that Laura was able to tape a butterfly needle in position on the back of the little chubby hand, and by the time Wolff straightened up from his task the microdrip administration set was ready to begin IV rehydration.

For all the severity of the child's condition on arrival, it wasn't long before the drug regimen had started to take effect.

'Right, Staff, if you can give a ring up to the children's ward and warn them that we've got a customer for them,' Wolff began, only to be interrupted by the child's mother.

'You're keeping him here?' she said with renewed fear in her voice. 'What's happening? Is he getting worse?'

'Not at all,' Wolff soothed with a smile. 'He's doing very well.'

'Well, why does he need to stay, then? Why can't I take him home?'

'I'd like him to stay for a little while for observation— just to make sure the drugs have done the job. If all goes well you'll probably be able to take him home later today.'

'But I'm supposed to be going to work later. . .I can't afford to wait.'

Laura was struck by the woman's apparently callous words. She'd been watching the way the mother's eyes had followed every move they'd made in their efforts to help her son and she'd been convinced that she really cared for him, but just now she'd sounded as if he was the least of her concerns.

If Laura hadn't been watching her so closely she wouldn't have seen the way her skin had paled and the way the expression in her eyes made her look like a trapped animal.

'Is there no one else to stay with your little boy while you go to work?' she asked gently, leading her a little way away from the youngster so that she would feel more comfortable about talking.

'There's only Mum, and she can't manage to look after him for long—she's waiting to have a hip replacement. She usually comes in to listen for him when he's asleep.'

'What about taking a day off work?' Wolff suggested,

but almost before he'd finished speaking the young woman was shaking her head.

'Can't,' she said bluntly. 'If I miss one more day of work I'll lose my job, and there's only me to look after Toby. His dad did a runner as soon as he knew I was pregnant.'

'Well, we'll have to see if we can sort something out with the children's ward,' Wolff said, his frown of disgust at the absent father's behaviour slow to fade. 'Perhaps they'll be able to keep him in overnight so you can collect him when you finish work in the morning. . . It will depend on how many beds there are free. . .'

His voice faded as he led the woman away towards Sister MacDonald's office, and Laura realised that he was going to hand her into that formidable woman's capable care.

Young Toby had barely disappeared into the lift, whisking him away to the paediatric ward, when the priority message came through from the ambulance centre.

'Five injuries from a robbery in the centre of town. One passer-by shot. Cranial injury. ETA seven minutes.'

CHAPTER FIVE

'ALERT X-ray and the labs, and make sure the ventilator is ready.'

'How much O-negative blood have we got on hand until we can get him cross-matched?'

'Contact someone from Neurosurgery and warn Theatre. They may not have much time to prepare if he needs to go straight up.'

'Draw some drugs up so they're ready to go—I'll need lignocaine for premedication, etomidate for anaesthetic and succinylcholine to speed intubation. I'll sort out the doses in a minute.'

The questions and orders emerged in an almost unbroken stream as the department was readied for the arrival of the injured, and by the time the approaching siren's ululation was cut off they were waiting by the door.

The double doors at the back of the ambulance swung wide and the trolley emerged as if jet-propelled, one uniformed attendant holding up IV bags while he kept pace with the swiftly moving cortège.

'He needs to be intubated,' one of the paramedics said. 'He's breathing on his own—just—but he doesn't sound good and he's unresponsive to stimuli. There was a stray gunshot during a robbery and he had the bad luck to be in the way. The injuries on the other four are mainly from flying glass and shock.'

He was only young, Laura saw as she looked down at

the poor man, struggling to draw a ragged breath then exhaling with a strange sobbing whistle.

Just twenty-two, the paramedic confirmed, and while he was swiftly transferred from the ambulance trolley the frantically moving staff who surrounded him were very careful not to touch the side of his head covered by the blood-soaked dressing.

One pair of hands was swiftly stripping his clothing away while another was slotting X-ray cassettes into position, ready for the first shot to be taken.

A mask connected to the piped oxygen supply was held tightly over his face to try to get as much of the precious element into him as possible before he was intubated, while additional IV's were being started and a detailed examination was being made of the rest of his body for other injuries.

Laura continued to monitor the patient's pulse and respiration as the correct doses of drugs were injected to sedate and paralyse his injured body for intubation, and soon saw him become flaccid and stop breathing.

The cervical collar had been opened at the front to aid the positioning of the laryngoscope and, with an expertise which spoke of much practice, Wolff began to slide the instrument into position.

'Can't see a thing,' he muttered, and there was a brief pause to suction blood and saliva away before he could see the vocal cords and finish positioning the laryngoscope.

'Tube,' he said, one hand reaching blindly.

Laura had it in her hand, ready and waiting, and within seconds he had passed it down into the trachea.

'Oxygen,' he ordered briskly, then listened to the sounds in the young man's chest for a minute to confirm that the tube had been positioned correctly before he straightened up.

'Hyperventilate to reduce swelling of the brain,' he directed as the O-negative blood was hung and a catheter inserted to drain his bladder. Then an orogastric tube was snaked past the endotracheal tube and down into the stomach to empty out the contents.

At intervals there was the familiar sound of the X-ray machine taking another of a series of shots of the skull and neck but it happened almost without comment, all of them so familiar with the signals that they were able to remain intent upon their own tasks.

'Blood pressure's stable but his Glasgow coma scale score was very low,' Laura heard Wolff say to the neurosurgeon as they stood in front of the X-ray view-box and he clipped the plates into position with a practised flick of the wrist.

'His whole skull is unstable—it looks as if the shock wave from the impact of the bullet has cracked it in five or six places.'

'God knows what sort of damage it's done to the brain itself, then,' Wolff's deeper voice commented.

'Quite. That's why I need to get him up to Theatre as soon as possible. I need to get a tube into the ventricles of his brain to relieve the pressure there—just in case,' his colleague replied, and they turned back towards the still, silent figure on the table.

'Just in case' his brain swelled as a result of the trauma, Laura interpreted, and, at the same time, 'just in case' he survived, in which case they didn't want to chance further brain damage from uncontrolled swelling.

Once again there was concerted activity as he was prepared for the journey upstairs, with notes, IV bags, oxygen and monitors stacked around his deathly still figure on the trolley.

Their hands moved with familiar speed and efficiency. There was no need to speak, the only sounds intruding on the edges of their concentration being the rhythmic bleep of the cardiac monitor and the suck-and-blow of the ventilator.

The room had hardly had time to be cleared of the debris when the phone rang.

'Damn.'

Wolff's muttered curse might just as well have been shouted for the impact it had on the remaining staff.

'No good?' Laura queried when he put the phone down, but the expression on his face had already told her the worst.

'He got the tube in but instead of clear cerebrospinal fluid the tube delivered chunks of brain matter.'

Laura's shoulders slumped. She knew as well as anyone in the room that this result meant that the young man's brain had been hopelessly damaged—and all because he'd been in the wrong place at the wrong time.

'Have we managed to trace any family?' Wolff asked. He was obviously thinking ahead to the task of explaining what had happened to the young man, and Laura could see the tension tightening his jaw. It was one part of his job which she would never envy.

'I'll find out,' Laura volunteered, and reached for the phone to connect her to Celia MacDonald. If anyone knew she would.

Within minutes she had the answer.

'They've contacted his parents—they're on their way

in. He was carrying a donor card and had put his name on the organ donor register.'

'Good lad,' Wolff said softly, a sad smile creasing the corners of his eyes. 'Now we've got the job of consulting his parents for confirmation that we can plan to harvest his organs but, hopefully, if he'd told them about his wishes...'

He stripped off his disposable apron and dumped it in the bin, then slid his arms into a fresh white coat.

'Sometimes I wonder why I chose this job,' he murmured as if he were talking to himself. 'So many of them never get a second chance.'

While Wolff talked to the bereaved parents in the small interview room Laura's work went on as she helped to take care of the other victims of the incident.

It was painstaking work to make a good job of repairing the numerous lacerations, caused by flying plate glass, and several of the cuts were very deep.

'I never was much of an oil painting,' commented one gentleman as the last of several dozen tiny stitches was put into a jagged wound down the side of his face.

'Well, once the stitches come out and the scar has had a little time to fade perhaps you'll be able to tell people it's a war wound,' Leo suggested.

'Better still, be mysterious and don't say where you got it,' Laura advised with a grin. 'Most women are a pushover for a wounded hero.'

'Really?' Their patient sounded sceptical.

'Of course,' she assured him, knowing that he really *wanted* to believe what she was telling him. 'You only have to look at the world's great literature—Jane Eyre's Mr Rochester must be one of the most famous.'

'Anyway,' Leo added, 'I've done my best to make certain that it heals neatly.'

'So I won't frighten the horses?'

'Or children and women of a sensitive disposition,' Leo confirmed with a grin as he taped a protective dressing over his handiwork. 'And if you can give yourself a vitamin boost to help your body heal quickly you'll soon be on form again.'

Laura escorted the gentleman towards the reception area and walked over to see who was next.

'One more for stitching?' she asked, and was handed the outpatient details.

Automatically she glanced down at them, read the phrase 'hit by a candelabrum' and blinked, the corners of her mouth curling up with the threat of a smile.

'Which one is he?' she enquired, hoping that her attack of humour would be under control before she had to face the man at close quarters.

'He's the one sitting round the corner out of sight,' the clerk told her in a grim mutter, not a smile in sight.

'You'll recognise him because he's the one handcuffed to the policeman.'

'Handcuffed. . .?' Laura was startled.

Suddenly she guessed who their next patient was, but that still didn't tell her how he'd come to be injured.

'A candelabrum?' she murmured, her mind boggling.

'It was a jeweller's shop he was trying to rob, and when the plate glass shattered one of the staff was quick-witted enough to grab a silver candelabrum and knock the beggar for six.'

Laura had been hoping to explain the circumstances to Leo before he was confronted by his next patient—just in case anyone made any unfortunate comments—but when she walked in it was Wolff waiting in the room.

He looked terrible, his face almost grey in spite of the deep colour he still sported from his time abroad, and his eyes had gone that empty icy colour again.

Laura's heart went out to him, especially when he saw who his next patient was. If he gritted his teeth any harder they would shatter.

She could only guess how the interview with the young man's parents had gone and, with the glowering young man in front of him being the cause of the tragedy, this was hardly the time to ask whether they'd had permission...

On second thoughts, she mused, remembering Wolff's anger at his feeling of helplessness in the face of the refugees' suffering, perhaps this was *exactly* the right time to ask about it.

'Did you see his parents?' she said quietly as she placed the suture tray ready. She'd already pulled a seat across so that the policeman could stay beside his charge and yet not get in the way.

Wolff was silent for a moment, a questioning expression on his face as he gazed at her. He knew that it was unlike her to talk about one patient while in the room with another, and he was obviously puzzled.

Laura flicked a glance down at the patient waiting for his attention and raised an eyebrow, knowing how quick on the uptake he usually was.

She saw the expression on his face change and he nodded briefly.

'Yes. I saw his parents,' he confirmed in an icily quiet voice as he reached for the prepared syringe and began to inject around the edges of the wound high up on the man's forehead to deaden it, ready for cleaning and stitching. 'Obviously they were devastated. He'd only told them yesterday that he was going to get engaged, and he was apparently looking at the rings in the jeweller's window.'

Laura knew from the way the policeman's head jerked towards them that he'd made the connection between their conversation and his prisoner, and the way that surly young man stiffened told them all that he'd understood, too.

'Did you ask them whether they were going to allow us to use his body for organ donation?' she asked after a brief pause.

'Yes. I asked,' he said gruffly. 'They knew that he carried a donor card but they hadn't realised—or didn't remember—that he'd filled in the form to be put on the organ donor register.'

'Did they give consent in the end?'

Her question seemed to hang in the air above their sullen patient, his pale brown eyes darting from one to the other as he waited silently for the reply.

'They did,' Wolff confirmed, then paused to position another stitch. 'The labs are doing the cross-matching and tissue-typing at the moment, and there's a computer search ready to run to match up with potential recipients.'

He snipped the thread and glanced up at Laura, totally ignoring the patient lying frozen with apprehension under the poised needle as he continued.

'Even though he's dead they're keeping his body alive on the life-support machine to keep it fresh until they get the go-ahead,' he said.

For just a second Laura wondered why Wolff was telling her something which she already knew, then she realised that he was pitching the level of his explanation so that the rest of his audience would be in no doubt about what was happening.

'If everything goes well they'll get the temperature-controlled containers ready and begin harvesting. We should be able to make use of his kidneys, his heart, his liver, his lungs, his pancreas, his corneas and maybe even some sections of his bones and strips of skin for grafting—I understand there are several programmes where they're experimenting with transplanting whole joints rather than using artificial ones.'

'My God!' croaked the man on the table under Wolff's hands, his face absolutely green with nausea as a result of their deliberately gruesome conversation. 'You're sick! You're talking about chopping him up as if you're butchers with a piece of meat!'

'Oh, no, sunshine!' Wolff said with bitter emphasis, the loathing in his icy blue eyes utterly intimidating as he bent forward again with his needle. '*We're* not the butchers...*We* didn't kill him. We're just trying to minimise the senseless waste of his life!'

The rest of the stitching was achieved in total silence, the young thug gazing up in terror at the icy disdain in Wolff's eyes as he finished the job with his usual attention to detail.

'You can take him away now,' Wolff directed the uniformed policeman as he stood up and stripped his gloves off. 'He won't need to come back here to have the stitches taken out—unless we're the closest hospital to whichever prison he's sent to.'

He glared down at the cowering lout one last time.

'All I can say to you is that while you're locked up I hope you think about some way of making your life count for something. Having killed someone, I reckon that means that you've got twice as much good to do in the world to make up for it.'

A shiver worked its way up the back of Laura's neck as she watched him stalk out of the room. She could almost feel the pain radiating from him, and if he'd been holding his spine any more rigidly it would have snapped.

For the rest of his shift he seemed very subdued, in spite of the fact that Leo had begun regaling the rest of the staff with anecdotes of the things the two of them had got up to when they'd been in medical school.

Laura took everything with a large pinch of salt, far more interested in watching Wolff's reaction to the stories than in the content of them.

One thing she noticed was that most of the tales either concerned feats of physical daring—such as the time-honoured placing of a bedpan on top of the ornamental cupola over the principal's office—or involved copious quantities of semi-naked females—such as the equally time-honoured setting-off of the fire alarm in the nurses' home at dead of night, much to the delight of the rest of the waiting camera-wielding male medical students.

While Wolff bore it all with a smile and the odd quiet disclaimer, Laura had the feeling that it was not so much equanimity which was helping him to cope with it as the fact that his thoughts were elsewhere.

She had just finished her shift and was on her way to collect her belongings before she made a quick dash out to the shops for some coffee and milk when she passed the door of the staffroom.

Several paces further along the corridor it dawned on

her that there had been someone standing in the dimly lit room, his figure faintly outlined against the window.

She paused a second then shook her head. For heaven's sake, she'd known the man for less than three days. There was no way that she could possibly recognise him from such a brief glance.

Her curiosity wouldn't let her continue on her way, though, and she found herself retracing her steps to the door and peering through the panel of safety glass.

The thump of recognition her heart gave was confirmation enough and, almost without realising that she'd done it, she saw her hand come up to push the door open and then she was walking in.

He was so still that she didn't think he'd heard her come in until his husky voice reached her, then she realised that he must have seen her reflection in the glass.

'Have you come to join me for a coffee?' he asked, and she willingly took the question as an invitation, making straight for the kettle and switching it on.

She turned to face him and realised that he hadn't moved. He was still facing the window, staring out at the dirty yellow tinge of the pseudo night sky with his hands wrapped around a mug.

'Is yours fresh or do you want a top-up?' she asked, marvelling that she had recognised him with so few clues to go on. She would almost defy a sophisticated computer to do better. . .

'Actually, I was just thinking that I don't want to be here but that I don't seem to have the energy or the inclination to move.'

Laura's heart sank into her eminently comfortable shoes with a sickening thud.

'You mean you're regretting coming to St Augustine's?' she enquired, almost holding her breath as she waited for his reply. Did this mean that as soon as Nick Prince returned he would be leaving? And why did it matter so much to her—he was just another doctor, wasn't he?

'At this precise moment, yes,' he admitted gruffly. 'But what I really meant was that I need to get out of here before the walls start closing in on me.'

'In which case,' Laura began as she reached across and switched off the kettle before it could come to the boil, 'let's sneak out before anyone notices we're going. You have finished your shift, haven't you?'

'And handed over,' he confirmed, turning towards her with a slightly arrested expression on his face. 'Where do you suggest we go?'

'Well, *I'm* going to that little corner shop in the side road behind the hospital. I need to get some milk and some coffee or I won't be able to get my eyes open tomorrow.'

She let the words die away while she waited to see what he would say.

Part of her wanted to invite him to come with her—to walk to the shop and then accompany her to her room to drink a cup of the coffee she was buying—but the habits of two years were hard to break. She couldn't afford to let anybody get too close—it hurt too much when they left. . .

'Would you mind having some company?' he asked, his tone unexpectedly hesitant. 'I don't usually let it get to me, but after that young man with the bullet. . .'

She'd had a feeling that his mood was somehow connected with that particular patient, out of all the ones he'd seen today, and that it was also connected to the things he'd seen while he'd been volunteering his time and expertise at the refugee camp.

'No problem,' she agreed easily as she turned away and began to walk towards the door, grateful that he couldn't see the idiotic grin which had just covered her face and the sudden leap in her pulse rate. 'It will be nice to have someone to talk to while I unwind.'

It was the work of seconds to grab her big puffy parka and her bag from her locker, and then they were walking out through the big automatic doors and into the dark of the November evening.

Much as Laura would have liked to prolong their time together, it was too cold to do anything but walk briskly. All too soon she had her purchases in her bag and it was time to go back to her room.

'You wouldn't. . .?'

'Could I. . .?'

They both began to speak at the same time, then both halted and laughed.

'Ladies first,' Wolff offered with an attempt at a smile, his teeth gleaming briefly in the shadows between two streetlights.

'I was only going to ask if you would like to join me for a cup of coffee,' she said, trying to sound as if his answer didn't really matter.

In actual fact, she had grown quite concerned when he'd hardly spoken during their walk. There was something weighty on his mind, and if there was any way she could help. . .

'I'd like that—in fact, that was what I was going to ask,' he said quietly, and gestured for her to walk beside him again.

The dimly lit lounge area of the nurses' accommodation was occupied by several people watching a situation comedy on the television so Laura's first choice of venue for their coffee had to be abandoned. If Wolff *did* decide that he needed to talk he wouldn't want an audience.

'We might as well drink it in my room,' Laura suggested quietly as she handed him one mug.

She turned away quickly, her cheeks glowing as she mentally crossed her fingers in the hope that they were all too engrossed in their programme to notice what was happening around them.

Still, it would be worth a little embarrassment if she could get him to relax enough to forget about whatever was playing so heavily on his mind.

She might not think it worth the price when any nurses who had noticed her disappearing towards her room with the newest and handsomest doctor on the staff started pulling her leg, but for the moment she didn't care what they thought.

By the time Laura had shut the door to her room and turned back to face Wolff he had slipped his jacket off and was standing at the foot of her bed, his mug of coffee all but forgotten as he gazed around at the small array of knick-knacks in the soft illumination of the bedside light.

'Make yourself comfortable,' she invited as she hung her own parka on the back of the door, before sitting on the edge of the only comfortable chair in the room.

Wolff took her words to heart and immediately appropriated her bed.

'Ah, bliss,' he groaned as he eased himself down onto the pile of colourful throw pillows stacked against the headboard and sprawled the rest of his long lean body bonelessly on the mattress like a lazy cat.

There was a long silence while they sipped their drinks, but it didn't feel uncomfortable. In fact, Laura was amazed just how comfortable she felt with Wolff in her room. Somehow it almost felt as if he belonged. . .

She heard him sigh deeply and her eyes were drawn to his face, unsurprised when it seemed as if he hadn't even realised that he'd made the sound—his coffee forgotten as he balanced it on his washboard-flat stomach.

Once again he was wearing that awful withdrawn expression, and she mentally crossed her fingers before she began to speak.

'Did today bring it back?' she ventured, and watched him blink while he focused on her words.

'The refugee camp? All too clearly,' he said, the corners of his mobile mouth pulling down in a grimace.

If he was surprised that she had followed his train of thought he didn't say so.

'Imagine today's event multiplied by ten, by twenty, and you'll have some idea of what it was like on a daily basis while the camp was being shelled. . .' He drew in another shuddering breath and shook his head.

'We didn't manage to save that young lad today in spite of unlimited medical supplies, personnel and all our sophisticated technology. Out there they don't stand a chance.'

Laura saw the darkness fill his eyes as the memories took over, and she couldn't remain sitting on the other side of the room with a mug in her hand as if she didn't care.

She wasn't even certain if he'd noticed when she perched on the edge of the bed beside him, but when she gently covered his clenched fist with one hand and relieved his other one of the forgotten coffee he stared at her as if he'd never seen her before.

'Ah, Laura, you can't imagine the things I saw,' he whispered, his husky voice sounding as if it was having to fight its way out through the tightness in his throat. 'You can't imagine how utterly frustrating it was to have to stand by and watch those defenceless people being systematically maimed and murdered. It didn't matter what I did—there weren't any second chances.'

He closed his eyes briefly but shook his head and opened them again as if he couldn't bear what he could see behind his eyelids.

'And every time you close your eyes you relive it all over again, especially after cases like today's,' she murmured softly, somehow knowing that it was true. 'And, gradually, because the nightmares keep waking you up you get more and more tired until you begin to feel like a rat caught in a trap with no way out.'

He gazed at her silently, and when she saw the thoughtful expression creep across his face she realised that her ready empathy had told him that she, too, was haunted by demons.

She tensed, dreading the moment when he asked her to explain—but it never came.

'Ah, Laura,' he murmured on a sigh as he wrapped one arm around her shoulders and pulled her closer.

Off balance on the squashy edge of the mattress, Laura couldn't stop herself toppling towards him and she ended up sprawled halfway across his chest.

For a moment she couldn't help the fact that the unexpected contact with the solid warmth of his body made every muscle grow tense, but when it became obvious that he only wanted to hold her for their mutual comfort she finally allowed herself to relax.

Gradually she became aware of a multitude of apparently insignificant details—such as the lingering scent of soap or aftershave she could detect on his skin, overlying his own musky warmth, and the teasing drift of his breath as it drifted over one side of her face.

His chest was broad, the fine white cotton of his shirt smooth under her cheek. Beneath the cotton there was the steady drumbeat of his heart.

When Wolff woke up it took him several seconds to work out exactly where he was, and less than one second more to decide that he liked being there.

Over the last few months it seemed as if he'd hardly spent any time settled in one place, and hardly more than a couple of nights in the same bed.

He glanced across at the bedside light and caught sight of the time shown by little alarm clock beside it with disbelief. If the glowing green figures could be believed he had just slept for seven hours without even a hint of a nightmare to disturb him.

Wolff felt a smile creep over his face as he looked down at the woman curled up beside him. The bed was so narrow that there was only room for the two of them when he held her tightly against his side, but he wasn't going to complain.

He tilted his head to get a better view of her face and marvelled at her elfin prettiness. She could only be about three or four inches above five feet, far smaller and daintier than his own six feet, but she had a strength of will and purpose big enough for an Amazon.

He frowned when he remembered the odd occasions when he'd seen hints of an enduring pain in her eyes. Last night he'd longed to ask her about her demons, had hoped that when he'd told her about his own that she would volunteer the information so that he could comfort her...but he could wait.

They hadn't known each other very long—he snorted softly; they didn't really know each other at all—but for the first time in his life he felt as if he'd found someone who understood how he thought and felt...

It was a slightly scary thought...almost as scary as the fact that for the first time since he'd arrived in that hell-hole of a camp he had actually slept deeply and dreamlessly, and the only reason he could see was the endearingly rumpled sprite who slept with her arms wrapped around him like a treasured teddy bear.

He looked down at her again, his eyes charting the shape of her face with its high cheek-bones, slightly pointed chin and the feathery blonde hair lying in wisps across her forehead.

Her eyelashes were several shades darker and cast fan-like shadows onto the soft peach bloom of her cheeks. And when they opened they would reveal eyes of such a dark green that the first time he'd seen them—when she'd joined him on the stage at that wretched ball—he'd thought they were black.

It wasn't until he'd turned her towards the light during that mind-boggling dance that he'd realised that they were green and all but shooting daggers at him.

He hadn't been able to resist taking advantage of the situation with that mad impulsive kiss, and he'd wondered several times whether that was the reason she'd been so wary around him.

Now that he knew that she was living with shadows too he was determined to take things slowly, to build up a friendship between them so that she would eventually learn to trust him enough to tell him about her pain.

His eyes focused on her soft pink lips and he remembered how they had responded to him, hotly and wildly, and he registered the swift reaction of his body with a silent groan.

He tightened his arm around her briefly, loath to let her go, but he had a feeling that it would be bad enough if Laura woke up to find that they'd slept together all night— no matter how innocently—without discovering that he was rampantly ready to destroy any semblance of that innocence.

CHAPTER SIX

'LAURA?'

The call was accompanied by a brisk tap on the door and Laura rolled over groggily.

'Come in,' she called, still more asleep than awake, as she glanced towards her alarm clock.

'Lazybones!' Hannah scolded cheerfully. 'You're usually up and ready by now. What happened? Did you forget to set your alarm? And why are you still dressed in yesterday's uniform?'

Laura glanced down at herself, and when she saw the way her bedspread was tucked around her crumpled form she suddenly remembered what had happened last night.

'I. . .er. . .must have fallen asleep before I had time to get ready for bed,' she mumbled as she dragged strangely shaky fingers through her tousled hair. She hoped fervently that the light in the room was too dim, and Hannah too busy with her barrage of questions, to notice that her face had just grown scarlet.

What *had* happened last night? All she could remember was curling up against Wolff in the close confines of the narrow bed. How long had he stayed? What had he thought when she. . .?

'Well, I hope you slept well,' Hannah continued brightly, 'because you've got just fifteen minutes before you're due on duty.'

'What? I'll never make it!'

Laura scrambled to her feet and looked wildly around the room, trying to decide what to do first.

'Oh, for goodness' sake!' Hannah said in exasperation. 'Have your shower and get dressed. I'll make you some coffee to see if we can jump-start your brain.'

'Thanks, Hannah. I don't know how I can have forgotten to set the alarm. . .'

She crossed her fingers superstitiously as she voiced the lie. She knew only too well how she'd come to forget to set her alarm. Once she'd been wrapped in Wolff's arms, with her head resting over the reassuring beat of his heart, the last thing she'd been thinking about was setting her alarm for work the next morning. She'd felt so comfortable and secure that for the first time in ages she'd slept as soundly as a baby.

So soundly, she thought exasperatedly as her mind went round in ever-decreasing circles, like the soapy water going down the drain, that she had no idea what time he had left her.

What must he have thought when she'd fallen asleep on him like that? She'd hardly been the most entertaining company. . .

'Here you are,' Hannah announced as she arrived with a steaming mug of coffee and a pile of hot buttered toast. 'Get some of that inside you.' She reached out and grabbed one slice for herself, and sat herself on the end of Laura's bed to watch her play the hairdryer over her wet hair.

'Thank you,' Laura mumbled around a crunchy mouthful. 'How am I doing for time?'

'OK so far. Keep going.' She retrieved Laura's shoes from under the end of her bed and nudged them towards her feet. 'It's not like you to be so disorganised,' she commented. 'You must have been very tired.'

'I certainly slept well,' Laura confirmed honestly. Well, it was true. She'd slept better in Wolff's arms that she had in...well, in years.

'Have you forgotten anything? Watch? Belt?' Hannah prompted.

'Brain?' Laura joked through the last mouthful of toast and chewed frantically, with the second half of her mug of coffee waiting to follow it down.

'All I can say is that it's a good thing that you're on half-day today,' Hannah teased. 'Perhaps your brain will catch up and you'll be firing on all cylinders by tomorrow!'

She continued to tease Laura all the way across to the A and E department, only allowing her to escape when Sister MacDonald wanted a word with her.

Laura had dumped her belongings in her locker and was on her way back to the reception area when Wolff appeared in the doorway of the kitchenette with a steaming mug in his hand.

Her eyes flicked over him in a lightning survey, noting with more than a spark of interest that while his clothes were different from those he'd worn yesterday his dark hair was nearly black with the remaining dampness from his own shower—and there was a tiny razor cut on the edge of his jaw, as if he'd had to shave in a hurry this morning.

'Good morning, sir,' she said, hoping that he couldn't hear the quiver of apprehension in her voice and that her face wasn't as hot as it felt.

So far, she hadn't had time to speak to anyone in the nurses' accommodation so no one had commented on the fact that she'd taken him up to her room last night, but she still wasn't confident that they hadn't been observed.

'Well, that answers one question,' he murmured in a husky voice, a teasing glint in his eyes. 'You called me "sir" so that must mean you still respect me the morning after.'

'Wolff!' she muttered with a nervous glance each way along the corridor. 'You start saying things like that and who knows how they'd be interpreted if people overheard?'

'I'm sorry,' he said, but his grin was unrepentant and so infectious that she couldn't help smiling back. 'Anyway, I'm glad I've seen you.'

'Oh?' Her heart skipped a beat and settled into a faster rhythm in spite of her silent battle for control.

He bent towards her, lending an air of intimacy to their conversation, and she was surrounded by the same mixture of fresh soap and indefinable musk which instantly reminded her of how it had felt to be wrapped securely in his arms.

'There were two things I wanted to talk about. . . First, I wanted to thank you,' he murmured, the silvery blue of his eyes skating over her face with a tender touch. 'I can't remember when I last slept so well.'

'You slept, too?' she demanded softly, helpless to stop the pleased smile spreading over her face. 'I thought I was the only one to drop off, and I've spent the last half-hour worrying about how rude I was.'

'It's all right. . .you didn't snore,' he teased, and she felt her cheeks heating again at the intimacy of the comment.

'What was the second thing?' she prompted, not quite certain how to cope with this new playful version of the tightly wound Wolff Bergen she'd thought she was getting to know. She hadn't taken part in this sort of repartee for years—shouldn't be indulging in it now—but there was something about him which she found absolutely irresistible.

'I wanted to ask you a favour,' he replied with an expression which was just too guileless to be true. 'I saw on the rota that you're on half-day today...' He paused, with one eyebrow raised in a question.

'Yes, but...'

'In that case, I wondered if you'd keep me company while I look at some flats this afternoon,' he said diffidently.

'Me? But...' Laura was quite startled by the unexpected request.

'I feel that I've burdened Leo long enough,' he explained. 'Especially as he hasn't been getting much sleep since I moved in with him.'

'By all accounts, he doesn't get a lot of sleep when you *aren't* there,' she replied with her tongue firmly in her cheek. 'Are you sure this isn't a male solidarity thing, and you just don't want to cramp his style any longer?'

'Either way, I've lined up some properties to look at and I'd like your input,' he said, swiftly sidestepping her comments about Leo's love life.

'But why me?' Laura asked in confusion. 'I don't know what sort of thing you're looking for.'

'Nor do I—in detail,' he admitted. 'But last night, when I saw how comfortable and individual you'd made your room in the nurses' accommodation, I thought that you would be a good person to spot the possibilities in a place.'

'Well...' She was aware that he was using his praise of the touches she'd added to her room in a deliberate attempt to butter her up, but she was no more immune to praise than the next person.

'I haven't really had time to make many friends yet,' he continued softly. 'And Leo's on duty this afternoon, and it's so *boring* looking at places without a friend along to bounce ideas off...'

'All right! All right! Enough!' Laura begged with a laugh. 'I'll go with you, if only to prevent you having to invent another half a dozen reasons to make me agree.'

'Great!' he said with a smile. 'Where shall I meet you?'

'For heaven's sake!' she exclaimed in exasperation. 'We'll be working in the same department all morning. It's hardly likely that we'll lose track of each other by lunchtime! Now go and do some work!'

Laura sent him a mock glare and set off towards the reception area once more, only just managing to turn the corner before the urge to skip along the corridor was subdued under a broad smile.

She still wasn't quite certain why Wolff had gone to so much trouble to persuade her to go with him this afternoon. Did he have some nefarious scheme up his sleeve, such as the exotic dance scheme of Leo's, or did he genuinely think of her as a friend he could call upon to keep him company while he did a boring chore?

Her thoughts were going round and round in her head while she dealt with the usual mixture of ills and ailments brought to the A and E department on a frosty November morning.

Wolff was such an unlikely candidate for a friend, she mused as she watched a young Lolita try to chat him up while he was examining her for possible appendicitis.

From what the precocious youngster was saying, Laura

thought there was a good possibility that the painful episodes she was complaining about were the result of pelvic inflammatory disease at best, or one of the more serious sexually transmitted diseases at worst.

Laura hid a smile when she saw the way the back of Wolff's neck reddened when his young patient volunteered to spreadeagle herself for examination without a trace of embarrassment.

She also heard genuine relief in his voice when he told the forward young hussy that he was sending her up to the obstetrics and gynaecology department where any necessary tests would be performed.

Laura would have loved to have teased him about his endearing embarrassment, but there was no time. By the sound of running feet their next patient was already on her way into the emergency room, her terrified screams making all the hair stand up on the back of Laura's neck.

'Please. . . Help my little girl. She's burnt. . .'

It was the mother who burst into the room first, wild-eyed, with her child clutched in her arms.

'She fell over and her hand went on the fire. . .' reported the ambulanceman who had followed immediately behind her at a run, an IV bag held aloft and an Entonox cylinder under one arm. 'She's been fighting the Entonox mask all the way in. . .'

Almost before the words were out of his mouth Laura was reaching out towards Wolff with a hypodermic needle in one hand and a container of analgesic in the other, while the ambulanceman finally managed to place the Entonox mask over the child's nose and mouth.

The mother was standing just inside the door with her little girl clutched in her arms, as if she was too scared to let go of her, but it didn't make any difference to the speed of Wolff's reaction to the emergency.

The pain-relieving injection was administered almost before the child had realised what he was trying to do, and a second IV line was put in position and taped securely just in case they needed to increase her fluid intake in a hurry.

While Wolff was concerned with the chemical management of the child, trying to make certain that she didn't go into shock as a result of the trauma, Laura was giving the injured hand an extra-liberal coating of Water Jel and covering it with a fresh dressing.

'Can you bring her over to the table?' he asked the distraught mother over her child's pitiful cries, and he demonstrated how he wanted her to sit on the stool he usually used when he was in for a long stretch of stitching. She could then rest her daughter's weight on the supportive surface of the table while she could continue to reassure her with her encircling arms.

As the Entonox and analgesic began to work the poor scrap's blood-curdling shrieks slowly diminished into hiccuping sobs and whimpers.

The ambulanceman was finally able to make his full report, and when he left the room Laura saw him glance back sadly at his tiny passenger.

Wolff had examined the little hand as far as he could without disturbing the now-silent child too much, and he beckoned Laura across for a quick word.

'Will you monitor her while I speak to the burns unit?' he muttered. 'I've only had a quick look at the injury but I'm afraid that it's going to mean amputation so I want her looked at quickly.'

Laura nodded and watched as he spared a few seconds

to reassure the young mother and stroke the back of one finger over her child's tear-stained little cheek.

'She's only just learning to walk,' the young woman said when the doors swung closed behind Wolff. She looked up briefly from her pretty daughter, but was obviously desperate to talk. 'My boyfriend's mum bought her these new shoes and she wasn't used to them...'

Her throat closed up, preventing her from speaking for a moment, and Laura watched as she pressed her colourless lips tightly together in attempt to control her tears.

'I'd just taken the fireguard away to put some more coal on when she tripped over the edge of the rug in front of the fireplace and fell towards the flames. She put her hand out to try to save herself...I couldn't catch her in time to save her...'

She shook her head, unable to continue for the force of her silent sobs.

'Dr Bergen has gone to see how quickly they can get a bed ready for her in the children's burns unit,' Laura told her, knowing that she would want to know what was going on. 'As soon as he gets back he'll tell you what's happening.'

There was no reason to tell her that he'd left the room to make his call because he also wanted to tell the consultant how serious the injuries were—there was plenty of time for the poor woman to find that out.

'Will I be able to go up with her? She's never been away from me before.'

'Of course you can,' Laura reassured her as she checked the child's vital signs again, smiling at the solemn expression in her watchful hazel eyes. At least the analgesic meant that she wasn't in pain any more...

'They've even got a limited number of beds available so that you can stay overnight,' she added, remembering the special arrangements the hospital made for parents of their younger patients.

'Oh, thank you.' She drew in a shuddering breath, a little colour stealing its way back into her face.

'I don't know how I'm going to tell my boyfriend what's happened. He's working shifts, and if I'm not there when he gets home he's going to worry where we are.'

'Have you got a neighbour you can call?' Laura asked. 'Perhaps they'd be willing to give him a message for you?'

Ideally, Laura would have liked to be able to contact the young woman's boyfriend so that he could come straight to the hospital. She had a feeling that the mother was going to need all the support she could get if the injury was as serious as Wolff thought.

'The lady over the road might. . .' she was musing aloud as Wolff returned.

'It's all organised,' he announced with a reassuring smile on his face. 'There's a bed on the unit and it will be ready and waiting by the time the two of you get up there.'

As he spoke a porter came through the door, pushing a wheelchair, and in no time they had her sitting in the chair with her daughter cradled safely in her arms.

Wolff gave a final check of the child's vital signs, filled in his findings on her chart and then draped the IV bags over the porter's shoulder ready for the journey.

'Good luck,' Laura murmured with a consoling squeeze of the woman's slender shoulder as she was wheeled away. 'They'll do everything they can for her.'

'How bad do you think it is?'

Laura couldn't help asking, wondering just what sort of

handicap the little scrap was going to have to grow up with.

'It looks as if she gripped the hot bar at the top of the fender in front of the hearth when she fell because at least two fingers received full-thickness burns. They'll probably have to take both of them away because they're too badly injured to survive and they daren't risk gangrene.'

'And the rest of the hand?' Laura asked, feeling slightly sick.

'She'll have scarring on the other fingers where they were seared by the heat but, with any luck, they'll still be viable.' His expression was grim. 'I suppose the only good thing we can say about it is that at least she didn't land on her face.'

Laura shuddered at the thought.

'Her poor mother is never going to be able to forgive herself,' she murmured as she completed the tidying-up routine. 'Every time she sees her daughter's little hand she's going to blame herself for not catching her in time.'

Wolff murmured his agreement and sighed.

'I'm ready for a break,' he said, and when Laura looked up at the clock on the wall she realised that she was due a few minutes off too.

'Whose turn is it to put the kettle on?' she asked, still subdued by the sadness of their last case.

'Mine, I think,' he said as he pushed the door open for her and they stepped out into the corridor.

'Doctor?' Celia MacDonald's familiar Scots accent floated along the corridor towards them. 'Could you come here a minute, please?'

Wolff grimaced and shrugged wryly.

'Obviously there's no peace for the wicked,' he grumbled as he set off after the senior sister.

'Do you want me to come, too?' Laura offered. The thought of a cup of coffee wasn't nearly as enticing if she wasn't going to be sharing Wolff's company at the same time.

'Please,' Wolff said with a smile, and Laura's heart grew just a little bit lighter.

'This is Sharron Ferguson,' Big Mac announced when they joined her in the far treatment room. 'She's fourteen years old and weighs twenty-two stones. This. . .' she indicated an even more gargantuan figure overflowing a chair beside the trolley '. . .is her mother.'

The introductions were interrupted by a rising moan from the daughter who writhed awkwardly, rather like a beached whale.

While Wolff read the notes Laura busied herself by gathering an examining tray and a fresh set of gloves until Sister MacDonald could make herself heard again.

'As you can see, she's suffering intermittent abdominal pain of rising severity. She's menstruating at the moment and she's never been sexually active.'

When she heard the last two details Laura's first guess—that the obese youngster was in labour—had to be replaced with several other possibilities.

Perhaps she had eaten something to which she had an allergy, or was very constipated or had some other form of bowel obstruction. Or it might be that her appendix was either about to rupture or had already done so, and she was starting to suffer the symptoms of peritonitis.

She listened while Wolff questioned the girl, watching him grow steadily more frustrated when her mother answered every question and gave him little or no useful information.

He'd waited until she was between bouts of pain before he tried to palpate the tender region of her stomach, but Laura could tell from the expression on his face that the girl was so grossly overweight that he couldn't determine anything helpful.

'So, Sharron,' he recapped after several minutes, 'you've been in pain intermittently for about twelve hours and you've been sick a couple of times. You've never been pregnant...'

'How could she have been pregnant when no one's ever touched her...down there?' interrupted her mother belligerently. 'I've told you. She only started her monthlies two years ago and they're not regular yet.'

'And you haven't noticed any particular weight loss or weight gain recently?' Wolff persevered.

'She's put on about six stone in the last year or so,' her mother confirmed wearily as her daughter's wails grew louder again. 'Look, when are you going to do something to help her? She's in pain.'

'Before we can do anything to help we have to know what's the matter,' Wolff said patiently. 'And to do that I'm going to have to take a blood sample and then examine your daughter so if you'd like to help her take her clothes off and put a gown on...'

'How many of her clothes?' demanded her mother suspiciously. 'I've heard about you doctors interfering with women...down there.'

'That's why the nurse will be with us the whole time,' he replied with admirable calm. 'To make sure that I can't do anything I shouldn't, and that I can't be accused of something I didn't do.'

'Well, that's as maybe but you still aren't touching her...down there,' she said stoutly.

In spite of Wolff's patient explanations, it seemed as if they had reached stalemate—until Sharron's pain seemed to grow suddenly worse.

For the first time it looked as if her mother was wavering in her conviction, and Laura pressed home the message.

'When the pain is that bad it could be a sign that there's something seriously wrong,' she said earnestly. 'The examination will only take a couple of minutes, and if we can find out what's causing the pain then we'll know what to do to stop it.'

Sharron began to writhe again, shouting out like a soul in torment, and her mother finally caved in.

Moving swiftly in case she changed her mind, Laura draped a sheet over the heavily sweating youngster and helped her out of her blood-stained underwear before Wolff sat himself on a stool at the foot of the trolley with a speculum in his hand.

He hadn't even had time to position the instrument when there was a sudden gush of blood-streaked fluid all down his disposable apron.

A wet shiny object covered in thick black hair appeared between his patient's legs, and it was so swiftly expelled that he only just managed to catch it as it fell towards the floor.

Laura gasped and Wolff looked up from his contemplation of the wriggling mass in his hands with a shocked expression.

Training kicked in then and, although they didn't usually end up delivering babies in the emergency department, Laura was quick to grab the right sterile pack so that Wolff could clamp and cut the cord and then suction the tiny nose and mouth.

'Here you are,' he murmured, seeming almost shell-shocked by the speed of events as he stood up and laid the baby boy on the new mother's stomach.

'That's not mine!' shrieked the youngster, looking at the blood-smeared infant in horror as he started to utter the familiar newborn's cry.

'That's not hers!' echoed her mother, glaring balefully at each of them in turn.

'Well, it's certainly not mine,' said Wolff with a masterful attempt at keeping a straight face. 'So, if you'll forgive me for a minute, I'll just let the maternity ward know that they've got another customer waiting for collection.'

It was another half-hour before Laura finally managed to sit down for a drink.

In the meantime, it seemed as if everyone in A and E had heard about Wolff's 'special delivery'.

'The local football team could do with him in goal,' joked one of the porters, the first person to stop her and ask for confirmation of the story.

'Does *everyone* know?' she asked Hannah after the twentieth comment.

'Well, it was a bit difficult to miss it,' Hannah pointed out with a grin. 'You must admit there was an awful lot of shouting going on in there.'

'It did get a bit noisy,' Laura agreed wryly as she remembered the combined volume of the belligerent mother and her beached whale of a daughter.

It still amazed her that the fourteen-year-old could still

deny having ever been touched by a man while she was in the throes of advanced labour.

But the saddest part, as far as Laura was concerned, was the fact that the first thing that gorgeous healthy little boy had known was instant rejection.

If he had been hers...

She squeezed her eyes tight shut, concentrating on controlling the temptation to cry at the unfairness of life.

The sadness hung over her for the rest of the morning, casting a shadow over her proposed outing with Wolff.

In all probability, once the nurses and midwives took Sharron and her baby son in hand she would realise that, although he was unexpected, there was no reason why the precious gift she'd been given should be unwanted or unloved.

The situation was still playing on her mind as she waited for Wolff to meet her at the end of her shift.

'Sorry to keep you waiting in the cold,' he panted after a swift sprint across the car park. 'Can you grab these while I unlock?' He thrust a sheaf of papers at her and rummaged through his pockets for his keys.

Laura gazed down at the bundle of estate agent's details he'd handed her, but out of the corner of her eye she was cataloguing the way his washed-to-death jeans fitted the lean perfection of his body. If there was anything which could take her mind off her own troubles it was this man...

'I did a quick detour after I handed over,' Wolff said as he settled himself behind the wheel of the car. He'd impressed Laura with his old-fashioned courtesy when he'd made a point of opening the passenger door first to let her get in out of the cold.

It had also given her a chance for some more surreptitious ogling as she watched his long fluid strides take him round the front of the car to his own door.

She liked the way he looked in his comfortably worn casual clothes. It seemed as if most of the nurses had commented on how different he looked after he'd been forced to change out of his suit trousers and leather shoes when baby Ferguson had liberally coated them with amniotic fluid.

She managed to subdue the smile which threatened and concentrated on his words.

'If something more urgent has come up I don't mind if you want to put this outing off,' she offered.

'No way!' he objected. 'I've been looking forward to this all morning. It was the only thing which made all the teasing after that unexpected delivery bearable!'

'You've been fending off enquiries and jokes, too?' she said and they both laughed.

'There's a map with those papers I handed you,' he said, pausing to concentrate on his driving as he turned out of the hospital grounds and onto the main road. 'Could you direct us to the first place I've marked—a red dot?'

Laura found the mark and gave him directions for their first port of call.

'Actually, that's where I went just now,' he said as he indicated for the first of several turns. 'I went to find out how "our" baby was doing.'

'How is he?' Laura demanded eagerly, all thought of navigating gone. She could have kicked herself for not thinking of doing the same thing. It would have stopped her worrying about. . .

'It doesn't look very hopeful,' Wolff said with a scowl as he indicated again and pulled up outside a very dilapidated-looking house, crudely divided into flats.

'What doesn't?' she enquired, muddled by the effort of sorting out two separate conversations. 'The flat?'

'Oh, *that* won't do at all,' he agreed as he pulled back out into the flow of traffic and asked for the next set of directions. 'But I was talking about the baby.'

'Why?' Laura demanded, worry jolting through her like a fierce blow. 'What's wrong with him? He seemed fine when he left us—his Apgar was almost perfect.'

'Oh, there's nothing wrong with *him*,' he said, rapidly putting her mind at rest on that score. '*He's* doing fine. It's his mother and grandmother who are the problem.'

'Why?' she repeated with a feeling of dread, her eyes deserting the map entirely to focus on the steely expression on Wolff's face.

'They've completely rejected the little chap,' he said angrily. 'They say they don't want him...that he's going to be put up for adoption.'

CHAPTER SEVEN

LAURA could hear from Wolff's voice that he was disgusted, but she was utterly devastated by the news.

How could people *think* about abandoning their own flesh and blood? She realised that Sharron was too young, but it wasn't as if she wouldn't have her own mother's help. How could they bear to just give her baby away? Didn't they want to watch him grow and develop...to watch the changes as he became a toddler, a schoolchild, a teenager and finally a man?

She was aware that her inner debate was making her a less than ideal companion, but she couldn't seem to switch it off.

Several times she caught Wolff's thoughtful gaze on her, his blue eyes seeming to try to work out what was troubling her. He was obviously making allowances for her strange mood, keeping up a flow of easy chatter as they criss-crossed the town looking at everything from detached gothic horrors to tiny modern flats whose fixtures and fittings were the epitome of yuppie self-indulgence.

If she'd had to pick her favourite Laura would have had to admit that the last one they visited had held her attention the longest. Its decorative mixture of soft neutrals and earth colours with honey-coloured wood seemed to welcome her with warmth as soon as they stepped inside, in spite of the fact that it was empty and the heating was turned off.

'What do you think?' Wolff said as he surveyed the

spacious-looking lounge again at the end of their tour. 'This one looks as if it's ready to move straight into.'

'It's very nice,' Laura agreed with a distracted half-smile. She was staring blindly at the fading daylight outside the bay window, the pain which she usually managed to keep hidden inside the darkest corner of her heart creeping out like some sort of virulent cancer to cast a pall over everything.

'Laura?'

The change in tone of Wolff's voice drew her attention back to him.

'What's the matter?' he questioned kindly. 'Aren't you feeling very well. . .or have I bored you into insensibility?'

'Oh, Wolff, I'm sorry,' she said, stricken to realise that she'd hardly done more than answer in monosyllables all afternoon. 'I've been an utter wet blanket, haven't I?'

'Is it. . .?' He hesitated. 'I don't like to sound like a male chauvinist pig, but it seemed to come on so suddenly. Is it what Mrs Ferguson would call your monthlies?'

Laura gazed at him in dismay, too shocked to feel any embarrassment at the topic of the conversation.

Of all the things he could have said, what on earth had put *that* into his head?

Suddenly the implications of the whole day overcame her and she burst into tears.

'Oh, God! Laura, I'm sorry,' Wolff muttered as he hovered beside her for one brief second as if he had no idea what to do with a weeping woman.

Then he acted, wrapping both arms around her and drawing her as tightly as he could against the warmth and security of his broad chest.

'I'm sorry,' Laura wailed, mortified that she'd lost control over such a stupid thing. In two years she had never broken down like this. 'Oh, Wolff, I feel such a fool.'

'Shh, Laura, shh!' he soothed as he cupped his hand around the back of her head and cradled it against him, rocking her as though she were a frightened child.

Eventually he produced a large handkerchief and proceeded to mop her face dry before he handed it to her to blow her nose and stepped away.

'Better?' he enquired, and when she nodded she saw him glance down at the slim watch strapped to his wrist.

'Have you got another appointment?' she asked, drawing in a shaky breath as she straightened her shoulders and prepared to leave.

'No. I was just checking to see if the estate agent's office was still open. I'd like to put my name down for this one before anyone else has a chance to.'

Laura was almost breathless with the speed of his decision, and totally distracted from her own concerns.

'Are you certain you don't want to see any others?' she cautioned. 'You've only been looking for a couple of hours.'

'I went through a small forest of details to draw up a short list of the ones which met my five most important criteria—they had to be the right size, within my price-range, empty. . .so that I can move straight in and within reasonable travelling distance of the hospital in case I get called in to an emergency.'

'And?' she prompted. 'You said *five* criteria—size, price, ready to move in straight away, distance and. . .?'

'And *you* have to give your seal of approval,' he said with an outrageous grin. 'So, as this one fulfilled all five, it must be the one.'

Laura wouldn't have thought that she would find herself laughing so soon, but Wolff seemed to be developing the knack for lifting her out of herself with nothing more than a bit of nonsense.

'Let's lock up and get back to the car,' he suggested, suddenly seeming to be in a hurry. 'I've got the mobile phone in there to get hold of the estate agent, and we can drop the keys off on the way back.'

Laura followed in his wake, casting one last look over her shoulder at the welcoming atmosphere in the little house before she resigned herself to the end of her outing with Wolff.

She sat beside him in the car while he made the estate agent's day with a speedy sale, but her thoughts were in a hopeless muddle.

In spite of her preoccupation, she'd enjoyed spending time with him. He'd been such good company that she wasn't looking forward to returning to her room, knowing that she would end up shut inside the four walls with the memories that, today, were haunting her more than ever.

It didn't take long for Wolff to leap out of the car and lean in through the office door to hand the bunch of keys to the agent, not even bothering to walk all the way inside the office.

Laura heard him promise to come back as soon as they let him know everything was ready for signing, and then he was climbing back into the car.

'When he hears that I found what I was looking for Leo's going to be a very happy man,' he commented wryly as he started the engine.

'I thought you were staying with him because the two of you were friends?'

'We have been for, oh, it must be ten years at least,' he agreed. 'But, as the saying goes, guests and fish stink after three days, and I've already been with him for four.'

Laura was still laughing at the wry accuracy of the quip when she suddenly realised that they were going the wrong way.

'Wolff, you should have turned the other way back there. The nurses' accommodation is the other side of the hospital.'

'Actually, I was hoping you'd help me to celebrate my new status as a nearly-householder,' he said casually. 'As you helped me to choose, the least I can do is offer you a cup of coffee or a glass of wine—if Leo hasn't found the bottle I hid in the back of the fridge.'

Laura was so pleased that their afternoon together wasn't over yet that she nearly missed the searching look he threw her way.

Suddenly she remembered just how sharp this man's mind was, and realised that his offer of hospitality was probably nothing more than an excuse to pin her down with questions until she told him why she'd broken down this afternoon.

Even though a shiver of apprehension raised goose bumps up her arms she still couldn't regret the chance to spend more time with him.

For all that he gave the appearance of being a typical footloose bachelor and far too handsome for his own good, she had discovered over the last few days that there was another Wolff carefully hidden under that façade—a Wolff who made her feel good about herself made her feel feminine and womanly for the first time in two years...for all the good it would do her.

It was that last thought which accompanied her as Wolff let them into Leo's little flat, but the sight which met her eyes as he shut the door behind them drove everything else out of her mind.

'Oh-h-h,' she breathed in horror when she saw the state of the room.

'Exactly,' Wolff muttered, sounding almost embarrassed about the chaos that confronted them. 'Leo's actually quite a tidy person, but you'd never know it from this mess. A flat this small was never designed to cram two sets of possessions into.'

'You're right there,' Laura agreed as she wondered where on earth they were going to sit to have the drink Wolff had offered her.

'Perhaps you can understand now why I was so keen to find a place of my own as soon as possible,' he said as he picked up an armful of belongings from the small settee, then looked around helplessly for somewhere else to put them.

'Here. . .' Laura amalgamated two piles on the sturdy coffee-table. 'Will that fit there?'

'Thanks,' he growled sheepishly as he deposited his burden. 'At least that clears a place to sit. Sometimes I wonder if it's actually breeding and we'll get buried under it one night and never be seen again!'

Laura chuckled at the thought as he went to get their drinks.

As she shrugged out of her parka she realised that there was nowhere obvious to hang it so she lay it over the high back of the settee, then settled herself onto its surprisingly comfortable cushions.

'Here you are,' Wolff said, holding out a glass of pale

straw-coloured liquid, the tiny bubbles rising through it like miniature strings of beads.

'Leo didn't find it, then,' she commented, suddenly nervous now that he'd come back into the room. She could see that there was only one place for him to sit, but she didn't know how she would cope with having him sitting so close.

It was one thing to innocently fall asleep beside him when tiredness overtook her, or to accept the comfort of his strong arms when she was upset, but the only other time she had been this close to Wolff Bergen had been the very first time they'd met when he'd danced with her as intimately as if they'd been long-time lovers.

'Relax,' he whispered and leant back into his corner, proving once again that he had an uncanny ability to discern her thoughts. It was a strange feeling, and the proximity of his long legs to hers didn't make it any easier.

She glanced up at him, his tanned face seeming even darker in the subdued lighting and his eyes strangely lighter as though lit from within with a soft radiance.

She took a sip from her wine and tried to calm her nervousness by thinking about the shift she'd just finished.

Suddenly she had a mental image of the second when Sharron and her jet-propelled baby had showered his smart clothes with unexpected fluids, and she couldn't help the grin which crept over her face.

'What?' he demanded, although she hadn't said a word.

'Nothing, really. I was just wondering whether your shoes will ever recover,' she said with a chuckle. 'And I'd love to be a fly on the wall when you take those trousers into the dry-cleaners and explain what sort of stain removal they're going to need.'

'Sometimes I think you've got a very twisted sense of humour,' Wolff complained in a pained voice, but then he met her eyes and they were both laughing.

Laura sipped again and slowly she lost her smile.

'He was a beautiful baby, wasn't he?' she commented as her mental replay of the morning's events rolled on and her throat grew tight.

'Beautiful?' Wolff questioned in a voice full of amazement. 'He looked like a very bald, very wrinkled, very angry old man. You women are all the same. You grow positively misty-eyed over every one of them, no matter what they look like.'

Laura knew he was teasing and tried to give him an answering smile, but her lips were trembling too much.

'Dammit, I've done it again,' she heard him mutter when he saw the tears glittering in her eyes.

He reached for the wine glass, which was perilously close to losing its contents, and deposited it under the coffee-table with his own, then he slid one arm behind her shoulders and pulled her close.

'Ah, Laura, tell me what's the matter,' he demanded softly. 'I can't bear it when you look so hurt and desperate, and I seem to be causing it...'

'No.' She shook her head and drew in a steadying breath. 'It's not you, Wolff. It's... It's...' How did she begin? *Where* did she begin?

'Shall I tell you how far I've got in working things out, and then you can tell me where I've gone wrong?'

He didn't wait for her agreement and she was grateful that she didn't have to try to make a decision.

'It doesn't take a genius to work out that it's got something to do with babies,' he began matter-of-factly. 'You were a little subdued after the baby was born this morning but you were perfectly all right earlier this afternoon—right up until I told you the Fergusons wanted to give their baby away.'

Laura was almost frozen with shock. She'd had two years of practice at hiding her thoughts and feelings and had no idea that she was still so easy to read.

'Now we come to the part I haven't worked out,' Wolff continued. 'As far as I can tell, you're about twenty-five years old...'

'Twenty-six,' Laura corrected, and he inclined his head in acceptance.

'Close enough for my purposes,' he conceded graciously. 'And, although I can't understand why someone as gorgeous as you hasn't been snapped up long ago and chained to a kitchen sink, twenty-six is far too young for you to be feeling as if you've been left on the shelf so it's unlikely that babies are setting off the alarm button on your biological clock...'

He let his voice die away in an obvious invitation for her to supply the *real* reason.

'Sorry. No prizes,' Laura said with a bitterness she couldn't hide. 'For some of us the biological clock starts ticking at a much faster rate than the rest, and we can run out of time before we even realise that there's a deadline.'

'What?' His forehead pleated in thought as he tried to decipher the meaning of her words. 'Do you mean that you've had an accident, or surgery, and it's affected your reproductive system?'

'You're getting closer,' she said lightly, trying to make a joke out of the situation before she embarrassed herself again. 'Only in my case it's endometriosis which has stopped my clock.'

'Stopped it?' he queried instantly. 'I know there are a small number of women who suffer from it early, but you're very young for it to be that advanced.'

'As far as my fiancé was concerned, it might just as well have done,' she said as the anger and despair welled up inside her. 'I'd been having some problems—ever since the onset of puberty, in fact—and when he proposed I decided to get things checked out.'

She stared blindly at the calendar hanging lopsidedly on the wall, not even registering what the picture was about as she remembered.

'We'd talked about when we wanted to start a family and how many children we wanted. . .' She drew in a shuddering breath and continued doggedly.

'The results of the tests came through the day we were going to celebrate our engagement, and when I told him I was so upset that it might disrupt all our lovely plans that he suggested putting off the party. I didn't realise that he meant to put it off permanently until he announced his engagement to one of my colleagues three months later.'

'Bastard,' Wolff hissed venomously as he tightened his arm protectively around her.

'He's not really,' she admitted, her voice seeming to echo in the emptiness inside her. 'He's a paediatrician and he's always loved children.'

'But if he were any sort of a man he'd be marrying a woman because he loved her, not because she was going to be his brood mare,' Wolff pointed out fiercely.

Laura had to smile at the way he'd instantly leapt to her defence and she rested her head gratefully on his shoulder.

They sat in silence for a moment, but she could almost hear the thoughts whirling round in Wolff's brain before he spoke again.

'Did your results say you'd never be able to have children?' he asked, obviously pursuing the loose ends of her story.

'The specialist said that my chances would decrease rapidly as time went on. He seemed to think that if I hadn't had any children by the time I reached thirty then it was unlikely I would ever conceive.'

She was proud of the steady way she had delivered his verdict, even though it felt just as though her heart were being cut out with a blunt knife.

'Did you ever consider artificial insemination?' Wolff asked.

His voice was as calm as if he were commenting on the weather, but it released a tornado of unexpected thoughts inside her head.

'I considered it,' she said with a lift of her chin. 'Like St Augustine's, my last hospital had a fertility clinic, but in the end there were too many factors against it.'

'Such as?' he challenged.

'Such as. . .the fact that I'm single and they understandably prefer to concentrate their limited resources on couples. Such as the likelihood of success in the limited time I would have available to try. Such as the fact that, although patients' records are supposed to have a degree of confidentiality, there's little chance of preserving your privacy when the hospital grapevine will pick up on the fact that you're seen going into the fertility clinic on a regular basis.'

'You don't mean you'd be put off by the possibility of embarrassment?'

'Not so much for myself but for the child,' she pointed out. 'Can you imagine what it would be like to have all your mother's colleagues and friends knowing all the private details of your conception?'

He conceded the point with a nod but it was absent-minded, as if his restless brain had whirled on to consider other things.

'I take it from your reaction to events today,' he began slowly and thoughtfully, as if he was working out something complicated as he spoke. 'I take it that you'd still like a family of your own?'

'Oh, Wolff,' she breathed as the longing welled up inside her again and she looked up into his fiercely intent gaze. 'If only you knew how much. . .'

There was a long moment of silence as he absorbed the fervency of her words.

'I've had an idea. . .' he murmured softly, and Laura could have screamed with frustration when he didn't continue.

'What?' she questioned eagerly with a sudden hopeful leap of her heart. 'What idea?'

He was silent for so long that she began to wonder if she'd imagined those hopeful words.

'No,' he said at last.

The word was so final that it was like a slap in the face and she gasped at the impact.

'Ah, Laura, I'm sorry,' he said when he saw the stricken expression which she knew must be filling her eyes. 'I didn't mean that the idea was no good, just that it's too soon to say any more. I need to do a bit of research before I tell you what I'm thinking of.'

'But...'

'I'd love to tell you,' he said, a strange electric excitement seeming to sizzle through him as he gazed deep into her eyes, 'but I don't want to get your hopes up until I've checked some details. Please...' he continued when she would have begged him to explain. 'Trust me?' he whispered.

Laura subsided, defeated.

She might have known him for only a few days but she *did* trust him, and if he said he needed to do some research before he presented her with his idea then she was just going to have to wait.

'How long?' she demanded impatiently, and he chuckled, the sound deep and rich in the cluttered room.

'I hope, for both our sakes, that I'll have found out what I need to know in a couple of days.'

'A couple of days!' she remonstrated and he laughed again.

'You sound like a child waiting for Christmas to come,' he said, and suddenly they both grew serious at the implication of his words.

A child...

'Oh, Wolff,' she whispered, her heart full to overflowing that he was interested enough to try to find a way round her problem. It was more than Peter had ever done, and *he* was supposed to have loved her enough to marry her...

'Thank you,' she said fervently. 'Even if it doesn't come to anything, thank you for trying. Thank you for being there and for listening...'

She reached up and cradled his cheek, loving the sandpapery roughness of his chin against her palm as she tilted his face towards her own and pressed her lips to his.

The sensation was electric, every nerve in her body responding to the warmth and the subtle sliding of his mouth as he took over control.

They'd kissed before, but the circumstances of that first time had been so outlandish that she hadn't believed that her memories could be accurate.

In the end she'd dismissed them as fantasies, produced by terror, embarrassment and too much wine.

Blood didn't boil like it did in her memory and nerves didn't sizzle...

Except that it was happening again, and this time neither of them had done more than sip a glass of wine.

She was vaguely aware that she was probably going to feel very embarrassed afterwards when she remembered how avidly she was wrapping herself around his body, her fingers revelling in the silky density of his thick dark hair and the warm strength of his neck and shoulders.

But for the moment the only fear she was feeling was that he might stop kissing her.

Wolff groaned when he finally tore his mouth away and rested his forehead against hers, and Laura echoed the sound, missing the soft stroke of his tongue across the tender inner surfaces of her lips and the possessive way he'd duelled with her own inside the warm darkness.

'Ah, Laura, if we didn't need to breathe...' he muttered, his voice huskier than ever, and with a wild leap of her heart Laura realised that he had been every bit as affected by their kiss as she had. 'And if Leo's car hadn't just pulled up outside...'

It took several seconds for the words to register, but

when they did Laura all but leapt out of his arms, frantically dragging her fingers through the short feathery strands of her hair to try to bring them back into some semblance of order. At least her clothing was still neat, even though she'd desperately wanted the constricting layers to disappear without trace not two minutes ago.

'Don't worry about it,' Wolff advised lazily as he sprawled back in his corner of the settee like a well-fed cat.

A wicked grin curled the corners of his mouth when he saw how flustered she was, but it wasn't until she saw the gleam in his eyes as they travelled over her that she realised that he was still consumed by desire, too.

'You look beautiful,' he murmured, his voice a husky purr which defied her to regain any sort of normal rhythm to either her heartbeat or her breathing. It sounded the way she imagined it would if they were in bed together, with even less between them than when she'd wrapped her arms around his naked shoulders on the stage.

She tried to block the mental image of what he would look like without the exotic waistcoat hiding the width of his chest, tried vainly to prevent herself from imagining what it would feel like to strip the rest of their clothes away until the two of them were naked and then. . .

'Laura,' he growled, a clear warning in his voice, 'if you don't stop looking at me like that there will be three very embarrassed people here when Leo walks in that door.'

Laura felt the heat rise in her cheeks and she couldn't look at him—*daren't* look at him—because, for the first time in years, she was enjoying the fact that her body was vibrantly aroused and Wolff seemed to be able to read her very thoughts.

'You're not the only one,' he muttered wryly as he shifted his position on the settee and leant forward to plant his elbows on his thighs. 'Leo would only have to take one look at me and he'd know what *I've* been thinking about.'

Laura couldn't help her sly smile of pleasure that *his* body's reaction was lingering, too. She'd been fully aware of his reaction to her the first time they'd kissed—it had been unavoidable, the way their bodies had been plastered together from breast to ankle—but their cramped position on the settee right now meant that she hadn't been nearly close enough to tell if their kiss had affected him the same way.

'Hi, Wolff,' Leo said tiredly as he swung the door closed with an elbow. He used the same elbow to hit the main light switch, then realised as brightness flooded the room that they had company.

'Oh, hello, Laura,' he added with less than his usual enthusiasm. 'Just to warn you for when you go in to work—it looks as if there's a bad batch of drugs on the street. We've had two doses so far, both fatal.'

He leant dejectedly back against the door with an armful of belongings, a carrier bag full of familiar foil containers and a miserable expression on his face.

'Leo, old friend,' Wolff greeted him with cheerfully smiling *bonhomie*. 'Before you sink into terminal depression at the trauma of coming home to this horrible sight at the end of a tough shift I've got some good news for you... I've found my own place.'

'Really?' Leo's strange golden eyes brightened instantly with guilty relief. 'That was quick. Where is it and when do you move?'

'It's a small house in a road on the other side of the

hospital from here, and it's in good enough decorative order for me to move in as soon as the legalities are taken care of. Laura helped me find it this afternoon.'

'Did she, now?' Leo said with a knowing tone in his newly vitalised voice and a roguish smile. 'In which case, Laura, I will be eternally in your debt. Ask anything you want and it shall be yours—my clothes, my body, my firstborn child—anything but my *moo goo gai pan* because I'm starving!'

They laughed when he tried to wrap his heavily laden arm protectively around the containers in the carrier bag and Laura noticed that his step was very much lighter as he went to get himself a plate.

He returned to the cluttered room in seconds, with his other belongings still clutched under one elbow.

'Can I help you with those?' Laura offered, jumping to her feet to relieve him of his ungainly burden. 'Where shall I put your jacket? Can I hang it up?'

'Thanks. If you could put it on the hook on the back of the door. . .' He pointed with an elbow.

There was the familiar shape of a hanger sticking out from under another jacket and Laura reached for it, intending to hang Leo's jacket up properly.

The only problem was that the hanger wasn't empty.

'Oh!' Laura exclaimed as she drew out a familiar waistcoat, the overhead light gleaming on the metallic threads the same way the spotlight had on the night she'd first met Wolff.

'Oh, no,' she heard his familiar husky voice mutter as she turned to face him, an impish smile curving her mouth as she held the hanger up.

'Yours, I believe?' she questioned wickedly. 'I seem

to recognise the waistcoat and the bow tie...but I don't remember seeing *this* part of the costume last time...'

She hooked one finger through the elastic and held up the skimpy matching G-string underwear, swinging it gently to and fro for a minute before she added thoughtfully, 'You know, if you'd worn *that* on the night you wouldn't have had to worry about *anyone* recognising you—they wouldn't have been looking at your face at all!'

CHAPTER EIGHT

LAURA was still chuckling when she went to bed that night.

The expression on Wolff's face had been priceless, especially the deep colour which had flooded his cheeks.

With the typical disloyalty of a friend of long standing, Leo had joined in with the story of Wolff's refusal to stand in for the professional dancer unless he was allowed to modify the costume.

'He was supposed to strip off to reveal that gorgeous little number before he danced with the winner but chickened out,' Leo had accused with a return to his usual wicked sense of humour. 'And it's not as if he's got anything to be ashamed of either. He's actually in quite good shape for an old man.'

'Old man?' Wolff had yelped. 'You're only two months younger than I am so watch who you're calling old.'

Wolff had straightened up out of the settee with his usual swift, economic grace and stepped aside to allow Leo access to the only available seat in the room.

'Here, sit down and rest,' he'd offered with a gleam in his eye which promised retaliation. 'You'd better save your strength for eating—while you've still got enough teeth. It's amazing how age can creep up on you.'

He'd suggested driving Laura back to her room then and, while she'd been loath to miss watching the easy way Wolff and Leo teased and insulted each other, she'd been glad to be leaving. So much had happened today that she'd needed some quiet time to absorb it all—not least the possibility that Wolff might have found a way for her to achieve her dearest wish.

Unfortunately, whatever lucky chance had been making certain that their shifts coincided had obviously deserted them now, and she'd been working with several other members of the A and E staff while they coped with another fatality and three near-misses as the bad batch of heroin took its toll on the drug-taking fraternity.

When Leo had told Wolff about the first two accidental doses Wolff had confirmed the newly familiar maxim in emergency care that if you had one get ready for several—and he'd been right.

Laura's memories and thoughts of Wolff were all she had to sustain her because for three days she hadn't seen him at all. Nor had he made any attempt to contact her outside the hospital.

Slowly the bright daydreams she had started to build about the fulfilment of her longing to be a mother started to fade, and the lightness in her step and the sparkle in her eyes dwindled into dull normality.

Even the prospect of a whole day off wasn't enough to cheer her up at the end of a long tiring shift.

She gazed out at the surrounding darkness as she zipped her parka up to her chin and braced herself to brave the bone-chilling rain.

The light streaming out across the car park showed her that the torrential downpour was being blown along almost horizontally by an unforgiving wind, and she shuddered in anticipation of the soaking she was going to get.

If only she'd listened to the weather report this morning

she'd have driven her car the few hundred yards around to this side of the hospital. Even if it had cost her money for petrol at least she wouldn't be getting soaked.

'Laura?'

Only half a dozen steps into her miserable journey her hair was already soaked and her ears were being buffeted unmercifully, but she could have sworn that she'd heard Wolff's husky voice calling her name.

'Hey, Laura! Over here!'

When the call was repeated she caught sight of a car in the no-parking zone to one side of the main entrance, an arm waving at her from the open window and a plume of white at the exhaust telling her that the engine was running.

Her heart leapt inside her chest when Wolff leant out of the open window to wave again, and she recognised the familiar shape of his head.

Laura hesitated for just a second, terrified by the implications of her joy at seeing him, but then she found that her feet were taking her towards him without conscious thought—unable to resist her strong desire to get closer to him.

It didn't seem to matter that he seemed to have ignored her for three days—she was still delighted to see him.

She'd only met him for the first time a week ago, and already she had noticed how big a gap there was in her life when he wasn't around.

After two years of avoiding any sort of relationship with a man she was finding that she missed the satisfaction of working with Wolff as part of the team, but most of all she missed seeing him on a daily basis—whether on duty at St Augustine's or outside the hospital.

'Get in quick or you'll drown,' he said through the open

passenger door, and as she ducked her head to slide inside she caught just a glimpse of his heart-stopping smile.

She pulled the car door shut to close out the raging elements and reached for the seat belt, drawing in her first breath of warm dry air permeated with the familiar mixture of soap and man as he started driving.

After one quick look at the way the passing streetlights highlighted the familiar features of his face she shut her eyes to savour his closeness and, in spite of the rain trickling down her face and inside her collar, she relaxed back against the seat as if she had finally found the place she wanted to be.

She was filled with a deep certainty that Wolff had found a solution to her problem but that wasn't the reason for her contentment.

For the first time since she'd heard that awful diagnosis and had realised what it meant for her future she wasn't certain that it *was* so all-important. For the first time she was wondering if the man who might have found a way around that problem might be more important than the solution he'd found.

'Here.' His husky voice drew her reluctantly out of her warmth-induced stupor and she saw the pale fabric he was offering in his outstretched hand. 'It's only a clean handkerchief but at least you could use it to dry your face.'

'Oh, thank you,' she said, touched by his thoughtfulness. 'It's all running off my hair down the back of my neck, and your seats are going to be soaked.'

Laura reached for the square of folded cloth gratefully, but her fingers brushed his and she nearly dropped the fine cotton when she felt the searing heat of his skin. It had felt almost like a shock from static electricity, and she was surprised that there hadn't been a visible spark between the two of them.

She glanced across at him to see if he had noticed, but either it was too dark to see his reaction while he was concentrating on his driving or he was much better at hiding it.

In a matter of minutes he was steering the car into a driveway and Laura suddenly noticed where he had taken her.

'This is your new place!' she exclaimed, pleased to see the house again. 'Have all the papers been signed?'

'And I've moved in,' he confirmed, apparently pleased by her enthusiasm on his behalf.

She peered through the rain streaming down the windscreen but visibility was too poor to discern any details about the place Wolff would now call home. She'd been so preoccupied the first time she'd been here that she couldn't remember much about it—just the fact that it had a warm and welcoming atmosphere.

'I hope you don't mind,' he said quietly as he took the keys out of the ignition and released his own seat belt to face her in the dimness. 'I'll take you back to your room if you'd prefer, but I wanted to have a word with you and I thought we would be less likely to be disturbed if I brought you here.'

'I don't mind,' Laura said, smiling at her understatement. It would have been more accurate if she'd said that she was delighted to be here...delighted to be with him...

'Well, then, let's make a dash for it,' he suggested, and flung his door open.

By the time Laura had followed him to the front door Wolff had unlocked it so that she could walk straight in.

He paused just long enough to aim the automatic locking device at his car before he shut the door and enclosed the two of them in his new house.

'Give me your parka and go through to the sitting room. I'll fetch a couple of towels,' he suggested.

Laura shed her wet jacket gratefully, then watched as he draped it over the newel post at the bottom of the stairs and set off up them two at a time, his long legs making short work of the distance.

Laura paused in the hallway just long enough to realise that she hadn't been mistaken about the atmosphere in the house. It felt as if each of the people who had lived here had left a little of their happiness behind in the air, and it was now settling around her shoulders like a friendly arm.

The sitting room was the one she remembered best from their inspection tour, but last time it had contained only the carpets left by the previous owners. Now it boasted curtains of a dark ivory colour and a suite of furniture framed in natural wood and upholstered in an earthy mixture of ivory and terracotta.

'What do you think?' Wolff demanded cheerfully as he held out a thick fluffy towel. 'It's gone together quite well, hasn't it?'

'It's lovely,' Laura agreed. 'I can't believe you've got it all done so quickly.'

'It's amazing how eager Leo was to help me move in,' Wolff said with his tongue firmly in his cheek.

'You mean how eager he was to help you move *out*,' she corrected with a laugh. 'I'm just surprised by how perfect it all looks.'

As she began to rub the moisture out of her hair she turned in a circle and spotted a row of low-level bookcases, filled with a mixture of well-thumbed paperbacks and more formal-looking medical tomes, a state-of-the-art hi-fi system and a richly gleaming coffee-table with the remote control for the television.

'It looks as if you've been here for ages,' she said in amazement. 'It doesn't seem possible that the whole place was empty three days ago—I didn't think anyone could move that fast.'

'I think my solicitor managed to find some short cuts,' he said vaguely. 'Anyway, I told him that, barring plans to knock it down and build a motorway straight through it, I wanted it. It's just perfect for what I need.'

'Well, I'm amazed,' she said with a shake of her head.

That reminded her that she needed to give her hair another rub. The warmth of the room had helped, but there were still chilly drips sliding off the end of each strand.

She emerged from the soft caramel-coloured towel with every hair standing on end and laughed.

'It's all right for you,' she complained as she tried to smooth the tangle into some sort of order. 'You had yours cut so short that it must just about dry by itself. I bet it was different when you had it long.'

She saw the momentary shadow cross his face as he remembered what he'd been doing when his hair had grown so long and she bit her tongue but it was too late to stop him remembering.

'Actually,' he began after she watched him deliberately pull down an invisible shutter on the memories, 'apart from the problem of keeping it free from lice, when the weather turned so cold so quickly it was very useful for keeping my head warm. I'm hoping I'll acclimatise to being shorn fairly quickly because, at the moment, I freeze every time I set foot outside!'

Laura laughed, pleased that he was able to make a joke instead of allowing the past to intrude between them.

'How about a coffee?' he offered as he relieved her of the damp towel. 'That should complete the thawing-out process.'

Laura accepted, but as she followed him through to the kitchen she sensed that he wasn't quite as relaxed as he appeared.

'Oh, I like this,' she said when he switched on the light. She didn't remember this room from their first tour but once again the colour scheme was a mixture of earth tones and natural wood, with matt ivory tiled walls and dark honey tiles on the floor. 'It looks sort of edible—a bit like *crème caramel.*'

In no time he had filled two large pottery mugs with the steaming brew and slid one across to Laura.

'Would you like a guided tour?' he offered, and she had the strange feeling that he had only suggested it as a way of procrastinating.

As she followed him out into the hallway she wondered briefly if her instincts had been wrong.

When he'd been waiting for her outside the hospital she'd been almost certain that the reason he'd been there was because he'd found a way to help her, but now. . .

Had he suggested showing her around the house to delay the moment when he would have to tell her that his idea *hadn't* worked out?

Knowing how sympathetic he'd been when she'd told him about her endometriosis, it would be quite likely that he would be worried about how she was going to take the bad news.

That would explain the strange air of tension which seemed to surround him...

She was preoccupied when he led the way upstairs, noting almost absent-mindedly that things looked far more sparse up here.

The bathroom was well appointed but spartan rather than opulent, with a shower head over the bath and no fancy extras, and the spare bedroom, which he told her he was thinking of turning into an office or study, was completely bare.

Then there was only one door left and Laura felt an unexpected quiver of nervous excitement deep inside at the prospect of seeing where he slept.

He pushed the door open silently and invited her to enter with a graceful gesture.

Laura stepped past him, careful not to brush against him, but even so she was aware of his eyes following her as if he needed to see her reaction to this most personal room.

Once again there were too few possessions in the room for it to look cluttered but, after a quick glance round, the one thing her eyes focused on was the bed.

'A *brass* bed?' she questioned in amazement. 'That's the *last* thing I would have expected.'

'And what *would* you have expected, always supposing you'd given it any thought?' he asked mischievously.

Oh, Lord! she thought as she felt the start of a blush. If he knew exactly how many times in the last week she'd imagined his bed and... On second thoughts, thank goodness he *didn't* have any idea...

'Oh,' she said airily, hoping it sounded as if she was

making suggestions off the top of her head. 'Perhaps a king-sized modern divan, or a Japanese futon, maybe even a solid wood four-poster—not one of those modern monstrosities with curlicues and frilly curtains but a genuine heavy antique one, built to last for centuries.'

'Quite a comprehensive list, with not a brass one among them,' he agreed. 'But, then, you couldn't have known that this one was passed down to me by my grandparents with generations of stories of good luck and happiness.'

Laura looked at it with new eyes, imagining how many lives had been entwined in the history of the bed, then dragged her eyes away again before she started imagining Wolff stretched out on it, his body entwined. . .

'Well, I'm absolutely amazed at how quickly you've settled in,' she reiterated with a last look around.

'I had a few things in storage—like the bed and the suite—but my last place was a furnished rental so there wasn't very much to unpack. Just my books and a few clothes.'

'No cupboards full of exotic underwear?' she teased, remembering his reaction when she'd found the costume he *should* have been wearing that night.

'If you're talking about that wretched costume again,' he growled as he trapped her gaze with his, 'I'd like to remind you about the rather obvious effect you had on me when we were dancing. *Then* tell me if you wish I had been wearing that skimpy bit of nonsense.'

Heat blazed in Laura's cheeks as she shared the potent memory of their mutual arousal, and suddenly she couldn't look away from him.

Several times since she'd met him she'd seen that predatory look directed at her from his icy blue eyes, but never with the same intensity as this.

They weren't cold now but seared her with a laser's heat that travelled through her like a bolt of lightning.

Every cell in her body seemed to be responding to him, her heart pounding and her breathing ragged as her breasts grew tight and her most intimate places liquefied with the need to join with him.

For two years she'd avoided getting close to a man, physically or mentally, but once she'd met Wolff it was as if she didn't have a choice any more.

The old fear of being let down, being hurt the way Peter had hurt her, surfaced briefly. At a time when she'd needed support and understanding he'd thought only of himself, and it had left her afraid to trust.

But Wolff was nothing like Peter, and she wasn't even the same person she'd been then...

While a myriad thoughts whirled around inside her head she realised that Wolff was waiting with a predator's patience, his eyes never leaving hers as he watched the progression of thoughts leave their mark on her expression.

Like his namesake, he had a hunter's instincts and she suddenly knew that when he was this hungry he would pursue his prey relentlessly...

She shivered, but she knew it wasn't fear which caused all the hairs to lift on the back of her neck. It was awareness.

As they gazed deeply into each other's eyes across the width of his grandparents' bed she realised that it was time to let go of all her old fears.

Wolff desired her, a fact she'd known instinctively from the first time they'd met, and—in spite of the fact that he knew about her problems—the message in the eyes looking at her now was that he still desired her. . .more than ever.

A surge of certainty lifted her heart and she felt a smile start to curve her lips.

There were no guarantees in life and precious few second chances, but if there *was* a chance for happiness with Wolff, no matter how short-lived, she was going to grasp it with both hands.

Slowly, never taking her eyes away from his, Laura took the first step towards him, her footsteps all but silent on the soft thick pile of the carpet.

As she drew closer she grew more and more certain that she had made the right decision, and the fire in Wolff's eyes was almost incendiary when suddenly the shutters came down and he turned away from her.

Laura's steps faltered, his reaction like a physical blow.

Had she been wrong? Was it wishful thinking which had made her see desire where there was none?

'Wolff?' she said uncertainly when he didn't say anything, and he glanced briefly in her direction without meeting her eyes.

'I. . . My coffee's gone cold,' he began almost hesitantly. 'Does yours need topping up?' She nearly laughed at the prosaic comment. She'd been expecting. . .hoping for. . .a proposition, and instead she'd been offered more coffee!

With a silent nod she followed in his wake as he led the way back downstairs, still not certain whether to laugh or cry at the way things were turning out.

She'd spent so long with her emotions locked away, and the very time she'd decided to set them free. . .

She wrapped her arms around herself, chilled to the core as questions proliferated inside her head.

He'd had time to think about what she'd told him. Had

he decided that, in spite of the fact that he found her desirable, he didn't want to get involved?

She needed to think.

She needed to shut herself in her room at the hospital and replay everything that had happened this evening, analysing it until she understood what was going on.

'Wolff, I think it's time I...'

'Laura, about that idea I...'

They both came to a halt and there was silence while they each absorbed the fragments of sentences they had heard.

It was Wolff who continued.

'Please, Laura, will you stay a little longer, or would you rather I took you back?'

'You said...' She drew in a sharp breath as her heart began to pound again, this time with a different sort of excitement, and her words began tumbling out one over the other in their rush to be spoken.

'Oh, Wolff, have you found something out?' she demanded. 'Is there a way of getting round the system and fooling the grapevine? Have you found some way for me to remain anonymous while I try to get pregnant?'

'Hold on, Laura,' he said, a strained smile on his face as he still avoided meeting her eyes. 'It's not quite as easy as that and...' He stopped, blew out an exasperated sigh and gazed up at the ceiling as if for inspiration.

'Please, Wolff, I'm dying of suspense,' she begged, carefully depositing her pottery mug of coffee on the work-surface before she snatched a nervous breath and continued.

'Have you thought of some way for me to try to get pregnant without the whole hospital finding out I'm going to the fertility clinic?'

'Yes, but...'

'Oh, Wolff!' She flew across the short distance between them and flung her arms round him, narrowly avoiding his own mug of coffee.

'Hang on, Laura!' he exclaimed, twisting to put the hot liquid in a safer place, but he didn't break her hold, and Laura noticed that he hadn't really tried very hard.

'Tell me, please,' she begged. 'How do I avoid being seen?'

'By not going to the fertility clinic,' he said simply.

'But. . .'

'Think about it,' he continued. 'You only need to go to the fertility clinic if you are physically incapable, for one reason or another, of becoming pregnant. Right?'

'Right,' she agreed. 'But. . .'

'And so far,' he continued, ignoring her rider, 'you have no reason to suppose that the endometriosis has irreparably damaged your ovaries. In other words, because of the irregularities in your system it might take longer to achieve fertilisation, but there's actually no physical reason why you shouldn't get pregnant eventually.'

Laura nodded seriously.

'No one has ever actually put it that clearly, Wolff, but of course you're quite right.'

'So, in actual fact, the only reason why you would need to go to the fertility clinic would be to have your own egg fertilised.'

'Exactly,' she agreed, whirling away to walk to the other side of the kitchen and back, suddenly frustrated that the conversation had circled back to the same point. 'And that's why I need to go. . .'

'So, really,' he interrupted quietly, 'all you need is a willing sperm donor.'

His soft words stopped her in her tracks and she spun back to stare at him.

'You're right,' she breathed, stunned by the simplicity of it, then she froze as the implications of what he'd said dawned on her, and as her heart went crazy inside her chest she found herself examining his face very closely.

He had that expression in his eyes again, the one that made her think of a hungry wolf on the prowl, and her heart began to beat heavily against her ribs as her thoughts suddenly became very clear.

Yes, she needed a sperm donor if she was ever going to become pregnant and, logically, she didn't need to go to the fertility clinic to find one.

But while her mind was calmly listing the basic facts her heart was filled with the sudden realisation that there was only one man she wanted to be the father of her child.

A hint of uncertainty made her drag her eyes away from the heat in his.

Was he hinting that *he* would be willing to be the donor, or was that just wishful thinking on her part?

'Well?' he demanded, his deep voice huskier than ever. 'What do you think?'

She flicked a glance back at him and was surprised at the hint of vulnerability in his expression. All she had to do now was choose her words carefully so that she didn't end up embarrassing both of them.

'What are you suggesting?' she asked faintly, tempted to cross her fingers for luck.

She watched him draw in a deep breath, as though bracing himself, and his chin inched up as if in expectation of a blow.

'I could do it, if you like,' he offered steadily, and Laura began to breathe again.

'You'd be willing to donate sperm for me?' she questioned as happiness flooded through her.

She hardly noticed the way he flinched at her words, too overjoyed that it was Wolff who had shown her how to fulfil her dream and Wolff who was willing to father a child for her.

'If you like,' he agreed tersely.

Laura sighed with relief as she uncrossed her fingers and then giggled, almost as giddy as if she'd been drinking. 'Oh, yes, I like,' she said. 'Oh, Wolff, how can I ever thank you? If you only knew...'

'Well,' he interrupted abruptly, his clipped tone bringing her feet back down to earth in a hurry, 'where do we go from here? When do you want to start, and how well regulated is your cycle?'

Laura looked up at him, puzzled by the hint of anger in his voice. He couldn't be regretting his offer already, could he? It was a sobering thought.

'I suppose I should start as soon as possible,' she suggested sensibly. 'Bearing in mind that I don't know how fast the endometriosis is progressing.'

One of the things she remembered very clearly from the consultation with the specialist was the possibility that her form of endometriosis could eventually damage her ovaries so much that she would become totally infertile. It could be just a matter of time...

'As for my cycle...' She paused to do some mental calculations and her pulse doubled at the result. 'I should be in my most fertile phase in about a week.'

'Fine.' He nodded, the expression in his eyes hidden

behind those sinfully long lashes as though he didn't want her to know his thoughts any more.

'I know you're taking people's temperatures all day, but do you know how to chart your basal body temperature so that you can tell when you ovulate?'

This was his doctor's voice, calm and professional, and it helped her to respond the same way.

'I know that there is a slight dip in my normal temperature when the egg is actually released, and then it rises a bit above normal until the end of my cycle.'

'Is it a clear difference?'

'Yes, I'm one of the lucky ones—apart from the fact that the endometriosis means that I can almost feel the egg being released.'

'What?' He seemed quite startled.

'Yes.' She smiled wryly. 'I get quite a sharp pain at the time of ovulation—*when* it occurs—but the cycles when there is no egg released are becoming more frequent. . .'

He nodded, an expression of sympathy warming his shuttered face for a moment.

'In which case. . .'

'Where did you. . .?'

Once again they had started speaking together, and he gestured for her to continue.

'I was only going to ask where you thought we should. . .do it?' she questioned diffidently, feeling the heat rise in her face again.

'Wherever you would feel most comfortable,' he replied easily, before adding with a frown, 'except it might cause gossip if I'm seen going in and out of your room.'

'Would. . .would you mind if we did it here?' she asked

with a swift mental image of the wonderful brass bed up in his room.

'I wouldn't mind at all,' he agreed with a small smile. 'It's more peaceful here, with no nosy colleagues keeping an eye on your visitors, and, anyway, if we're successful it would be one more happy story to add to the tale of my grandparents' bed!'

Laura smothered a gasp of shock. Had he been reading her mind?

'Do you think we've covered everything?' he asked while she was still enmeshed in visions of herself lying in the middle of his family heirloom bed.

'I. . .I think so,' she stammered, scrambling for her common sense.

'In which case, I'll wait for you to tell me when the time is right,' he said, and her heart took a sudden dive when he began fishing for his keys.

'*And* hope that the two of us aren't on shifts at opposite ends of the day when the time comes,' she added wryly. 'I know of several nurses married to doctors who reckon a hospital duty roster means they don't need contraceptives—they're never home at the same time for there to be any risk that they'll get pregnant. . .'

Wolff chuckled briefly, his expression lightening a little at the typical hospital pessimism.

'Well, Nick Prince is due back this week after his honeymoon in Brittany,' he pointed out. 'That should take the pressure off *my* timetable. Do you want me to see what I can do to synchronise the two of us?'

'Don't you dare!' she squeaked, secretly delighted that he would even suggest the idea. 'Never mind the department gossiping—the whole hospital would have a field day if you did that!'

'It might be worth it,' he suggested cheekily. 'I haven't started to build up any sort of a reputation yet—apart from the rather adolescent one Leo has been trying to revive.'

'You'd certainly have a reputation if you were seen to be involved with me, and then several months later I start looking as if I've swallowed a watermelon!' she reminded him.

He grinned at her but she saw his eyes flick down to her slender waist and linger for a moment, as though he was imagining what she would look like with her body swollen with his child, and when he met her eyes again he was looking strangely thoughtful.

CHAPTER NINE

'NURSE?'

Laura looked up from the trolley. The department had been frantically busy this afternoon and she'd been left on her own in the treatment room to finish clearing away after a mammoth session of stitching up hooligans after a bottle fight outside the local football ground.

She'd been checking the level of supplies of needles and sutures when the tentative voice broke into her concentration.

'Can I help you?' she asked him with a smile. 'Are you lost?'

Automatically her eyes travelled over his pale, clammy-looking face. He could just be nervous but, patient or visitor, she didn't like the look of him.

'My chest hurts. . .and my arm. I don't feel very well. . .'

He doesn't look very well, either, she thought, and was almost certain that he was a prime candidate for a heart attack.

'Come and sit down,' she said, clearing off the top of the trolley with a speed born of adrenaline and intuition and putting a hand under his elbow to help him hitch himself up.

'In fact, you might as well lie down and be comfortable,' she suggested, supporting his shoulders as she lowered him easily on to his back. There was hardly anything of him, she thought as she reached for the phone. He hardly weighed any more than she did, and he was several inches taller—hardly the picture of a typical heart-attack victim.

Sister MacDonald answered on the second ring and Laura spared a glance at the man, lying there with his eyes shut, before she turned away to muffle her voice a little.

'A patient has just walked into treatment room two, apparently without being processed through Reception. He's pale and clammy and suffering chest pain,' she said succinctly, hoping that the man couldn't hear her speaking because he would be able to tell from her tone that she thought it was something serious.

'I've got him lying down but I'm the only one here and I need assistance,' she finished calmly.

'Good lass,' Celia said. 'Hang on and I'll send the team. He'll need the heart monitor and IVs, oxygen and blood for testing. In the meantime, start on his vital signs.'

In the absence of any case notes, Laura grabbed a drug company's promotional notepad, coincidentally advertising a tablet designed to combat high blood pressure, and began jotting down her findings.

As she spoke calmingly to him she was able to add details of the man's name and date of birth, but what she was really waiting for was the team to arrive before something major happened.

She had a nasty feeling about him.

It seemed like hours until there was the sound of hurrying feet in the corridor, and within seconds they were surrounded as the monitor leads were attached and IVs set up.

There was a brief pause when the bloods were sent up to the lab, and Laura had perched herself on a stool near the man's head to copy the details she'd scribbled down onto his new file when he made a funny sound.

She looked at his face and, if anything, he looked worse than when he'd wandered in, in spite of the oxygen mask and the two IVs.

Suddenly the rhythm of the heart monitor changed and a quick glance up at the screen showed her the horribly familiar pattern for ventricular tachycardia.

At that moment she was the closest person to the patient, and she knew that if something wasn't done fairly quickly his heartbeat could degenerate still further into ventricular fibrillation or even full cardiac arrest.

There was no time to think, no time to speak. She just leapt to her feet, vaguely aware that the sheets of paper in the carefully ordered file had just tumbled to the floor as she locked her fingers together into a double fist and thumped him in the middle of his chest.

'Good girl. You beat me to it,' said Wolff, his husky voice coming from just behind her shoulder as they both looked up at the monitor and confirmed that the sudden shock had converted his rhythm back to normal.

'You've got good reactions,' he said approvingly as he checked the man over and confirmed that his heart and breathing rhythms were back to normal again. Then he looked over at her to share a brief smile of success before it was back to business.

'Can we get that box of tricks to spit out an ECG trace as fast as possible? Then we can get him organised for a trip to the cardiologist,' Wolff said to the team, as calmly as if they hadn't just nearly lost their patient. 'He walked in here just in time on the right day, and Laura managed to react fast enough just now to keep him going. He's had a second chance and I think he deserves to get three out of three so let's get moving.'

Laura went to retrieve the scattered notes and saw a slightly nonplussed expression on the patient's face, as if everything was happening too fast for him to take it all in.

'I'm sorry I had to hit you,' she murmured apologetically. 'Are you all right?'

He smiled, his face carrying a little more colour now that the first drugs were stabilising him, and tilted his head towards Wolff.

'If he said he reckons I should get three out of three then I'd jolly well better be all right, hadn't I? Thanks for whatever it was you did just then...I couldn't catch my breath for a minute.'

It wasn't long before their unexpected patient was on his way upstairs, and Laura surveyed the debris left behind with a sigh before she set to again to put the room to rights.

She was on late shift today, and had been feeling rather tired and lethargic for several hours. At least tomorrow was a day off again and, noise permitting, she'd be able to catch up on some sleep.

It didn't seem possible that it was over a week since Wolff had been waiting outside the hospital and had given her a lift to his new home.

The last thing she'd been expecting when she went with him was the startling offer he'd made, and several times during the last week she'd wondered if she'd dreamt the whole thing.

But then she would catch sight of him around the department, and when he lifted one dark eyebrow in a silent question she knew that it had actually happened.

At odd times, when they were on the same shift, he seemed to deliberately take his breaks at the same time as she did, almost as if he wanted to build up some sort of rapport with the woman who was hoping to carry his child.

While she was nervous of allowing herself to become too drawn to him, she had to admit that she enjoyed his company and she'd already found out that they shared the same wry sense of humour.

The trouble was that there were too many observant eyes around them and, at some stage or another, both Leo and Hannah had spotted Wolff and herself silently communicating their opinions of events going on around them.

When the A and E consultant himself had sent them a questioning look after an unexplained simultaneous chuckle, she had blushed scarlet and wished that the ground would open up and swallow her—but she couldn't make herself regret the growing closeness she felt towards him.

'No change?' a husky voice murmured for the second time that day, and she nearly jumped out of her skin.

'You again!' she muttered, glancing around quickly to see if they could be overheard. 'I thought the arrangement was that *I* would let you know.'

'Yes, but. . .'

'But nothing,' she said fiercely. 'If we carry on this way everyone's going to wonder what's going on and, anyway, this could be an anovular cycle, and if there's no egg released my temperature *won't* change.'

'All right, all right!' Wolff held his hands up and backed off with a grin at her unaccustomed snappishness. 'Don't kill me, you might want me later.'

'I'm too tired to dig a six-foot hole,' she said darkly. 'So you're safe—for now.'

He was still chuckling as he strode away down the corridor, leaving her to her thoughts.

That was the problem in a nutshell, she complained

silently. He'd joked about the fact that she might be needing him later but, if her X-rated dreams were anything to go by, she already needed him now—desperately.

She'd tried to rationalise her feelings, reminding herself that he'd only offered to be a sperm donor—not a husband—but she couldn't get her stupid heart to listen.

Now every time she was near him, even when they were in the middle of a traumatic situation, she was aware of his presence beside her, and when his shift was over she felt lonely, although she was surrounded by the usual throng in the department.

Apart from the fact that Nick Prince and his new bride were still the focus of all sorts of jokes, today was much like any other day in the A and E department.

They could tell that the flu season was already in full swing by the number of people turning up convinced that they were dying—or else coughing so badly that they wished they were.

There had been the usual mixture of time-wasters and the genuine emergencies which sent the adrenaline pouring into her system and kept her on her toes, but nothing seemed to keep her mind away from Wolff Bergen for long.

Just this afternoon there had been a particularly harrowing asthma attack when an eleven-year-old girl had suddenly gone into cardiac arrest.

She'd had to be shocked before they could get her back, but when she had finally been stabilised and sent off on her way to the ward they'd all looked at each other with a communal grin of success.

Suddenly Laura realised that she was beginning to feel as if she'd been accepted as a full member of the team, and she couldn't help the smile of delight she threw in Wolff's direction.

Finally, it was the end of her shift and she made her way gratefully towards her room.

On the chest of drawers lay the cylinder containing her thermometer and she pulled a face at it, wondering if it was worth bothering with it tonight. It looked as if this cycle was going to be one of her increasing number of anovular ones, and she was going to have to cross her fingers and wait until next month before she could make her first attempt at conceiving.

She shrugged and finally reached for it, slipping it under her tongue to 'cook' while she rummaged for a fresh towel and got ready to take a long hot shower. Perhaps then she'd feel as if she'd got a bit more energy or, if not, she could always have an early night and hope to feel better in the morning.

When the time was up she glanced disconsolately at the silvery line of mercury and prepared to shake it back down, ready for tomorrow morning, then froze and looked again.

'It's dropped!' she whispered in disbelief, and suddenly realised why she'd been feeling off-colour all afternoon. 'It's dropped!' she repeated, her hand beginning to shake so that she couldn't see the evidence any longer.

All at once her mind went blank, and she couldn't remember what she and Wolff had arranged to do when this happened.

She had to contact him. . .but how?

By telephone. . .but what was his number?

He wrote it down on a piece of paper. . .but where had she put it?

Suddenly she was racing round her room like a madwoman, opening and closing drawers and peering in pockets.

'Think!' she ordered herself as she stood in the middle of the room. 'What did you do with it when he gave it to you?'

She closed her eyes and remembered the mock-furtive way he'd handed her the tightly folded scrap of paper—as if he were a desperate spy, handing over international secrets.

'In my pocket!' she muttered triumphantly, then remembered that it had been several days ago and the pocket in question had been washed—probably twice by now.

A vague picture formed in her mind of the last lot of washing she'd sorted, and she remembered emptying several unwanted messages into the bin. Had Wolff's been one of them?

She sank to her knees and prepared to sort through cleanser-soaked cotton-wool and paper hankies to see if the precious number was lurking at the bottom—but the bin was clean and empty, and she remembered tipping all the rubbish away when she'd cleaned her room this morning before she went on duty.

Laura stood in the middle of the room with fists planted on her hips and groaned aloud.

What was she going to do now?

The gleam of light off her small bunch of keys drew her eyes and, finally, her brain was working again.

She knew where he lived, and she knew that he was off duty this evening. All she had to do was turn up on his doorstep and apologise for coming without warning.

The thought that he might have visitors with him was

daunting but she could always offer to come back later. It wasn't as if the process was going to take very long...

She slid her arms back into her parka and grabbed a small carrier bag from the little stack she'd saved from her shopping trips. A quick glance inside her wash bag confirmed that the items she'd put ready were tucked into the side pocket, and she slid the whole thing into the camouflage of the plastic bag before she grabbed her keys and let herself out.

All the way over to Wolff's house she was assailed with last-minute doubts and fears.

Was she doing the right thing?

A swift mental image of herself cradling a dark-haired infant while he suckled at her breast sent a shaft of longing through her. Just the thought that it might never happen if she didn't seize the chance she'd been offered was enough to dispose of that qualm.

But was Wolff still willing...?

That was something she wouldn't know until she'd told him that she'd ovulated and had watched the expression on his face.

She drew her elderly Mini to a halt outside his house and saw from the thin sliver of light showing down one edge of the curtains that there was someone home.

The time for procrastination was over. Now all she had to do was to get out of the car and knock on his door.

'Laura!'

At least he sounded pleased to see her, she thought as her knees knocked like castanets.

'Come in,' he invited, standing back so that she could enter the welcoming warmth of the hallway. 'This is a surprise. What can I do for you?'

He stood there, surrounded by the smell of exotic food and looking absolutely delicious, and asked her what he could do for her? If her heart kept misbehaving the way it was he was going to have to practise cardiac resuscitation off duty.

What *had* she come here for?

'I...I'm sorry to just turn up like this,' she said nervously as she remembered the reason for her journey. 'But when I looked I couldn't find the piece of paper...with your telephone number on it...and...'

'And?' There was a gleam of patient humour in his eyes at her stumbling explanation.

'And it's gone down,' she announced baldly. 'This evening when I got back to my room I took it and it's gone down.'

She saw the second when he finally realised what she was talking about.

'You mean your temperature dipped? You've ovulated?' The expression of fierce gladness in his eyes took her breath away.

If she'd had any lingering doubts about his continued willingness to help her get pregnant they were dispelled in that instant.

'Ah, Laura, I'm so pleased for you,' he said, and drew her into his arms for a spontaneous hug. 'All week I've seen you getting more and more tense as you worried about it, but now...' He lifted her off her feet and swung her round in a circle until she laughed out loud.

'Wolff, you idiot! Put me down!'

'Certainly not,' he retorted, and, instead, reached down to hook one arm under her legs so that he was now carrying her in his arms as he set off towards the kitchen.

'What are you doing, you crazy man?' she demanded as he deposited her on the first chair inside the door.

'Settling you at the table before I feed you,' he announced, and reached out towards the stove to turn the heat on again.

'Feed me? But...'

That wasn't what she'd expected to happen when she'd come here to make her announcement.

'I haven't eaten yet, and I doubt whether you've had time to.' He raised an eyebrow in her direction and she had to shake her head.

'I was actually expecting to feed Leo tonight,' he explained. 'It was supposed to be a thank-you for putting up with my mess while I looked for this place, but he called off at the last minute. Apparently, he's swapped shifts tonight for some reason. And as I happen to have enough food prepared to feed an army you are quite welcome to share.'

He turned back towards the stove and tipped the first lot of ingredients into the wok, stirring the sizzling mixture with casual competence. Several aromatic and pungent additions later he tipped everything into the large serving bowl he'd placed to warm in the oven and carried it over with the two ready-warmed plates, a chilled bottle of white wine under his arm.

'Fork or chopsticks?' he offered with a grin, and she accepted the challenge.

'Chopsticks, on condition that I don't have to clean the floor!'

She laughed at his disgusted expression, then proceeded to show him that she was as adept at handling them as he was.

By the time they'd argued over the last of the cashew nuts and snow peas and taken the last of the wine through to the sitting room to linger over while they talked, Laura was so relaxed that she had almost forgotten why she'd come to his house.

As she drained the last sip of the deliciously crisp wine from her glass and leant back into her corner of the settee she half-heartedly offered to help with the washing up, but he shook his head.

'I'll do that in a little while,' he said quietly, his eyes suddenly intent as he met her questioning gaze, and instantly her nerves began to tighten again.

'Should I. . .? Do you. . .?' She stopped and snatched a quick breath into suddenly constricted lungs.

'Hey, Laura, relax,' he murmured and reached one hand out towards her along the back of the settee.

He combed his fingers through the silky strands of her hair and cupped her cheek, a gentle smile playing over his mouth.

'It will be all right. . .' he said softly. 'I promise. . .'

'I'm sorry, Wolff.'

She drew in a calming breath and forced herself to meet the concern in his eyes. 'I do trust you, but. . .I'm a bit nervous. I've never done this before.'

'In which case you'll be glad to hear that I've done some research on the subject,' he announced with a perfectly straight face.

'I've never heard it called that before,' Laura said, and couldn't help chuckling.

'I don't mean *that*!' he retorted, trying to sound offended. 'I actually meant that I've done some research into the guidelines offered by the fertility clinics to maximise the chances of conception.'

'Oh,' Laura breathed, and felt the wash of heat along her cheek-bones. 'I see.'

'Not yet, but you will!' he promised with a wicked smile. 'Now listen while I give you your instructions.'

'Yes, sir!' She gave him a mock salute.

'That's good!' he said. 'Start as you mean to go on! Now, while I do the washing up, I want you to go upstairs and do whatever will make you comfortable. You're welcome to have a bath or a shower and just help yourself to anything you need.'

Laura nodded and swallowed, unable to meet his eyes as she scrambled awkwardly out of the comfortable settee and hurried up the stairs.

It hardly seemed as if five minutes had passed before she heard the sound of Wolff's feet coming up the stairs and she froze just inside his bedroom door like a frightened deer, poised for flight.

As she'd expected she heard the click of the bathroom door, followed by the sound of the shower running and then silence...

Her cheeks grew fiery as her imagination ran riot. She'd left everything ready for him on the shelf by the basin, knowing that he would be bound to find it.

All she had to do while she was waiting was remember to keep breathing—or he might just come in and find her unconscious on the floor.

'Laura?'

She hadn't heard him leave the bathroom and the sound of his husky voice so close behind her gave her such a shock that she jumped visibly and whirled to face him.

'Wolff?' she whispered, her breath completely stolen away by the sight of him, all golden tan and long powerful muscles, the broad wedge of his torso covered with a scattering of damp silky hair arrowing down towards his lean waist and hips.

His towel was a much smaller version of the large one she'd borrowed to wrap around herself, and it scarcely hid the bare essentials.

For several long seconds her eyes travelled admiringly from his shoulders to his feet and back again, and she wished she'd had the courage to ask him to impregnate her the traditional way.

But he'd only offered to be a sperm donor and, instead, they'd be using the syringe she'd left ready for him in the bathroom, and she would just have to be grateful for that.

She cast one last covetous look over his broad shoulders and forced her eyes up to meet his—to discover that he was frowning.

'Is. . .is there a problem?' she asked when she finally realised that he was empty-handed.

'Yes and no,' he answered cryptically, his husky voice seeming deeper than ever as he stepped close enough for her to feel the heat radiating from his body.

'Didn't you find. . .? Couldn't you. . .?' The words wouldn't come past the lump in her throat as embarrassment overwhelmed her and she subsided into silence.

'Laura?' He hooked one warm finger under her chin and tilted her head up until she finally met his eyes. 'Do you trust me?' he asked, and she could see in his eyes that her answer mattered to him.

She nodded.

'Yes, Wolff,' she whispered, knowing that it was true.

'Then will you trust me to do my best to help you achieve your dream?'

She gazed up into his eyes, puzzled by his intensity as she tried to work out the significance of his questions.

As she searched his face for clues she watched the way his own eyes kept returning to her mouth as if it fascinated him, his pupils dilating as though just the sight of it was arousing.

Suddenly she knew what he was asking—what he wanted—and she drew her breath in on a gasp of relief and delight.

'Oh, yes, Wolff,' she said, her voice quivering with the intensity of her emotions. 'I'll trust you,' and she surged up on tiptoe to touch her lips to his.

For a second he held himself in check, as though he wasn't certain he could believe what was happening, but then his arms circled her and he covered her mouth with his, a deep groan wrenched from him as she met his marauding tongue eagerly.

Long minutes later he pulled away just far enough to allow her to catch her breath.

'Ah, Laura,' he whispered, his own breathing laboured as he gave a husky chuckle. 'If we do much more of that I'm going to have the same control problem as an adolescent, and that won't help you at all!'

He pressed one last kiss to her forehead and turned her towards his family heirloom bed.

'Let's add another chapter to the saga of the brass bed,' he invited softly, and led her across the room.

The overlap on the towel she'd wrapped around herself lasted just long enough for her to sit on the edge of the mattress before it was overcome by gravity and pooled around her waist.

'Oh!' Laura tried to retrieve it but Wolff was faster, his hand resting over hers to prevent her covering herself again.

'Let me look at you, please. You're so dainty...so beautiful.' He worshipped her with his eyes before he gave in to the temptation to touch, and once she felt his hands on her body she was lost.

As if in an enchanted dream, she followed his lead as he removed first her towel then his own and helped her to slip under the covers.

When he wrapped her in his arms it didn't feel in the least bit like the coldly clinical attempt at impregnating her that she'd been expecting, and when he explained the various theories about the best positions and optimum methods for conception to occur his husky murmur in her ear sounded far more like erotic foreplay than a scholarly dissertation.

Then he proceeded by degrees to show her all the things he'd described, with a pile of pillows underneath her hips so that they were tilted just right, before he parted her quivering thighs and joined his body with hers.

Even when his own pleasure was complete he continued to pleasure her, his hands teaching her things about her body she'd never dreamt about as he explained that her own orgasms would hasten the journey of his seed inside her.

When at last they both lay still Wolff curled around her, persuading her to stay on her throne of pillows with her legs draped over the hard support of his thighs so that she could stay comfortably in the most favourable position as long as possible.

Utterly replete, she revelled in his possessive care and

at some stage, just before she drifted off into a deliciously decadent doze, she realised with a sensation of absolute inevitability that she had fallen in love with him.

Several times during the night she was woken with kisses and gentle caresses as Wolff roused her to new heights of ecstasy, and each time she was aware that her love was growing deeper—until she had to bite her lip to prevent herself from blurting out her discovery.

The smell of coffee tantalised her and Laura lifted heavy lids to find Wolff, sitting on the edge of the bed in all his naked glory and sipping a steaming mugful as he waited for her to wake up.

'If you can spare a mouthful or two of that I might be able to focus,' Laura mumbled.

Her heart had leapt when she'd realised that he was sitting so close and for a minute she had worried what she must look like, sprawled in the tumbled wreck of his bed.

Then she realised that she didn't care if he could see more of her than she was accustomed to anyone seeing at this time of day. He had already seen and touched every inch of her during the long night, and her newly discovered love meant that she trusted him—even if he was being very mean about sharing that delicious-smelling coffee.

A slow heavy pulse began to beat deep inside her as she thought about the pleasure he'd given her through the night. They both had a day off today, and she could only imagine what delights he might initiate once she was awake enough to respond. . .

'You can have some coffee in just a minute, sleepyhead,' Wolff promised with a deep chuckle. 'First of all, open your mouth for me.'

He'd used the same words several times last night and her stomach clenched in anticipation.

Something cold and hard nudged at her lips and when she parted them in surprise she felt the familiar length of a thermometer sliding between them.

Suddenly she remembered exactly why she was lying in Wolff's bed with her hips angled up on a pile of pillows, and the effect on her was as shocking as having cold water dashed into her face.

CHAPTER TEN

AFTERWARDS, Laura could never remember what she'd said to persuade Wolff that she needed to return to her room.

The next thing she knew was that she was sitting on her bed with her arms wrapped around her waist while she rocked silently backwards and forwards.

She didn't know whether she was hoping that she *was* pregnant, so that she would always have a part of Wolff to keep with her for ever, or hoping that she *wasn't*, so that she could legitimately spend another ecstatic night in his big brass bed.

Either way, she felt emotionally shredded that, while she had fallen in love with him and had believed that they were beginning to form a deep and lasting bond, he had never lost sight of the fact that she was only in his bed so that he could help her to become pregnant.

For ten days she wondered and worried while she worked her shifts alongside him, trying to treat him as though he meant no more to her than Leo or Nick.

She knew that he had noticed the difference in her attitude towards him, and where once she would have welcomed any chance to spend time with him now she actively avoided him. It hurt too much to spend time with him, knowing that the love she felt for him was not returned.

Sometimes she felt his eyes on her, their laser intensity

almost burning, and she'd seen that terrible empty look return to their icy blue depths.

'Laura?' Hannah began tentatively when it was their turn for a coffee-break. 'Is something the matter?'

'Not that I know of,' Laura replied defensively, while the persistent little voice inside her cried out about broken hearts and broken dreams.

'I wondered if you were sorry you moved to St Augustine's after all. You don't seem to be very happy. Did...?' She paused, as though uncertain whether to ask the question on her tongue, then continued, 'Did you and Wolff have some sort of bust-up?'

'Wolff and I?' Laura did her best to sound amazed and amused, and apparently pulled it off.

'Well, you did seem to be getting on rather well when he first came here, and I began to wonder if there was the possibility of something developing between you... But then, suddenly, you were hardly speaking to each other and Wolff was growling at everyone.'

'Oh.' Laura's brain whirled as she tried to come up with an explanation, then decided to stick as close to the truth as possible. 'He did a bit of research for me several weeks ago...about endometriosis. But that's all there was between us.' Apart from the most fantastic night of love-making she would ever know in her life, but that was something she wasn't ever going to confide to anyone else—whether it had resulted in a pregnancy or not.

'Endometriosis?' Hannah questioned, and then she nodded as if that explained something she'd wondered about. 'I remember you having problems sometimes when we were training. Is that what it was?'

Feeling guilty about being unable to confide the details

of her arrangement with Wolff, Laura compromised by telling her about the demise of her relationship with Peter.

'Luckily, once I transferred to A and E we didn't work too closely together so I just gritted my teeth and got on with the job.' And cried private tears about all the lost dreams.

'So how soon after did he marry her?' Hannah asked with quiet understanding in her tone.

Laura gave a wry laugh. 'I couldn't help myself following what was happening, and I was bracing myself for the big event to happen fairly quickly but it didn't.'

She shook her head, knowing that the old hurts were clear in her voice but suddenly needing the catharsis.

'I thought that perhaps she wasn't too willing to give up a good career to be a brood mare, and I even found myself fantasising that he was delaying committing himself to her because he was regretting breaking up with me. . . But then, a couple of months ago, everything went ahead with a big splash.' She drew an unsteady breath.

'It was only when the grapevine dissected the reasons for the sudden rush to the altar that I found out his new bride was nearly three months pregnant—he'd obviously taken the precaution of making sure she could give him the children he wants.'

'What a rat!' Hannah said with more venom than Laura would have expected, and suddenly she realised that Hannah had her secrets, too.

Something similar must have happened to *her* in the time since they'd last been together.

She vaguely remembered that her friend had been seeing a specialist about something. . .

'If there's anything I can do you know I'm always willing,' Hannah offered, her voice banishing Laura's attempt at remembering.

'Unfortunately, some things can't be mended with a hug or some superglue,' Laura murmured, returning to her own concerns. 'And we can't always have our dreams, no matter how much we want them.'

'Too true,' her friend agreed with a touch of bitterness in her usually cheerful voice. 'Very few of us get a second chance at happiness.'

There was the sound of approaching footsteps and Laura recognised Wolff's voice among the others.

'Well,' she said, rising briskly to her feet, 'time I was back at work.'

Before Hannah could utter a word she had tipped the last of her coffee down the sink and rinsed her mug.

By the time the small knot of people had entered the room she was already waiting to leave, her eyes carefully averted so that she couldn't possibly catch Wolff's eye.

She knew how cowardly it was to run from the situation, but until she knew the results of the night they'd spent together she couldn't bear spending time with him. It tore at her heart to know that while she had been falling more and more deeply in love with him he had merely been performing a biological function.

Not that she could blame him. After all, that was all he had offered and, having listened while he'd talked about the tragic things he had seen at the refugee camp, she could understand that he was unconvinced about the worth of a committed relationship.

In spite of her attempt at avoiding him, she looked up at just the wrong time as she went to leave the room and met his eyes full-on for the first time in over a week.

Her heart gave a sick jolt when she realised that he didn't look any happier than she felt, his eyes empty of expression, and she could have wept when she had to restrain her automatic action to reach out and comfort him.

As she dragged her eyes away and continued on her way she sternly reminded herself that she had no right to touch him, no right—other than as a fellow human being—to care that he was unhappy and wonder why.

She tapped on the door and started to walk into Sister's office before she suddenly realised that it was already occupied by a totally oblivious couple.

'Sorry,' she muttered, full of embarrassment, and smartly reversed direction.

'Don't go,' called Polly as she disentangled herself from her husband's arms. 'We're the ones who should apologise—it was totally unprofessional to be caught like that.'

'At least we're married,' her husband pointed out in their defence. 'And it was a one-off thing.'

'I hope not,' Polly muttered swiftly, then went red when she realised that she'd said the words out loud.

'What I meant,' Nick continued smoothly, to spare her blushes, 'was that the kiss was a celebration of a special event and not a habit we'll be indulging in while we're on duty.'

Laura tried not to look curious, but realised that she'd obviously failed when Polly laughed.

'If I tell you can you keep it quiet for a little while so we have time to savour it before it gets on the grapevine?'

'You don't have to. . .' Laura began awkwardly, feeling that she was intruding on something intensely private.

'I'm pregnant,' Polly blurted, and smiled lovingly up at

the big man, hovering protectively over her. 'I've just had official confirmation.'

For a second envy made the smile freeze on her face, but then the natural joy at their happiness took over.

'Congratulations. I don't need to ask if you're pleased.'

'Ecstatic,' Polly confirmed with a giggle.

'Whether she'll still feel the same when it comes to early morning feeds and changing nappies remains to be seen,' Nick warned, but it was obvious that he was just as delighted as she was.

The touching scene played on her mind all day, and the more she thought about it the more she realised that the situation between Wolff and herself couldn't go on like this.

She didn't want to leave her job, not now that she'd been accepted as a valuable member of the team and especially with the excellent career prospects ahead of her. On the other hand, knowing that Wolff had just bought a house, she knew that he would be very unwilling to move again so soon.

They were two intelligent adults, for heaven's sake. There must be some way of sitting down and thrashing out their differences or it would sour things for everyone.

A little quiver of apprehension settled deep inside her when she thought about confronting Wolff, but she promised herself that she *would* do it—just as soon as she found out whether she was pregnant or not.

She didn't have to tell him that she'd fallen in love with him, she reminded herself as she detoured into a chemist's shop on her way back to her room and stood, contemplating a display of pregnancy indicator kits. And at least once she had a result she'd have a reason to approach him to initiate the conversation.

She made her choice and cursed silently at the stupidity of a qualified nurse who at work dealt calmly and efficiently with every intimacy inside and outside the human body at work yet blushed betroot-red over buying a pregnancy test kit.

There were new road-works creating havoc on her way back to the nurses' accommodation, and she had to take the long way round before she could park her scruffy little car and scurry through the dark into the light and warmth of her room.

There had been headlights following her before she'd stopped, and when the car had drawn past her she'd imagined that it had been the one Wolff had given her a lift in when...

'Stop it,' she hissed into the silence of her room as she kicked off her shoes and hung her parka on the back of the door.

It was time to concentrate on reading the instructions on the packet and carrying them out. *Then* would come the time for seeking Wolff out and...

'Bother!' she muttered as the leaflet slid out of her fingers and fell neatly down the back of her chest of drawers. 'How am I going to get *that* out?'

She dropped to her knees in the space between the cupboard and the door of her room and tried to wriggle her fingers into the narrow gap to fish it out, but before she had any success there was an enormous roar and the sound of shattering glass as the lights went out and she was plunged into darkness.

The first thing she noticed when the noise ended was

that she was cold, then she realised that there was a heavy weight pinning her down and that it was difficult for her to draw in a breath.

The unearthly silence which had followed the roar was now filled with screams and further crashes, as well as the sound of water cascading somewhere nearby. In the distance there was the familiar reassuring sound of the siren on an approaching vehicle.

'Laura!'

She peered into the darkness, certain that she'd heard someone shouting her name, but with all the noise going on around her she could easily have been mistaken. She knew to her cost that wishful thinking could have you believing all sorts of things. . .

'Laura!'

The voice was coming closer, and this time she could hear that it *was* calling her name. She tried to call back but couldn't draw in a deep enough breath. It felt as if she had half the building sitting on her chest.

'Laura!'

The voice was right outside her room now, and if it hadn't been for the fear distorting it she would have sworn it was Wolff's voice.

'Oh, God! Please, not Laura. . .not Laura!' the voice begged, and the familiar husky tone told her that it *was* Wolff outside her door.

'Wolff. . .' she tried to call, but it emerged as nothing more than a whisper and the effort made her cough.

'Laura?' He must have heard the choking sound she made because the word was a demand this time. 'Can you hear me, Laura?'

'Yes,' she breathed on a shallow sigh, but he heard her.

'Oh, thank you, God,' she heard him mutter before there was the sound of crashes and bangs not far from her head.

Outside, too, there was a cacophony as the emergency teams began to get to grips with the situation. There was the sound of a powerful generator starting up and a bright light suddenly flooded her room as floodlights were switched on around the scene.

'Laura?' Wolff called to her again, his voice sounding as if it was just inches away from her head. 'Are you hurt?'

Laura experimentally tensed the muscles in each of her limbs but, apart from the cupboard pinning her against the wall, she seemed to be all right.

'Trapped,' she muttered succinctly with her limited air supply.

'Trapped?' he repeated.

'Yess.'

'By masonry?' he demanded, but she didn't bother making the effort to reply. He'd never have heard the soft breathy sound of the word 'no' over the sounds of rescue.

'Furniture?' he guessed, and she hissed briefly in agreement.

'Are you near the door?' he asked, and she could hear from the forced patience of his questions that he wasn't nearly as calm as he was pretending to be.

'Yess,' she whispered again, the effort quite exhausting her as she dragged the next breath in.

'If I try to open the door will I injure you more?' Wolff demanded, his patience obviously wearing very thin.

Laura turned her head this way and that while she tried to judge how firmly the furniture was wedged into the corner.

Now that there was light coming in from outside she could see that there must have been some sort of explosion because nearly half of the outside wall had been blown into her room, the glass from her window glittering in deadly shards as far as she could see.

Exploring with the hand not trapped, she worked out that if she could...

'Laura? Are you still with me?' The anxiety in his voice dragged her out of her musings.

'Yess,' she answered, a tired smile creeping over her face when she realised that he was worried about her. It wasn't the same as loving her, but at least she knew he cared.

'I'm going to try to open the door,' he announced, his endurance obviously at an end. 'I'll go slowly so if you need me to stop just hiss. OK?'

'Yess,' she agreed, her heart lifting at the thought of release.

She heard the door catch release and braced her hand against the heavy piece of furniture pinning her down. Hopefully, when he started to push against it the angle at which it had landed would allow it to slide just far enough up the door to relieve the pressure on her ribs.

She heard his involuntary groan as he put his weight against the door and slowly, slowly, watched the deep score being gouged in the wood as he forced it to slide up.

By degrees the weight on her ribs eased until at last she was able to draw her first normal breath.

'Wolff?' she called, the residual ache in her chest still restricting the volume of her voice.

'Yes?' The grinding sounds stopped as he paused to listen.

'If you can get your hand round the edge of the door, about a foot from the floor, you could grab the cupboard.'

There was a brief shuffling sound on the other side of the door and she could imagine him altering his position against it so that he could reach in through the gap he'd created.

She watched the shadowy corner and saw his hand appear. It took only seconds for him to locate the edge of the chest of drawers and, although the restricted access through the narrow gap must have made it almost impossible, she watched his tendons tighten as he began to lift.

Once it had started moving momentum worked in his favour, and within seconds he had heaved the obstruction far enough to get his other hand through to help.

'Wait,' she called, and he stopped pushing instantly.

'What's the matter?' he demanded through teeth gritted with effort.

'I'm in the way...' She clenched her teeth and forced herself to roll over carefully so that the door could swing open. 'It's clear now,' she confirmed, and she saw the cupboard rock back onto its base when Wolff gave one last heave.

'Laura? Where are you?'

He swung the door open slowly so that he didn't hit her and stepped into the devastated room, his feet crunching on a mixture of glass and masonry as he came into view.

'Down here, catching my breath,' she panted, conscious that she was aching all over.

He crouched down beside her, one hand reaching out tentatively towards her face as though he couldn't quite believe that she was there.

'Ah, Laura, I thought I'd lost you,' he said gruffly, and cradled her cheek in his trembling palm.

Laura gazed up at him in amazement, hardly able to believe what she was hearing.

'Hey! Wolff? What are you doing here?' demanded Leo's voice, and the two of them looked up to see the first of the rescuers, working their way along the corridor, the reflective bands on their emergency uniforms ghostly in the strange light.

'You're not supposed to be in here,' Leo pointed out sternly. 'It's rescue personnel only until they tell you it's safe to come in.'

'I was already in,' Wolff told him shortly. 'I was in the stairwell on my way up when it happened. What the hell caused it? It sounded like a bomb.'

'Gas main blew,' Leo said succinctly as he focused a torch on Laura's face. 'How are you doing?' he demanded, his voice as gentle as his hands as he quickly examined her. 'Fingers and toes all in working order?'

'Apart from feeling as if I've been run over by a steamroller, I feel fine,' she confirmed.

'In that case, we'll just get you over to A and E for a quick checkover,' he decided. 'Your room seemed to take the brunt of the explosion, and if you come out of it with nothing more than a few bruises then we've come off very lightly. Nobody lower down in the building got any more than shock and cuts from flying glass, and you were the only one up here on this side of the building.'

Wolff had stayed in the background while his friend did his job.

As the St Augustine's Hospital emergency team doctor, Leo had been trained to cope with such emergencies, and even though Wolff had probably had more experience of such situations in the last three months than Leo had had in a couple of years there was still the matter of professional courtesy.

Finally Laura was loaded onto a stretcher, her neck protected in case she'd injured it without realising it.

'It doesn't feel right, being the patient. I feel so helpless,' she mumbled, and Wolff smiled briefly, his face still showing signs of strain as he accompanied her out to the ambulance waiting to transport her.

'You don't have to stay with me,' she said, trying to be brave. 'If they need you to take care of other injured people...'

'I'm concentrating on one patient at a time,' he growled, and tightened his hand around hers. 'And when you've got the all-clear I'm taking you home where I can keep an eye on you!'

Wolff's husky voice made it sound like a threat but it was music to her ears.

He drove his car behind the ambulance to the emergency entrance and waited more or less patiently while her neck was X-rayed and declared clear. Then he wheeled her out of the department as if she were made of spun glass and settled her in the passenger seat.

As he drove silently out of the hospital grounds she caught a quick glimpse of the damaged corner of the nurses' accommodation and, remembering the glitter of all that glass, suddenly realised just how lucky she'd been. If she hadn't been trying to fish the instruction sheet for the pregnancy test out from behind the chest of drawers...

The memory flooded over her and her hand crept over to lie protectively across her stomach. She hadn't even had time to take the test so she still didn't know whether she was carrying Wolff's baby or not.

The X-ray department had made certain that her lower body was safely covered by a leaded shield before they'd taken their pictures, but that was a routine precaution they would have taken for any woman of child-bearing age...

Her scattered thoughts ground to a halt when Wolff drew up outside his house.

'I'm sorry,' he said gruffly into the sudden silence, 'I seem to have kidnapped you without giving you a choice as to whether you wanted to come here.'

'I want to be here,' Laura confirmed, her heart racing at the thought that he'd wanted to take her to his home, 'but I haven't got anything with me—no wash kit or clothes. Nothing.'

'You can worry about that in the morning,' he said as he released her seat belt for her and then went round to help her out of the car.

She hardly had time to swing round and put her shoeless feet out before he'd scooped her up into his arms and was carrying her up the path.

'Wolff! You'll hurt your back!' she warned with a soft laugh, hanging onto his neck with both arms as he juggled with the front door lock and took her inside.

The door swung closed behind them but he made no effort to switch on the light as he leant back against the door and held her cradled in his arms, the tension in his body overwhelming.

She could feel the way his heart was pounding against his ribs, his breathing ragged against her cheek, and she started to worry about him. He'd hardly said a word since she'd been rescued...

'Wolff...' In spite of the darkness surrounding them, she cupped his cheek unerringly with her hand and found that the skin was wet although it hadn't been raining tonight.

'Wolff, are you all right?' she demanded softly, wishing that she could see his expression. Were they tears on his face? Was he crying and, if so, why?

'Oh, sweetheart, I thought I'd lost everything,' he said hoarsely into the darkness, his voice sounding raw as he slanted his head over hers and rubbed his cheek softly over her hair. 'When I realised that there'd been an explosion and you could be injured—even dead—I couldn't bear it...'

He drew her closer against his chest, as if he couldn't bear to have any distance between them, and she tightened her arms around his neck—utterly content for the first time in days.

'As I ran up the stairs,' he continued, his voice sounding almost rusty, 'all I could think of was that I'd never told you that I love you and that it might be too late.'

'Oh, Wolff,' she breathed as happiness bloomed inside her. 'And all I could think of as I was lying trapped under that chest of drawers was that I couldn't breathe and that if I died I'd never have the chance to tell you that I love you.'

She felt the impact of her words as he froze.

'You love me?' he questioned, open disbelief in his tone. 'But you've hardly looked at me since we spent that night together, let alone spoken to me. I thought you'd only wanted me to make you pregnant.'

'I know,' she admitted guiltily. 'And I'm sorry if I hurt you but...I was in love with you and I was afraid that I might say something.'

'What? That's crazy!'

Suddenly he strode across the empty hallway and into

the sitting room, his elbow finding the light switch and flooding the room with brightness.

'Sit there,' he ordered, plonking her down on one end of the settee and marching across to shut the curtains.

Laura was quite giddy with the sudden change of pace. One minute they were standing quietly in the darkness of the hallway while they murmured loving words to each other and the next he was dumping her on the settee as if he was angry with her.

'You were in love with me and you didn't want me to know? What sort of idiocy is that?' he challenged as he sat down with his knees touching hers.

'You told me about your time in the refugee camp and you said you didn't think that relationships had a chance. You'd seen the pain and heartbreak and you didn't believe in second chances.'

'That was *then*,' he said indignantly. 'This is now—and us.'

'And that makes it different?' she queried hesitantly.

'Yes! Of course it does!' He caught her hands and wrapped them in his, bringing them up one at a time for a tender kiss.

'Then why didn't *you* tell *me*?' she demanded softly. 'Out in the hallway you said you love me, but why didn't you say it before?'

'I was going to,' he said with a wry smile on his face as he tightened his fingers around hers. 'That's why I was on my way up the stairs when the gas main blew—I couldn't bear the waiting any longer.'

'The waiting?'

'To find out if my gamble had worked—to find out if you were pregnant,' he explained. 'I've spent ten miserable days not knowing whether I wanted you *not* to be pregnant so I could persuade you to share my bed again—and maybe persuade you to fall in love with me—or whether I wanted you to be pregnant so that I could try for the gratitude vote.'

'The gratitude vote? Vote for what?'

'Marriage, of course,' he said, as if it was obvious. 'That's what I've wanted ever since you stepped up on that stage, your eyes spitting fire at me for daring to embarrass you.'

'Actually, it was fear, not fire,' she said with a smile. 'After two years without a problem I hardly had to look at you and my hormones went into overdrive...'

He smiled at her with a wolfish gleam in his eyes.

There was just one shadow lingering in a corner of her mind.

'Wolff, I still don't know the result,' she murmured softly, determined that there would be no secrets.

'Result?' he queried distractedly, his eyes intent on her mouth.

'Of the pregnancy test,' she explained. 'I still don't know if we managed to...'

'Laura, it isn't the baby I want—it's you. I love *you*, and any children we have will just be a special bonus.'

Laura heard the words and knew that he meant every one of them. Was this the man who didn't believe in second chances? Ever since she'd met him he'd been taking chances—with his heart, with her love...

'Anyway, it doesn't matter,' he said confidently. 'We've got plenty of time for second chances now. If we didn't manage it last time I'm sure you won't mind trying again...and again...'

'And again,' she echoed with laughter in her voice as he swept her up in his arms and made his way towards the stairs.

* * * * * * * *

Third Time Lucky is the climax of Josie Metcalfe's trilogy.

Meet Hannah Nicholls, who has her work cut out trying to tame the ultimate playboy doctor – registrar Leo Stirling!

THIRD TIME LUCKY
by
Josie Metcalfe

CHAPTER ONE

'OH, DAMN!' Hannah muttered with feeling as she clenched her fist tightly.

She'd only just found time to stop for a drink, and it wasn't until she'd reached out to switch on the kettle that she'd realised how badly her fingers were shaking.

It had been all right when she'd been busy. She hadn't had time to think of anything except the shocked and injured patients, firmly closing her mind to the fact that she knew so many of them.

Now, in the quiet of the staffroom, she was alone and the post-adrenaline reaction was setting in.

The explosion had happened so suddenly...

She snorted in disgust at the inane thought...as if an explosion could ever be anything other than sudden! But the fact that the blast had damaged the St Augustine's nurses' accommodation had been unbelievably shocking.

As the emergency team had swiftly donned their protective clothing and grabbed their prepared kit, she'd found herself hoping that she would be able to ignore the fact that she was actually going to have to deal with her own colleagues.

In the shattered remains of one corner of the building there was the possibility that she could find her friends trapped, maimed or even dying...

No amount of experience could have prepared her for this eventuality, but she'd managed to do as she always did if she wanted to do her job efficiently—shut down the personal emotions which would slow her reactions—

and concentrated on following the other members of the specially trained team into the fray.

'Ah-h!' she breathed as she leaned her hips back against the edge of the mock-onyx work surface and took her first sip of the wickedly strong brew, both hands wrapped firmly around the sturdy mug—as if the hospital's notoriously super-efficient heating had failed.

In spite of the warmth, she shivered, remembering the way Leo Stirling had followed the firemen into the debris-strewn corridor, the word DOCTOR glowing eerily across his back under the emergency lighting and acting as a beacon for her to follow.

She'd dogged his footsteps as the rescue squad searched the building systematically and provided a supportive arm as each of the shocked inmates they located had been led out to the care of the paramedics to be ferried the short distance to the accident and emergency department.

It wasn't until she'd remembered following his long-legged stride up the stairs that the shaking had grown suddenly worse—remembered the way a heavy dread had settled in her chest when she'd been unable to shut the fear away any longer.

The gaping hole she'd seen from the outside of the building had seemed at first sight to have been right where her friend's room was, but she'd refused to admit to herself that anything could have happened to Laura.

They'd known each other for years—ever since they'd met during their training. If she'd lost Laura her best friend and a large part of her past would be gone for ever...

Oh, she realised that it was partly her own fault that she didn't have a wider circle of friends at St Augustine's, but she was too aware of the problems she could have if she allowed people to come too close—the explanations she would have to make...

She still shuddered when she remembered the embarrassment of a shopping trip with a group of her new colleagues shortly after she'd arrived to work at the hospital.

After an indulgent coffee-cake-and-chat session, where she'd been told all the inside stories about the rest of the staff on A and E, they had unexpectedly ended up in the evening-dress section of a large department store.

'Let's try on the wildest and most expensive things they've got,' one of her colleagues had suggested, and a third member of the group had eagerly agreed.

When Hannah had adamantly refused to join in it had cast a pall over the afternoon, and when the next outing they'd suggested had been a trip to the local swimming pool she'd realised that she wasn't ready for her problems to become common knowledge.

Sadly, she'd decided that, in spite of the fact that she'd always been a gregarious person, the only way she could cope now was to keep herself to herself.

The only person she'd felt she might be able to confide in was Laura, and ever since her friend had joined her on the staff at St Augustine's she'd been trying to pluck up the courage to tell her what had happened in the time since they'd last worked together.

Now Laura was somewhere in the rubble of the room up ahead, and she might never have the chance to talk to her again.

'Hey! Wolff? What are you doing here?' she heard Leo demand through the buzz of her thoughts, and knew he was questioning his friend about his presence in a restricted area. Until it had been declared safe only emergency personnel were supposed to enter.

'I was already in,' a deep voice replied from inside

the gaping horror of Laura's room. 'I was in the stairwell on my way up when it happened. What the hell caused it? It sounded like a bomb.'

'Gas main blew,' she heard Leo reply as he stepped into the room, his feet scrunching on shattered glass as he crouched down just out of her sight.

'How are you doing?' she heard him ask, and held her breath until she heard the reply.

'Apart from feeling as if I've been run over by a steamroller, I feel fine,' she heard Laura's familiar voice reply, and released her breath in one long sigh of relief.

That relief had made Hannah almost light-headed, and buoyed her up through the time-consuming routine mechanics of protecting her friend's neck, stretchering her out to the waiting ambulance and her own return to the department.

With the last few nurses needing careful stitching to repair the damage caused by flying glass, as well as the usual cross-section of 'routine' patients, Hannah barely had time to notice the way Wolff had shadowed her injured friend through her check-up in A and E.

At some stage it dawned on her that Laura wouldn't have a room to return to, and while she knew that the hospital management would have willingly found her accommodation she thought her own alternative would probably be the more attractive option—a chance to get right away for a few hours.

Perhaps she might even find the courage to talk to Laura and tell her about the events of the last two and a half years.

She waited the last few minutes to the end of her shift, but when she went to offer her friend a bed for the night in her own little flat it was to discover that Wolff was already helping her into his car.

She shrugged, initially piqued that Laura hadn't turned

to her for help, but when the light fell across her friend's face and illuminated the expression in her gaze as she looked up at the darkly brooding doctor, leaning so solicitously towards her, she suddenly understood.

Ruthlessly ignoring the sharp twist of jealousy which pierced her again at the memory, Hannah buried her nose in the fragrant steam rising from her mug and took another sip.

She wasn't looking for a husband so why should she feel jealous of the fact that it looked as if Laura had found herself one. . .?

'Hey, beautiful, any more of that going?'

Hannah jumped with surprise when the cheerful voice accosted her from the other side of the room. She'd been so lost in her thoughts that she hadn't even heard Leo come into the room.

'I expect the kettle's still hot,' she murmured, glancing up warily as she stepped aside to allow him access.

'Hey, Hannah, how are you doing?' he demanded brightly, and she smiled wryly to herself. In his own inimitably charming way he'd obviously called her 'beautiful' without having any idea who she was.

She spared him a brief glance, then tightened her hands wrapped firmly round her own half-empty mug. There was no way she was going to risk letting him see how badly she was shaking—it would feel as if she were letting herself down in front of him. . .

They'd been working together for over eighteen months now, and she'd never come so close to letting her guard down in front of him—in front of anyone.

'That was a scary one,' Leo commented against the rising rumble of the kettle as he waited for the water to reheat.

Hannah kept quiet, hoping he would drop the subject, then groaned silently when he continued.

'Somehow it seemed much worse to know that it was our own we were going after, especially when we saw that great hole in the wall. It looked almost like the newsreel pictures of Beirut or. . .'

'Stop it!' Hannah said through clenched teeth, squeezing her eyes tightly against the pictures he was drawing in her mind. 'Please, just stop talking about it. . .' She couldn't go on and stood silently, shaking her head.

'Hannah?'

She heard the surprise in his questioning voice but refused to look at him, heat rising in her cheeks when she realised how badly she'd let herself down.

'Hey, Hannah, come on,' he coaxed, his voice strangely gentle as his hands descended on her shoulders.

Hannah froze.

'Leo. . .' she began as she tried to twist away from the contact, but he wasn't having any of it.

'You're shaking,' he murmured, as though he'd just made a startling discovery, and before she could formulate a single excuse he turned her towards himself and wrapped his arms around her, pulling her firmly against the solid warmth of his own broad chest.

'L-Leo,' she stammered breathlessly up at him, stunned by the sudden turn of events. 'Why. . .? What are you. . .?'

'Hush, woman. Can't you tell I'm giving you a hug?' he muttered in her ear as he brought his head down beside hers.

When Hannah felt the slight rasp of his emerging stubble against her cheek she drew in a startled breath, and with it an indefinable mixture of soap, laundry starch and male musk.

'But why. . .?' she began breathlessly.

'Shh. . .and put your arms round me,' he murmured just below her ear, and sent a sudden shiver skittering up her spine to lift the hairs on the back of her neck. 'I'm enjoying this, even if you aren't—a full-frontal cuddle with a beautiful woman is just what the doctor ordered at the end of a long hard day...'

At the sound of his husky voice she found herself complying mindlessly, and her arms wrapped themselves around the taut muscles of his lean waist, her hands flattening themselves against the stiff fabric of his white coat.

She drew in a deep shuddering breath at the overwhelming feeling of comfort that surrounded her and her heart produced an extra beat, almost like an exuberant skip in its normal rhythm. She was struck by a sudden light-hearted urge to giggle.

'Idiot!' she muttered as she tried to step backwards out of his encircling arms, feeling a little ridiculous now that her shaking was subsiding. 'There are any number of beautiful women in the hospital who would be willing to oblige you with a hug—Sexy Samantha, for instance,' she added in a burst of inspiration.

'Don't!' Leo protested with a shudder, his arms dropping away from her as if she'd just admitted to carrying a deadly plague. 'It's bad enough having to duck and run when I go past Obs and Gynae, without you taunting me about that barracuda!'

Hannah laughed at his terrified expression, not believing for a moment that he meant what he was saying— his reputation among the nurses was far too colourful for that!

Still, bringing up the voluptuous nurse's name had achieved what she'd hoped and there was now sufficient distance between the two of them to allow her to breathe more easily.

While he concentrated on making himself a mug of coffee Hannah took her own drink across to sit in one of the few high-backed chairs, curling her feet up under her for comfort.

For some time the two of them chatted easily about the events of the day, and Hannah was amazed how effective Leo's 'hug treatment' had been. There was hardly a trace of the awful shaking which had consumed her such a short time ago.

She allowed her mind to wander as her eyes took in the way her companion had sprawled himself across one of the small settees. She knew from standing beside him that he must be at least six feet tall but he looked much more than seven inches taller than she, with his long legs stretched out across the floor towards her own.

Her eyes travelled up the length of his dark trousers, the crease still sharp in spite of the long day, and she noticed the intricately braided belt around his waist.

Her attention was caught briefly by one of his collection of colourfully modern silk ties, bisecting his pale blue shirt, the knot of which hung low beneath the button he had loosened at the collar.

In spite of the fact that it was midwinter his skin still carried the remains of the colour he'd caught during the summer, and against the dark upholstery the tawny gold of his rumpled hair gave him the look of an indolent lion, apparently bonelessly relaxed but with the underlying feeling that he could leap into action at the slightest provocation.

'Do you know,' Leo began in a musing voice, drawing her eyes up from their idle contemplation of the width of his shoulders to meet the striking golden fire of his own eyes, 'I think that's the first time you've ever really looked at me?'

Hannah was trapped by the intensity of his gaze, unable to look away from him in spite of the slow tide of heat which swept up her throat and into her cheeks.

'Don't...don't be silly,' she blustered shakily. 'We've been working together for more than a year.'

'Eighteen months,' he corrected her softly, almost as if he'd been keeping count. 'And the fact that we've been working together all that time doesn't mean that you've ever seen me as anything more than a colleague—until now.'

Hannah drew in a shaky breath, realising with a deep quiver of unease that he was right.

She dragged the fingers of her free hand distractedly through her hair, feeling them catch on the tousled curls while she frantically cudgelled her brain to find the words to refute his assertion.

The sudden burst of sound as a group of colleagues trooped into the room broke the tension between them and she sighed with silent relief as he released her from the curious captivity of his eyes.

Strangely fearful that he might try to continue the conversation before she'd had a chance to marshal her thoughts, Hannah waited just long enough for Leo to begin talking to one of the group and then made her escape.

It had been a full day, with the added stress of the explosion in the nurses' home on top of everything else, and all she wanted to do was get back to her tiny flat as quickly as possible so that she could begin to unwind.

The last thing she wanted was a discussion with Leo about the fact that he was the first man she'd really looked at since Jon had changed his mind about marrying her...since he'd told her so bluntly that she was unlikely to find *any* man who would want to marry her.

'Wolff?' Hannah called as she hurried after him the following afternoon. She was on her way towards the staff canteen for her meal break and had just caught sight of him in the distance.

'Dr Bergen,' she called again, using the more formal mode of address when she realised how close they were getting to another group of staff. 'Can you wait a minute?'

'Hi, Hannah. What can I do for you?'

Wolff smiled as he turned and paced slowly back towards her, waiting for her to catch up to him before he propped his hips on the narrow windowsill overlooking the winter-bare hospital grounds and folded his arms loosely across his chest.

'Sorry to hold you up,' Hannah began apologetically as she stopped in front of him.

The whole department had been only too aware of just how short-tempered he had been over the last couple of weeks and, although Hannah realised that she was probably the only one who had guessed that his bad mood had something to do with her friend, she didn't want to risk getting off on the wrong foot with him at the start of his shift.

'No problem.' He dismissed her apology breezily. 'I've got a couple of minutes.'

He smiled again and Hannah suddenly noticed what a change there had been in him over the last twenty-four hours. This wasn't the same man she'd worked with yesterday. *He* would have bitten her head off, rather than smile at her so easily.

'Oh... Well...' she floundered, completely put off her stride by the cheerful glow surrounding him. 'Actually, I just wanted to know how Laura is.'

'She's wonderful,' he said fervently, then cleared his throat when he realised what he'd just said. 'Sorry, that's not quite what you wanted to know, is it?'

'I don't know. Was it?' Hannah queried, bemused by

the wash of colour riding high on his cheeks. What on earth had gone on between the two of them since she'd watched him helping her friend into his car last night?

'Laura's a bit battered and bruised from being trapped under the furniture but otherwise...' he shook his head in amazement '...she had a very lucky escape.'

'Do you know when she'll be back to work...and when the hospital is going to be finding her alternative accommodation? She's going to need some of her things in the meantime. Shall I bring her the basics after work?'

'I'll get her to give you a call about her things. If you *could* sort out a few essentials at the end of your shift I could take them back with me. I've told her she's taking a couple of days off—just until the stiffness goes away—but she won't be going back into staff accommodation.'

The last pronouncement was made in a very decisive tone of voice and Hannah's ears pricked up, especially when she saw him throw an almost furtive glance either way along the corridor. 'Actually, she's going to be moving in with me...permanently.'

'With you? But...' To say that Hannah was surprised was an understatement. She was almost speechless.

It hardly seemed more than a few hours ago that Laura had been telling her the details of the heart-breaking reasons for her decision to transfer to the A and E department at St Augustine's.

Although she'd known almost from the first that her friend was very attracted to the darkly handsome doctor, Laura hadn't known him very long and had given no hint about an ongoing relationship with Wolff.

Had the situation been precipitated by the traumatic events of last night? Was it gratitude for her deliverance from a life-threatening situation which had persuaded Laura to move in with...?

'I've asked her to marry me,' Wolff announced softly,

his husky voice cutting across her scurrying thoughts as he met the concern in her eyes with his own icy blue gaze.

For the first time Hannah was allowed to see the depth of the emotions he'd been keeping hidden, and suddenly she wasn't worried any more.

'We had a...a misunderstanding a couple of weeks ago and we've still got a few problems to sort out but I've told her I won't wait more than...'

'Married!' Hannah whispered, and a smile began to curve the corners of her mouth as his words sank in. 'That's wonderful! Oh, Wolff, I'm so happy for you both...!' She flung her arms around his shoulders and planted a noisily enthusiastic kiss on his cheek as he hugged her tightly, lifting her from her feet and swinging her around before he deposited her back on her feet again.

Hannah found herself beaming up at him, genuinely delighted that whatever had been making the two of them so unhappy for the last couple of weeks had apparently been resolved.

'Hey, Leo!' Wolff called over her shoulder and Hannah froze briefly, before wriggling herself hurriedly out of Wolff's friendly grasp and smoothing down her uniform as she turned to face the man striding towards them.

She'd hardly seen more than distant glimpses of him all day—almost as if he was avoiding her—and for her own peace of mind she needed to confront him to confirm the fact that her unexpected reaction towards him last night had been nothing more than her imagination working overtime.

After their strange interlude together she'd gone home to the quiet isolation of her tiny flat, bemused by mental images of his long-fingered hands wrapped around the steaming mug as he focused his tawny gaze on her.

She'd even imagined that there was a new heat in that

gaze, a strange intensity in their deep golden colour which had made her quiver deep inside with a prickly awareness of her long-ignored femininity.

A sudden high-pitched bleeping made all three of them look towards the pager clipped at Wolff's waist. He pulled a face, but it was obvious to Hannah that nothing was going to be able to dim his happiness today.

'Got to go,' Wolff announced as he killed the noise. 'I'll see you later?' he reminded Hannah, referring to her offer to gather up some of Laura's belongings, and—at her nod—turned to his friend. 'I'll leave it to Hannah to tell you the good news, Leo,' he said with a beaming smile and a friendly clap on his shoulder, then he bestowed a totally uncharacteristic kiss on Hannah's cheek before he strode away.

'And what's put him in such a disgustingly cheerful mood?' Leo enquired as he shared a frown between Hannah and his friend's departing back. 'He's looked like a thundercloud for so long now that I was beginning to wonder if he'd forgotten how to smile.'

'Marriage,' Hannah explained with a broad smile as she began to lead the way towards the staff canteen. 'He proposed last night.'

'He did *what*?' Leo demanded, sounding utterly shocked as he came to a dead halt in the middle of the corridor, his hands clenched into tight fists at his sides.

To Hannah it almost seemed as if he'd gone pale at the very idea.

'Not everyone is as gun-shy as you are, Leo!' she teased, grinning up into his frozen face as she patted his sleeve consolingly. 'Some men actually decide they'd *like* to get married—like Nick Prince did, and now Wolff.'

'And you accepted?' he grated, his voice sounding almost rusty as it emerged from deep in his chest.

'*Me?*' Hannah squeaked in disbelief and burst out laughing. 'Of course I didn't. He propos—'

She clapped a hand over her mouth and glanced around guiltily before she continued in a much quieter voice, remembering that it wasn't her place to spread the news around the hospital—no matter how accidentally.

'He didn't propose to *me*, you idiot!' she snarled as she dragged him to one side of the corridor, out of the way of a small group of curious junior nurses on their way out of the staff canteen. 'It's *Laura* he's in love with, Leo. He asked her to marry him when he took her to his house after the explosion.'

'Laura?' he repeated blankly. 'And she accepted?'

'Of course she did,' Hannah confirmed with a gleeful chuckle, wholeheartedly approving of the way things had worked out for her friend. 'Why wouldn't she? She's been in love with him almost since she clapped eyes on him with all those acres of bare muscles exposed by that exotic waistcoat at the Ball.'

'So...' She watched as Leo drew in a rib-cracking breath and considered the information. 'I suppose I can take the credit for engineering the meeting, can I?' he suggested, with the start of a smile lightening the golden colour of his eyes.

'Hey, it was my idea, too,' Hannah reminded him. 'Especially the part about swapping my ticket with Laura's. Otherwise *I'd* have been the one to go up on the stage with him, and he might have fallen for me instead.'

Leo muttered something under his breath, but before Hannah had a chance to ask him to repeat it his pager went off too and he made for the nearest phone.

'Drat,' she muttered as she helped herself to a tray and made her selection from the menu. She'd been looking forward to the chance of talking to him while they had their break.

Now that she thought about it she was quite enjoying the fact that once again the two of them were in the position of knowing privileged information about their colleagues, and she'd wanted the chance to gloat a little before the news became common knowledge.

At least she had one less worry on her mind, she thought as she drained her glass of orange juice at the end of the meal. The confrontation in the corridor had proved once and for all that she had no need to worry about Leo becoming interested in her—no need to worry that she might damage his ego by turning him down.

He'd obviously hardly noticed her in the eighteen months they'd been working together because he'd never have imagined for a minute that she'd accept a proposal of marriage from Wolff if he'd known anything about her.

And, she reminded herself as she approached A and E for the last part of her shift, she had no intention of entering into any sort of involvement with *any* man.

Especially not, she stressed to herself, a highly sought-after bachelor such as Leo Stirling, who had a ready smile for any female from six to sixty-six.

Furthermore—she continued her silent lecture—the situation was exactly the way she wanted it, and there was absolutely no reason why she should have felt a twinge of disappointment that he hadn't even noticed her, other than to sound aghast that his friend might have proposed to her.

Her inner debate continued for several hours as she worked beside Leo in the department.

She'd helped him to check over the young woman who had given birth to her first baby two weeks early while the ambulancemen transporting her had tried to battle their way around a choked temporary one-way system caused by yesterday's gas explosion.

'Here's a treat for sore eyes,' Ted Larrabee announced, beaming as he carried in his tiny blanket-swathed charge, Mike Wilson following closely behind with the surprised mother. 'Makes the whole job worthwhile.'

After a quick check-up Leo gave both mother and daughter a clean bill of health and they were transferred across to the maternity ward, leaving the A and E staff temporarily wreathed in smiles because they'd seen the beginning of a new life rather than more of the pain and ugliness they usually dealt with.

Unfortunately, the euphoria didn't last long.

The next patient brought in by the same ambulance crew meant a return to the grislier side of their job.

'Thirteen-year-old. Suicide attempt with paracetamol,' Ted detailed as he handed the belligerent youngster over.

Flushing the enormous number of tablets out of Sam's stomach was a task Hannah hated, and the whole situation was made so much worse when the distressed youngster cursed them for saving his life.

Hannah shared a horrified glance with Leo across the skinny body between them.

'I'll do it again,' the youngster rasped through a throat turned raw by the procedures he'd undergone, his eyes dull with resignation. 'If you send me back there I'll do it again, and next time I'll make certain that no one finds me in time.'

'Back where?' Hannah heard Leo ask as he waited for the next set of toxicity results to tell him how much of the drug had already been absorbed into the boy's system before it had caused the youngster to vomit and had given away his condition.

Although he wouldn't still be in A and E by then, she

knew that it could take anything up to five days before they could tell how badly his liver function had been damaged.

In the meantime, there was Parvolex dripping down the IV line into his arm, mixed with copious quantities of five per cent glucose to keep up his fluid levels.

'Where?' Leo repeated, keeping his tone even. 'Send you where?'

'To the home,' Sam croaked despairingly, and as he turned his head away from them Hannah caught sight of the single tear which slid across his temple and into his hair. 'I won't go back. I can't bear it any more. . .'

'Can't bear what?' Hannah prompted gently as she cleaned the evidence of the last hour's events from his face and wiped away the traces of the tear she was sure he'd never meant her to see.

'The polecat,' he muttered through gritted teeth, utter loathing in his voice. 'He's horrible and he smells and he does bad things to us kids. He hurts us.'

For the first time his determination and bravado had deserted him and his last three words had made him sound like the young child he was—only the stark fear and loneliness evident in his voice should never have been there.

Once again Hannah's eyes met Leo's and they shared silent communication about their suspicions.

'I'll just go and hurry those results up,' Leo announced quietly, and left Hannah beside their troubled patient to keep him company.

She knew that they both suspected that the lad had been the victim of some form of abuse in the home, and knew also that they were legally obliged to report their suspicions.

It would depend which paediatrician was on duty—Leo would be contacting them at that precise moment—

but she knew that hospital policy would mean that the youngster would be admitted to one of the small sidewards so that he could be interviewed about his situation.

She could almost feel sorry for the misguided abuser, if it was, indeed, proved that the youngster had been injured in any way, because Ross MacFadden was the sort of consultant who believed absolutely in a child's right to happiness and love. She'd seen in the past how he went in to bat on behalf of his young charges without fear or favour, no matter how illustrious the abuser.

A member of staff in a position of trust at a children's home, whose activities had driven a young lad to attempt suicide, could expect no leniency.

'Right, Sam. I've got some good news and some bad news,' Leo announced when he returned, and Hannah watched the skinny shoulders go rigid as he waited to hear the worst.

'The bad news is that we're going to have to admit you to keep an eye on your blood until we know how many of the tablets have gone into your system. That means you could be here for several days.'

Hannah felt her eyes sting when she saw the relief flood through the youngster, his breath whistling out in a jagged stream. He'd obviously been terrified that, now that they'd emptied his stomach of its deadly burden, they were going to send him back into his nightmare...

'And the good news?' he croaked, finally meeting Leo's eyes.

'That you're going to be one of the lucky ones who gets a room all to yourself so you can choose the channel on the TV without an argument!'

'That'll make a change,' Sam commented wryly, the first hint of normal childish spirit lighting up his face. 'I might even get to hear the sound as well...'

CHAPTER TWO

BY THE time she came to the end of her shift Hannah was feeling quite cheerful in spite of the fact that the weather had deteriorated and there was rain lashing down in the darkness outside the windows.

Before she'd left the department to change out of her uniform word had filtered down from the ward that the lab results on Sam's baseline liver function and prothrombin time were looking good so far.

Her pleasure was tempered by the knowledge that the tests would have to be repeated every twelve hours to make certain that Sam wasn't going to deteriorate into liver failure, but she had a feeling that he was going to be one of the survivors.

His fear of returning to the home was a different matter, she thought with a touch of resentment as she scurried through the driving rain with a double load of belongings.

As far as *that* was concerned, she realised that it was unlikely that she would hear anything further about it unless Leo chose to speak to the paediatric consultant about the case and passed the information on to her. Even then, patient confidentiality meant that. . .

'No! You can't *do* this to me!' she wailed aloud in the chilly confines of her little car, smacking her hands on the steering-wheel in helpless frustration before she tried again to start it. 'Come on, you useless bucket of rust. Start!'

This time the engine barely whined at her and she gave up the attempt, staring out at the pouring rain in disgust. Her jacket was already sodden from her dash across the car park and her feet were soaking from the puddles she'd not seen in the dark.

Now the insides of the windows were rapidly misting up with the resulting condensation.

'What do I do next?' she muttered, agitated by her helplessness. She had no idea why the car wouldn't start, and there was no way she was going to stand about in the pouring rain while she tried to work it out.

'I can either run back inside the hospital to phone for the rescue service, and then hang around developing pneumonia while I wait for them to come, or I can pay for a taxi to take me home now and sort out this rotten heap in the morning.'

Hannah dropped her head back against the restraint and sighed loudly when she realised that either option meant that she was going to have to brave the elements again.

She nearly jumped out of her skin when something tapped sharply on the window right beside her head.

For several seconds she sat there, with her heart trying to pound its way out of her chest. The windows were so opaque by now that all she could see was a looming dark shape outside the car, silhouetted against the yellow lights of the car park...and in her hurry to get out of the rain she'd completely forgotten her usual safety precaution of locking herself in the car.

Sudden dread caught at her throat when she remembered the way a colleague at her previous hospital had been stalked by an ex-patient, and the level of her fear went up like a rocket.

She couldn't even reach back towards the lock to press the button down because she was afraid the movement would be visible and would tell whoever was outside that the car was unlocked.

'Hannah?' called a male voice, the sound distorted

into unrecognisability by the noise of the raindrops drumming on the car roof and splashing into the acres of puddles around it.

'Have you got a problem with your car?'

This time the voice sounded closer, and when she peered at the shadowy form outside the window she realised that he was now bending down so that he was level with the car window, his head just inches away from her own on the other side of the glass.

'Who. . .who is that?' she stammered in a shrill voice, her teeth chattering with a combination of fear and cold. She hardly dared to lift her hand to wipe the condensation away because while it would give her a clear view of the person outside it would also make her as visible and as vulnerable as a goldfish in a bowl.

'It's Leo, you idiot. Wipe the wretched window and look out before I drown out here!'

'Oh, thank God,' Hannah breathed, her first instinct being relief as she raised a shaky hand to swipe at the obscuring condensation.

Then anger roared through her.

'You're the idiot!' she shouted, her voice tinny in the confined space. 'You nearly scared me to death, tapping on the window like that!'

She glared out at him, getting her first good look at him.

Leo was even wetter than she was, his thick blond hair flattened against his head and so wet that it looked nearly as dark as Wolff's—a solitary strand curving down over his forehead to direct an annoying stream of raindrops down his nose.

'Has the car died, or do you just need a push?' he asked, apparently unmoved by her tirade, and she suddenly realised what a shrew she was being.

Knowing how temperamental the winder on her

window was, Hannah opted to release the catch on the door and swung it open a scant inch so that they didn't have to shout at each other.

'I've got no idea what's the matter with it, Leo,' she said in exasperation. 'It was fine when I drove in this morning but it sounds as if the battery's too flat to turn the engine over now. Listen...' She tried the key again with the same miserable results.

'Did you leave anything switched on that could have drained it? The radio? The windscreen demister? The lights?'

Hannah had been shaking her head at each of his suggestions until he reached the last one.

'The lights?' she repeated, her hand going out to test the appropriate switch before she groaned. 'It was the lights. I had them on during a cloudburst when I set off from home this morning, but it must have cleared up by the time I got here so I forgot to turn them off.'

'Easily done,' Leo commented as he straightened up and grasped the top of her door. 'Now you need to decide what you want to do.'

Hannah peered up at him through the gap around the door while she tried to decide which of her options would be quickest, then realised that the poor man was getting wetter and wetter while she messed about.

'Look, Leo, there's no point in you hanging about drowning. I can either phone the rescue service or phone for a taxi and sort it out in the morning. You might as well go home and get dry.'

'Better than that,' he suggested. 'I could give you a lift home first. If we take the battery out of your car I could charge it up overnight so it will be ready to go back in tomorrow. Have you got a tool kit? It'll be bolted down and I'll need to take the leads off the terminals.'

'There's no reason why you should get filthy doing

that—I can phone for the rescue service in the morning and—'

'You're wasting time, Hannah, and I'm getting wetter by the minute,' Leo butted in impatiently. 'Now, be a good girl—find the spanners and release the catch so I can get at the battery.'

He was standing beside the car with his fists on his hips, as immovable as a statue. His jacket collar had been turned up against the rain but, standing like that, the front edges had parted and his pale blue shirt was plastered over the breadth of his chest like an extra layer of skin.

Guilt at his sodden state made her give in without another word.

She scrabbled about in the glove compartment and came up with an adjustable pipe wrench.

'Will this do?' she offered meekly.

He pulled a wry face as he took it from her and disappeared around to the front of the car.

There were several scrapes and bangs behind the upraised bonnet of her car before he straightened up again with a familiar object in his hands.

'Right,' he said when he came round to her window again. 'You can grab your stuff while I unlock my car. And don't forget to check that you've locked up,' he called over his shoulder as he strode away towards his own vehicle.

'There's not a lot of point locking the wretched thing—I don't think anyone's going to be desperate enough to steal a dead car,' she muttered under her breath as she dragged her eyes away from his long legs. She hadn't realised just how well muscled he was until she'd seen the way his wet trousers moulded around his thighs and along the lean length of his calves.

She shivered as she found herself doing as he'd said, gathering up her bag of belongings and the second carrier beside it before she remembered what it contained and where she had intended taking it.

'I've got a bag of things to drop off at Wolff's,' she announced apologetically as soon as she'd dived gratefully into the dry interior of Leo's car. 'They're some of Laura's clothes, rescued from her room.'

'No problem,' Leo said calmly, and her level of guilt rose another notch. He was absolutely soaking wet and it was all her fault. And now she was getting him to drive all over the place, running errands, when he needed to be going home and getting dry.

'Which bag?' he demanded. The words were startlingly loud in the heavy silence between them, and Hannah suddenly realised that the car was already parked behind Wolff's. She'd been so preoccupied that she hadn't even realised that they'd arrived.

She checked the contents of each and silently handed over the right bag, then watched while he loped swiftly up the path and rang the bell.

Light flared out briefly over him from the open door as he handed it over but he didn't linger—just a brief salute to his friend sufficing before he was on his way back to the car again.

He'd hardly closed the door before his whole body was convulsed by an enormous sneeze and her feelings of guilt escalated sharply.

'Would you mind if I stopped off at my place to grab a jumper?' he asked with a brief sideways glance towards her as he leant forward to flick the heater control up high.

For one brief second she longed to insist that he took her home first, but the lights from the dashboard were gleaming on the rivulets of water trickling down his face from his wet hair and she didn't have the heart.

'Of course I don't mind,' she agreed faintly and leant back in her seat again in a deliberate pretence of relaxation. It wouldn't matter so much if he did another detour—how long could it take him to get a dry jumper?

Hannah vaguely recognised the route they were taking, but it was on the other side of town from her own tiny flat.

She was quite surprised when the car drew up outside a building very similar to the one she lived in.

'This is where you live?' she queried. 'I would have thought you'd have something a bit bigger.'

'It's big enough for one,' he said in a quiet tone, which didn't invite any further comment.

As he pushed his door open to get out the wind caught it and flung it wide. In the space of the few seconds the door was open and the warm confines of the car were filled with a raw sample of the increased fury of the rising storm.

Suddenly it didn't feel quite so cosy any more and as she watched him walk around the front of the car she could see the way the wind was whipping his partially dried hair around his head in the few seconds before the rain plastered it down again, and she found herself wrapping her arms around her waist in an attempt to preserve her remaining heat.

'Come on,' Leo said shortly as he jerked open the passenger door. 'You'll freeze if you stay out here.'

'Oh, but. . .it's hardly worth me getting out just for you to grab a jumper,' she objected, strangely reluctant to go inside his flat.

She would be seeing the place where he lived, and even though they had been working together for eighteen months their relationship had been purely professional.

Somehow the thought of seeing where he relaxed and slept and entertained seemed far too intimate.

'No arguments,' he continued, brushing her objection aside as he reached for her elbow. 'Doctor's orders— I'll even throw in a cup of coffee to help thaw you out.'

Hannah grimaced, but once again did as she was told. She knew there was no point in debating the issue any further. If Leo had made up his mind. . .

'Ah, thank goodness for central heating!' he said gratefully as he unlocked his front door and they walked into the welcoming warmth.

He only paused long enough to drop the catch behind them before he shrugged his way out of his jacket and reached for the hanger on the back of the door.

As Hannah watched, wide-eyed, he slid the knot of his tie down until it unravelled and then began to unbutton his shirt, his fingers struggling slightly with the stubborn wet fabric until it, too, was peeled away and wadded into a ball between long-fingered hands.

'I. . .' she croaked, then paused to clear her throat, suddenly concerned that he was going to continue to strip until he stood stark naked in front of her.

The only trouble was that she didn't know whether it was embarrassment at the idea of seeing her hospital colleague without his clothes or a secret excitement at the prospect of seeing even more of the virile perfection which had frozen her voice in her throat.

'Leo?' She tried again, and this time her voice worked. 'Shall I put the kettle on for coffee?'

'Wonderful idea,' he said with a grin as his hands reached automatically for the catch on his waistband. 'You'll find a coffee-maker in the corner, all ready to switch on, and there might be a packet of biscuits. . .'

His voice faded away behind her as she made her escape, aiming for the other door leading off the main room of his flat.

She flicked on the light switch in the kitchen and stood with her hands braced on the work surface, her head hanging forward as she mentally berated herself for her cowardice. If she'd stood her ground just a few seconds longer he'd have undone his trousers and she'd have seen...

'Here.'

His husky voice interrupted her heated musings and she whirled to face him with a scalding blush starting its way up her throat.

If he had any idea of the things she'd been imagining before he'd spoken he...

Her thoughts screeched to a halt when she saw him standing there, covered only by the towel wrapped around his hips.

'Here,' he repeated, holding out the twin to his own towel. 'You need to get out of that jacket and rub some of the wet out of your hair.'

Numbly she reached out for the bundle of soft towelling, her eyes darting helplessly from the width of his shoulders to the narrowness of his hips to the length of bare hair-sprinkled legs revealed by the towel before they returned to the amusement beginning to gleam in his strange golden eyes.

'You're covered in goose bumps,' she said, blurting out the first coherent words which popped into her mind.

After a second of startled silence Leo burst out laughing.

'Talk about keeping things in perspective!' he spluttered when he'd regained his breath. 'There I was thinking you were admiring my manly body!'

I was, I was, she declared silently while she fought to keep her eyes on the mock dismay filling his face. Even then his eyes were filled with good-natured mischief.

'You don't need me to stroke your ego by telling you that you're good-looking,' she said with a teasing smile of her own, proud of her steady voice. 'I'm probably the last nurse on the staff to see the proof, if the hospital grapevine is to be believed.'

For a second she thought she saw a shadow darken the light-hearted expression in his eyes, but it was gone so quickly that she couldn't be sure.

'You might be surprised,' he murmured cryptically, and padded away on elegant bare feet, leaving her with the enticing image of tight male buttocks moving rhythmically under the precarious cover of his towel.

Hannah forbade herself to wish that the knot at his waist would magically unravel itself, horrified at the lascivious way her mind was working these days. Leo would be just as horrified if he knew what sort of fantasies were weaving their way through her head.

'Keep busy,' she muttered under her breath as she peeled her parka off and spread it open over the back of a chair in the vain hope that some of the wetness would have gone by the time she put it back on.

Not that she held out much hope—the rain had been falling so heavily that it had soaked right through her thin jumper.

She plucked at the damp fabric, horribly conscious of the way it was clinging to her and outlining the edge of her bra and hoping that was *all* it was revealing...

The coffee was made and Hannah was buried under the towel, briskly rubbing the worst of the wetness out of her short dark hair, when she felt a prickling sensation on the back of her neck.

Cautiously she peered out from the edge of the cloth and found Leo watching her as he leant against the frame of the kitchen door.

This time his lower half was covered in a disreputable pair of well-worn jeans, the seams rubbed so white that it was a wonder they still hung together and the waistband loose enough across the hollows of his belly to show her the path of the tawny hair that arrowed down from the width of his naked chest.

His towel was now draped around his neck, the hands holding each end curled into tight fists as his golden eyes spread fingers of fire over her body everywhere they touched.

Nervously Hannah cleared her throat, allowing her own towel to fall away from her head as she dragged her fingers through the tangled strands of her hair.

'Y-you wouldn't happen to have a comb I could borrow?' she asked huskily, consciously avoiding meeting the unexpected heat in his eyes. 'I—I left mine in your car.'

'As long as you don't mind sharing.'

One hand delved behind him into his hip pocket and came up with his wallet. As he padded silently towards her he flipped it open and slid out a narrow stainless-steel comb.

'Allow me,' he offered, beckoning with the comb.

'I can manage,' she said with a quick smile, holding her hand out for it. 'When I towel-dry my hair the ends can get in an awful tangle.'

Hannah started working her way through the knots and suddenly realised that Leo had returned to his position by the door and was still standing there watching her.

She froze, knowing that although it had nearly dried in the warmth of the room her thin jumper would be drawn tightly across her body by the position of her arms.

She glanced over at Leo and found that he had made the same discovery, his eyes making a very male examination of the visible curves and hollows revealed by her position.

Hurriedly, she lowered her arms, wrapping them around her ribs in a deliberately protective gesture.

'This isn't a very hygienic place to do this,' she commented as she tightened one hand around the comb until the teeth bit into her palm. 'Is it all right if I finish off in your bathroom?'

'No problem,' he said easily. 'You could have a shower, too, if you want. There's unlimited hot water and I can always find you some clothes to travel home in.'

'No!' she blurted, horrified by the idea of stripping off her clothes anywhere near him. It wasn't until she saw his frown that she realised how abrupt she'd been, and hurriedly began again.

'It's a lovely idea—especially in view of the fact that my hot water supply can be a bit erratic,' she said, smiling up at him while she frantically tried to find a cast-iron reason not to take him up on his offer, 'but I. . .I think I'd rather wait until I get back to my own flat then I can climb straight into bed afterwards.'

'As you like,' he agreed, his eyes travelling over her once more before he looked across towards the coffee. 'Did you find everything you needed?'

'The coffee's made but I hadn't looked for the milk yet.'

'I thought you took it black?' he said with a slight frown as he reached for the fridge door.

'During the day I do,' she agreed, unreasonably pleased that he'd noticed. 'But this late at night I usually adulterate it with milk so I can still get to sleep.'

She'd been watching the way his well-worn jeans hugged his rear as he bent over to reach for the bottle of milk, and had nearly missed the official-looking notice painted in ornate black letters on the white door.

'"Hangovers installed and serviced",' she read out, and couldn't help laughing.

'That's a legacy of my student days,' Leo said with an answering smile as he straightened up with the familiar container in his hand and nudged the door shut with one lean hip. 'I shared a ghastly semi—'

'With Wolff?' Hannah butted in, remembering that the two of them had met during their training.

'And two others.' He nodded as he poured milk into her outstretched mug. 'We had a party to celebrate passing some exam or other, and one of our guests left us with an artistic reminder of the event.'

'And you kept it?' Hannah blew on the steaming brew and sipped at it gingerly to test the temperature, before downing half of it in one welcome draught.

'When we came to the end of our tenancy the landlord took exception to the sentiments, and we had to replace it or lose our deposit. As it was still in working order I took it with me when we left.'

'And the fact that you've still got it doesn't have anything to do with sentiment at all?' Hannah teased light-heartedly, grateful that Leo's attention had been drawn away from her.

'Well, in mitigation, it *is* the only remaining evidence of my misspent youth,' he said with a grin, his eyes gleaming at her across the top of his own mug.

'You hope!' she shot back. 'We nurses get to hear all sorts of rumours about the things that go on during medical training—usually from the nurses who were invited to participate!'

'Not guilty!' he vowed with an innocent expression on his face, his free hand raised in surrender. 'I spent every night bent over my books, burning the midnight oil. . .!'

The mocking tone of Hannah's laughter told him just how much credence she gave that idea, but his words reminded her that she still had things to do before she could go to bed and she glanced up at the clock on the wall over his cooker before she hastily drained the last of her coffee.

'Speaking of midnight oil,' she began, turning back to

face him. She was smiling as she met his eyes but when she saw the strangely hungry expression in his gaze suddenly it was as if there was no air left to breathe and the tension, which his nonsense had dispelled, returned full force to tighten all the muscles in her neck.

For the last few minutes they'd been talking and laughing in the same way they did in the department. Now all she could think about was the fact that the two of them were completely alone in his flat.

It wasn't a frightening thought—she couldn't imagine feeling physically threatened by him—but her emotions were a different matter entirely. . .

'Well, Leo, I'm on earlies tomorrow so I ought to be getting back,' she said, feeling the warmth rising in her cheeks when she heard how false her cheerful tone sounded.

She reached out to retrieve her parka but he got there before she could peel it off the back of the chair, one warm hand covering her own much cooler one.

For a moment he paused and she thought he was going to try to persuade her to stay, but then he took the heavy garment away from her.

'There's no point putting this back on or you'll be soaking wet again,' he pointed out. 'I'll lend you something of mine to keep you warm.'

'Oh, but. . .'

'Doctor's orders,' he continued, cutting across her objection as he led the way out of the kitchen. 'You can let me have it back tomorrow.' He threw her a strangely impersonal smile, as if he, too, was creating a distance between them.

She paused as he disappeared into his bedroom again and her foolish imagination ran riot as she listened to the sound of drawers being opened and closed.

Within minutes he returned and she wasn't certain

whether she was pleased or disappointed that the upper half of his body had finally been hidden under a chunky-knit sweater.

'Here you are—this should keep you warm until we get you home.'

He handed her a deep blue sweatshirt, and when she put her hand out to take it she discovered that she was still clutching his comb tightly in her hand.

Awkwardly exchanging one of his belongings for another, she pulled the fleecy-lined garment over her head and breathed in a familiar scent. Was it his washing powder or fabric conditioner—or was it his own male essence transferred to the clothing by proximity?

Whatever it was, it made her feel strangely secure—as if she was once again being held in his arms instead of just being surrounded by his clothing.

'Ready?' he questioned when she slid her arms into the sleeves and found exactly how far they dangled past her fingertips.

'I would be if I could be certain that this jumper hadn't decided to swallow me up,' she quipped wryly as she tried to roll the cuffs back. The hem reached halfway down her thighs but, in the circumstances, that wasn't a problem—it would just make sure that there was less of her exposed for another soaking.

'Come on, then, little bit. You look like a child playing dress-up!'

'I'm not much more than six or seven inches shorter than you—less if I'm in high heels,' Hannah objected, stung by his indulgent tone.

'True,' he admitted as he came to stand in front of her and took over the fiddly task of rolling up the second sleeve. 'But your shoulders aren't as wide so the jumper droops down a lot further... Anyway, what's wrong with being petite? It can be very attractive to a man—brings out our protective instincts.'

She scowled up at him fiercely and he grinned back, tapping her on the nose with one finger.

'Of course,' he continued with a wicked gleam in his eyes, 'I wouldn't dare mention that with that expression on your face, and with your hair all tousled like that you make me think of a cat who went to sleep in a washing machine and didn't escape until she'd been fluff-dried.'

Before she had time to do more than draw in an indignant breath he'd swooped down and planted a swift kiss on her startled lips.

'Home,' he declared as she stood staring up at him with wide eyes, her lips still seared by a startling flash of heat at the unexpected contact.

A week later Hannah was still thinking about the lightning flash which had shot through her when Leo had brushed his lips over hers.

She still had no idea why he'd done it—there had been no warning that he was going to kiss her, and he hadn't even mentioned what he'd done either during her journey home or during their numerous meetings since.

She'd even begun to wonder if she'd imagined the whole thing...if it was some kind of mental aberration which proved that she was no more immune to charming bachelor playboys than any other woman.

Unfortunately, every time she saw Leo around the department her heart would give that silly skip and she could feel her cheeks grow warmer. In contrast, he seemed to be completely oblivious to anything other than his work, while he effortlessly charmed every woman between six and sixty.

When she realised that she'd been allowing the event

to dominate her thoughts for a whole week she decided it was time she gave herself a stern talking-to.

'Enough is enough,' she muttered aloud, squaring her shoulders with determination as she stood up after donning her boots at the end of her shift. 'There are more important things going on in my life than endlessly replaying a. . .a mere brush of the lips that the wretched man obviously forgot about as soon as he'd done it.'

In fact, one of the things which she had promised herself after Laura had been rescued was that she would finally take her courage in both hands and tell her about the events in her life since they parted company two years ago.

With the decision made, she set off to track Laura down and invite her for supper.

She hadn't cooked a meal for guests in all the time she'd been at St Augustine's, and it was about time she did.

CHAPTER THREE

'LAURA?' Hannah called as she saw her friend just disappearing around the corner.

'Yes. . .? Oh, it's you, Hannah,' Laura said with a big smile as she stuck her blonde head back around the corner. 'Come and join us. We've got time for a coffee before it's time to go.'

'Actually,' Hannah began as she caught up with her friend, 'I was wondering if you were busy this evening.'

She'd fallen into step with her smaller colleague as they continued towards the staff lounge and she couldn't help noticing an unmistakable eagerness in Laura's stride and an aura of happiness surrounding her—such a difference from the subdued person she'd been when she joined the staff at St Augustine's such a short time ago.

'This evening?' Laura queried with a slight frown as she pushed the door and held it open for Hannah.

'Yes. I was hoping to persuade you to come round for a meal—it seems like ages since you started work here, and we still haven't had a chance to catch up on each others' lives.'

Laura looked a little puzzled.

'Oh, Hannah, I would love to but. . .didn't Wolff get a chance to speak to you alone this afternoon? We were hoping you would join *us* this evening. . .' She lowered her voice conspiratorially. 'It's a bit of a celebration, and it just wouldn't be right without *you* there.'

Hannah only had to look at the shining happiness in her friend's elfin face to guess what was going on. It was obvious that she wouldn't be returning to a room in the nurses' accommodation—Wolff had evidently made her a better offer...

'Oh, Laura,' she murmured with a delighted smile, keeping her voice low as she reached for her friend's hand and squeezed it. 'So this evening is by way of a celebration. I hardly need to ask if you're pleased with the situation?'

Laura beamed and nodded, her happiness spilling over like sunshine.

'In which case, I'd be delighted. Just tell me when and where.'

'At last,' a deep male voice grumbled before Laura could answer, and Hannah saw the way the soft colour swept up her friend's cheeks when she saw Wolff waiting for her, his on-duty white coat and charcoal-coloured suit trousers long discarded in favour of a pair of smartly casual chinos.

For several seconds the two of them gazed silently into each others' eyes, their feelings so easily read that Hannah looked away, feeling almost like a voyeur.

'And another one bites the dust!' murmured a familiar husky voice in her ear, and she whirled around as if she'd been stung.

Leo.

She hadn't realised he was in the room, too.

'What do you mean?' she demanded, angry with herself when her voice emerged sounding as breathless as if she'd just run a marathon. Her heart had given that silly skip again, as though it were the first time she'd seen him in a week.

'Didn't Laura tell you?' he asked quietly, in deference to their friends' privacy and the scattering of colleagues around them. 'It's by way of a formal announcement.'

As she gazed up into his strange golden eyes Hannah was hit by a maelstrom of emotions. First was the brief second of hurt that Laura had only agreed with her that the meal this evening was a celebration, rather than explaining what the occasion was, but this was followed by a renewed burst of pleasure that her friend had found such happiness.

Hannah felt the smile lingering on her face even as the familiar shadows crept out of their hiding places to taunt her that she was forever doomed to watch other people from the sidelines. Such happiness could never be hers. . .

'I take it you didn't know anything about it,' Leo said, his voice drawing her out of her less than happy thoughts.

'No. . . Apparently, Wolff was supposed to deliver the invitation but. . .' She shrugged in resignation.

Leo's eyes flicked down over her washed-to-death jeans, and she suddenly realised that he, too, was looking very smart—no well-worn jeans emphasising his masculinity tonight.

'Oh, Lord,' she breathed as she glanced across at the other couple and suddenly understood what was happening. 'It's not a pot luck meal—it's a fancy restaurant do and the rest of you are all done up to the nines.'

'Hardly,' he scoffed gently. 'But I think you'll find that Laura's got a dress on under her coat, and I know Nick was taking Polly home to change—they're going to meet us there.'

Hannah hadn't realised that their boss and his new wife were coming, too, and when Leo mentioned the name of the venue she recognised it as one of the more exclusive little places on the outskirts of town—ideal for a once-in-a-lifetime special event like this.

Unfortunately all she knew about its location was that it was on the other side of town, and her heart sank when she glanced at her watch. There was no time for her to go back to her flat to change, then return to the hospital in time to follow the rest of them to the restaurant.

'In that case, I'm going to have to drop out,' she said with a wry smile and resignation in her tone. 'I'm not dressed for the occasion and there isn't time for me to go home to change, without making everyone else late.'

'There would be if I gave you a lift,' Leo pointed out, one hand already delving for his keys.

'What difference would that make?' she objected. 'You don't drive that much faster than I do, surely—unless that car of yours has hidden wings?'

'No, but I do know where we're going and I could take us both straight there when you've changed. . .' He left his words hanging in the silence between them, one dark tawny eyebrow raised questioningly while he waited for her to think.

'Laura would be upset if you didn't come,' he murmured persuasively as she was still undecided and with those words the decision was made.

Almost before she'd verbalised her agreement he'd grabbed Wolff's shoulder and, in a few low-voiced words, had told him what was happening.

'Let's go, then,' Leo declared briskly as he cupped her elbow in one warm palm and ushered her towards the door. 'They're just going to have a coffee and then they'll make their way to the restaurant. That gives us about twenty minutes to get you home and dressed.'

Hannah was having difficulty keeping up with his much longer legs as he strode along the corridor towards the closest exit to the car park or she might have found enough breath to challenge his choice of words.

As it was, the mental image he'd evoked of the two of them in her flat, getting her dressed together, had made her heart give its newly familiar skip, but it wasn't until the pictures in her head started to reverse the procedure—with his hands helping her to remove her clothing item by item instead—that she was able to regain grim control of her fantasies.

While Hannah fastened her seat belt she made certain to clamp down on her wayward imagination, and by the time she let herself into her flat she was able to be perfectly matter-of-fact about his presence there.

'Grab a cup of coffee, if you want. You could drink it in front of the television,' she offered as she made her way towards the bedroom. 'I shouldn't be much longer than ten minutes.'

'I'll believe that when I see it,' he scoffed, raising his voice so that it carried all the way through the flat. 'I've never yet met a woman who could get ready to go out in less than an hour.'

'In which case, you'd better keep your fingers crossed that I'm the exception to the rule or you're going to miss out on the first half of your meal,' she retorted as she rummaged speedily through her drawer for a clean set of underwear.

There was no problem in choosing what she was going to wear—there was only one item left in her wardrobe which was dressy enough for such an occasion. Everything else had been given away to a charity shop when she'd realised that she was never going to be able to wear them again. . .

'No time to think about that,' she muttered as climbed into the cubicle and had one of the shortest showers of her life.

In no time at all she had a towel wrapped around her dripping hair and was fastening her bra over skin which was still slightly damp.

Her legs weren't quite dry enough either and the tights she'd chosen for speed wouldn't slide up smoothly.

'Damn!' she muttered when she stuck her finger through them and made a huge hole. She knew she didn't have another pair so she'd have to go back out to the bedroom to replace them with stockings.

She wrapped her tatty old dressing gown around herself and opened the door, pausing a moment until she heard the sound of the television from the other room before she ventured out.

It wasn't that she thought Leo was so desperate for female company that he would resort to ambushing her in her own bedroom—it was just that she always felt so vulnerable when she came out of the bathroom without being fully clothed.

Her hands didn't stop shaking until she finally fastened the top of the silky midnight jersey outfit and smoothed it down over her hips. The wrap-over bodice was draped and pleated, cleverly disguising the fact that she was completely covered up to her throat—the whole design relying on subtlety to hint at the shape of the body it concealed.

Finally Hannah approached the mirror, rubbing her hair briskly for a moment before she ran a comb through it in the stream of hot air from her dryer. This was one time when she could be grateful for the fact that her natural curls would take care of themselves.

By the time she'd emphasised the deep blue of her eyes with a toning shadow her face didn't need any blusher, just a quick coat of her favourite lipstick and a last glance in the mirror at her hair.

With practised ease she scooped up her watch and bag with one hand and nudged her feet into slender-heeled shoes as she reached for the jacket hanging on the back of the door with the other.

'How was the coffee—nearly finished?' she asked as she walked into the other room, her attention on the watch strap she was trying to fasten one-handed. 'Have I taken too long?'

When there was no reply she glanced across the room, knowing that he would have found the only comfortable seat in the flat, and met Leo's intent gaze.

'What?' she demanded nervously, her hands growing still as his eyes travelled over her from head to foot. 'I'm sorry... Isn't it suitable?'

He blinked, almost as though he were waking up after a sleep and shook his head.

'Oh, it's suitable all right,' he confirmed, his voice sounding strangely husky. He cleared his throat and she felt a swift frisson of heat flicker over her skin at the unspoken pleasure in his eyes before she saw him drag them away to check his own watch. '*And* you made it inside the ten minutes!'

'Will you refuse to act as chauffeur if I dare to say I told you so?'

'Come on, woman,' he growled. 'It isn't nice to gloat.' He turned and led the way to her door, leaving Hannah to follow.

They arrived at the restaurant just as Nick Prince was helping Polly out of their car.

Something about the way he held her arm caught Hannah's eye and she paused thoughtfully as she waited for Leo to lock the car.

'What's the frown for?' Leo murmured as he reached her side. 'I thought you approved of the match.'

'Oh, I do,' Hannah agreed fervently, careful that her voice didn't carry as far as the other couple. 'If you remember, I did my best to push the two of them together.'

'Then why the frown?' he repeated, leaning back against the side of the car with his hands pushed deep into his pockets, apparently immune to the winter chill.

'It's nothing, really.' She dismissed his question but

the intent expression in his eyes told her that he wasn't moving until he was satisfied.

'Well,' she capitulated, 'I was just watching the way Nick was hovering over Polly. He seems even more protective than usual, and it made me wonder. . .' She looked across, her eyes following the two of them as Nick ushered his wife into the restaurant, apparently so intent on her care that he was completely oblivious of his audience.

'Wonder?' Leo prompted.

'Whether *they've* got something. . .'

'Hey! You two!'

Wolff's call cut between them before she could voice her suspicions that there was more than one celebration going on tonight.

'Are you going to stand out there all night?' he demanded. 'There are people in here starving to death!'

Leo straightened up from his slouch against the car and waved.

'We're on our way,' he called back, and held out a hand to invite Hannah to precede him.

They were immediately surrounded by a welcoming warmth as they stepped inside the foyer and were escorted through to their table straight away.

'Here. . .let me,' Leo murmured as he helped her to removed her jacket and handed it to the hovering waiter.

His breath tickled the back of her neck as he bent over her to help her into her chair. It wasn't the first time in the last few days that she'd noticed this strange new awareness whenever he was near. She didn't need to look to know that he was standing close behind her, and the realisation set a tide of heat rising in her cheeks. She didn't know how she was going to manage to concentrate on her meal when he was sitting just inches away from her.

'Drinks, everyone?' Wolff offered.

'Just a minute,' Nick interrupted. 'In view of the occasion, I insist that this one's on me.'

'Certainly not,' Wolff retorted. 'Laura and I invited you all to help us celebrate. . .'

'And just beat us to the punch,' Nick continued mysteriously with a grin towards Polly. 'I suggest that we crack a large bottle of champagne.'

'That sounds promising—two colleagues arguing over who's going to pay for the bubbly—but I'm going to have to decline,' Leo said regretfully. 'It's orange juice for me.'

'Oh, Leo, no,' Laura commiserated. 'You're the one with the pager tonight?'

'John Preece is on duty, but if it gets too hairy. . .' Leo pulled a face and shrugged.

Hannah knew he didn't have to say any more. They all knew how easily a quiet night in A and E could turn into a bloodbath, with every available hand working flat out. All they could reasonably hope for was that Leo managed to get to the end of his meal undisturbed.

As expected, the food was wonderful—one perfect course following another—and as the six of them chatted easily among themselves Hannah found she was able to relax in spite of the the way Leo's arm tended to brush against hers.

As was usually the case with colleagues, the conversation began to veer towards work but Hannah wasn't surprised—with all of them working in the same department of the same hospital it was almost a forgone conclusion that it would.

'Ladies and gentleman,' Wolff said portentously when the dessert dishes had been replaced with liqueurs and coffee.

'Who?' mocked Leo, looking around as if wondering at Wolff's audience. 'You can't mean *us*!'

'Leo...!' Nick admonished with an attempt at a frown. 'Let the poor man have his time in the limelight.'

'I thought he'd already had that at the Autumn Ball,' Leo muttered in an aside to Hannah.

'And very nice he looked, too,' Hannah said with an answering grin. 'Beautiful tan, good body—and a lovely mover.'

'Hey!' Leo objected indignantly. 'You're supposed to be *my* date—you're not supposed to be ogling other men, even in retrospect!'

The burst of laughter from the other four told them that their conversation had been overheard and robbed Hannah of the chance to point out that she *wasn't* Leo's date. It had been purely coincidental that he'd been the one to bring her to the restaurant.

'If you two have finished wrangling?' Wolff asked pointedly, before he turned towards the green-eyed blonde beside him and captured her left hand in his. 'I would like you all to know that Laura has consented to marry me.'

While they applauded he slid an emerald and diamond ring onto her third finger, then raised her hand to his lips.

When Hannah saw the expression in her friend's eyes as she looked up at the darkly elegant man bending over her hand she felt the warning prickle of tears. She didn't think she'd ever seen her look so happy...

'And while you're all in the mood for celebration,' Nick added as he reached for Polly's hand and squeezed it, 'we'd like to tell you that we're expecting our first baby.'

'First...?' Polly squeaked, but her voice was drowned under the chorus of congratulations.

'*That's* what you were hinting at outside,' Leo muttered in a soft-voiced aside to Hannah. 'Was it just a lucky guess or had someone given you a hint?'

'I just noticed how protective he was being as he helped her out of the car—as if she was made of spun glass—and...' She shrugged.

'Well, I'm beginning to feel quite left out,' Leo complained to the group as a whole. 'You four are so happy it's almost abscene. There's Dr Prince grinning regally as he contemplates the start of a long line of princes and princesses, and there's Wolff smiling wolfishly as he volunteers to put his head in the trap...'

His awful puns on their names drew groans around the table, then he turned towards Hannah, his eyes gleaming at her like candlelight through expensive whisky.

'Well, Hannah, that just leaves the two of us,' he announced with one of his patented ladykiller smiles as he captured the hand closest to him. 'It seems to me that it would be a *sterling* idea if we got married as soon as possible.'

There were more groans and one exclamation of 'Leo! How unromantic!' from Laura, but Hannah was so startled by the unexpected declaration that she was grateful for the interruption, her mind going from blank surprise to utter turmoil in the blink of an eye.

Shock had adrenaline pouring into her system, altering her pulse and breathing in an instant as she stared up into his strangely intent expression.

He couldn't be serious, could he? It must be just one of his interminable jokes—the sort of thing which he could prolong for a whole shift if he found enough staff and patients willing to play along.

Deep inside, the vulnerable woman she'd once been relished the idea of his proposal, no matter how off-hand, but the eminently controlled, sensible woman she'd had to become knew she had to marshal a response...quickly.

'Oh, Leo,' she began, her voice far huskier than she would have liked, 'if only I'd realised earlier that you were feeling so left out I could have done something to make certain you felt wanted and needed...'

She'd been gazing into his eyes as she said the teasing words, pretending to simper up at him, until suddenly she realised that his pupils had dilated—almost as if he were becoming aroused—their strange colour darkening from whisky to brandy and their expression almost fierce.

'And if you'd realised?' he questioned, his voice deeper than ever. He was concentrating on her so intently that it was almost as if they were alone in the room...alone in the world... 'What would you have done to make sure I wasn't so lonely?'

Hannah blinked, wondering how she'd got herself into this situation—and how she was going to get herself out of it without making an utter fool of herself. What on earth had she been thinking of to tease him like that? Anyone would think she was flirting with him...that she had finally joined all the other females between six and sixty who kept trying to catch his interest.

In a blinding flash she had her answer, and she felt her lips curve into a smile.

'Easy,' she whispered with a hint of a pout as she dared to run the tip of one finger along the freshly shaven curve of his jaw. 'I'd have invited Sexy Samantha along to keep you company...'

'You teasing witch,' she heard him whisper under the hoots of laughter from the rest of the group.

'Oh, well done, Hannah,' cheered Wolff. 'You set him up beautifully for that one. Have you ever done any acting? That was definitely Oscar quality.'

Hannah found that she couldn't join in their amusement. She had seen the quick flash of challenge which replaced his pique at being bested, and wondered just how far Leo was likely to go if he did decide to reciprocate. Was she going to regret baiting him in front of their friends?

Nervous about travelling back with him, she waited until the general mêlée of retrieving coats before she tried to approach one of the couples for a lift, but it was almost as if Leo had read her mind.

'Here, Hannah,' he invited, holding her jacket open for her to slide her arms into the sleeves. 'It won't take long for the car to warm up but you might as well take as much warmth with you as you can.'

'Oh, but...' she began, glancing from the wicked gleam in his eyes to the other couples performing the same ritual.

'Scared of me?' he taunted softly as he leant close to her ear, his warm breath aromatic with the scent of coffee. 'Scared enough to want to play gooseberry to either of those sets of lovebirds?'

He could hardly have chosen anything more likely to put the missing starch back into her spine.

'Of course not,' she hissed as she jerked her chin up a defensive notch. She knew as she said it that it was just the knee-jerk reaction he had been looking for, and the fact was confirmed when she saw the swift gleam of triumph lighten his eyes.

'Well, then, beautiful, let's go home to bed,' he invited with a wicked grin, his voice just loud enough for his words to carry to the rest of the group.

The expressions on their faces ranged from shock and surprise to speculation and concern, but Leo didn't give her a chance to explain that they would be returning to their own separate beds.

There was just time for a swift farewell before he was ushering her rapidly towards the door and out into the darkness, his silent efficiency leaving her almost breathless.

She hesitated about berating him for his deliberate *double entendre* in front of their friends, realising that it wasn't safe to argue while he was trying to concentrate on his driving, but he apparently didn't have the same scruples.

'Your place or mine?' he questioned slyly once they were on the road, the car's heater efficiently dispelling the wintry chill from her feet.

Hannah drew in a slow silent breath as she chose her words, tempted to let fly. How dared he presume that just because she had accepted a lift in his car they would be spending. . .

At the last second sanity prevailed and she realised that outraged reaction was probably exactly what he wanted. She knew from working with him that he was a past master at stirring people up.

A second slower breath gave her time to rein in her anger and consider a different course.

'Whichever is more convenient for you,' she said calmly as she unknotted her fingers and folded them neatly one over the other on her lap. 'If you'd rather not drive the extra distance I can always walk. It's not that far.'

There was silence for a moment, as if she'd startled him, then she heard a soft chuckle and she dared a glance at him just in time to see the wry expression on his face in the intermittent glow of the streetlights.

'You know, Hannah, if you worked at it you could be very bad for my ego,' he murmured.

'Really?' she said, hardly daring to believe that he was already prepared to joke about the situation. She'd known other men who wouldn't have been able to accept such a calm dismissal without pushing the point.

'Yes. Really,' he confirmed, obviously having to try very hard to sound disgruntled as he fought a grin. 'I use my very best chat-up lines on you, and what do you do...swoon with delight...scream with excitement...accept with alacrity...? No such luck. *You* remain perfectly unaffected and suggest walking home!'

Perfectly unaffected? Hardly, she thought as she mentally replayed the images which had assailed her when he'd first said he was taking her home to bed. She had a good enough imagination to know that the naked, golden-skinned body she'd imagined in that bed was a fair approximation of Leo's, but if he ever found out that she'd so readily imagined herself in the bed with him she'd never hear the end of it.

'Your very best chat-up line?' she scoffed, latching onto something...anything...which would take her mind away from the image of a stark naked Leo sprawled across her bed like an indolent lion. 'Your place or mine?' she repeated and forced a chuckle.

'You don't mean to tell me you've heard that line before?' he demanded in horrified tones, and the chuckle turned into shared laughter.

Within minutes he was drawing up outside her flat, and she was startled to realise how much she was regretting the fact that their time together was over.

'Well, thank you for the lift,' she mumbled as she searched feverishly for the doorhandle. The sooner she could shut herself inside her flat the sooner her brain could start functioning normally again. 'There's no need for you to get out...'

Too late. She was talking to his knees as he straightened up out of the car and shut his door.

Hannah huffed out an exasperated sigh as she swung her feet out to the pavement, then resigned herself to making polite conversation for a few minutes while Leo did the gentlemanly thing and escorted her to her door.

As he took her elbow she admitted secretly that she

actually enjoyed the feeling of security his hand gave her. She wouldn't dare to admit it among her more feminist friends but she regretted the fact that so many of the old-fashioned courtesies between men and women were dying out.

'I enjoyed myself this evening,' Leo said suddenly as they reached the step in front of the door, the angle of the building sheltering them from the chilly wind.

'You sound surprised,' Hannah said with a smile as she turned to face him. 'Weren't you expecting to?'

'Yes and no.' His expression was wry as he went on to explain, his breath forming a frosty halo around them. 'The three of us—Nick, Wolff and I—have been friends for a long time, and with the demands of our careers we've sometimes gone months or even years without getting together.'

'Rather like Laura and I?' Hannah suggested.

'Probably.' He nodded, the light over the door striking gleams of gold off his hair and highlighting the clean masculine lines of his face. 'But, even so, when we *do* see each other it's as if we can carry on the conversation exactly where we left off.'

'Laura and I are like that,' she confirmed with a laugh. 'I was a bit concerned when she said she was coming to St Augustine's. I was afraid that in the two years since we last worked together we might have grown too far apart to pick up the threads or that new friendships, such as mine with Polly, might have taken over.'

'*That's* what I was afraid of tonight—that with the new bonds the other two had formed with Polly and Laura the bonds between the three of us would have been broken.'

'And instead?' Hannah prompted, interested to hear his thoughts in spite of the fact that the cold was gradually creeping through the warmth of her jacket.

'Instead, it's as if the bonds have somehow stretched to accommodate the changes in the relationship. . .as if Polly and Laura have slotted into niches that were ready and waiting for them. . .'

He paused when she couldn't hide her shivering any more, his eyes moving swiftly over her as if he had forgotten how lightly she was dressed for the time of year.

'Oh, Hannah, I'm sorry,' he apologised, wrapping a penitent arm around her shoulders, as though to share his own heat with her. 'Here I am prattling on about nothing while you're freezing.'

The warmth of his body seared her from shoulder to thigh as her questing fingers found the key in the bottom of her bag and, in spite of their insidious trembling, she managed to unlock the door on her first try.

'I wouldn't have listened if I wasn't interested,' she pointed out as she stepped into the warmth of the minuscule hallway and then, on an impulse, held the door open to invite him to follow her inside.

'Coffee?' she offered, a different sort of shivering beginning inside her when she realised exactly how long it had been since she'd invited a man into her home.

Leo's face creased into his trademark ladykiller smile as he followed her inside, but before he could speak there was a familiar high-pitched bleep.

Hannah's heart sank with swift disappointment but the expression of disgust on Leo's face as he batted the thing into silence made her chuckle aloud.

'The phone's through here,' she offered as she led the way into her sitting room and switched on the lamp on the side-table.

'Thanks,' Leo said, his voice preoccupied as he concentrated on tapping out the familiar number.

The conversation was brief and to the point, and

Hannah soon realised that there had been an horrendous crash of some sort on the motorway.

'How many trapped?' she heard him demand, and she could visualise the sort of scene which would have met the rescue services—she'd seen it often enough at first hand since she'd become a member of the mobile emergency team.

'I'm sorry, Hannah, but I've got to run,' he said as soon as he broke the connection. 'Can I take you up on the offer of coffee another time?'

'I expect so,' she said absently, her concentration more on the last words of his conversation on the phone. 'Did I hear you say they were having difficulty contacting one of the team members?'

Leo nodded and threw the name of one of Hannah's nursing colleagues over his shoulder as he made his way back towards the door.

'She's been off with flu. They thought she was ready to return but she's not answering so it looks as if the team is going to have to be short-handed tonight.'

'Not necessarily,' Hannah said decisively as she kicked off her strappy high heels and stripped off her best jacket and flung it haphazardly towards the arm of a chair. 'If you can give me ten seconds to grab my anorak and a pair of trainers I can take her place.'

CHAPTER FOUR

'SOMETIMES I don't know which I hate most about an English winter—when it rains or when it doesn't rain,' Hannah said with a heavy sigh as she crumpled up another length of used disposable sheeting.

'Why's that?' Tina Wadland glanced up from her own task, her gloved hands continuing to wipe down blood-spattered surfaces.

'Well, when it rains some stupid idiot will always forget how slippery wet roads are and travel far too fast and too close to the car in front. Then something goes wrong and everyone has to brake suddenly, and we end up with this. . .' She gestured with the bowl of blood-soaked swabs before she disposed of it.

'So?' Tina's hands had slowed into a repetitive circular movement. 'Surely it's better when it doesn't rain?'

'Ah, but at this time of year when it doesn't rain they're so delighted that they forget how low the temperature can drop at night and forget about black ice so that when they have to brake suddenly. . .'

'A clear case of heads you lose, tails you lose,' a familiar husky voice broke in, and Hannah whirled to face Leo, her eyes racing over him with guilty pleasure.

He was leaning lazily against the work surface closest to the doors, his ankles crossed and his white coat pulled back by the hands thrust casually into his trouser pockets, his pale blue shirt adorned by yet another of his collection of brightly patterned silk ties. This one was an abstract symphony of terracotta and turquoise in the midst of the hospital monochrome.

He hardly looked as if he'd missed hours of sleep last night, she thought as her eyes finally reached his face, peeved that he looked as alert as ever while she was feeling distinctly ragged.

Mind you, she admitted silently, that could be because he'd gone straight to sleep when he finally got to bed while she'd tossed and turned, endlessly reliving the events of the evening like a tape loop in a projector. It had been after three o'clock the last time she'd glared at the glowing numbers on her alarm clock.

'Any news on those people last night?' Hannah questioned when she managed to find her tongue.

'We haven't lost anyone else,' he confirmed, his smile dimming as he, too, remembered the horrific events which had been the culmination of the previous night.

He hadn't bothered arguing with her spontaneous offer of assistance—a nod and a briefly muttered 'see you in the car' had been enough to indicate his acceptance.

Within a minute they'd been on their way to the hospital, the journey virtually silent as they'd geared their minds up for the task ahead.

'A minibus went out of control on the motorway,' was the greeting they'd received when they'd arrived. It hadn't been until Hannah had seen eyebrows going up that she'd remembered that the two of them had still been dressed for their celebration meal, but everyone had been too preoccupied to comment. Tomorrow would be different. . .

'Fire and police on the way, and we've called in an additional mobile medical team from St Mary's as they're not the designated hospital. Estimates of fifteen casualties, several trapped.'

The briefing went on as Hannah stepped behind a convenient stack of shelving to don her protective clothing. There was no time for niceties such as changing in a cloakroom—people could be dying.

She was still pulling on her reflective tabard over her green arctic anorak as she slid into the back of the vehicle, the layers of tracksuit and waterproof boiler-suit making her feel terribly clumsy after the soft clinginess of the dress she'd just removed.

There was a quick burst of static on the radio before they left the shelter of the hospital building, then they were on their way, speeding through the darkness.

'Any more information yet?' Leo demanded, leaning forward against his seat belt.

'They think the driver of the minibus either fell asleep at the wheel or had a heart attack. The vehicle swerved across the road and, of course, everyone else started trying to get out of the way...'

Hannah saw him shrug. He didn't need to say any more.

'Mayhem,' Leo muttered, confirming her thoughts, and slumped back against the seat again.

For the first time Hannah saw the fourth member of the team sitting on his other side.

'Hi, Nia,' she murmured when she saw the familiar outline of the other nurse.

Nia Samea smiled, her teeth very white against her dark olive skin in the subdued light.

'Wish we didn't have to meet like this so often,' she commented in her softly lilting voice. 'But at least this time we've not having to rescue our friends.'

'We do seem to have had more than our share of call-outs recently,' Hannah agreed.

'One of the hazards of working in a front-line hospital with all the latest bells and whistles at our disposal,' Leo added wryly, then sat up straighter as the brightness of the emergency floodlights up ahead told him they had arrived.

'Oh, my...' breathed Nia when she caught her first glimpse of the chaos which awaited them. 'There are bodies everywhere...'

The vehicle detoured on the direction of one of the policemen at the scene, and they came to a halt at the command centre beside the generator which was supporting one of the towering floodlights, illuminating the carnage.

'How far have you got? Where do you want us first?' Leo demanded as soon as his feet hit the littered tarmac.

'We've set up a casualty collecting station,' confirmed the senior policeman who was obviously in control at the command centre. 'Two paramedics from the ambulance service have started triage, but there are too many victims. Can your team split up...one half to the collecting station and the other to those still trapped? Obviously, in these sort of temperatures the faster we can get them shipped back to St Augustine's the better—we don't want to add hypothermia to their problems.'

Leo turned to their group to direct them.

'John, will you and Nia take the collecting station and sort the wheat from the chaff? Hannah, come with me.'

He set off at a brisk jog, his bag carried as easily as if it were just an extension of his arm, the fluorescent bands on his uniform gleaming eerily in the harsh light.

Several members of the fire service were clustered around the minibus, the jaws of life already being positioned to scissor their way through the front doors to provide access to the injured trapped inside.

'Doc...over here!' called a voice, and Leo veered around the back of the vehicle towards the fluorescent striped beckoning arm, with Hannah close on his heels. 'Can you check these two before we begin?'

The expression on his face let them know that he wasn't hopeful for the outcome of the venture, but that obviously wasn't affecting the efficient way he did his job.

The impact of the crash had come primarily at one side of the front of the vehicle, and the diagonal forces as another car had slammed into the back had twisted it so badly that none of the doors could be opened.

Leo reached in through the shattered windscreen, the reflective bands on his own protective clothing almost blinding at close quarters.

Over his shoulder Hannah could see him trying to find a pulse in the patient's neck. She was only a young woman, Hannah thought as she waited alertly in case Leo needed her to pass something. From what she could see, the patient was probably much the same age as herself but one side of her head and face had been badly injured, probably on impact with the side of the window frame, and her long blonde hair had an ominously large dark patch right down one side.

Leo's gloved hand was bright with blood when he withdrew it, shaking his head.

'No hurry for that one,' he muttered succinctly as he stepped back to look for the best way to clamber over the wreckage towards the person in the driver's seat.

'Nor that one,' the fire officer added bluntly, grabbing Leo's elbow to save him the journey as he gave his crew the signal to continue. 'He was partially decapitated on impact, but there are others trapped inside.'

He indicated the route they had started clearing through the side panel of the minibus, their machinery opening it up like some monstrous tin-opener.

While he waited for the space to be widened sufficiently Leo strode towards the car which had rammed into the back of the minibus. It looked as if the engine must have ended up on the driver's lap...

'Has this one been checked?' he called as he bent down to peer inside.

'No good,' the fire officer called back over the noise surrounding them. 'Broken neck—probably instantaneous on impact.'

Hannah watched Leo straighten up, his expression grim as he strode back to the bus, arriving just in time for a large panel to be peeled back.

'Can we get some more light in this side?' he called as he was cleared to approach and leaned inside.

'God, what a mess,' Hannah whispered when she saw the state of the interior. 'Where do we start?'

Leo's mouth tightened as he silently held his bag out towards her and climbed gingerly between the ragged edges of the hole. She stepped closer so that when one hand reached out she was ready with the handle within reach.

'Is there room for me?' she asked, peering into the jumble of seats and upholstery, people and belongings she could see tangled together.

'Give me just a minute...' There was a pause of a few seconds before several armfuls of extraneous baggage came sailing out into the road. 'OK, Hannah, you can come in now, but watch yourself—there's a lot of glass and sharp metal...'

One of the fire crew took charge of her bag but it wasn't until she tried to climb up into the bus herself that she realised how much easier Leo's long legs had made it for him.

Another fireman took pity on her predicament and solved it instantly by lifting her up bodily so that she could thread her feet into the hole.

'Thanks,' she muttered with a brief smile as she twisted back to retrieve her bag.

She turned to focus on the interior of the minibus and the outside world ceased to matter.

Several of the passengers were obviously unconscious, if not worse, but some were coherent.

'Please, help me,' whispered one crumpled figure as she raised a hand in supplication. 'I hurt so much. I—I think my leg's broken.'

Hannah crouched beside her, carefully manoeuvring between the severed upright struts of one of the damaged seats.

'Where does it hurt?' she asked gently as she began her examination, her fingers automatically reaching to feel for the woman's pulse.

In the end she didn't need the young woman to tell her where the injury was—the jagged edges of the shattered bone sticking up through the blood coating her thigh told their own story.

'Leo,' Hannah called, knowing just how quickly such an injury could cause a patient to go into shock from the amount of blood lost into the thigh itself. With an exit wound as large as this, the loss could even cause death. 'I've got a compound fracture of a femur here.'

She heard Leo relay the message outside and, as she reassured the increasingly drowsy young woman that help was on its way, she swiftly found a vein in the patient's hand.

By the time the ambulancemen arrived to work out how they were going to stabilise the leg and extricate the patient she was ready to attach the bag of fluids to the needle she had taped in position.

It took nearly ten minutes to help the poor woman out, her cries of pain muffled by the Entonox mask as they finally lifted her out through the gaping hole.

Two of the women were unconscious but, apart from large knots on their heads, they appeared to be uninjured.

'Sorry to take so long getting them out of your way but we have to put a neck collar on each of them and get them on boards, just in case there's any spinal damage,' one of the younger ambulancemen explained, totally unnecessarily.

Hannah didn't comment. She knew that safety first was the best maxim if they weren't to cause further damage to their victims in the process of getting them out. It would be dreadful if one of the passengers had survived the crash, only to be paralysed by an injury to the spinal cord in the rush to get her out of the vehicle.

She was just about to work her way forward to the next victim when a sound in the corner behind her drew her attention.

'Has anyone mentioned that they were carrying pets on board?' she asked as she warily made her way towards the noise—a strange mixture of panting and growling.

'It's all right,' she said soothingly as she got closer to the shadows, worried that an injured animal might lunge out at her in panic. 'I'm not going to hurt you,' she continued in as reassuring a tone as she could manage while she peered at what appeared to be a large mound of clothing.

'Please... Help me...' whispered a hoarse voice, the words broken up by ragged breathing. 'It's... My baby's coming... It's too early...'

Hannah's blood ran cold when she heard the terror in the voice emerging from the shadows, and she scrambled forward as fast as the obstructions would allow.

'Woman in labour,' she called over her shoulder as she cleared a space for herself at the woman's side, and heard Leo swear succinctly.

'How is she? Any injuries?' he demanded across the

shambles separating them. 'I've got my hands full for a minute...'

'Were you hurt in the crash?' she asked the labouring woman as her moans began to escalate. Hannah's fingers automatically reached for the hand she could see in the dimness, seeking a pulse.

'My arm...!' yelped her patient. 'It hurts like...like hell...'

Now Hannah could see that the poor woman was cradling one arm with the other.

'Is that the only place you're hurt?' she asked, frustrated by the fact that the lights didn't quite reach this corner. 'What about your head?'

'No, that's... Oh, God... Here comes...another one...'

Hannah had begun to stroke the dark hair back from the woman's forehead while she asked for details, such as her patient's name and age, but when she realised that the contractions were almost continuous she knew there was no time to waste on bedside manners.

She'd just turned to shout for the ambulancemen to bring the supplies she'd need to help Sara Pethick bring her baby into the world when the young woman caught her wrist in a grip of steel.

'It's coming,' she panted suddenly. 'I can feel it...down there... I want to push...'

'No!' Hannah ordered fiercely. 'Don't push... not yet!'

'Oh, but... I've *got* to...!'

'Pant! Please, you must pant until I can check that the baby's all right.'

'But it's ready to come...' Sara wailed as she tossed her head restlessly from side to side. 'I can feel it!'

'Just give me a minute to check that everything's ready,' Hannah pleaded. 'You've still got your underwear on and...and you don't want to hurt the baby, do you?'

It was half plea, half emotional blackmail, but it seemed to work.

'Quick! I need some more light over here,' Hannah snapped over her shoulder as she helped her patient out of her underwear, moving as quickly as she could. 'And an oxygen cylinder and a sterile obstetric kit.'

She longed to ask questions about the prematurity of the infant, but she didn't dare distract the mother-to-be from her panting. Not until this contraction faded and she was able to make her examination...

As someone angled a powerful torch towards her the level of light increased in her niche behind the back row of seats, and she suddenly saw what was happening.

'Oh, God,' she breathed, then closed her lips firmly, hoping the young woman hadn't heard the horror in her voice.

'Leo,' she called over the cacophony surrounding the vehicle, fighting to keep her voice calm as her discovery forced her to rearrange her plan of campaign. 'She's got a prolapsed umbilical cord.'

She mentally crossed her fingers that the words would be meaningless to her patient, but she and Leo both knew that the young woman's unborn baby was now in great danger.

She heard the urgency in Leo's voice as he handed over the care of his present patient to another pair of willing hands, then heard his voice getting nearer.

'I'm bringing the oxygen and the upholstery from one of the seats to elevate her hips.'

Hannah had to shuffle across on her knees to allow him to wedge himself in the limited space beside her, immeasurably relieved to have him working so closely with her.

'What's happening?' the young woman demanded

hoarsely as the urgency to push died away for a moment. 'Is something the matter with my baby?'

'Your baby's fine,' Leo said soothingly as he signalled silently for Hannah to help him lift the young woman's hips. 'We just need to put a cushion under you...'

The upholstery from one of the broken seats was slid into position as easily as if they'd practised the manoeuvre many times, tilting Sara's hips to help relieve the pressure on the protruding cord.

A gloved hand passed Hannah the sterile obstetric kit over her shoulder and she tore it open immediately, careful to touch only the outside of the package until she'd had time to clean her hands.

'Here,' a disembodied voice said over her shoulder, and she turned to see a bottle of povidone-iodine scrub solution apparently suspended in mid-air.

'Thanks,' Hannah muttered as she stripped off her contaminated gloves and held her hands out under the liquid, grateful that whoever the administrator was had recognised the need for speed.

As soon as her hands were clean she leaned away to reach into the open kit for a fresh pair of gloves, allowing Leo to take his turn with the scrub solution.

She turned back to their patient just as the next contraction began building.

'Pant!' she reminded Sara when she groaned, pleased to see that Leo had been able to position the Entonox mask and hoping that it would be enough to dull the urge to push. 'Keep panting!'

'I'm going to have to catheterise,' Leo murmured. 'If I can get half a litre of saline into her bladder and clamp the catheter shut then the full bladder will alter the pressure between the head and the pelvis and help to stop the blood supply to the placenta being cut off.'

Hannah nodded her comprehension, carefully keeping

her hands out of the way. She knew that when the cord arrived ahead of the baby the danger was that it would become trapped between Sara's pelvis and the baby's head. If that happened the baby would be asphyxiated, its brain dying when its supply of oxygenated blood was cut off.

'Are you ready for a bad case of cramp?' he muttered under his breath.

'Ready.' She nodded again and bent forward to position her fingers against the baby's emerging head and push it gently back up into the vagina until the cord was free, the thick dark loop once more pulsating strongly.

As she settled her fingers around the tiny head she tried to find the most comfortable position—she knew that Leo hadn't been joking about the probability of cramp.

As she watched him swiftly catheterise the woman, carefully timing the task between contractions, Hannah knew that, no matter how uncomfortable she got, if they wanted to save the baby's life she was going to have to hold the position of her hand against the baby's head until they managed to get the young woman out of the minibus and into the ambulance which would transport her to hospital.

Only when there was someone else there to maintain the pressure against the baby's head would she be able to relinquish her position.

Leo leaned around her to cover the exposed cord with a sterile dressing moistened with saline, and draped an apparently endless supply of towels and blankets around the shivering woman to preserve her body heat.

When Hannah heard him draw in a breath she knew he wasn't relishing having to explain to the young woman exactly what was going on and, while she maintained her own position, she watched as he gently broke the news about the baby's problem and what they were doing about it.

It took an agonising half-hour for the combined teams of firemen and ambulancemen to extricate Sara from the minibus, time that Hannah spent quietly talking to the increasingly agitated young woman, encouraging her to stay calm for her baby's sake.

Leo had received an urgent call elsewhere to administer morphine and make a decision about a possible emergency amputation and had been forced to remove himself from the scene, but the time he had spent gently explaining the complication seemed to have allayed Sara's most pressing fears for the time being.

Hannah was amazed at Sara's resilience when she heard later that the young woman had actually been able to crack a joke with the ambulanceman who'd taken over her intimate task for the duration of the journey to hospital.

As Hannah ruefully massaged her hand she watched the ambulance speed on its way towards St Augustine's, grateful that Sara had been far too involved in her own predicament to think about the fate of her fellow passengers.

After her baby was safely delivered would be soon enough for that.

In the meantime... She flexed her fingers one last time before she retrieved her bag and set to work again.

It was another two hours before the last ambulance left for the hospital, this one travelling without flashing blue lights. There was no need for haste with its final sad burden—the bodies of those who had lost their lives.

'Let's get back to base,' Leo murmured as he wrapped a comradely arm around her shoulders and gave her a brief squeeze. 'You must be shattered.'

'Well,' Hannah conceded as she slid gratefully into

the comforting upholstery of their rapid response vehicle and leaned back, 'all I can say is it certainly isn't dull, spending time with you.'

'All the girls say that,' Leo quipped smugly. 'I'm well known to be a fun person to date.'

'Are you two going out together?' Nia demanded from her corner, instantly interested enough in the gossip potential of what she'd heard to rouse herself from an exhausted slump.

'No...!'

'Yes.'

They answered simultaneously, but Hannah couldn't believe what he'd said. Didn't he realise that this wasn't the sort of thing to joke about if he didn't want it to spread through the hospital like wildfire?

She glared at him.

'No, we *aren't* going out together,' she said, firmly contradicting him.

'So where were we earlier this evening?' he demanded mildly, both eyebrows raised in interrogation and a fugitive smile playing at the corners of his mouth.

'At a restaurant with Nick and Polly, and Laura and Wolff,' Hannah said impatiently. 'But—'

'And who took you there and brought you home?' he continued inexorably, obviously playing to the gallery as both John and their driver were now listening too.

'*You* did,' she confirmed. 'But—'

'I rest my case,' he interrupted, not allowing her to continue.

He finally allowed his wicked grin to show. 'I took you out to a meal in a restaurant with a group of friends, then brought you home again. Now, doesn't that sound as if she's going out with me?' he demanded, turning to appeal to Nia.

Much as she would have liked to set the story straight,

Hannah was too tired to argue and had to be satisfied with turning her back on the wretched man and his far too interested audience until she could get away from them.

Even when they arrived back at the hospital, it didn't prove easy. She'd been thanking her lucky stars that her own car was still parked in the staff car park and she wouldn't need to rely on Leo for a lift, but he was still waiting for her when she emerged from the cloakroom, dressed once more in her 'dining-out' finery.

'Hannah. There you are.' The familiar husky voice startled her. She'd been hoping that he would be otherwise occupied until she could make her escape.

'Leo.' She smiled wanly up at him, her breath hitching in her throat when he captured her elbow and began to escort her towards the exit closest to the car park.

'You don't need to walk me to my car—there are plenty of lights for safety...'

'I just thought you'd like an update on Sara,' he said mildly, totally ignoring her objection as he ushered her out into the frigid darkness.

'How is she?' Hannah demanded, totally sidetracked by his change of topic.

'She had a little girl and she says she's going to call her Hannah in your honour.'

'Oh, Leo...!' she breathed, emotional tears flooding her eyes. 'Is she all right...are they *both* all right?'

'Little Hannah is apparently raising the roof and couldn't be better, and Sara's getting plastered!'

'Oh, I'm so glad. She was so brave. She went through everything without a murmur, in spite of her broken arm.'

'And it couldn't possibly have anything to do with the calmness and courage of the nurse who held more than her hand throughout!' Leo teased as he turned her to face him, cradling her cheeks in his hands and gently wiping a single escaping tear away with his thumb.

'It was a team effort,' she objected, in spite of the warmth his praise sent flooding through her. 'The whole team was fantastic—we didn't lose anyone else at the scene of the accident, and...'

She bit her lip, suddenly aware that she was babbling. Had the warmth of his hands short-circuited her brain?

Leo was smiling down at her, his teeth very white in the artificial light and his eyes seeming to glitter as he looked down into her face.

Hannah shivered as a strange tension began to grow between them.

'Well, it's certainly been an eventful evening,' he said, his voice almost distracted as his eyes travelled from her eyes to her mouth and back again. 'Perhaps we should try it again some time...?'

Hannah gazed up at him, not quite certain what he was suggesting, but before she could ask his head had swooped down and his lips brushed over hers.

CHAPTER FIVE

THE memory of that fleeting kiss had haunted the hours of darkness.

One moment Hannah was reliving the soft warmth of his mouth on hers and revelling in the accompanying surge of excitement, and the next she was chastising herself for overreacting to what was little more than a friendly salute.

But why had he done it? She'd been working with him for nearly two years now and he'd never shown any interest in her before. Was he at a loose end with no new partner in sight? Had that kiss been part of his infamous seduction technique—the one that was rumoured to turn knees to jelly in every department in the hospital?

She snorted in silent disgust at her own nonsense.

As if someone as downright handsome and charismatic as Leo was likely to restrain himself to such a milk-and-water effort. It was only because it had been so long since she'd received *any* kisses that she was reacting this way.

Anyway, there was no point in getting herself in a state over it—it wasn't as if there would be any more kisses to worry about. Jonathan had let her know in no uncertain terms that no man would ever be interested in her unless he was desperate, and Leo certainly wasn't desperate. He could take his pick of the most beautiful. . .

'Hey! Hannah! Are you asleep on your feet?'

It was Tina Wadland's voice which called her back to the present, and she blinked owlishly as she looked around.

What was she doing? What was she supposed to be doing?

'Sister MacDonald was looking for you,' Tina continued once she knew she'd got Hannah's attention. 'She wanted to know if you'd come back from your break so she can send the next lot off.'

'I'm coming,' Hannah confirmed as she swung herself round on the stool in the corner of the tiny kitchenette and slid her feet down to the ground. She grimaced when she saw the state of her cold coffee and tipped it down the sink. 'Just give me two minutes in the bathroom and I'll be firing on all cylinders.'

'Thank God for that,' Tina commented as she began to walk away. 'The world and his wife seem to have decided to pay us a visit today, and there's a new woman on duty in Reception who seems to think it's her right and duty to make everything as difficult as possible.'

'As if life isn't difficult enough,' Hannah muttered to Tina an hour later when she'd ushered out yet another patient who had spent the entire time he was being treated complaining about the receptionist's obstructive attitude. 'Enough is enough.'

'What are you going to do?' Tina called as Hannah began to stride away down the corridor.

'I'm going to bring in the big guns,' Hannah said, and threw a grin over her shoulder before she elaborated. 'I'm going to set Big Mac on her!'

Hannah entered the main reception area and looked around for the familiar spry figure of the diminutive senior sister, knowing that she was just as likely to be seen out here as closeted in her office.

The doors slid open silently and a tall man strode in, with a child of about eight cradled in his arms. Father and son bore such a striking resemblance to each other that there was no mistaking the relationship, and they were both looking pale and worried.

It wasn't until he gently deposited the boy on the floor by the receptionist's desk that she saw that one hand was wrapped in a blood-soaked towel.

'My son's put his hand through a glass door,' the man said, one arm comfortingly around his child's shoulders, regardless of the fact that his immaculate suit was in imminent danger of getting blood-stained.

'Name?' demanded the receptionist, with barely a glance in his direction as she began tapping self-importantly on the computer keyboard.

'Ben Thomas.'

'Is that Ben or Benjamin?' she asked disapprovingly, her hands suspended over the keys like petrified spiders.

'Benedict,' he supplied patiently.

Click, tap, tap, tap. . .

'Address?'

Once again he supplied the information in a calm voice but Hannah could see that it was only a façade he was maintaining for his son's sake and she set off quickly towards him.

'Date of birth?' Click, tap, tap. . .

The next question coincided with the limits of the man's patience. Hannah had seen his agitation rising as he watched the spreading pool of blood dripping from his son's elbow, his free hand clenching spasmodically in his frustration.

'For God's sake, woman!' he exploded just as Hannah reached his side. 'He's damaged an artery and he's bleeding heavily. If this nonsense goes on much longer I'll be able to give you his date of death as well!'

For the first time the officious woman actually looked up from her keyboard.

'Well. . .!'

'If you'd like to follow me, sir,' Hannah suggested quietly, cutting across the woman's outrage.

'I can't let him go *yet*, Sister. He hasn't finished filling in the details. . .' she began pompously.

Much as she would have liked to have given the woman a piece of her mind, Hannah ignored the bleatings going on behind her and led the way swiftly towards the trauma room. It was enough for her that she'd seen Celia MacDonald bearing down on the reception desk with fire and brimstone in her eyes.

Later she would make certain that Sister had heard both sides of the story, but for now her job was to take care of one brave but very frightened young lad.

Once his father had settled him on the high bed he retreated to the other side and held his son's free hand.

Hannah carefully unwound the once-white towel and found that the gash on the youngster's arm was every bit as bad as she'd imagined, running diagonally almost the length of his forearm.

The towel was almost saturated with blood and the poor child was beginning suffer shock.

'How did you do this?' she asked, partly for information and partly to take the child's mind off what she was doing.

'Ant—my little brother, Anthony—pinched my car and I was trying to catch him. He ran inside the house and pushed the door shut behind him to try and stop me.'

'And you put your hand up to stop it shutting?' she questioned as she quickly wrapped a sterile dressing over the gaping wound.

'Yes, and the glass broke. . .' He hissed with pain as she applied pressure to slow down the bleeding, and Hannah apologised.

She caught sight of the expression on his father's face when he saw his child's discomfort and swiftly enlisted his help, showing him how to take over the job of maintaining pressure over the damaged artery. As she'd expected, he was only too pleased to feel that he was doing something to help.

'If you can hold on there for a second I'm just going to grab the doctor from next door,' Hannah said, and quickly suited her actions to her words, her hands held out of contact with the doors as she used her hip and shoulder to exit the room.

'Leo,' she called softly as she pushed open the swing doors to the room next door, easily recognising his burnished hair and broad-shouldered physique as he bent over his own patient.

'I need you next door for a moment,' she continued, sternly dragging her eyes away from her unaccustomed appreciation of his physique. 'I've got a young lad next door who's put his arm through a pane of glass. It looks as if he's nicked the radial artery and he's bleeding pretty badly. I've got him head down because he's already in borderline shock.'

Leo's head turned towards her, his eyes tiger bright over his disposable mask.

'Nerves? Tendons?' he rapped out over his shoulder as he turned back towards the still figure in front of him.

'Probably,' Hannah said, correctly interpreting his shorthand as a demand to know about the involvement of other structures in the boy's arm.

'Get a saline IV up and running straight away and send blood samples up to the lab for cross-matching, ready for Theatre. I'll be with you in two minutes.'

Hannah ducked out through the doors again and turned immediately into the next set.

'Right, Ben,' she said. 'I need some information from you.' Out of the corner of her eye she saw his father begin to bristle, but she surreptitiously winked at him and watched him subside into watchfulness.

'Tell me, do you ever watch any hospital programmes on television?'

'And vet programmes.' The bright-eyed youngster nodded, obviously determined to fight the side-effects of his accident. 'Dad says I'm the bloodthirsty one in the family.'

'So you know a bit about the equipment we use?' she asked as she collected the items she needed. 'Like masks and gloves and needles and transfusions?'

'Yes,' he nodded, the slightly wary look which entered his eyes telling her that he was intelligent enough to have worked out just where this conversation was going.

'So, if I was to talk about an IV you would know what I meant?'

'It's a needle with a tube on it for putting something into someone,' he said. 'Is that what you're going to have to do to me?'

There was a slight quiver in his voice and Hannah longed to give him a reassuring hug. He might be trying to be very grown up and brave, but he was still only a boy...

'You've been losing blood ever since you cut your arm, and we need to put some liquid back into you so you won't dry out and blow away.'

'What sort of liquid? Blood? Will it...hurt?'

Hannah couldn't help smiling and was glad she was wearing a mask so he didn't think she was laughing at him. It was touching the way his keen inquisitiveness had given way in the end to natural fear.

'You'll probably be having some blood put in later, but at the moment I'll be putting some saline in—that's water with a tiny bit of salt in it. It might hurt just for a second when the needle goes in,' she admitted honestly, 'but when we put the saline solution in you won't feel a thing.'

'Oh.' He gazed up at her for a moment before he looked back at his father for support and drew in a shaky breath. 'OK!' he said, and held his little paw out to her.

'Good boy,' Hannah praised, then concentrated on getting the needle in as quickly and as painlessly as possible.

'How's that?' she said when she straightened up. 'Did I do it as well as they do on TV?'

'Yes, but...you said I was losing blood so you had to put s-saline in—' he hesitated over the unfamiliar word '—but then you took some of my blood *out* and squirted it in a tube.'

'That's right. And now I'm going to write your name on the label and send it up to the labs. They're going to test it so they can match it up in case you do need to have some blood put in.'

'There's a chance that he might be AB negative,' his father interrupted, 'in which case you can have some from me—I'm a regular donor.'

'How long ago did you last donate?' Leo asked as he walked into the conversation and grabbed a fresh pair of gloves.

'Nearly six months ago—the mobile unit comes round twice a year and they're due soon.'

While he'd been talking Leo had gestured for him to release his hold on the dressing over his son's arm. After he'd done so Leo gently peeled it back to have a look at the damage.

'Well, there's some good news and some bad news,' he said when he straightened up after a thorough examination, one hand supporting the injured arm as he applied pressure over the vital area. 'The good news is that the cut is so clean and sharp that there's a good chance that it will mend just as cleanly.'

'And the bad news?' Mr Thomas prompted, his face still very grey.

'The bad news is that he's going to have to go up to Theatre for this to be stitched up.'

'Why?' Ben demanded shakily. His eyes had been going from one adult to the other while the conversation went on across him. 'Can't *you* do it?'

'It will need the special microscopes they have up in the operating theatre so they can see clearly enough to join everything up in the right order,' Leo explained with a patient smile. 'You've cut one of the arteries in your arm and you also caught some of the tendons so we want to make absolutely sure that we don't miss anything.'

Mr Thomas was looking as if he would rather go through the whole thing himself than sit by and watch his son suffering, but the youngster seemed to have accepted the situation remarkably quickly.

'Will I be able to see the microscope?' Ben demanded as Hannah took over and rewrapped his arm and then, at his request, let his father resume responsibility for maintaining pressure over the wound.

Meanwhile, Leo's long-legged stride had taken him over to the phone and he was waiting to be connected with the surgeon who would do the job.

'That's all arranged, then, Ben,' he announced when he turned back to them. 'As soon as you're ready to go up the surgeon will give you a quick look at his operating microscope, and then you'll be put to sleep so that he can use it on you.'

'Really?' He might be pale and injured, but there was nothing wrong with his enthusiasm.

'Thank you, Doctor,' Mr Thomas said with a tired smile as the tension began to show. 'You've been very kind.'

'It's the least I can do for Ben. After all, he made two bad mistakes today.'

'Two?' Ben questioned looking from one adult to another with a frown.

'Yes. The first one was in putting your hand through the glass in the first place, and the second one was in putting the *wrong* hand through it—even after the operation you won't have to miss any school!'

Ben's groan was nearly as loud as his father's chuckles.

With a quick salute and a grin Leo left the room, and it wasn't long before Ben was on his way up to Theatre, his trepidation lightened by the prospect of a glimpse at hospital technology.

Hannah set to putting the room to rights.

Last time she'd looked there had been a queue of people waiting—some more patiently than others—and all wanting attention.

By the time she came to the end of her shift she felt as if she'd attended to half of the population of the town. They were at the beginning of the annual flu season but this year it seemed to have started early, with every other person complaining of a cough, a high temperature or a headache.

In between there had been splinters to remove from a large naked bottom, the owner of which refused to detail how it had happened, and stitches to be removed from under a child's chin, collected as the result of an argument with a school playground.

There had also been four assorted lacerations, three broken limbs, two suspicious chest pains, 'and a partridge in a pear tree,' Hannah muttered as she reached for the small pile of letters in the 'N' section of the internal mail system and sorted through for any with her name.

'Just one,' she sighed as she peeled the flap open. She quickly scanned the computer generated appointment letter and her heart sank like a stone.

Had time really passed so quickly? Was it time for her next check-up already? At least they hadn't given her too long to think about it.

She stuffed the letter back into the envelope and shoved it roughly into the pocket of her parka.

'Bad news?'

Hannah jumped and whirled to face the owner of the voice. She hadn't even realised that Leo had entered the room, let alone that he'd been standing right behind her.

'No. . .just an appointment I'd forgotten about,' she said with a calmness which belied the trembling inside.

That had been too close, she thought. He could have seen the letter over her shoulder and then her secret would have been revealed. He certainly wouldn't be smiling at her if he *had* seen what the letter was about. . .

'If it's something you want to talk about,' he offered softly, and she suddenly realised that her thoughts must have been mirrored on her face, 'I've got broad shoulders, if you need to use one. . .?'

She cast her eyes over the width of his chest and slid them upwards. He certainly did have broad shoulders, and they looked as if they would be infinitely comforting to burrow against if everything went wrong again.

If she'd had someone like Leo to rely on last time when her whole world had fallen apart everything would have been so different. As it was, she'd been totally alone and had been forced to turn inside herself and draw on her own strengths.

That was when her self-sufficiency had been born, and she hadn't regretted it for a moment until now. . .

'Thank you,' she murmured quietly, bending forward to pick up her bag to avoid meeting the keenly analytical look which had replaced the puzzlement in his whisky-coloured eyes. 'I'll bear that in mind.'

Suddenly the last couple of days caught up with her and she couldn't wait to reach her own tiny haven and lock the rest of the world out for a few hours.

'See you tomorrow,' she said with a quick dismissive smile, and hurried out of the room.

As she drove through the freezing darkness she laughed bitterly to herself.

Leo would never know how lucky he was that she hadn't taken him up on his offer. Knowing what a devil-may-care sort of character he was, he would probably have been horrified if she *had* told him about her problems.

The most frightening thing was that, for the first time, she had actually been tempted to tell someone all about it, just for the relief.

She hadn't even told Laura yet, and they'd been friends for years, so why on earth she should think about confiding in someone like Leo. . .?

Perhaps it would be better if she erected the barriers again and kept the world at its customary distance. She would hate to ruin the wonderful working relationship she'd built up with her colleagues, and she knew that if they found out about her past then everything would change.

Her preoccupation with her impending appointment made it all too easy for Hannah to keep everyone at arm's length—even Laura.

It had felt as if something inside her was tearing apart when she saw the hurt in her friend's eyes when she repeatedly turned down invitations to join her to make up a four or a six with Nick and Polly or Wolff and Laura.

Unfortunately she knew who the other member of the

group would be, and she'd already seen his expression harden when she'd refused his every invitation—even a cup of coffee when their breaks coincided.

Oh, she'd made certain that no one could complain about her attitude to her work—she was still just as dedicated and hard-working, and she still joined in the jokes and laughter within the department—it wasn't in her nature to mope around with a long face.

The trouble was that she couldn't help her attraction towards Leo. It seemed that once her feminine awareness of him had awoken it refused to go back to sleep, and working with him only made her realise what a genuinely nice person he was.

Many was the time over the next few weeks that she sat alone in her tiny flat and chuckled at the memory of some bit of nonsense he'd perpetrated during her shift...some trick he'd played on another member of staff or a joke he'd told a frightened patient to try to help them relax.

She'd laughed longest at the running battle he seemed to have, trying to stay out of Sexy Samantha's predatory clutches—his detours into sluices, behind curtains and into linen cupboards descending into farce as he begged the A and E staff to save him from her.

His behaviour seemed very out of character for one of the most charismatic bachelors on the staff and, in spite of her determination to keep out of his way, Hannah found herself aiding and abetting his avoidance tactics with growing glee.

It was two days before Christmas before she realised that her wish had come true. In the discomfort of the aftermath of his kiss and all it could represent she had longed for a return to the relaxed relationship that the two of them had always enjoyed when they worked together.

As she reported for the start of her shift she glanced

at the board to see which other members of the team were sharing the duty with her, and was pleased to see Leo's name without a qualm—in fact, she was actually looking forward to spending the time with him.

She smiled at the prospect of the seasonal silliness he was bound to bring with him and refused to admit that she still harboured a niggling regret that she hadn't been able to risk seeing where that fleeting awareness might have led the two of them.

The Leo who reported for duty was anything but the embodiment of life and energy she had been expecting. When he walked through the doors his face was almost grey and his stunning golden eyes were dull and red-rimmed.

'Heavy date last night?' taunted one of the charge nurses with an all-men-together leer on his way through, and blinked when his words were totally ignored.

'Late night, Leo?' He tried again, obviously expecting to see the trademark grin and cheeky reply.

'Something like that,' Leo replied sombrely and walked away.

Hannah filed his response away and determined to find out what was wrong. She hoped that Leo saw her as a friend now and, as far as she was concerned, friends cared about each other and Leo wasn't happy.

After a morning of his strange mood, Celia MacDonald was obviously concerned, too, and readily agreed to release Hannah for her break as soon as she saw Leo disappearing in the direction of the staff lounge.

'Here,' Hannah murmured a few minutes later as she held out a steaming mug full of black coffee.

He hadn't even looked up when she followed him into the room and set about filling the kettle and switching it on.

He'd gone across to the window and perched one hip

on the corner of the sill so that he could gaze out at the dull wintry scene outside.

'What. . .? Oh, thanks, Hannah,' he murmured absently, wrapping both hands around the thick pottery mug as though he were freezing, before he returned his gaze to the depressing prospect of soggy brown grass and bare trees.

'Is. . .is there anything wrong?' she ventured, her heart going out to him. He seemed as if he had turned in on himself in the few hours since she'd last seen him.

He'd been his usual cheerful self yesterday. . .

The last time she'd seen him, when she'd been on her way out of the department at the end of her shift, he'd been teasing one of the junior nurses about what presents she wanted from Father Christmas.

What had happened in the meantime?

He barely acknowledged her question, just shrugging briefly without breaking off his blind contemplation of the small patch of the hospital grounds visible out of the window.

'Leo. . . Can I do anything to help?'

This time he did turn to look at her, and his eyes were so full of pain that she nearly cried out.

'No. . . No one can help,' he said, his voice sandpaper rough as if his throat were raw.

'Are you ill? Is it this flu bug that's going round?'

He chuckled, but there was no humour in it.

'I wish it was something that simple,' he murmured, and glanced at her again.

She had the sudden impression that he wanted to talk but, with the chance of others coming in very high, the staffroom definitely wasn't the best place.

'Do you want to go for a walk?' she suggested, unable to think of any other way they could guarantee seclusion.

He glanced significantly out at the dismal prospect and raised one eyebrow.

'Well, at least we'd have it to ourselves,' she pointed out with a tentative smile.

'On the assumption that the rest of the staff have too much sense to go out there?' he said, but she was pleased to see that, in spite of the resignation in his voice, he was getting to his feet.

Hannah dumped her coffee in the sink with hardly a glance. There would be other cups of coffee, but Leo needed her now.

'I'll grab my parka and meet you by the side-door,' she suggested, and crossed her fingers that she wasn't giving him time to regret his decision.

She breathed a sigh of relief when he joined her outside and, hands stuffed deep in pockets for warmth, they both began pacing slowly around the damp paths surrounding this end of the hospital buildings.

Hannah virtually had to resort to biting her tongue while she gave him time to decide whether he wanted to confide in her. She'd even begun to take note of the bank of shrubs they were passing which *hadn't* lost their foliage when he turned and began to pace towards the hospital again.

Her heart sank when she thought that the whole miserably chilly exercise had been a waste of time, but suddenly he halted and swung to face her.

'Do you ever wonder if it's all worthwhile?' he demanded quietly, his eyes darkly intent.

For just a second she was tempted to voice the sort of flippant reply she would give to any other questioner, but this was Leo and he was hurting.

The spiteful breeze flipped the ends of his tie up into the air but his reactions were too slow to prevent it flicking his face.

Hannah realised that it was still the same eye-catching composition he'd worn yesterday and he certainly didn't look as if he'd had much sleep since then...

'Often,' she admitted, finally answering his question. 'Some days all I seem to do is wonder whose stupid idea it was that I trained as a nurse.'

'And?' The word was almost a challenge.

'And then I have days when someone names their baby girl after me,' she reminded him with a wry grin. 'Somehow that seems to redress the balance.'

He closed his eyes and sighed deeply, his broad shoulders slumping as though from an insupportable weight.

'But what happens if there are too many bad days and not enough good? Too many days when you don't seem to be able to help enough people, too many people who are beyond helping?'

'And too little sleep...and too much stress...and not enough time to allow your soul to recover before the next onslaught,' Hannah enumerated with a sigh of her own.

There was silence between them then, but this time the air didn't contain the sharp-edged knives she'd felt before. This time Leo just seemed so...discouraged?

'Leo?' she began tentatively, then threw caution to the winds. 'Would a hug help?' she offered.

'A what?'

He blinked at her as if he had just woken from a strange dream.

'A hug,' she repeated, and hoped he would think the increased colour in her face was due to the sharpness of the wind.

Leo closed his eyes again, the smile which lifted the corners of his mouth almost painfully slow in appearing as he silently opened his arms.

'Oh, Hannah,' he murmured as she stepped closer and he wrapped them around her. 'You'll never know how much I needed this.'

CHAPTER SIX

'WHAT happened last night?' Hannah prompted softly from her position just under Leo's chin, his broad shoulders sheltering her easily from the chilly breeze.

He stiffened slightly as she broke the silence between them but she tightened her arms around his waist and burrowed her head deeper against him, as though she was settling in for the duration.

In fact, she had been quite prepared for him to make some excuse to push her away once the initial offer of a hug had been delivered, but he didn't move—almost as if he was weighing up his options.

Slowly she felt the tension drain out of him and he settled his arms more securely around her, one hand encircling her shoulders and the other nestling against the curve of her waist through the thick padding of her parka.

Under her ear she could hear the steady double beat of his heart and marvelled at the warmth and strength he radiated. He felt good...smelt good, in spite of the lingering hospital odour of antiseptic.

Today he seemed just a little rumpled around the edges but he'd obviously taken the time to shave, the fresh clean smell of the soap on his skin affecting her senses more than any artificial cologne—her breathing deepening unconsciously as she drew it into herself.

It had been so long since anything like this had happened that she'd almost forgotten how good it felt to be held like this...how easily it could help you to forget about all the miserable things happening in the world.

'A patient died last night,' he murmured in a husky

voice, his words dragging her back to the real reason they were standing out here in the cold with their arms around each other.

The echo of pain was clear in the rough tone.

Hannah's heart jerked in response, then sank. She would never get used to the apparently senseless loss of life.

'One of the crash victims?'

She had a mental image of a very pregnant Sara as she had seen her last, and found herself surreptitiously crossing her fingers that nothing had happened to her or her baby.

'No...a young lad up in Birch Ward—ten years old.'

'Birch?' For a second she couldn't place the name— it wasn't one of the wards that A and E had much contact with. Then she remembered where it was—in the complex where cancer victims came to stay when they were undergoing courses of chemotherapy—and she nodded briefly to show she'd realised the significance.

'He had leukaemia.' Leo went on, and Hannah could have wept at the pain in his voice. 'We thought he'd beaten it—he seemed to be doing so well—but in the end...' He drew in a shuddering sigh.

'Was he a relative?' she asked. Perhaps the ten-year-old had been a nephew or even a young cousin.

'No, not a relative, but I'd known him for so long that it felt as if he should be part of the family. He was admitted the day after Lisa was.'

'Lisa?' A strange stab of jealousy forced her to ask, even though deep inside she didn't want to know who the woman was. Her intuition was telling her that she wasn't going to like the answer.

'My...my fiancée,' Leo said softly, hesitantly.

'Your...?' She stiffened, unable to say the word as her heart turned into a lump of cold lead inside her.

He had a fiancée? Leo was engaged—or at least, he had been when he first met the young lad who'd died last night?

She loosened her hold on him, feeling strangely betrayed. When she would have stepped back it was Leo's turn to tighten his hold.

'She died three years ago, Hannah,' he murmured, his breath warm against her cheek, and she felt suddenly guilty for the relief that flashed through her—not relief that Lisa had died, she hastily told herself, but relief that the woman was no longer in Leo's life.

'How long had you known each other?' she asked in a vain attempt at reminding herself that *she* didn't have any place in Leo's life either. They were colleagues— friends who cared enough about each other to want to offer comfort, but that was as far as it went. . .

'Most of my life, it seemed,' he said wryly. 'Her parents and mine were friends since before they were married—they were my honorary uncle and aunt throughout my childhood.'

Hannah stayed still and silent, knowing that he was far more likely to continue reminiscing if she didn't remind him that she was listening. In spite of the fact that the last thing she wanted to hear was how happy he and his Lisa had been, she knew instinctively that he needed to talk about it—especially after his young friend's death last night.

'She had just started planning the wedding when the leukaemia was diagnosed, but she swore both sets of parents to secrecy, hoping to get better before I found out.'

'What?' Her question was involuntary. How on earth had his fiancée thought she was going to hide something like that, and why would she *want* to hide it from the man she was going to marry?

'She wasn't involved in a medical career,' Leo explained wryly. 'She hadn't realised what sort of effect the chemo would have on her, nor could she have known that she would react so badly to it.'

He sighed softly, his attention focused on the pieces of gravel he was pushing around with the toe of his shoe while he retreated into the memories.

'I went to visit her,' he said, glancing up at her briefly. 'She was supposed to be staying with an old schoolfriend but her mother let something slip about visiting hours.'

He shook his head. 'They'd just told her that her only chance would be to have total body radiation and a bone-marrow graft, but all she could think about was the fact that she wouldn't be able to give me a family.'

He looked up at Hannah with anguish in his eyes.

'She told me to forget about her and find someone else, but there *wasn't* anyone else. . .I loved *her*.'

He shook his head as words momentarily failed him.

'I suggested bringing the date forward, but she insisted that the wedding couldn't take place until she was fit and well again. She wasn't going to walk up the aisle until she was looking her best—and certainly *not* with a wig on. . .'

Hannah hid a smile of admiration for the courageous woman and, as she listened to the rumble of his voice deep inside his chest, her initial petty jealousy died and was replaced by the wish that she could have met her. Leo deserved someone like his Lisa in his life. . .

'What happened?' Hannah asked, finally daring to lift her head from its comfortable resting place to look up at him. She knew that Leo wasn't likely to stop telling her the story at this point, and for some unexplained reason she felt she needed to see his expression while he was talking about Lisa.

He was looking out over her head, his whisky-coloured

eyes staring blindly at the lacklustre scenery around them—as if his whole concentration was on the events inside his head.

'We couldn't get her into remission and she went downhill quite rapidly.' He drew in a deep sigh and finally looked down into her upturned face. His eyes were dark with painful memories and Hannah's heart clenched with the helpless need to comfort him.

'As the original date of the wedding drew closer she became very depressed. Her parents even approached the hospital chaplain about the possibility of conducting the wedding on the ward but she wouldn't hear of it.' His brief chuckle owed little to humour and sounded as if it had been forced past a huge obstruction in his chest.

'She said. . .she said I was far too young to be a widower and far too good-looking and, anyway, she'd lost so much weight that she'd look terrible in her wedding dress—like a scarecrow. . .'

His words ended on a whisper and because she could see he was fighting tears she looked away to give him some small measure of privacy—as much as she could with his arms wrapped so tightly around her.

She heard him swallow heavily before he began to speak again, his voice sounding almost rusty in the chilly air.

'I spent so much time on the ward with her that I got to know the regulars quite well—there's a special atmosphere up there that you rarely find on any other ward.'

Hannah smiled. She'd spent part of her training on a children's ward, and she knew what Leo meant about the atmosphere there.

'Simon was one of the ones who looked as if he was going to make it—until his blood count a month ago. I've visited him most days—partly to give his parents a break together—and I was just about to go home at the end of my shift last night when he sent a message down that he wanted to see me.'

'And you went up and sat with him,' Hannah guessed as everything fell into place.

In spite of her efforts at maintaining a sensible emotional distance between the two of them, she had learned so much more about Leo Stirling than she'd known on the night of the Autumn Ball. . .certainly enough to know that he had willingly given up a night's sleep to keep his young friend company during his last few hours.

The strident sound of an approaching ambulance shattered the silent bond which had wound its way between them, and the outside world reappeared around them.

Suddenly realising that she still had her arms wrapped around him, Hannah loosened her hold on his waist and tried awkwardly to step back.

Leo resisted for a moment, pulling her back against his lean length for one last squeeze.

'Hannah?'

The hesitant tone in his voice drew her eyes up to meet his again in spite of the embarrassment which coloured her cheeks when she realised how their embrace would be interpreted should anyone see them. She'd been so isolated within the little cocoon they'd woven around themselves that it had taken the sound of the siren to make her see what they had been doing.

She could only be grateful for the bank of evergreen shrubs which had screened them from prying eyes—she certainly hadn't been thinking about the effect it could have on their reputations.

'Thank you,' Leo said sincerely, his slow attempt at a smile a painful imitation of his usual ladykiller grin—but it still managed to jump-start her pulse rate. 'Thank you for listening. . .for being there for me.'

'There's no need for thanks,' she began, conscious that she was trying to dismiss his effect on her senses as much as deflect his gratitude.

'Ah, but there is,' he insisted, his hands gripping her shoulders as he towered over her. 'Double thanks, in fact. Once from me, for allowing me to weep all over your shoulder, and once from the department, who will now be able to work with me for the rest of my shift without fear of being shouted at in spite of doing their best.'

The expression in his eyes matched the sincerity in his tone and she had to fight the prickle of response in her own eyes.

'S-so,' she said on a shaky breath, 'I'm responsible for pulling the thorn out of Leo the Lion's paw for the sake of peace in the jungle?'

After a startled second of silence Leo threw his head back in a quick burst of appreciative laughter.

'Now, isn't that just typical of you, Hannah?' he said with a chuckle as he turned her back towards the side-entrance they'd used at the beginning of their break.

In spite of the fact that they were now in full view of anyone who bothered to look out of the window, he wrapped his arm around her shoulders and pulled her close to his side for a one-armed hug.

It wasn't until they were walking back along the path that she realised how cold her feet were. She hadn't noticed all the while they were talking but suddenly she was worried about how long they'd spent outside. Was she going to be late back on duty?

She fished inside her parka for the watch pinned to the front of her uniform and was surprised to see how little time had actually passed since they'd come outside—it seemed as if they'd been talking for hours if the amount of ground they'd covered was anything to go by.

'Whatever happens,' Leo said as he pushed the door

open for her and ushered her into the enveloping warmth of the hospital building, 'you always seem to manage to come up smiling.'

Hannah was glad he couldn't see her face when his final words registered.

Not always, she thought sadly as she hurried to put her parka away. There had been times, over the last couple of years, when it had taken every bit of acting ability she possessed not to break down and cry, regardless of where she was or who might be watching.

Sometimes it was only the thought that there were other people in far worse situations which kept her going.

Sternly she pushed the unhappy memories into their dark corner in the back of her mind and set off towards the main reception area. If the noise of sirens was anything to go by, she would soon be too busy to think about anything other than her job.

'Sister Nicholls,' a familiar Scottish voice called almost as soon as she appeared through the doors.

'Yes, Sister.' Hannah hurried across, knowing the tone denoted urgency.

'Will you take Michelle through to three? She's been vomiting for nearly eighteen hours. I'll send Dr Stirling as soon as possible.'

The young girl sitting in the wheelchair had so little colour in her face she looked almost grey. Her skin was sheened with sweat and her pale silky hair was plastered to her head.

'Mum, *I* want to have a go in the wheelchair. Why is *she* having all the rides?' whined a petulant voice just behind her, and Hannah glanced briefly in its direction then blinked.

If it hadn't been for the fact that the whinging child had so much more colour in his face, the two of them would be indistinguishable. The likeness was too marked for them to be anything other than twins.

'Are you Michelle's mother?' she asked, pausing only briefly on her way to the examining room. 'Do you want to follow me?'

The offer was just a formality because most parents would fight to be allowed to accompany their children when they were ill.

'Oh, no.' The overweight woman's chins wobbled as she shook her head and glared in her daughter's direction while she put a comforting hand on her son's shoulder.

'Poor Michael doesn't like seeing people being sick— I'm certain she's only doing it because she knows it upsets him. I told her to stop it last night when she made a mess of her bed, but she didn't take any notice. Selfish, that's what she is, just plain selfish. . .'

As Hannah wheeled her charge swiftly away from the rambling diatribe she had to press her lips tightly together to prevent herself from telling the stupid woman what she thought of her.

There was no way this frail angel of a child could have deliberately made herself sick for eighteen hours. The strongest will in the world couldn't have made her bring herself to such a state of collapse, nor have given her such a high temperature.

'She's badly dehydrated,' Leo confirmed when he arrived a couple of minutes later. 'Get an IV going as soon as possible to get some fluids into her.'

He continued his examination, gently questioning their apathetic patient and trying to tease her into some sort of a response, but she was obviously too overwhelmed by everything that was happening to her.

'Ouch!' Her cry of distress was hardly more than a mew as Leo palpated her abdomen, her enormous blue eyes swimming in tears.

'Positive McBurney's...acute,' he muttered after he'd soothed their little patient with a heartfelt apology for having to hurt her, then grabbed for a bowl and held it for her while she retched helplessly.

Hannah took over, wiping the girl's pasty little face with a cool cloth as Leo strode across to the phone and tapped out the code to connect him to Theatre.

While he was arranging for Michelle to go straight up for prepping Hannah mentally patted herself on the back that her own diagnosis of a badly inflamed appendix had been confirmed.

Now they needed to get her ready to go up as quickly as possible, and that included getting her awful mother to sign the parental consent for the operation.

'I don't understand it,' Hannah told Tina when they were finally freed for a coffee-break. 'That woman has the most beautiful set of twins and she seems to be lavishing all her love and attention on one of them and ignoring the other.'

'How's the little girl doing? Did we get her on the table in time?' her young colleague questioned with concern.

'Only just,' Hannah confirmed with a shudder when she remembered the message relayed from Theatre. 'Her appendix was already gangrenous when they opened her up. If her mother had left her suffering for another few hours it could have perforated, and it might even have been too late to do anything.'

'Well, all I can say is thank goodness we sometimes get lighter moments,' Tina commented when Hannah subsided a little. 'Did you hear about Mrs Myfanwy Griffiths?'

Hannah shook her head. 'A patient this afternoon?' she asked. She was still angry about events earlier but was willing to have her attention diverted.

'Yes. A Welsh lady with a very pronounced accent,' Tina said with a creditable imitation. 'She was in a lot of pain—apparently she'd probably passed a gallstone and she's been sent up so they can look for more.'

'Don't tell me—she was fair, fat, female, fertile, forty, feverish and flatulent,' Hannah enumerated, counting the well-known indicators on her fingers.

'Very!' Tina agreed with a laugh. 'She was talking nineteen-to-the-dozen, telling us about the concert she had been hoping to go to tonight while Dr Stirling was palpating her abdomen. Suddenly she released a noisy gust of wind and she went purple with embarrassment.'

'The poor woman,' Hannah said with a chuckle.

'That's not the best of it,' Tina said, really getting into her stride. 'Dr Stirling said to her, "Was that Purcell's Trumpet Voluntary?" and she said, quick as a flash, "No, Doctor, more like Griffiths's Trumpet *In*voluntary!"'

An appreciative laugh ran around the room, everyone's attention having been caught by Tina's clever imitation of Mrs Griffith's Welsh accent.

The silly story had finally taken the edge off Hannah's anger and she was idly looking towards the clock on the wall when she did a horrified double-take. If she didn't get moving she was going to be late for her appointment.

As she hurried through the hospital she couldn't help a wry chuckle at the realisation that she had been so wrapped up in the events in the department that afternoon that she'd almost managed to miss the appointment which had been hanging over her like a big black cloud for the last few days.

Now remembrance returned with the force of a tsunami, obliterating everything in its path.

Hannah pushed open the door of the department, conscious for the first that her hand was visibly shaking.

A quick glance around the empty waiting area told

her that she wouldn't have long to wait—at least the consultant was sensitive enough to realise how stressful these appointments were and made certain there was as little hanging around as possible.

Half an hour later it was all over for another six months, but her hands were still trembling when she returned to the department.

Hannah had surprised herself by confiding the nature of her appointment to Celia MacDonald when she'd asked for permission to leave the department. Her superior hadn't asked for details but had been concerned that she ought to go home when she'd finished, but Hannah had been adamant that she would far rather be kept busy.

Anyway, she thought as she reported back, there was only another hour to the end of her shift.

She was just in time to take her turn to stand on the apron of the emergency entrance as another ambulance reversed swiftly towards her, the doors flying open almost before the vehicle was stationary.

'OD,' Ted Larrabee said crisply as he unlocked the trolley and pulled it towards himself with an expertise which spoke of much practice. 'Female, name unknown, age approximately early thirties,' he continued, while his colleague concentrated on the rhythmic count of resuscitation. 'She's taken a complete cocktail, by the look of those...' He pointed at the plastic bag beside the ominously still body and the assortment of bottles visible inside.

Hannah found herself running along beside the trolley as the young woman was whisked through, and she briefly crossed her fingers and sent up a prayer for their unhappy patient as the team swung into its horribly familiar routine.

They did everything they could, working hard to save

the life of someone who apparently hadn't valued it herself, but it was all in vain.

It wasn't until Hannah had time to go through the clothes they'd taken off her to see if she could find some sort of identification that she found the note.

'Leo, I've found something,' she called as she began to read. 'Her name was Tamsin French and... Oh, God...' she finished on a whisper when she turned the piece of paper over and found the reason for the young woman's suicide.

Suddenly there was a strange buzzing sound in her head and the room seemed to go slightly out of focus.

As if from a great distance, she could hear Leo calling her name and she could see him coming towards her, but he almost seemed to be moving in slow motion as her knees refused to hold her weight any longer and she sank silently into darkness.

'Hannah?' called an insistent voice. 'Hannah, can you hear me? Open your eyes, now.'

It was an effort just to lift her eyelids when she would far rather have stayed in the silent anonymity of the dark. Something told her that she wasn't going to like what she found out when she woke up properly, but that voice was accustomed to being obeyed.

'Good girl,' Celia MacDonald said briskly when Hannah finally peered up at her. 'How are you feeling?'

Hannah blinked and tried to sit up.

'Now, then, you know better than that,' the senior sister chided as she put a firm hand on her shoulder and pushed her back down. 'Just stay still for a moment until you catch your breath.'

She subsided, horrified by how weak and shaky she felt. What on earth had happened to her to make her feel so...?

'Oh, Lord,' she groaned as her lapsed memory returned in glorious Technicolor. 'Please...tell me I didn't faint.'

'I could tell you but it wouldn't be true,' retorted the bustling little figure as she trapped Hannah's wrist in expert fingers and counted her pulse without a pause in the conversation.

'You went out like the proverbial light. It was a good job Dr Stirling was quick on his feet or you'd be sporting a fine crop of bruises.'

Hannah groaned again as she remembered her impression that Leo was walking towards her in slow motion. He must have been moving a great deal faster than she'd thought if he'd managed to catch her before she'd hit the floor.

'I knew you should have gone home after your appointment,' her superior said, dropping her voice so that she wouldn't break confidentiality. 'That's not the sort of thing you can easily shrug off—far too much stress involved.'

'It...it wasn't that,' Hannah said, stumbling to her own defence. 'It was the suicide they brought in.'

'What? That young woman? Was she a friend of yours?'

'No, but she had just been diagnosed with cancer.'

Hannah knew she didn't have to say any more when she saw comprehension dawn on Celia MacDonald's face.

'Och, lass. I'm sorry.'

'How is she feeling now?' interrupted Leo as he strode across the examining room. 'Any idea why she keeled over, Sister?'

Hannah's eyes zeroed in on his face. How long had he been there? How much of their conversation had he heard?

'It was probably a combination of reasons, the way it

usually is,' the senior sister said diplomatically. 'But, whatever the reason, it's time she went home.'

'Well, as I've already handed over to Nick, I'm just the person to make sure she gets there safely,' Leo declared as he offered Hannah a hand to help her to sit up. 'Take it slowly until you're sure you aren't going to flake out on us again.'

'I don't need someone to follow me home,' Hannah said, horribly aware of the petulant tone in her voice, but her emotions were in such turmoil that she was almost afraid to spend too much time in his company.

'No, you need someone to *take* you home—don't you think so, Sister?' Leo demanded evenly, his eyes far too intent for her peace of mind.

Hannah glared at him for enlisting her senior's agreement. There was no way she could go against both of them and he knew it.

'So, what was all that about?' Leo demanded.

He'd hardly given her time to fasten her seat belt before he drove away and already the inquisition had begun.

'All what?' she queried cautiously—there was no way she was going to volunteer information unless it was strictly unavoidable.

'Oh, come on, Hannah,' he snapped. 'You've been as jumpy as a cat on hot bricks for half the day, then you disappear for some mysterious appointment and almost as soon as you come back you pass out.'

That was one way of putting the facts together, she supposed. At least it meant that he hadn't heard enough of her conversation with Celia MacDonald to make a connection with the unfortunate woman who'd committed. . .

'And what was that business with the suicide note?'

he continued, blowing *that* idea to smithereens and winding the tension up another notch as she searched frantically for a way to explain the inexplicable.

Why did the man have to be so sharp-witted?

She'd just been getting used to the idea that they could be friends, but if he forced her to tell him. . . She sighed heavily. She knew that everything would change. . . again. . .and she'd be left alone and hurting. . .again.

'Please, Hannah, talk to me,' he said into the darkness of the car, his voice calmer and more even now, as though he'd managed to find a degree of control.

'Oh, Leo. . .' She blinked furiously to beat back the threat of tears, saddened by the fact that she couldn't confide in him.

Since Laura had fallen in love with Wolff their friendship had altered, and Leo had slowly become the closest friend she had but even so. . .

Leo parked the car outside the front of her house and she reached for the seat belt release, but before she could use it he'd turned towards her and rested one hand over hers to hold her still.

'Hannah. . .are you pregnant?' he asked softly.

'Wh-what? No!' she squeaked in horror. 'Of course I'm not pregnant, Leo.'

'Then what *is* it?' he demanded, one fist thumping the steering-wheel. 'You went white as a sheet and crumpled into a heap. There must be *something* the matter.'

He caught her hand and cradled it between both of his, rubbing it gently as if she needed warming.

'Please, Hannah, I'm worried about you. I. . .I care about you.' He lifted her hand and brushed a gentle kiss over her knuckles.

The sweetness and unexpectedness of the caress was her undoing, an electric shiver travelling over every nerve ending as she fought for control.

How could she ignore the thread of hurt in his concern when deep inside she longed to be able to speak openly about the things going on in her life? But, equally, how could she bear it if she confided in him and ruined their fledgeling friendship?

Was there some way she could tell him enough of her history so that he would understand the nightmares which haunted her, the way she'd told Celia MacDonald only as much as she *needed* to know?

Almost unconsciously she wove her fingers between his and returned the pressure, her decision made. If she had to carry the burden alone much longer she really would be in danger of going round the bend.

'It was the young woman committing suicide which blew my fuse,' she began in a shaky voice, but she was pleased to hear that it became stronger with each word.

'I've. . .I've already lost four members of my family to cancer—my grandmother, my mother and two aunts. I'm. . .' She had to pause for a deep breath before she could continue. 'I'm the last one left,' she finished on a whisper, her lips quivering uncontrollably.

'Oh, God, Hannah, I'm sorry,' Leo said as he tried to gather her into his arms for comfort, but the seat belt thwarted him.

Hannah sat there with tears slowly dripping off the edge of her chin as he found the release and triggered it, then he paused and cradled one wet cheek in his palm.

'It's my turn to give *you* a hug this time,' he said determinedly. 'And as I can't to do it in the front seat of a car you're going to have to let me into your flat.'

Hannah's breath caught in her throat at the thought of Leo coming into her flat, and she stared up at him in the darkness of the car with silent tears still sliding down her cheeks.

Her emotions see-sawed between excitement and fear

but most of all she realised that she needed to be held, needed the comfort of Leo's strong arms around her, even if it was just for a short while.

'A-all right,' she whispered as she swiped at her tears with shaky hands, before fumbling for the doorhandle. 'I—I could make you a cup of coffee, if you like.'

His murmured reply was lost in the sound of opening car doors and she could only presume that he'd agreed.

The wind had grown much colder and the remains of her tears felt icy on her cheeks as she hurried to the main door and tried to fit the key in the lock.

'Here, let me,' Leo offered gently when her third failure started the tears falling again and he took over the task.

'I'm upstairs,' she whispered as she gestured towards the stairwell. 'It...it's not as convenient as a ground floor flat, but it does mean that I don't have to put up with other people's feet stamping about over my head...I'm sorry...you've already been there and...and I'm so wound up I'm babbling like an idiot...'

She bit her lip and sniffed helplessly as he used the other key to unlock her front door and ushered her into the softly lit hallway with a solicitous arm around her shoulders.

'Don't worry about it, my love,' he murmured as he leant back against the door to close it behind them, and pulled her into his arms. 'I think you can be forgiven for babbling today.'

My love? Had he really called her 'my love'?

The endearment was so sweet and so unexpected that it dried her tears and she stared up at him speechlessly, startled by how easily he'd said the word.

'Ah, Hannah, we both know how it hurts,' he whispered as he cradled her head against his shoulder and tightened his arms around her. 'We know what it's like to watch the ones we love fading away when their bodies just can't fight any more, and we know what the loneliness is like when they're gone...to want someone to hold you and tell you the hurt will go away...'

'Does it ever go away?' she whispered brokenly. 'Don't you just carry it with you for ever, with each new generation going through the same fear and torment?'

'Ah, shh, Hannah, shh.'

He framed her face between his palms and brushed his lips over hers as though to banish her words.

Hannah froze at the intimate contact, her breath trapped in her throat.

CHAPTER SEVEN

'HANNAH?' Leo whispered, the word a simple question as his breath flowed warm against her chilled skin.

Hannah's eyes were drawn upwards, widening when she saw the expression on his face—a haunting mixture of desire and desperation.

'A hug isn't enough this time, is it?' he breathed. 'I want to kiss you... I *need* to kiss you...'

As he wrapped his arms even tighter around her and pulled her between his spread thighs she discovered the unmistakable evidence that he was heavily aroused, and she drew in a shuddering breath.

Her own body softened in response and she leant helplessly against him, her head tilting back and her lips parting in surrender without a conscious decision.

'Do you want me to kiss you?' he whispered, and she gazed drowsily up at him out of half-closed eyes at lips poised just millimetres from her own as if he wanted to tease her to death. 'Hannah, I need to hear you say it,' he demanded hoarsely. 'Do you want it as much as I do?'

It was his intensity which helped her to find the last of her reserves of strength as she slid her hands up behind his head and speared her fingers through the silky strands of his hair to cup the curve of his skull.

'Yes...' she hissed as she surged against him and tightened her grasp on the back of his head to close the final distance between them.

It was never like this before, she thought in a flash of ecstatic revelation as lips slid sensuously over lips and tongues duelled in the heated darkness. Until this moment no one has ever made me feel as if they were the other half of my soul, as essential to my life as air or water.

As if the move had been choreographed by years of intimate knowledge, their hands were mapping each other's contours—the intimidating breadth of his shoulders and the trim slenderness of her waist, the muscular strength of his back and the sleek curve of her hip.

And yet it wasn't enough.

As tightly as they were wrapped in each other's arms, they couldn't get close enough or kiss deeply enough to satisfy the desire which soared out of control.

'Please,' he whispered, his breath searing her lips with heat and his hands delving beneath the hem of her uniform to slide up the silky length of her trembling thighs.

At first he seemed content just to cup her bottom in his hands and pull her against his own body, and Hannah revelled in the sensations, her body rocking against his and savouring the evidence of his desire for her.

Suddenly it wasn't enough and impatience took over as his hands tried to find a way through her underwear to make contact with her naked skin.

Hannah stilled for just a second as she realised what he was doing, but then she realised with a jolt of excitement and acceptance that she wanted it just as much and leant back just far enough to allow him to reach his objective.

'Ah, Hannah,' he groaned when she shyly took advantage of the change in position to deliver caresses of her own, her hands tentatively exploring his heat through the fine fabric of his trousers.

Soon she felt the same impatience, and it was the work of seconds to find the tab of his zip. Even though her fingers were trembling it slid down easily to allow her access to explore yet more intimately.

For just a second, as his heat branded itself into her

cool hand, he stood stock-still and gave an agonised groan. Hannah froze in the middle of her fascinated exploration, suddenly afraid that she'd displeased him.

She looked up at him...up into tiger-bright eyes which seared her to her soul with the demanding intensity of their golden fire, and when she realised that his breathing was as laboured as if he'd been running a race she understood for the first time just how tightly he had been controlling his desire.

For wordless moments they gazed into each other's eyes and then she moved her hand again, encompassing his quivering length in a graphic answer to his unspoken question.

Desire exploded between them as they tore at each other's clothes, unable to wait once the decision had been made, doing nothing more than removing the bare necessities of clothing to allow their bodies to merge in that ultimate communion.

For a single instant Hannah was conscious of the fact that Leo had been so impatient that he'd torn her tights away, and that she'd wrenched the button off the waistband of his expensive trousers to pull them down his straining thighs...but then he had wrapped his powerful hands around her hips and lifted her up against him, before holding her in the perfect position for his fierce thrust.

'Leo...!' she cried as all the breath was forced out of her lungs in an explosive rush, and he froze.

'Oh, God, Hannah, did I hurt you?' he demanded in tones of anguish, and the muscles in his shoulders and arms contracted as he began to lift her.

'No...' she groaned, and wrapped her legs tightly around his slim hips, trying to tighten her arms around his neck. 'Don't take it away...'

She felt his ribs jerk as he chuckled and then he pressed his forehead against hers.

'To tell you the truth, I don't think I could,' he whispered as he allowed her to pull them tightly together again. 'It feels too good, being like this, to want to move at all.'

Hannah knew what he meant and wreathed her arms around his shoulders to maintain the ultimate closeness between them, revelling in the fact that the two of them were as united as a man and woman could be.

She also knew the moment when just being close wasn't enough, and the warning spasms in the nerves and muscles deep inside her drew answering twitches from the tumescent member buried there that the need to move was growing uncontrollable.

'You're doing that on purpose,' Leo growled as he palmed her bottom and tried to stop her moving by pulling her tightly against himself, but it was as much use as trying to stop an earthquake.

The closer their bodies were the closer they wanted to be, and in the end the apparently haphazard friction gave way to the driving rhythm which could only have one result.

'Oh, Hannah, I'm sorry,' she heard Leo groan when he finally draw a deep enough breath to speak.

'Sorry?' Hannah repeated in a whisper as her heart clenched inside her and she awkwardly began to unwind herself from around him.

She was suddenly distressingly aware that to an outside observer it would look as if they hadn't bothered to do any more than uncover their sexual organs before they'd coupled like ravenous animals.

How was it possible to go from ecstatic closeness to uncomfortable vulnerability in the space of seconds, without shattering into a million fragments? If, after the most earth-shaking experience of her life, all he felt were regrets...

'Hey! Where are you going?' he demanded indignantly as he refused to loosen his hold, maintaining the contact between them.

'But...' Hannah stilled self-consciously, feeling a bit like a butterfly on a pin. 'You said...'

She was confused. He'd apologised...sounded so full of regret...but when she'd tried to leave him he'd stopped her.

Had she misunderstood?

Didn't he want her to go?

There was only one way to find out.

'Why did you say you were sorry?' she demanded, bravely meeting his eyes with her own.

'Well, it certainly *wasn't* because I regretted what just happened between us, if that's what you were thinking,' he declared fervently. 'My only regret was that it happened too fast for any sort of consideration or finesse!' He glanced around at her dimly lit hallway and gave a disbelieving laugh. 'I hardly let you get inside your front door, for heaven's sake!'

A flood of relief immersed Hannah in new warmth and she tightened her hold around his neck. Her spirits rose like a helium balloon on a hot day and tempted her to a teasing retort.

'There are those who might say that I hardly let you get inside my front door before I leapt on you,' she pointed out, and revelled in his sensuous chuckle as she buried her face against the warmth of his neck to revel in the scent of his continuing sexual arousal.

'Shall we give it another try?' he whispered against her ear, as if he was sensitive to the direction of her thoughts, his lips caressing her even as he spoke. 'How about starting off with a bit of novelty and undressing each other before we go any further?'

He tightened his hands suggestively around her bottom and arched himself against her, as if to remind her that they were still intimately joined. 'I can't wait to see all those curves I've been admiring for so long.'

Her renewed awareness of his body inside hers nearly prevented her from hearing his final words, but once they registered in her brain everything came to a screeching halt.

'Wh-what?' she gasped, suddenly cold and trembling inside at the thought that he wanted this encounter to continue. It wouldn't have been so bad—in fact, it would have been fantastic—if he'd only wanted an action replay of the explosive encounter they'd just enjoyed.

Unfortunately Leo naturally wanted variations on the theme, and that just wasn't possible.

Hannah cringed at the thought of having Leo take the rest of her clothes off and fear sent her pulse into overdrive.

What could she say?

How could she tell him that this utterly intoxicating episode was all there could ever be between them without telling him why?

'Hey! You haven't gone to sleep on me, have you?' he chided huskily as he nuzzled her temple, and she nearly hugged him with relief as she realised that he had just handed her the perfect excuse.

'Hmm?' she murmured with just the right amount of sleepy question in the sound.

'Oh, Hannah, you're hell on my ego,' he complained softly as he brushed a tender kiss over her cheek. Hannah kept her eyes tightly closed but his gentleness filled her chest with an enormous ache as he shifted her in his arms and carried her carefully through to her bedroom.

She couldn't help the way her body tensed when he deposited her on her bed, and she rolled away from him and wrapped her arms defensively around herself as though subconsciously conserving heat.

'Hey, sweetheart,' he coaxed. 'Let me help you get undressed...'

She feigned oblivion and sighed silently when he quickly gave up the attempt, having to content himself with sliding the covers out from under her and tucking them around her apparently sleeping body.

'Good night, my love,' she heard him whisper as he smoothed one hand over her tousled hair. 'I'll see you tomorrow.'

Over the erratic thumping of her heart Hannah heard him move through her flat, and even imagined she could hear him retrieving his scattered clothing in her tiny hallway before there was the very final sound of the lock catching as he shut her front door behind him.

Safe in the knowledge that he'd finally gone, she rolled over and lay staring up at the ceiling as the full horror of the situation poured over her.

She'd just made love with St Augustine's A and E department's resident heart-throb, Leo Stirling, the first man she'd made love to since Jonathan broke their engagement—the first man she'd even *noticed* as a man since then—and suddenly she realised that her life was made up of two inescapable truths.

The first was that, in spite of her determination not to let anyone get so close to her that she became emotionally involved with them, she had fallen in love with Leo and every exasperating, irrepressible enigma that he'd turned out to be.

The second truth was the one which made her newly vulnerable heart feel like lead—that she was never going to be able to do anything about her love.

She sighed deeply as she accepted that final inescapable fact and rolled over again to curl herself up in a tight ball under the warmth of her thick duvet.

A taunting voice inside her head told her that it wasn't as warm or as comforting as Leo's strong arms would be, but she firmly ignored it, banishing the erotic mental images of the two of them generating enough heat not to *need* a duvet over them.

She didn't have time for such heated imaginings.

What she had to do now was rack her brains for some way of facing him in the morning. Playing possum tonight might have put off the evil hour, but she had no doubt that Leo wouldn't be content to leave it at that.

'All right, poppet, all right,' Hannah crooned as she tried to soothe the unhappy child in her arms. She'd managed to take his clothes off, but he didn't seem to want to allow himself be wrapped up in a blanket by some strange woman and kept trying to struggle out of her grasp.

'I know you're feeling rotten, sweetheart,' his mother said as she stroked a consoling hand over his head, 'but the nurse is going to see what she can do about it as soon as possible.'

'Good morning.'

While her young patient's worried parents swung towards the deep-voiced pleasantry, Hannah found herself stiffening devensively.

Even without looking, she knew that the man behind her was unmistakably Leo, and it was the first time she'd seen him today...the first time since she'd feigned sleep in his arms...

'Good morning, Doctor,' she began endless seconds later when she finally forced herself to turn to face him with the unhappy child still in her arms.

She was horribly conscious that the quiver in her voice

was probably audible to everyone in the room, and a slow heat crawled its way up into her cheeks.

'This is Liam O'Malley and his parents. He's eighteen months old and he's had five days of fever, rash, vomiting and swollen glands. They've been to their GP several times, but Liam's no better and they're beginning to get very worried about him.'

As usual, Leo paused to crouch down to his little patient's level to pull a funny face and smile at him. He'd told Hannah long ago that he believed such direct contact was invaluable when the time came for him to actually need to do something to the child because he had already begun a form of communication between them.

'Hey, big boy, aren't you feeling so good?' he demanded as he gently smoothed one palm over the child's head and stroked the back of a finger over his cheek. 'Shall I ask your mummy and daddy what's been going on?'

He straightened up and stepped back to introduce himself to the young couple.

'I'm Dr Stirling, Mr and Mrs O'Malley. Can you tell me what's been happening the last few days? When did Liam become sick? Which symptoms arrived first?'

Hannah could see from their body language that the two of them were under a great deal of stress, her hand clutched tightly in his as though they were afraid they might fall apart if they didn't hold onto each other.

As if it wasn't bad enough that their child wasn't well, Hannah realised from their recounting of the events of the last few days that repeated visits to their GP hadn't seemed to have brought them any closer to knowing what was wrong with Liam, nor what needed to be done about it.

'The first time we took him he was a little bit warm and he'd been sick. The doctor told us to give him a liquid painkiller and said that he was probably teething,' Mr O'Malley told them. 'We took his word for it because they're supposed to know—'

'He more or less told us that we were making a fuss over nothing,' his wife broke in, 'but when his glands kept getting bigger and he still had a temperature we took him back twice. He finally decided to give us an antibiotic for him and said it was a simple infection or inflammation—probably something to do with his ears.'

'Did that help him?' Leo asked as he gently felt around Liam's jaw. Standing so close to him, Hannah could see the slight frown which pleated his forehead and knew he'd found the enlarged glands too.

She flicked back one layer of the enveloping blanket, knowing that he would be wanting to check other sites on Liam's body such as those in his armpits and groin.

'It didn't seem to make any difference,' Mrs O'Malley said as her anxious eyes tracked his every move.

'In fact,' her husband continued, 'he'd started developing other symptoms by then.'

'Such as?' Leo prompted as he continued his exploration.

'As you can see, his hands and feet are very red and swollen—it almost looks as if he's got inflated rubber gloves on—and his mouth started to get red and sore and now it's gone cracked and bleeding.'

'How long have his eyes been this red?' As Leo thumbed back the lids, Hannah could see just how bloodshot they were and was quite horrified—she'd never seen anything like it before, especially on a child this young.

'Must be nearly three days now,' Mrs O'Malley confirmed. 'And the skin on his hands and feet just doesn't feel right—it seems all dry and leathery.'

'Have any tests been done?'

'Not so far.' Mr O'Malley scowled. 'The GP said that

as it obviously wasn't meningitis it was a waste of time and money doing tests on babies this young because by the time the results came through they had invariably recovered and were up and running around again as right as rain.'

'We weren't happy with that,' his wife added. 'So finally he said if Liam wasn't any better by the beginning of next week he might send him to the hospital for a lumbar puncture... Doctor, is that because it might be meningitis after all? There's been such a lot about it on the television the last few years, but they always say that you should take your child to the doctor straight away.'

'You're quite right.' Leo glanced up from his careful examination of little Liam's peeling feet with a quick smile. 'If you think your child might have meningitis it's *essential* to make the diagnosis quickly, but I'm almost certain that your doctor got it right—that Liam *hasn't* got meningitis.'

'Thank God for that,' muttered Mr O'Malley, and Hannah saw the quick glance he threw his equally worried wife. 'Do you have any idea what *is* the matter with him?'

'Yes, I'm fairly certain that I do,' he said as he straightened up with a smile. 'If you'd like to take a seat for a minute, I'm just going to telephone Great Ormond Street Hospital. There's a friend of mine there and he's made this his special interest. I'd like to speak to him for confirmation, and then I'll be straight back.'

His long legs took him swiftly out of the room, and Hannah took pity on the two of them as they hovered uneasily, their eyes travelling helplessly between their child and the door as it swung silently closed behind the departing doctor.

'Mrs O'Malley, would you like to perch yourself on the edge of the trolley and give Liam a cuddle while we're waiting for Dr Stirling to come back? The little chap's been very good for us so far, but I think he'd be much happier if it was his mum holding him.'

The poor woman almost leapt at the chance to have him in her own arms again, and the way her husband stood close enough to run a gentle finger over his little son's downy dark hair told Hannah how much he loved the boy.

Leo would be like that, she thought, the words surfacing in her head from nowhere. He would be the sort of father who liked to hold and stroke his children...to cuddle them and tease them...

She gave her head a single fierce shake to rid herself of the impossible dream that they would be *her* children Leo would be treating so lovingly, and made herself concentrate on checking that the child's notes were complete.

'Right, Mr and Mrs O'Malley, we're in business!' Leo declared as he strode back into the room with a pleased smile on his face. 'We're ninety-nine per cent certain that we know what's the matter with Liam and, if he's only been sick for five days, it's been caught in time.'

'What is it, Doctor?' Mr O'Malley seemed utterly bemused by the tall doctor's ebullient attitude. 'What's the matter with my boy?'

'It's called Kawasaki disease,' Leo announced, as if he were pulling a rabbit out of a hat, and Hannah felt a smile of comprehension curl up the corners of her mouth as she recognised the name.

'Kawasaki?' questioned Mrs O'Malley. 'But...that's the name of a motorbike, isn't it?'

'Quite right,' Leo confirmed with a smile. 'But it's also the name of a disease little children can suffer from.'

'Is it a new one—one of these superbugs?' her husband asked fearfully. 'Are they still trying to find a cure for it?'

'It's relatively new—it was first described about thirty years ago—but, providing it's caught in the first ten days and the right treatment given in time, we're over ninety per cent successful with it.'

'What *is* the treatment? Is it very painful?' Mrs O'Malley tightened her arms around her little son protectively. 'And what would happen if he didn't get it in time?'

'If he doesn't receive the treatment in the first ten days there's a thirty per cent chance that the disease can cause serious heart damage because it attacks the arteries around the heart and causes weak patches that can blow up like balloons. Eventually it can cause heart failure.'

'And the treatment?' prompted Mr O'Malley, his face suddenly ashen at the thought of such things happening to their precious son.

'It's as easy to administer as a blood transfusion,' Leo explained with a reassuring smile. 'In fact, what we'll be putting into his vein is just one part of what naturally occurs in whole blood. It's called gamma globulin—it's one of the plasma proteins and contains high levels of antibodies.'

'How long will it be before you can start the treatment? Does it take a long time?' The young mother was a different person altogether now, her tension all directed towards getting the treatment started.

'It will take a few minutes to sort out all the formalities to admit Liam to the ward, but once he's up there. . .'

'Admit him?' she interrupted fearfully. 'Oh, Doctor, can't you do it here so we can be with him?'

'There's nothing to worry about, Mrs O'Malley,' Leo soothed with a liberal application of his famous smile. 'You can go up with him and stay while the gamma globulin is administered—you'll be much more comfortable there, I promise, and the paediatric consultant is a very nice man.'

Hannah turned away to hide her wry smile. Once again the ladykiller smile had done its job and the poor woman was like putty in his hands.

For a few minutes the room was full of activity as Hannah took blood samples to send up to the lab for cross-matching purposes and Leo contacted Ross MacFadden to tell him what was on the way.

Hannah breathed a sigh of relief when the little family were finally on their way up to the ward, taking one lingering look at Leo's broad back as he followed them out of the room before she turned to the job of stripping the trolley and preparing it for the next patient.

At least their first meeting had gone off all right, she thought with relief as she finally allowed herself to think about it. They had both behaved as professionally as ever in spite of the explosion of passion they had shared last night.

How much of that was due to the fact that they had both been occupied by a sick child and a couple of worried parents she didn't know, but if there was some way of making certain that they were always surrounded by other people then he wouldn't have a chance of saying anything personal to her.

Now all she had to do was stay out of his way until. . .

'Alone at last, you gorgeous creature!' growled a voice behind her just before her shoulders were seized and she was drawn around and tilted back over a muscular arm in a dramatic parody of a silent-screen kiss.

'L-Leo. . .!' she squeaked breathlessly, but there was no time to say any more as his lips met hers and stole her breath away completely.

At first her hands clutched at the lapels of his white coat as she tried to keep her balance, but when the tip of his tongue demanded entry and effortlessly recreated the same passionate onslaught of the night before she realised with the tiny corner of her mind which was still functioning that her arms had crept up to twine their way around his neck in surrender.

Dimly she became aware of a high-pitched bleeping and she'd begun to wonder vaguely whether it was a warning that her pulse rate had just exceeded safe levels when Leo dragged his mouth away from hers with a groan.

'Damn pager,' he muttered as he straightened up.

His gaze was fixed fiercely on her face, flicking from her kiss-swollen lips to her desire-drowsy eyes, as his hands sensuously massaged the curves of her shoulders as though he couldn't bear to let go of her.

It took several seconds before she could focus properly and realised the significance of what she was seeing.

She felt an extra twist of arousal deep inside when she realised that he was every bit as reluctant to part from her to answer the summons as she was to let him go.

'Stirling,' he growled when he reached out and grabbed the phone, and she was certain that the number had been tapped out by luck more than careful attention.

Hannah started to come to her senses while she watched his frown of concentration and realised that he still had one arm wrapped firmly around her shoulders, as though he was intending to continue where he'd left off when his pager had interrupted them.

Part of her would like nothing better than to do just that, but the sane, sensible person that she'd had to become over the last two years knew that there was no point in allowing it to happen.

Subduing a pang of regret for yet another set of might-have-beens, she slid out from under his arm and managed to evade his distracted attempt at recapture to put herself out of his reach.

She hadn't realised exactly how wobbly her knees were until she tried to walk out of the room, but if she didn't put some distance between them before his call ended there was every chance that he would take it as an invitation to continue, and she was honest enough to admit—to herself at least—that she didn't think she'd find the strength to drag herself away from his arms again.

'Hey...! Hannah...!' she heard him call as the door swung shut behind her, and she took off up the corridor like a scared rabbit.

She had a terrible feeling that she couldn't afford to let him catch up with her before she'd regained her equilibrium or she'd be falling into his arms like a ripe plum—again!

CHAPTER EIGHT

'DIABETIC collapse on the way in,' Polly called as she put the phone down. 'ETA four minutes.'

Hannah raised a hand in acknowledgement and reached for a fresh set of gloves, pulling them on as she set off towards the doors.

It was her turn again to act as reception committee as the ambulance arrived, and she wasn't looking forward to it—the weather had turned decidedly cold today, and unfortunately the emergency entrance was situated on one of the bleaker sides of the building.

Oh, the architects had thoughtfully provided the area with a canopy so that staff and patients were sheltered from the worst of the weather, but it was still horribly draughty.

At least the ambulance was nearly here so she shouldn't have to wait long. . .

There was the distant sound of one of the new-style sirens and she wrapped her arms around herself and stepped outside. . . But suddenly she couldn't hear it any more and shook her head in confusion as she glanced down at her watch. The ETA was down to two minutes so she *should* be able to hear it by now. . .

Another ten minutes of waiting and shivering passed and she was just beginning to wonder if the call had been a hoax after all when she heard the siren's unmistakable new *'wa-wa-wa-shh'* sound again.

'What kept you?' she chided Ted as she rubbed her hands up and down her arms and danced from one foot to the other. 'It's far too cold at this time of year to get stood up!'

'We picked up an extra passenger,' he said as he backed expertly down the steps, without having to look to see where he was going. 'Someone stepped out in front of us on the way in.'

'What?' Hannah gasped. 'You didn't hit them, did you?'

'No, no... They were flagging us down for their friend who'd just hit his head...'

He paused as he grabbed his clipboard and the whole cortège moved swiftly into the warmth of the building.

'Who have we got here?' demanded Leo as he met them in the emergency room, and Ted correctly took it for an invitation to start his report.

'This is David Lyall. He's a twenty-year-old who's been a diabetic for three years. He was studying late last night and forgot to set his alarm to wake him up in time to have breakfast this morning. Collapsed running for a bus. When we got to him he was staring vacantly into space and his skin was cold and clammy. Rapid pulse— one-twenty plus—dilated pupils and muscle tremors.'

While Ted was speaking Leo's hands were competently making their own assessment, but it didn't stop him from paying close attention to Ted's words.

'We gave him oxygen while we checked his blood-sugar level and it was almost too low to read so I gave him a glucagon injection to keep him going while we brought him in—didn't want him going into a coma on us.'

'Well, he's certainly coming out of it better than he might have done,' Leo muttered, and Hannah knew what he meant. It had only been a week or so ago that they'd had another young diabetic collapse in an almost identical way, mistakenly hoping that as long as he took his insulin on schedule he could catch up on his meal when her had time.

Unfortunately, *he'd* gone into cardiac arrest before anything could be done for him.

In David's case, the energy he'd used running for his bus had probably been the final straw which had flipped his system into hypoglycaemia.

If his friends had hesitated about calling for an ambulance when he'd collapsed, or if Ted's crew hadn't been free to race to his help, they could have been entering the details of another pointless waste of a young life.

She saw the notation Leo put on David Lyall's file and smiled wryly. He would be receiving a visit from the diabetes counsellor before he was released from the hospital to remind him—if today's scare hadn't been enough—that he couldn't afford to mess about with his routine, even if late-night studying for his exams was essential. The type of insulin he was on didn't give him the same warning he'd have got on the older type.

'And I suppose this is your hitch-hiker?' Leo enquired as he turned towards the second trolley, leaving Hannah to finish the setting-up of the second slow administration of dextrose through the wide-bore IV.

He was going to have to wait until his levels were testing normal before he was set loose on the world again.

'Doctor?' David Lyall interrupted, the panic in his shaky voice drawing Leo back to face him again. 'What about my exams? I'm supposed to have been starting one at half past nine this morning and I've got another one this afternoon, and if I don't attend I'll automatically fail and then my grant might be cut off and—'

'Whoa! Calm down, calm down,' Leo ordered as he waved a placating hand at his agitated patient. 'Don't get yourself in such a state. I can write you a certificate to present to your college principal—it's not as if you've been swinging the lead this morning. At least that should give you a chance for a resit exam if they can't let you through on your coursework so far.'

The young man subsided with a heartfelt, 'Thanks, Doctor,' and submitted with rather more equanimity to Hannah's attentions.

'Sorry about that,' she heard Leo say as he returned to his second patient. 'Now, what have *you* been up to?'

Hannah hadn't had more than a glance at the young man on the other trolley and had only seen the fact that he had a large handful of blood-soaked dressing held against his head.

'This is Steve Wright,' Ted began when it seemed that the patient wasn't up to answering for himself. 'He's a nineteen-year-old trainee carpenter, working on one of the houses damaged by the gas blast the other week. According to his workmate—the one who flagged us down—he was doing a repair on a sash window when the thing came adrift and fell on his head.'

'Did he lose consciousness?' Leo asked as he tested the young man's ocular reflexes with his penlight.

'Knocked him out cold for a good five minutes, apparently. His friend had helped him out of the house to get some help but he was staggering around and was still pretty groggy when we picked him up. He knows his name but doesn't seem to be quite with it.' Ted shrugged. 'We put the neck collar on him as a precaution, even though he was already on his feet.'

'In that case. . .' Leo began, then paused. Out of the corner of her eye Hannah saw him frown as he tested the young man's eyes again. He was obviously concerned about something.

'Right, Ted,' he said decisively. 'You might as well get back to your trusty chariot. Thanks for these two. . .'

Ted acknowledged his appreciation for Leo's thanks

with a brief wave and, collecting up his own equipment, left them to it.

'How are you doing over there?' Leo murmured as the X-ray technician bustled about, setting things up.

She'd seen him straighten up from his inspection of the damage under the dressing and scrawl something on Steve's notes, his bold slashing writing achingly familiar to Hannah.

'Oh, Mr Lyall and I have got to the boring bit now,' Hannah said from the other side of the room, smiling to cover up the fact that watching Leo work was turning into a refined sort of torture while her heart was still aching with all the things she couldn't have. 'We've just got to keep an eye on the readings at intervals until we can get the insulin and sugar properly balanced.'

'In which case, as soon as we get the all-clear from Mr Wright's neck X-ray you could lend me a hand here while I sew him back together. The quicker we get it done the better job it'll be.' He paused for a moment in thought, the top of his pen tapping idly against his chin.

'Then,' he continued suddenly, as though there had been no break in the conversation, 'I'll have to see if I can find him a bed for a while so that someone can keep an eye on him.'

'Ocular reflexes?' Hannah said questioningly, wondering how badly concussed their patient was if Leo was intent on admitting him. Had something about the way his pupils had reacted to light given him cause to be worried that there might even be hidden damage inside the young man's skull?

Leo gave a slight grimace, showing that she'd rightly guessed at his concern, and then, as the X-ray results were given the thumbs-up, he beckoned her to come closer.

Hannah resigned herself to another half-hour of intimate contact with the only man who raised her pulse level. Every time she had to hand him anything, or their bodies brushed each other, she would be reminded by a surge of that strange electricity which seemed to pass between them that they had been so much closer than this last night—more abandoned and somehow very much more intimate than she'd ever been with any other man...

'It's a shame the wound is too extensive for us to superglue it together,' he murmured as they waited for the local anaesthetic to take effect, and Hannah murmured her agreement as he concentrated on clearing the field of operations by clipping the hair back along the edges of the wound.

She watched with approval as he took the time to make a good job of neatening up the ragged edges of the torn skin to achieve better approximation. She knew only too well how much difference the care taken at this stage could make to the appearance of the finished scar—and if the young man was lucky enough to avoid going bald this scar might even spend most of its time completely hidden under his thick thatch of hair.

'I'm going to need five-oh monofilament for this, and if all goes well they'll be able to come out in five days,' Leo muttered, half his words directed at her and half at the young man under his hands.

He might as well not have bothered for all the interest his patient was taking, his expression as blank as if it were all happening to someone else.

Hannah retrieved the necessary supplies and acted as handmaiden as she watched Leo tie a neat row of stitches along the length of the wound, knowing that he'd chosen to use non-dissolving ones to make certain that the edges couldn't accidentally be released too soon.

As the whole process continued she grew more and more concerned that their patient did little more than grunt in answer to their attempts at conversation and was finally forced to say as much to Leo.

'Do you think he's usually this taciturn, or could it be a result of the blow to his head?' she asked quietly.

'Could be either—he took a heck of a crack to make this sort of mess of himself. At a guess, he must have the mother and father of all headaches and doesn't feel much like socialising.'

In spite of Leo's rational explanation, Hannah felt the worried frown pleating her forehead as she kept an eye on their taciturn patient... She had the strange feeling that there was another explanation.

'Right, old man, that'll do for you,' Leo announced cheerfully as he snipped the tail of the last stitch and dropped everything into the bowl Hannah held towards him, dragging his disposable mask down to dangle around his neck. 'Now, I'll just see whether I can arrange a bed somewhere...'

Hannah happened to be watching the young man's face as Leo continued speaking, and noticed that for the first time he seemed to be concentrating properly, a grimace tightening his lips when Leo mentioned arranging for him to stay in hospital.

A glimmer of an idea came to her and she pulled her own mask down before she spoke.

'How long do you think he'll have to stay in hospital?' she asked as Leo stripped off his gloves and automatically disposed of them as he strode across the room.

He paused with one broad shoulder against the door, ready to push it open, his puzzled expression probably the result of her unusually deliberate way of speaking.

As she'd hoped, their young patient's eyes had flicked across to Leo, as if he was waiting for him to answer, his eyes fixed intently on his face.

'If there are no complications he'll probably go home

tomorrow—tonight, even, if there's someone responsible who can keep an eye on him at home.'

'Yes-s,' hissed their young patient hoarsely, and Hannah saw Leo's startled blink of surprise.

'Ah, you're with us again, are you?' Leo asked as he came back across the room.

Hannah touched the young man's hand to draw his attention before she began speaking.

'I don't think he ever left us,' she said slowly and clearly, making sure their young patient could see her face while she was speaking. 'I think he needed to be able to *see* us talking to read our lips, and he couldn't when we were wearing masks.' She flicked the offending object hanging around her neck.

'Yes-s,' Steve repeated with a wry smile, an intelligent gleam in his eyes as he pointed to his ear. 'Hearing not good... Lost hearing aid... Headache bad... Hard to concentrate.'

'In which case, I apologise,' Leo said with a smile of his own and the offer of his hand. 'If I'd only realised, I would have made sure I explained what was going on before we did it. It must have been very confusing for you.'

He paused for a minute in thought.

'When you said yes, did you mean that there's someone at home who can keep an eye on you?'

'Yes-s. My mum,' he said succinctly, and fumbled for his trouser pocket to draw out a wallet. 'On the telephone,' he continued in his strangely monotonous voice, pulling out a piece of paper with an address and telephone number clearly printed out. 'She worries about me,' he added with a typical male grimace.

'Well, that shouldn't take long to arrange,' Leo said with an easy smile then paused again, before adding cautiously, 'It was a nasty knock so I'd still like you to stay with us until this evening but then, if everything's OK, you can go home.'

'OK,' he agreed with a more cheerful thumbs-up and settled his head gingerly back against the pillow as Leo turned and strode out of the room.

Hannah drew in a deep breath, feeling as if there was suddenly so much more air to breathe in the room now that his larger-than-life presence was out of the way.

She quickly disposed of the soiled swabs and dressings, replenished the trolley and set it to rights, before pushing it neatly out of the way against one wall, then ran the next check on David's insulin and sugar levels.

She'd hardly completed that task when Leo breezed back into the room with Tina Wadland and a wheelchair-pushing porter in tow.

'All arranged,' he said as he scanned Steve Wright's notes and initialled them before he turned and spoke directly to their young patient. 'You're being admitted upstairs for observation until we're certain you're not going to keel over on us.'

'OK, Doctor,' he said. 'Head too bad to argue.'

Leo chuckled. 'The painkillers should take that away soon,' he promised before he turned towards the room's other occupant.

'In the meantime, Nurse Wadland is going to check Mr Lyall's sugar levels and keep him company to make certain he behaves himself.'

He winked at the young man who had definitely improved enough to be showing signs of interest in the pretty nurse walking towards him.

'Now, Sister.' Leo turned his attention on Hannah and her heart gave a sudden thump before she firmly got herself under control.

'If I could have your assistance. . .?' he continued as he led the way briskly out of the room, and Hannah had no option but to follow him, expecting that he was leading her into one of the other treatment rooms to help him with the next patient.

Instead he continued to stride away down the corridor, and she almost had to run to keep up with his long-legged stride.

'Leo. . . Dr Stirling?' she called, suddenly mindful of hospital etiquette. 'Where are we going?' she demanded breathlessly when she finally caught up with him just as he pushed open the door leading to the emergency stairwell.

'Out here,' he said as he gently grasped her elbow to pull her through the door after him, 'in the vain hope that no one will think of looking for us until we've had five minutes alone.'

His words were so unexpected that it took Hannah several seconds to understand what he'd said, then her heart clenched tightly in her chest with foreboding, her elbow still feeling the heat of his hand even though he'd now released her.

She'd honestly thought that as long as she kept calm and made certain that there was always someone else in the room with her Leo wouldn't bother forcing this confrontation—she'd even hoped that he might eventually forget all about the unfortunate episode last night. . .

She should have known better.

He might have seemed perfectly calm as they were treating patients just a few minutes ago, but now that they were alone he seemed filled with an almost feverish intensity as he turned to face her, his hands clenching and unclenching as though he needed some physical activity to disperse the tension inside him.

Hannah drew in a deep breath and released it slowly while she collected her scattered thoughts, but when she realised that his gleaming eyes were quietly cataloging her every movement and expression she felt her shoulders stiffen with renewed determination.

She had made her decision, she reminded herself silently, conscious that her chin had come up a belligerent notch.

It didn't matter that she had fallen in love with him—she knew that Leo would never...*could* never...fall in love with her in return.

His confession about the pain of losing his fiancée to leukaemia had only reinforced her view of him as a confirmed bachelor so she would just have to cope with her unwanted feelings on her own.

The way she always had...

While she waited for him to start the conversation the little voice inside her head insisted that she remembered that she was no milk-and-water wimp to be intimidated into doing or saying anything she didn't want to. She was, after all, a responsible mature adult who had made a calm logical decision about her life.

She had no reason to explain any more than she wanted to and, knowing who and what he was, she certainly had no need to fear that Leo might try to force her to change her mind.

'Well?' he said, the word a mixture of boyish eagerness and impatient demand, as if he'd actually been waiting for *her* to start the ball rolling.

His voice sounded deeper and huskier in their echoing surroundings and she was almost overwhelmed by the feeling that he was having difficulty holding himself in check.

'Well, what?' she returned blankly, not certain what he was asking.

Her own voice sounded infinitely less substantial than his, almost thready as it hovered between them in spite of the fact that she'd tried to make herself sound calm and in control.

For just a second she thought she saw an expression of hurt cross Leo's face, but it was gone so quickly that she couldn't be sure.

He distracted her by taking a step backwards to lounge back easily against the fireproof door, crossing his ankles and hooking his thumbs casually in his trouser pockets.

Suddenly she realised that, intentionally or not, he had positioned himself so that the only way she could avoid this conversation with him was to climb up the echoing stairs to the next floor or brave the bitter weather outside.

'Suppose we start with the basics,' he said heavily, all the eagerness gone from his voice. 'I'll ask you how you are and you'll answer.'

'I'm fine, thank you,' Hannah replied, wondering exactly where this strange conversation was going to end up.

'Are you really?' Leo asked, abandoning his exasperated tone for one filled with concern, his eyes darkly intent on her. 'You almost seemed to pass out on me. . .afterwards.'

The hint of embarrassed colour along the high curve of his cheek-bones made her feel even more guilty about her pretence.

'I—It was late. . . I was. . .exhausted. . . The day. . .it was exhausting. . .' She stumbled to a halt in confusion when she saw the wicked grin start to creep up over his face.

'Oh, but worth every second,' he said, his husky voice sounding like a vow. 'Personally, I wouldn't mind exhausting you like that on a regular basis—who knows, sometimes you might even be able to stay awake long enough to kiss me goodnight?'

'No!' she gasped, horrified that he'd totally misunderstood what she'd been trying to say. 'I didn't mean *that*! I meant... I meant that I was tired after all the stress...the stress at work...the suicide...and...and then you gave me a hug and...and then we...but it didn't mean that we...it didn't *mean* anything...!'

Her impassioned words sounded like a frantic plea as they echoed around the bare stairwell and she was vaguely aware that she was wringing her hands together in her agitation.

Surely he didn't think that the two of them were ready to embark on some sort of red-hot liaison, just on the strength of one misguided encounter—no matter how mind-blowing it had been for her.

A bachelor like Leo, with his brand of stunning good looks and ladykiller smiles, had beautiful women queueing up for miles waiting for a chance to go out with him. He might be ready to think about entering a relationship now, but why on earth would he want to limit himself to her?

'Didn't *mean* anything?' Leo repeated heatedly as he straightened abruptly away from the door, scowling as he ploughed the fingers of one hand through his hair to leave it standing up in disarray. 'We made love for the first time last night and you didn't think it *meant* anything?'

'Well...' Hannah blinked in surprise. She hadn't expected him to react like this. He sounded...angry...? Hurt...?

She'd thought that by downplaying the significance of the event she would be be telling him what he wanted to hear—after all, it had been three years since he'd lost Lisa and he'd now reached his early thirties without looking for a permanent relationship. Had she been wrong in assuming that he didn't have any intention of settling down?

'Well, what?' he demanded.

'Well. . .I didn't think it would mean anything to someone like you,' she began tentatively, trying to feel her way through the minefield she seemed to have landed in.

'Someone like me,' he repeated ominously. 'What exactly do you mean by someone like me?'

Obviously, her choice of words had done nothing to defuse the bomb.

'S-someone footloose and fancy-free, a. . .an eligible bachelor with women running after him for. . .for his good looks and personality. . .'

She ground to a halt, closing her eyes tightly with embarrassment when she heard the echoes of her babbling words.

There was a long silence and she didn't dare to look at him, opting instead to wait in silence for the explosion.

Only it never came.

Instead, she heard the first rumbles of a deep chuckle, fighting its way up from the depths of his chest.

'So you think I have personality and good looks?' he questioned and chuckled again, the sound strangely smug as it wrapped itself around her and heated her cheeks.

Her eyes popped open and she saw that he was leaning back against the door again, and his grin was equally as smug as his voice.

'Well, of course you're good-looking,' she snapped with the impatience of embarrassment. 'You know that—you only have to look in the mirror to see it.'

'But I didn't know that *you* had noticed,' he murmured huskily, his eyes gleaming wickedly at her again. 'In all the time we've been working together you've paid me no more attention than. . .than a stack of bed-pans—perfectly functional but not in the least interesting if you're looking for a hug.'

'Bed-pans?' Hannah choked, and couldn't help the

spurt of laughter which escaped her control. 'Leo, you're crazy!'

'Crazy enough to make you laugh,' he pointed out with a return to smugness.

'Oh, Leo,' she sighed, realising uneasily that he was right—he did seem to have the knack for cheering her up and. . .

'So, when can I take you out?' he asked, his soft-voiced question breaking into her wistful thoughts.

'Take me out?' she said with a frown.

'Yes, take you out,' he said encouragingly with a boyish grin. 'You know how it works. . . We find out which evening we're both off duty, and then we arrange to go out somewhere together or stay in together. . .' He allowed the husky words to die away suggestively as his heated gaze slid over her face and started its incendiary journey down her body.

Her own eyes started a similar journey from the tawny gleam of his hair across the width of his broad shoulders and down the long lean length of his body.

Her heart began to beat out a rapid tattoo against her ribs and her memory supplied the X-rated pictures for what had happened the last time the two of them had been alone.

If she agreed to go out with him she knew what would happen, knew how they would both want the evening to end—except that *this* time he wouldn't be satisfied with a repeat of their frantic mating against her front door but would want to take her to bed and undress her, and then. . .

She shuddered as she imagined the way that scene would end and shook her head.

'No, Leo. I can't,' she said softly, hoping her shaky voice didn't reveal just how much she wanted to agree. 'It. . .it wouldn't work.'

'Why not?' he shot back. 'We work well together in the department, and we get on well outside work—very well,' he added huskily as he straightened away from the door and prowled silently towards her.

'But what about afterwards?' she demanded as she took a nervous step backwards to try to avoid contact with his reaching hand.

'Afterwards?' he repeated in a preoccupied way as he ran the tips of his fingers down the skin of her inner arm and sent a shudder of awareness right through her. 'What do you mean—afterwards?'

'When you finish going out with me and start on your next conquest,' she elaborated stiffly as she folded her arms to keep them away from him. She couldn't concentrate properly when he was touching her.

'Have you thought how awkward it would be for both of us?' she continued hurriedly when he would have broken in. 'It would be far worse than the situation with Sexy Samantha—at least she works in another department on another floor. Can you imagine what it would be like for the two of us to try to work together when the relationship ended?'

Leo was silent for a moment, as though he was thinking carefully about her point of view, and she started to breathe more easily at the thought that she'd managed to avert a potential disaster.

'But what if the relationship didn't end?' he suggested seriously. 'It doesn't have to, you know.'

Hannah gasped and the world stopped spinning for an eon as shock rocked her to her core.

'Don't...don't be silly,' she spluttered breathlessly when her lungs began to function again. 'Th—the hospital grapevine has been keeping count ever since you started working here, and you've never gone out with *any* of your dates more than a handful of times.'

'And I've never made love with any of them either,' he whispered as he caught her fluttering fingers and drew them up to the soft warmth of his lips.

'N-never...?' She felt her eyes widen as she gazed up at him in renewed shock.

'Never wanted to,' he added slightly awkwardly as a wash of colour crept up his face.

'But last night you...we...'

Hannah was speechless with the unexpected confession, her brain whirling as she tried to understand the new implications of what had happened between them the night before.

What *did* it mean?

What was he trying to tell her?

'Do...do you mean you've been impotent?' she suggested hesitantly, wondering if that was why he wanted to go out with her again. If his condition had corrected itself then that would explain why he wanted to...

'Good God, no!' he exclaimed with a mixture of horror and laughter. 'Far from it!'

'Then...then why?'

'You mean, apart from the fact that promiscuity is a very risky option these days?'

She nodded, suddenly conscious that he was still holding her hand when he brought it up to his lips for another kiss, then followed up with a gentle nibble on her knuckles and a soothing glide of his tongue which sent goose bumps right up her arm.

'Perhaps it's because I was waiting for someone special enough to come along,' he suggested softly as his warm breath bathed her hand. 'Someone who would make me want to throw away restraint in a glorious explosion of passion.'

Hannah drew in a startled breath as her body tightened

deep inside in reaction to his graphic words, then firmly brought her emotions back under control.

'All very poetic,' she commented wryly, 'except that we've been working together for two years so why me and why now?'

'Perhaps it's because you've only just noticed me,' he suggested, just as his dreaded pager burst into manic life.

'Just noticed you!' she scoffed with a burst of startled laughter, and she snatched her hand away. Before he could think about blocking her access to the door she stepped around him and opened it. 'Pull the other leg— it's got bells on!'

CHAPTER NINE

OVER the last few years, Hannah had found that she didn't enjoy Christmas very much any more—it was such an essentially family time and she didn't have any family to share it with.

It seemed as if it was going to be particularly empty this year, especially as Laura and Polly were totally wrapped up in their new relationships.

Hannah had felt very noble when she'd volunteered for the lion's share of the holiday shifts to allow her friends to spend time with their loved ones, but she hadn't realised that Leo had decided to do the same thing or she might not have accepted their thanks so blithely.

'The trouble is that I don't know whether to keep my fingers crossed that we're quiet—when Leo will have plenty of time to torment the life out of me—or hope we're frantically busy—when he'll probably manage to make certain that we're all but laminated together at the hip!' she complained to her two friends when she found out what had happened to the rosters.

Polly and Laura laughed at her disgruntled expression.

'Of course, there *is* one other thing you'll have to worry about,' Wolff suggested as he came in on the end of the discussion.

'Oh, no,' Hannah groaned. 'What?'

'A revenge attack from Sexy Samantha?' he suggested. 'She won't be very happy that you're getting to spend so much time with the object of her relentless quest.'

'As if she'd see *me* as any sort of competition,' Hannah scoffed with a hidden pang for the painful truth. 'She must be the most beautiful woman on the staff, and I've never seen her with a single hair out of place.'

'She is rather stunning,' Wolff agreed, then yelped as Laura dug her elbow in his ribs before he continued thoughtfully, 'I must admit, though, I sometimes think it's only a matter of time before Leo succumbs to her charms.'

'Before Leo succumbs to *whose* charms?' demanded the man in question as he strode cheerfully into the room, his eyes zeroing in on Hannah as if she were the only one in the room.

His dark gold hair gleamed with jewelled fire as he prowled towards her past the string of Christmas decorations which someone had strung around the top of the cupboards, the colours rivalling his gaudiest tie yet.

'If you're talking about Hannah here. . .' He dropped an unanticipated arm around her shoulders and pulled her close enough to the lean length of his body to press a brief kiss on her tumble of dark curls before he released her, startled and breathless.

'I'm ready to succumb to her charms the moment she crooks her little finger at me, and I've told her so!' he declared boldly.

He winked broadly as if the whole idea was a joke and the rest of the group joined in the laughter.

Only Hannah knew how hollow hers sounded.

'Are you counting on the principle of third time lucky, Leo?' demanded Wolff as he lifted Laura out of her chair and settled her on his lap. He curved his arms tightly around her as if he couldn't have her close enough, then continued speaking.

'You missed out the first time when Polly chose her Prince. . .'

'And I got the Big Bad Wolff,' Laura butted in with an impish grin at the man wrapped around her, tilting her head back to deliver a noisy kiss on his cheek.

'So you think I'm after Hannah to make it third time lucky?' Leo sounded bemused at the idea, his eyebrow cocked up towards Hannah as if he was daring her to comment.

'Well, if we're sticking to fairy-tales and wise sayings,' she mused aloud, 'he might be unlucky enough to find out that there's only Beauty and the Beast left.'

'Hey! Be careful of my ego!' Leo objected, but his exclamation was drowned out by the chorus of laughter.

As she looked back, Hannah realised that at least that light-hearted conversation had helped to set the tone of the rest of the holiday period, with various members of the accident and emergency staff taking Hannah's side when Leo's pranks and innuendos began to get out of hand.

It had started with the mistletoe.

Just one little sprig of green with two translucent berries, but as fast as one member of staff spotted its resting place and warned her so Leo would move it to another location and catch her unawares, his sexy mouth swooping down to deliver yet another earth-shattering kiss.

It wouldn't have been so bad if she hadn't wanted his kisses so much. As it was, each new episode left her lips tingling and her body trembling with renewed desire.

Dammit, she was in love with the man and all he was doing was taunting her with something she could never have.

It was almost a relief when the department received a warning that a bottle-fight had broken out between rival gangs in the centre of town at the height of the New Year revelries leading up to the striking of midnight.

Suddenly there was no time for kiss-chase games as

the department was inundated with so many wounded that it began to look like a battleground.

Apart from a larger than usual number of drunks and several people who were suffering from shock and hysteria, there were at least fifteen serious injuries due to arrive, two with suspected fractured skulls.

Once again the department swung into action like the well-oiled machine it was, with the triage team sorting everyone as they arrived.

'Thank goodness we're still on holiday rosters,' mumbled Tina as she swiftly cleared the debris from the previous patient and set everything up ready for the next one.

The speed and confidence with which she could achieve the job spoke volumes about the way she'd progressed since she'd first joined the department just three months ago.

'That's a point,' Hannah agreed as she replenished the trolley. 'At least we know they won't have had to cancel any routine admissions or defer any cold surgery because so few are booked to come in during Christmas and New Year.'

They'd barely finished speaking when the doors swung open and a partially clothed young man was wheeled in, with blood pouring down his face and neck and congealing in his dreadlocked hair.

'I got bottled,' he announced in a drunken voice as he gazed blearily around at his strange surroundings, his clothes reeking of alcohol and urine. 'Some bugger 'it me 'ead wiv a bottle.'

'He refused to lie down,' muttered the porter as he delivered his passenger to the side of the trolley and set the brakes. 'It was as much as I could do to persuade him to use the wheelchair, even though he's none too steady on his legs.'

As he spoke their patient made an abortive attempt at getting out of the wheelchair and nearly ended up measuring his length on the floor.

'Gently does it,' Hannah soothed as she caught his elbow just in time and directed his lunge towards the freshly prepared trolley. 'I think you'll be more comfortable if you lie down on here.'

He swung his matted head towards her, one arm raised threateningly in her direction until he caught sight of her.

'Hey...! You're a good-lookin' bit,' he slurred with a drunken leer. 'Too bloody clean, but I c'n soon take care of that... Jus' climb up 'ere with me—I'll soon make yer sweat a bit...'

The rambling came to a sudden halt as he lost his battle with gravity and slumped onto his back with a profane groan.

'Are you all right?' Leo muttered in Hannah's ear, and she swung her head to look up into golden eyes full of concern.

'No problem,' she assured him. 'He's too drunk to do anything more than talk.'

'It's that sort of trash that makes me tempted to start stitching without an anaesthetic,' he growled, and she couldn't suppress an answering grin.

'Still,' he continued, 'we have to take our pleasures where we can find them, and one of mine will be getting rid of this disgusting bird's nest so we can repair the damage.'

He picked up several rancid ropes of blood-soaked hair and lifted them gently away from the young man's head while Hannah leant forward to sever them with a satisfying snip of very sharp scissors.

'He'll hardly know himself when he wakes up,' Tina commented a few minutes later when the shearing job was finished to reveal the full scale of the damage to the young man's scalp.

'He certainly won't *want* to know himself when he finds out about his hangover in the morning,' Leo commented wryly as he irrigated the deadened wound thoroughly, checking for any fugitive shards of glass, then prepared to begin the painstaking task of piecing together the multiple gashes in the young man's scalp.

'Still,' he commented a few moments later, 'he should be well used to the experience by now—I reckon this is at least the third time someone's practised their embroidery on him.'

To Tina's horror, he pointed out the tracery of previous injuries which ran across his head in several directions.

'You'd think he'd learn after the first time,' the young trainee commented with a pained expression on her face. 'Is it really worth the agony over and over again, just for the sake of a few drinks?'

'Ah, well, some people are very slow learners,' Leo said cryptically as his eyes gleamed tiger-bright at Hannah over the top of his mask, full of hidden messages. 'They have to keep repeating something until they finally get it right. Who knows, perhaps this will be third time lucky for this young man?'

Hannah had to turn away for a second, pretending to check the arrangement of the suture tray in an attempt to hide the heat washing over her cheeks.

Wretched man.

He must know what those strange golden eyes did to her equilibrium, and as for referring to the conversation about his apparent pursuit of her. . .

'Well, at least it gives me plenty of practice with my stitching,' Leo added philosophically, as if he'd been talking about their patient all the time, and he held out his hand for the first needle. 'Perhaps, when I've finished,

I'll check up on the computer and see if the other stitches were done here, too—find out whose handiwork the rest are and see who did the neatest job. . .'

He bent his head over the brightly lit table, but before he concentrated on placing the first stitch he managed a surreptitious wink at Hannah and set her pulse racing all over again.

'What *is* going on between you two?' Laura demanded when the last of the roisterers had departed to continue their singing and shouting elsewhere, and the staff could afford to collapse for five minutes with welcome cups of coffee.

The final tally had included over a hundred stitches, two broken collarbones, numerous skinned knuckles and black eyes, a broken wrist and a hairline skull fracture, apart from a near-riot when the rival groups came face to face in the middle of the reception area.

Hospital security had welcomed the assistance of a small contingent from the local police station to sort that little lot out without any further bloodshed, but now that the cleaners had been through with their mops and buckets the department had finally returned to normal.

'Which two?' Hannah murmured as she leaned her head back into the corner of the squashy settee and groaned with relief as she slid her feet gratefully out of her shoes.

'You and Leo, of course,' Laura said impatiently, as though it should have been obvious.

'There's no "of course" about it,' Hannah said in a flat monotone, without even bothering to open her eyes. 'There's nothing going on between the two of us, other than a very long-running, very tiresome joke.'

There was a long silence and it sounded as if Laura

had accepted her words until Hannah felt the cushions dip and realised that she was leaning closer.

'I don't believe you,' Laura murmured. 'Every time you see him, or his name is mentioned, you try to hide your reaction but you go all pink and flustered... And, as for him, he can't keep his eyes off you—if I wasn't crazy about Wolff I could feel quite jealous. But if it's still a big secret, and you don't want to tell me about it...'

It was the soft sound of hurt in her friend's voice that made Hannah open her eyes.

'Laura...' Hannah began and then paused, not quite certain how to continue.

What *could* she say to her friend when she honestly didn't know what was going on?

'It's all right, Hannah, I understand,' Laura said hurriedly as she moved away from her friend and leant forward to reach for her coffee. 'I realise that our friendship is changing, especially now that I've got Wolff in my life, but I thought you would at least let *me* in on the secret.'

'But that's just the point!' Hannah exclaimed, then glanced around furtively and lowered her voice again. 'There isn't a secret to *tell* you, Laura. The whole thing is just one of Leo's many elaborate pursuits, and you've probably realised by now that he never chases anyone *too* hard in case he catches them.'

'Then there really isn't a secret romance going on between you?' Laura asked, the disappointment on her face almost comical, if Hannah had felt like laughing. 'Oh, Hannah, I was so hoping that you were going to be as happy as Wolff and I are.'

'But I *am* happy,' Hannah insisted. 'I've got my own home, a career I love with good prospects for promotion and a circle of caring friends—of course I'm happy.'

'But you're not content,' Laura said shrewdly, her dark

green eyes full of sympathy. 'I can see it in your face—and in your eyes,' she added when Hannah would have disputed the fact. 'I can recognise the loneliness you feel inside because I used to see the same thing when I looked in my mirror.'

'Oh, Laura,' Hannah sighed, knowing she was conceding that her friend was right.

'So what's gone wrong?' she probed gently, careful to keep her voice low enough to deter eavesdroppers. '*Is* it a case of Leo chasing you without any intention of catching you while you wish he would?'

'If only it was,' Hannah said wearily, and rubbed both hands over her face. 'For some crazy reason, he seems to have got it into his head that the two of us would make a good couple and he won't let go of the idea.'

'Well, what's so wrong with that?' Laura demanded pertly. 'You're obviously just as crazy about him so what's stopping you?'

'I'm *not*!' Hannah objected with a knee-jerk reaction, but when she saw the open scepticism in her friend's raised eyebrow she subsided with lips pressed tightly together.

'You're right, dammit,' she muttered when Laura had allowed the silence to drag on for several tantalising minutes. 'For all the good it'll do me,' she added in a soft whisper as her heart swelled with familiar misery.

'But. . .I don't understand,' said Laura, her forehead creased in a frown. 'He's in hot pursuit and you're in love with him—so what's stopping the two of you? The electricity the two of you generate when you're near each other could set off a nuclear reactor!'

Hannah felt the surge of heat in her face as she remembered the explosion of passion she and Leo had set off in her flat, and could have died of embarrassment.

Unfortunately, Laura was too close to miss the tell-tale signs.

'Oh-ho!' she chortled and rubbed her hands together gleefully. 'This looks promising! Tell me...tell me...'

Hannah closed her eyes and sighed.

'It was only the once,' she admitted.

'And...?' Laura prompted with a giggle. 'Did it blow your socks off?'

'Actually, no. It happened so fast we only got as far as removing the essentials.'

'Wow!' Laura breathed, her dark green eyes gleaming. 'But if it was that good why haven't you scheduled a re-match?'

'Because that's as good as it can get,' Hannah said cryptically. 'If I gave in to him and let him get too close I'd be left with just the memories.'

'But that's all you've got now,' Laura pointed out with stubborn logic.

'Yes,' Hannah agreed. 'But at least they're all *good* memories, and if I said yes to making love again he would want to spend the night with me and then I would have to tell him...to show him...' She halted, unable to finish the sentence.

'Tell him what? Show him what?' Laura demanded, obviously totally puzzled by the turn of the conversation.

Hannah drew in a shuddering breath and forced herself to meet her friend's eyes.

'The...the scars,' she whispered as her own eyes brimmed with tears. 'He'd have to see the scars...'

Her eyes were still slightly red when she came back from her break, in spite of the cold water she'd splashed on her face.

Laura had offered her some make-up but her skin tone

was so much paler that it was no use, simply making Hannah look as if she'd seen a ghost.

Laura had escorted her to the nearest bathroom when she'd broken down, shielding her from curious eyes until their privacy was guaranteed.

It had taken her some time to tell her friend about everything that had happened since they'd worked together at their previous hospital—from her discovery that her mother's recently discovered cancer had metastasised, to her funeral just six weeks later, to the revelation that there was a strong genetic link between all the cancer deaths in her family which had left her without a single living relative.

The story had come out in a torrent as she put the whole horror into words for the first time.

'Oh, Hannah, I'm so sorry I wasn't there for you,' Laura said with an impulsive hug. 'But you've come through it so well—I can't believe you're so frightened of telling him. If anything, you're stronger than you were when we were training and you know that Leo's just a big pussycat, in spite of his name.'

'A very big, very sexy, very good-looking pussycat who can have his pick of all the beautiful people in the hospital,' Hannah pointed out miserably. 'What on earth would he want with damaged goods?'

Inside her head she heard the echoes of her ex-fiancé's voice as he'd broken off their engagement, his words seared into her soul like a brand.

'You ought to carry some sort of declaration,' Jon had declared with a twist to his mouth. 'You know, like the ones manufacturers stamp on faulty goods when they're trying to sell them off cheaply—"Imperfect" or "Seconds"...' He'd held his hands up as if he were outlining the words in bold type. 'Or how about "Returned to maker unopened—Unwanted gift"?'

Even those insults hadn't been enough for him. He hadn't been satisfied with pointing out how much the sight of her offended him—he'd had to go on and attack her whole sense of self-worth, fragile as it had been at the time.

'Still, never mind,' he'd said with a sneer as he pocketed the sapphire and diamond engagement ring he'd told her he'd chosen to match the sparkle in her dark blue eyes. 'I understand there are some sickos out there who like to get it on with disabled people such as amputees so, who knows, you may get lucky one of these days. . .?'

'You've got to go and see Leo,' Laura said fiercely, breaking into Hannah's bitter memories and dragging her back to the painful decision she was going to have to make. 'You've got to talk to him.'

'But. . .'

'Look,' she interrupted before Hannah could voice her reservations, 'it's taken you months to tell me what's been happening to you, and I'm only your friend. If you love Leo as much as I think you do surely he deserves your honesty, too?'

In her heart Hannah knew that she was right but the memory of Jon's rejection was still fresh and raw, like an open wound.

Her determination to keep the rest of the world at arm's length had been so strong that she hadn't allowed herself to realise that she was falling in love with Leo—until passion had exploded between them and opened her eyes.

The trouble was that it had taken her such a long time to admit that she loved Leo—it had probably been growing, unrecognised, from the first time she'd seen his handsome face and distantly admitted to his sex-appeal—

and that now if he, too, rejected her she didn't think she would ever recover.

'But what if he doesn't—can't—?'

'Enough of the what if and maybe, Hannah!' Laura exclaimed forcefully. 'You're doing the same as I did, and it's tearing you apart all the while you're in love with him and wanting to be with him and not having the guts to talk to him to find out how he feels one way or the other.'

'Oh, Laura, it makes me feel better just to know that you went through something like this, too,' Hannah said as she returned her friend's hug. She was all too aware that just the thought of talking to Leo was making her quiver inside, but she knew that Laura was right.

'OK,' she said, and drew in a steadying breath. 'I'll collar him at the end of the shift and. . .and suggest he comes back to my place for coffee and a chat.'

'Make sure you do,' Laura warned with an admonishing finger. 'You've got big enough circles under your eyes to audition for a panda. It's about time you started smiling again.'

Hannah showed Laura that she'd crossed her fingers for luck as they went back to work, and she hoped there wouldn't be too many patients in the hours before the end of her shift. There was no guarantee that she was going to be able to concentrate properly on what she was doing if she was trying to compose her invitation in her head.

'Leo, would you like some coffee?' she practised under her breath, then shook her head. That was no good—he'd probably think she was offering to make him one in the little kitchenette, and there was no way they could have their talk *there*.

'Leo, are you free this evening?' she tried next, and grimaced as she realised that the words could sound as if she was asking him out on a date—the rest of the department would love to hear that one.

'Leo, would you like to come home with me...for coffee?' Lord, this was getting worse by the minute. Now she sounded as if she was propositioning him.

'Leo, I need to talk to you...' No, that was no good because he would only ask her why and she didn't want to start explaining until they were a long way from any eavesdroppers. What she had to tell him was not something she wanted to have broadcast on the hospital grapevine.

'Leo, I need...'

'What?' a deep voice demanded behind her and Hannah nearly jumped out of her skin.

'Oh, Leo, there you are,' she squeaked breathlessly, while her brain refused to produce a single one of the sentences she'd been trying out and she was left gazing up at him in silence.

'Hannah?' he prompted patiently. 'You said you needed something?'

'Oh, did I? I mean, yes, I did. I needed...I needed...' She gulped and drew in a sharp breath before she began again. 'Oh, Lord, Leo, I've got to talk to you before I go completely out of my head.'

He was silent, and for a horrible moment she was afraid that he was going to refuse—until she saw the gentle smile start in his eyes.

'And about time, too,' he murmured in a husky voice. 'Just tell me where and when.'

In the end it had all been so ridiculously easy that she hadn't had time to sort out the practical details, and she looked at him blankly.

'At the risk of sounding trite—your place or mine?' he suggested with a hint of a chuckle.

'Yours...no, mine,' she decided—at least she

wouldn't have to drive away from him if everything went badly but, then, if it *did* go badly she'd probably have to move flats because the rooms would be full of the memories of...

'What time?' Leo asked, his tone telling her that it wasn't the first time of asking.

'Is seven-thirty all right?' she offered hesitantly.

He agreed easily and his smile was a warm benediction that spread hope through her body before he strode away down the corridor. And then, as her eyes lovingly followed him until he turned the corner, she could have kicked herself.

Seven-thirty was *hours* away—far too much time for her to get her nerves knotted with anticipation and dread. What on earth had made her suggest it? If she'd said six...

Celia MacDonald's precise Scots accent hailed her urgently, breaking into her mental self-castigation, and in an instant everything else was pushed to a back corner of her mind as she whirled and set off briskly.

'Ah, good, Hannah,' the senior sister said with a shadow of her former briskness as she beckoned her into her room. 'The police are bringing one of our nurses in. She's going to need your special touch—she's been raped.'

Hannah's heart clenched in her chest.

It didn't matter that she'd had special training for these cases or that she'd seen so many of them. The feeling never went away—an overpowering mixture of compassion and anger. Compassion for the victims of this particularly loathsome form of violence and anger that *any* man thought he could get away with it.

This time it would be even worse because the victim was one of their own—one of the extended 'family' of hospital employees.

The anger was under control at the moment, but by the time she'd finished the necessarily intimate job of examining the victim and taking samples for any possible court case she would have spent a long time with her patient and would probably have heard enough details about the attack to make her look nervously over her shoulder for weeks.

What she *did* know was that if she met the man who'd done this thing she'd probably be so incensed by then that she'd willingly castrate him on the spot—at least he wouldn't ever be able to rape again. . .

'Hello, Su, I'm Hannah,' she said gently as she let herself into the room and closed the door quietly behind her.

The slender young woman had been leaning against the wall on the other side of the room, her straight dark hair a concealing waterfall around her face and shoulders as she huddled into herself with her arms wrapped protectively around her ribs.

At the sound of Hannah's voice she whirled to face her, and Hannah couldn't help gasping at the state of her face.

'Oh, Su, your poor face,' she murmured, and she took an involuntary step towards her before she got herself under control.

Su gazed at her out of a face that was hardly recognisable as human, both eyes already almost swollen shut and with bleeding cuts on her cheek-bone and lips. One side of her face was so raw that it looked as if she must have been dragged along the street.

'Have. . .?' Hannah had to stop and clear her throat, giving herself a stern reminder that the young woman needed her professional expertise as much as her sympathy.

'Have you been told what we need to do?' she asked

gently. 'Did the police tell you what the routine is?'

Su shook her head briefly and a single tear slid out of one discoloured eye.

'They wanted me to see the police surgeon,' she whispered through puffy lips. 'I told them I'd rather come here.'

She drew in a shuddering breath and winced, tightening her arms protectively around her ribs.

'I—I know most of the staff on A and E—by sight at least—and I trust you to do what you have to...'

'OK.' Hannah nodded, accepting her unspoken trust. 'You know you're safe here so the first thing I need to do is take a medical history.'

'My details are all in the hospital computer—I'm Sister Su Yuen and I work up on the special care baby unit. I'm twenty-seven, s-single and...and...'

'Hey, Su, take it easy,' Hannah soothed as the young woman started to lose control. She longed to be able to offer her the physical comfort of a hug but knew it wasn't possible yet, the only option being to distract her. 'Will it help if you focus on answering straight questions?' she asked instead.

'O-OK.' She nodded jerkily. 'Fire away.'

'Good girl,' Hannah said, amazed by her strength of will. She wasn't certain that she'd be holding up this well if it had happened to her.

'You're doing well, Su,' she said encouragingly. 'Are these the clothes you were wearing when you were attacked?'

'Yes,' she whispered. 'T-the police picked me up in the street after...after it happened and I made them bring me here.'

'Good. So you haven't been to the toilet or had a wash?'

'No.' She closed her eyes on a single sob. 'I

remembered that part of the lecture during our training...'

'Well, in that case, I'm going to put on protective clothing so that I can't contaminate any of the evidence, and then I'll help you to take your clothing off and seal it in bags to go for forensic examination.'

Limiting herself to questioning Su about her injuries, Hannah quickly but thoroughly noted down her observations about the state of her clothing and her physical and emotional state, very conscious that her notes would constitute a legal document in any court case.

Su had caught her hand in a death-like grip when Nick Prince had come in to take swabs and make the necessary internal examination, and by the time she'd combed the poor woman's pubic hair for foreign samples, taken internal swabs and scraped under Su's fingernails for traces of her attacker's skin Hannah was feeling completely drained.

It seemed like hours before the young policewoman stepped in to take charge of the various items of evidence, her sympathetic smile apparently the last straw for the traumatised young woman.

'It's all a waste of time,' she wailed as she finally gave in to hysterical tears. 'They said the evidence won't do any good because there were too many of them... And...and they said they'd tell Mike I wanted them to do it...that I like a bit of rough stuff...'

The policewoman stopped in her tracks as if she'd hit a brick wall, her expression one of total horror.

'What?' Hannah whispered in disbelief as she closed her arms around the terrified young woman, who trembled against her like a wounded animal. 'Do you know who did this to you?'

CHAPTER TEN

'SOMETIMES I could willingly commit murder,' Hannah muttered as she coaxed her elderly car into life, her mind still consumed by the details Su Yuen had finally given the young policewoman.

The Mike that Su had mentioned was her fiancé, an orthopaedic registrar at St Augustine's who had raced to be with her as soon as he heard that Su had been hurt.

Amidst her entreaties that she should be allowed to tell Mike the details herself, she'd told the sympathetic officer that they'd only been engaged for a month and that her attackers today had been his team-mates from the local rugby club he'd joined shortly after he began his medical training. She'd only met them for the first time the previous week at their engagement party at her parents' Chinese restaurant.

'They got drunk at the party,' she'd told the two of them through her tears. 'In front of both of our families they told Mike he was making a mistake in wanting to marry me. That everyone knew Chinese women were the best whores in the world—trained to please from the cradle...'

When the young officer's questions had finished Hannah had pieced together a tale of Mike's disgust with his team-mates' behaviour and his decision to quit the club, in spite of his leading part in the team.

It seemed as if their attack on Su had been a particularly sick form of revenge when the team had lost an important game without Mike on their side, and in their drunkenness they had actually made themselves believe that once they had all used her Mike would dump her and rejoin the club.

It was just an added agony for the young woman that she'd been a virgin, determined to save herself for the man she loved on her wedding day.

She was late, but there was no way she could have left Su before she was certain that she had someone else there to care for her.

Mike had been pacing a furrow in the corridor outside and tears clogged Hannah's throat when she remembered the gentle care with which he'd wrapped his injured fiancée in his arms.

The clock on the dashboard showed that it was already seven-thirty by the time she drew up behind the other cars parked outside her flat, and she sighed tiredly.

Hannah was just thinking that the only good thing about the events of the last few hours was that they'd stopped her thinking about her own problems when she saw the door on the car immediately in front of her open, and Leo climbed out and straightened up.

'You're late getting back,' he commented as he came forward to relieve her of one of her bags. 'Big Mac told me what was going on. Does your invitation still stand or would you rather make it another day?'

The coward inside Hannah wanted to grab at the chance to postpone their discussion but she knew that she couldn't bear to wait any longer. She had to know whether there was a chance for the two of them to build some sort of relationship together, and the sooner she knew the better.

'No. This evening's fine, provided you're not expecting the place to be tidy.'

She had a vivid memory of how neat his own flat had

been when he'd taken her there to dry off—not at all the typical picture of a bachelor's domain.

'It *must* be better than mine,' he commented while he waited for her to find her key in the muddle at the bottom of her bag.

'Yours? You must be joking!' she exclaimed in surprise. 'I've only been there once and it was immaculate— quite put me to shame!'

'Ah, well, that must have been the day that Audrey was there,' he said with his familiar ladykiller grin.

Hannah bit her tongue to stop the jealous words escaping, but it was no use.

'Audrey?' she heard herself echo. 'Who's Audrey?'

'Audrey's a wonderful woman who comes every week to shovel up my mess and put me straight for another week—every bachelor should have an Audrey!'

'Not just bachelors,' Hannah said, glowering to hide her relief that the mystery woman in his life was his cleaner as she pushed the door open and carried her bag through to her tiny kitchen.

She grimaced at the neat pile of crockery and cutlery waiting in the sink. 'It would be wonderful to come home, knowing that a good fairy had come and washed up the breakfast things in my absence.'

'In which case, it's a good thing I had time to pick this up,' Leo said, holding up the carrier bag dangling from his other hand.

Suddenly Hannah's nose was assailed by the tempting smells of Chinese food, and her stomach rumbled loudly.

'I hope that's what I think it is,' she said fervently as she reached up into a cupboard for two plates. 'Do you want chopsticks or forks?'

'Chopsticks,' he voted with a grin. 'I like showing off!'

Hannah handed him a tray on which to set the foil

containers, and while he carried them through and put them on the table she collected serving spoons and soy sauce and followed him through to sit on the other side of her tiny table.

After his implied boast, Hannah had been prepared for Leo to be a dab hand with chopsticks so it came as rather a surprise to find that he was dropping more than he managed to carry to his mouth.

'Leo!' she laughed when he lost control of yet another chunk of chicken and was left with his mouth open like a baby bird in a nest. 'You're going to starve at this rate!'

She reached out and neatly scissored her own chopsticks around a plump button mushroom and lifted it towards him.

'Here,' she offered. 'Open wide.'

Leo's eyes flared as he fixed them on her own and she suddenly realised how intimate a gesture she'd made when she watched his lips close over the smooth shape of the mushroom.

'Mmm,' he murmured as he made short work of the mouthful. 'More, please.'

Hannah hesitated, aware that her hand had started to tremble, but his eyes gleamed at her, daring her to feed him again.

'It's your turn this time,' she said, her voice huskier than usual. 'Turnabout's fair play.'

His eyes darkened as he accepted the challenge and suddenly he was able to manipulate the slender implements with no difficulty at all, tempting her with a succulent strip of chicken.

'You cheat!' she mumbled with her mouth full. 'You were only pretending you couldn't manage!'

'It worked, though, didn't it?' he teased gleefully, chuckling as he scooped up a goodly portion of fried rice and transferred it to his mouth without losing a single grain.

'But why the pretence?' she demanded as she fished for another sliver of chicken.

'Because I wanted an excuse to feed you,' he admitted simply, his laughter gone as he held out a perfect prawn and touched it to her lips. 'Open up,' he whispered, his eyes flicking from her mouth to her eyes and back again.

Suddenly Hannah was nervous of his intensity, and the tip of her tongue darted out to collect the moisture he'd left there.

'Oh, God, Hannah,' he groaned, and abandoned the chopsticks with a clatter. 'I can't think about eating when I see you licking your lips like that. All I can think about is kissing you and tasting the sweet and sour sauce on your tongue.'

He reached out to take her own chopsticks away, her hand frozen around them in spite of the fact that she'd completely forgotten they were there.

'Leo,' she heard herself whimper as he stood up and reached over to lift her from her own chair and enfold her in his arms.

'Kiss me, Hannah, please,' he whispered as he pulled her tightly against his body and angled his head towards her. 'I need you.'

His husky words caused a sharp twist of desire deep inside her and she was helpless to refuse him, her head settling against his shoulder and her lips parting for him almost before his mouth touched hers.

It was like coming home.

Only with Leo did she have this sensation that she had found the place she belonged, and when his tongue took possession of her mouth she knew that her submission to his penetration was only the symbol of her willingness for a far deeper surrender.

Her head was swimming by the time he lifted her in his arms and cradled her against his chest.

'This time I refuse to rush anything,' he declared roughly as he set off across the room towards the door of her bedroom. 'This time I want us to be able to take our time and make love in comfort, and if you fall asleep on me again I want to be able to cuddle your naked body next to mine until you're ready to wake up and start all over again.'

As he spoke he was sliding her down his body so that her feet touched the floor and she was achingly aware of every virile inch of him.

His husky words should have been as exciting as the evidence that his tautly muscled body was already fully aroused and ready for love-making but on Hannah they had the same effect as a dousing with a bucket of icy water.

'No, Leo,' she gasped as panic overtook her and she tried to step back out of his arms. 'I can't. . . We can't. . . Not until. . .until. . . Oh, Leo, let me go. . .!'

He must have recognised the anguish in her voice because he released his hold on her so suddenly that she nearly fell over.

'Hannah?' He caught her elbow again and steadied her, a confused frown pleating his forehead when she froze in his grasp. 'Sweetheart, what's the matter? What's wrong—don't you want to make love?'

'Oh, Leo. . .' Her throat closed when she saw the mixture of hurt and puzzlement in his eyes. 'Yes, I want to make love with you, but I can't—not until I've had a chance to tell you. . .to warn you. . .'

She shook her head. How was she ever going to find the words?

'Hey, sweetheart, whatever it is it can't be so bad,' he said supportively. 'If you want to talk to me then we'll talk, but we might as well make ourselves comfortable.'

Hannah felt for the edge of the bed behind her shaky knees and sank gratefully onto it, lacing her fingers together into a Gordian knot as she tried to find the words to start.

'What's it all about?' he prompted as he sat himself beside her, gently lifting her white-knuckled hands into his own and smoothing their chill away with his own warmth.

'I—I suppose it's about my family, or rather my lack of one,' she finally began, deciding it was easier to start at the very beginning. 'Since my mother died just over two years ago there's only been me.'

'I'm sorry, sweetheart. And I can't offer you much more—just a set of parents I don't have time to visit very often.'

'How old is your mother?' she asked, and saw him blink at the apparent change of topic.

'She was fifty-seven this year. Why?'

'My mother was thirty-nine when she died. My aunt—her older sister—was forty-one and their mother was thirty-five.'

'Was there no one else?' He was still frowning as he tried to see which way the conversation was going.

'Just my cousin. She died when she was twenty-nine.'

'I take it from the tone of your voice that there is some significance to all this?' His voice, too, was sombre and she knew his mind would be working with the speed of a high-powered computer as he tried to piece the picture together.

'All of them died of breast cancer,' she said bleakly. 'We're now one of the families that have been written up by researchers in the race to isolate and find a treatment for the breast cancer gene.'

'Have you been tested?' he asked, his tone as calm

and even as if he were asking the time, every inch the professional doctor in spite of the fact that he was sitting beside her on the edge of her bed.

She nodded briefly.

'Just after Mum was diagnosed—too late for treatment—I caught part of a television programme about a woman who traced her family and found that a very high proportion of them had died of a particular type of breast cancer. As soon as I realised the significance of my own family history I asked if I could be tested, too.'

She gritted her teeth and started undressing herself, ignoring his startled glances as she first unclasped the ornate buckle she wore so proudly then started on the front fastening of the uniform she hadn't had time to change in her hurry to get home.

She forced herself to continue speaking, her voice trembling as much as her fingers as she relived the past and dreaded the future.

'At the same time as I was waiting for the chromatography results I also had a mammogram, and they found a small suspicious mass. It could have passed unnoticed if they hadn't been looking for it—but it was malignant.'

By this time she'd shrugged out of her dress and was reaching for the front fastening on her eminently practical bra.

'I had to make a decision,' she continued through a throat filled with tears as she forced herself to allow the bra to fall away from her body. 'The surgeon agreed that in view of my family history the only possible course of action was to take both breasts off.'

There was the brief sound of his sharply indrawn breath, and then silence.

Hannah closed her eyes, unable to bear to look at him—afraid what his expression would tell her.

'Ah, Hannah, love...' he murmured softly, but she

couldn't tell whether the tone was of pity or compassion.

She forced herself to open her eyes just in time to see his hand reach out towards the scars, and she flinched away from the contact.

'Still painful?' he asked.

'More emotional than physical,' she admitted as she fumbled awkwardly to settle the flesh-coloured prostheses in her bra and fasten it in position again.

'Was there some reason why you didn't undergo reconstruction immediately?' he demanded, and she smiled inwardly at the evidence that his medical brain was still functioning as usual.

'At the time I was so depressed with the combination of my mother's death and my own diagnosis—' *and Jon's hurtful derision*, her silent inner voice reminded her '—that I didn't see the point of having the implants done. It seemed like a waste of time when none of my relatives had survived more than a few months after diagnosis.'

'But that was more than two years ago and your prognosis is good—surely you've made fresh enquiries about having implants at one of your check-ups?'

'I manage,' she said woodenly. 'It seemed like an awful lot to go through just for the sake of vanity. . . another operation, more scarring, and they still wouldn't be real breasts. . .'

Distracted by her memory of Jon's derision at the pointlessness of her original intention to have implants— and his scorn that they might make her *look* normal to anyone else but he'd know better—she was struggling to pull her uniform up over her shoulders again and didn't realise that he'd reached out to help until he brushed her naked skin.

She froze like a small creature caught in the beam of a bright light, unable to move while he was touching her.

He started to lift his hand away and then grew still, his warm fingertips still in contact with her cooler flesh.

She could almost hear his brain working—hear him calculating and analysing, sifting the information she'd given him and reading between the lines for the things she *hadn't* said.

'Who was he?' Leo demanded suddenly with anger in his voice. 'Who's the bastard whose shoes you've got me wearing?'

He leapt to his feet and strode to the other end of the bed, then whirled back to face her.

'Who was the insensitive clod who tried to destroy your self-confidence at a time when he should have been supporting you?' he demanded, his eyes fiercely intent.

'J-Jon. . .my fiancé,' she confessed, unable to withstand the force of his glittering glare. 'H-he couldn't help. . . He couldn't look. . . T-the sight of the scars. . .' She shrugged helplessly.

She saw Leo's hands clench into fists and suddenly knew that he was imagining what he would like to do to Jon. . .

The thought that Leo wanted to punish Jon for his shabby treatment of her was like balm to her soul, but it didn't alter the fact that. . .

'And *that's* the reason why you wanted to invite me here,' he said suddenly as comprehension and icy anger clashed in his voice. 'I was starting to be a nuisance, chasing after you when you weren't interested in anything more than a one-night-stand, and you thought you'd hit on the perfect way to get me out of your hair.'

'No!' Hannah gasped, horrified that he could have misunderstood so completely. 'It was for *your* sake—so you wouldn't waste any more time on. . .on someone like me when there are so many beautiful women you could have been going out with. . .f-falling in love with. . .'

'Damn you, Hannah,' he said harshly, his face ashen. 'Do you think I'm *that* shallow? Do you think so little of me that you think I can't see past external appearances?'

'No, Leo! I only—'

'Dammit, woman, I'm in love with you,' he continued, totally ignoring her attempt at explaining. 'I've been in love with you ever since I met you and you'd never give me more than a vague smile. . . But I still hoped. . .'

'Leo. . .' She didn't know whether to laugh or cry. He *loved* her. . .

'As if it makes the slightest difference to me whether you've got breasts or not,' he exclaimed furiously. 'It. . .it's as if you fell in love with a man, then decided you couldn't love him any more if he lost a leg in a crash!'

He whirled away from her and strode out of the bedroom, and suddenly Hannah came out of her happy daze with the realisation that he wasn't coming back.

'Leo?' She scrambled to her feet and sped after him, arriving just in time to see him thrusting his arms into his padded jacket. 'Leo, you can't go yet!'

'There doesn't seem to be a great deal of point in staying,' he said curtly, hardly glancing in her direction.

'But. . .'

She drew in a shuddering breath.

How on earth could she get him to stay long enough for her to explain. . .?'

'You said you love me. . .' she began, holding on tightly to the miraculous revelation.

'For all the good it does me,' he growled, swinging to face her like an angry bear. 'You obviously don't love me in return or you'd never have believed that your sad little striptease would have any effect on my feelings for you. What were you thinking? That all it would take was one look at you and you wouldn't see me for dust?'

'But I didn't know...' she began, then had to bite her lips when they quivered uncontrollably, tears horribly close when she realised how badly she'd misjudged him.

He squeezed his eyes tight shut and shook his head.

'I'm sorry,' he said on a deep sigh. 'Sorry that I put you through this...this...' He waved an expressive hand and shrugged. 'I'll see you at work and I promise not to embarrass you any more in front of the rest of the department.'

And before she could draw another breath he was gone.

'Good morning,' Leo said politely as she arrived for work, but his expressionless eyes struck Hannah like a blow.

It had been a week since he'd left her to her tears, the remains of their meal congealing on the plates as a mute reminder of how well the evening had started.

If only she'd spoken to him without resorting to the melodrama of showing him her mutilated body... If only she'd known that he loved her then everything would have been different.

Now he was so distant and so excruciatingly polite that sometimes she felt like screaming.

Her eyes followed his long-legged stride helplessly as he walked away from her towards the staffroom and another of the cups of lethally black coffee he'd started drinking.

Her heart clenched with despair.

She couldn't stand this much longer. She couldn't sleep, couldn't eat and her concentration was completely shot. If something didn't change soon they'd be coming for her with a strait-jacket.

She turned and had begun to walk towards the reception area when she came to a halt in the middle of the corridor.

'This is stupid,' she muttered as she whirled and set off briskly after him. 'He said he loves me, and I love him. For goodness' sake, we're two adults—we should be able to talk to each other...'

She paused by the door and peered in through the safety glass. If the room was crowded she'd have to try to catch him later, but if there was a chance of talking to him now she was certain she could explain how everything had got so muddled...

Her thoughts ground to a halt at the sight that met her eyes.

Leo was laughing, his solemn face wreathed once again in his familiar ladykiller smile as he leant forward to kiss... Sexy Samantha...

Hannah's eyes lingered for a moment on the other nurse's radiant face and voluptuous body and she felt her heart shatter inside her.

Leo might have vowed that her mastectomy didn't matter, but facts spoke for themselves when he replaced her so quickly with someone so spectacularly endowed.

Hannah straightened her shoulders and turned swiftly away, hurrying back towards the duties which awaited her.

At least now that she knew Leo had replaced her she wouldn't have to worry that he was still hurt by what she'd done. Now she'd be able to return to her original determination to make a lifetime's career of her nursing.

'Hannah? Trauma team,' Ceila MacDonald called as she returned the phone to its cradle. 'Another one in the suicide pit.'

Hannah groaned and turned to make her way swiftly to the emergency room, already able to guess what she'd be facing at the end of a high-speed journey—someone was trapped in the 'suicide pit' under a train.

Her mind was full of the last horrendous episode when a child had slipped and fallen off the edge of the platform in his excitement at his first train journey.

'I hate these,' Nia Samea muttered as the two of them zipped themselves into their protective clothing. 'Apart from the fact that we can't get at them properly to help them, it's always so bitterly cold—even in summer.'

She slid quickly into the emergency vehicle and Hannah followed her, crowding closely against her to make room for the last member to climb in.

'Ready,' Leo's deep voice announced as he pulled the door closed, but she hadn't needed to hear him to know who was sitting beside her.

Everywhere they made contact she seemed to feel the heat radiating out of his body, a strange sort of electricity which had never happened with anyone else and probably never would.

'Any details?' he demanded coolly, as if he hadn't even noticed who was sitting beside him.

'A jumper, apparently,' John Preece supplied from his seat beside the driver, using the common term for an attempted suicide. 'Whose turn is it to go under with him?'

'I'll go,' Leo offered, without the usual friendly banter about who'd done the dangerous, dirty job last time.

They arrived to find that the man was badly trapped, with one foot partially amputated. Hannah could see that they wouldn't be able to do much for him until the train was out of the way and she felt dread grip her.

She'd heard about this happening, but she'd never been present before when the potentially lethal manoeuvre was carried out.

'Has the electricity been switched off?' Leo demanded as he prepared to climb down onto the tracks. The last thing he needed to do was touch the live rail. . .

A railway employee confirmed that all the rails were safe, and Hannah watched Leo make his way along the side of the train until he reached the man trapped by the heavy steel.

She couldn't hear what he was saying, but she watched him trying to conduct some sort of examination between the wheels. Even in his protective clothing his arm looked so vulnerable against the sheer size of the machinery.

'Hannah, I need you down here,' he called, and she jumped in surprise. She'd honestly expected him to call for Nia's help.

With heart in her mouth, Hannah clambered down and made her way towards him.

'I'm going to have to go underneath with him,' Leo announced. 'I'll have to lie on top of him to hold him still while they drive the train off him. There isn't room to move and he's bleeding badly.'

Hannah had to clench her teeth to prevent herself from crying out against the idea of Leo putting himself in danger. All she could do was offer up a swift prayer for his safety and ask him what he wanted her to do.

It took a good five minutes for Leo to wriggle himself into position, and in the meantime Hannah had managed to set up an IV and had enlisted one of the station personnel to crouch on the platform above to hold the bag of fluid.

When the time came for the train to be moved it would have to be tucked underneath where the IV line couldn't be severed by the passage of the wheels, but at the moment at least it was doing something towards replacing the alarming amount of blood which seemed to be seeping out along the track.

'Hannah?' Leo's muffled voice called. 'I'm in position. Tell them it's safe to start moving the train—slowly!'

She relayed the message, but when Leo tried to get her to climb back up to the safety of the platform she refused.

'I've got to stay down here in case you need help,' she insisted. 'Everyone else will be too far away to hear, especially if the train is moving. Just tell me which rail to keep away from when they switch on and I'll be fine.'

He tried to argue but she wasn't listening.

'Switching power back on,' called the senior railway employee, and Hannah repeated the message for Leo who flattened himself over the young man trapped beneath him.

Hannah's eyes were flicking continuously between the rails and the wheels, waiting to see the first sign of movement, so she nearly missed Leo's convulsive activity as his patient started to revive and began to fight his captivity.

Unfortunately his convulsive bid for freedom coincided with the first lurch as the train began to move, and Hannah was the only one to see the back of Leo's head struck by some unrecognisable lump of machinery.

Almost instantly he slumped bonelessly over the man beneath him, apparently unconscious.

'Stop!' Hannah shrieked as she saw his hand flop dangerously near the live rail. 'Switch the power off— quickly!'

There was a screech of brakes and the train came to a shuddering halt as her voice still echoed around the high ceiling of the station building.

'What's the matter?' John shouted as he tried to lean over far enough to see what had happened.

'The train hit Leo's head,' Hannah called back as she scrambled between the carriages and lowered herself to the track. 'He's unconscious so I've got to protect him while they get the train out of the way.'

'Let me do it,' John insisted as he prepared to climb down.

'You can't—not enough room,' Hannah called back, not bothering to voice her determination that if anyone was going to take care of Leo it was going to be her. After the way she had hurt him it was the least she could do. . .

It was dark and cramped under the carriage and very cold, but none of that mattered when she ran her fingers through Leo's hair and felt the large lump coming up on the back of his head.

There was blood on her gloves when she drew her hand away so she knew the skin had been broken, and he wasn't responding to her voice.

Her heart thumped with fear as she slid carefully over the two men, grabbing hold of arms and checking that legs were out of harm's way as she spread herself over the top of Leo's inert form.

'Ready,' she called, careful to turn her head to the side as she tried to stay as low as possible. With a groan and a clank the heavy vehicle started moving again.

John and Nia were waiting as daylight finally poured down on her, but when they would have helped her up she refused their assistance, concentrating on examining Leo's injury while they took care of their original patient.

'Leo,' she called softly as she ran her hands over his head again, fearful that she might have missed a more serious injury in her first assessment.

'Oh, my love, are you all right?' she murmured frantically. 'Oh, Leo, I love you. Speak to me. . .'

She crouched over him to shelter him from the chilly wind, hardly aware of the activity going on around her as a temporary tourniquet was applied to the suicide patient's leg before he was loaded swiftly onto a stretcher and lifted onto the platform.

She was hardly aware of what she was saying as she stroked Leo's thick hair away from his forehead in an agony of remorse. She could have lost him, without ever telling him that she loved him...

'Sister?' another voice intruded. 'If you'll give us a bit of space we'll get him out of there. You can travel in the ambulance with him.'

She looked up into the familiar friendly face of Ted Larrabee and coloured when she realised how unprofessional she was being.

'Sorry, Ted,' she muttered, and felt the heat of embarrassment fill her face in spite of the bitter cold. 'I'll get out of your way.'

'Oh, no, you don't,' mumbled a familiar husky voice as Leo grabbed her hand and held it in place against his face. 'You're not going anywhere until you repeat what you said, but this time you're saying it in front of witnesses.'

'Leo... Are you all right?' she demanded as relief flooded through her.

'Not yet,' he mumbled as he rolled over to face her and trapped her other hand. 'But I will be as soon as you tell me what I want to hear. Tell me you love me. Tell me you can't resist me.'

'Oh, Leo, you idiot,' Hannah laughed through her tears.

'She must love you,' Ted butted in. 'It isn't every woman who'd climb under a train to take care of her man.' *Her man...*

Ted's words reminded her of the way she'd last seen Leo—laughing with Samantha and kissing her—and she remembered that Leo wasn't her man any more.

'No, Ted,' she corrected bravely. 'He's going out with Samantha from Obs and Gyn...'

'He certainly is not,' Leo objected, his eyes snapping fire. 'Whatever gave you that idea?'

'I saw you...this morning...' she began, then paused when she saw the glee in his face.

'You're jealous,' he whispered tauntingly as he pulled her towards himself. 'Jealous over nothing.'

'Nothing?' Hannah said, and bit her lip as hope began to blossom.

'She wanted to tell me that she's getting engaged— to that big good-looking physio that Tina's had her eye on. She apologised for chasing me and said it wasn't until she realised how I felt about you that she let herself notice the man who loved her.'

'Really?' Hannah squeaked, and felt a smile spread over her face.

'Really,' he confirmed. 'So now there's no reason why you shouldn't tell me what I want to hear.'

He sat there between the railway tracks with a boyishly expectant expression on his face.

'Oh, Leo, I *do* love you,' she said fervently, and framed his face in her hands for a kiss.

Time ceased to exist as their lips met, and it was only the sound of Ted insistently clearing his throat that brought the two of them back to their surroundings and the round of applause echoing across the platform.

'Your place or mine?' Leo offered huskily under the cover of the sound, his eyes darkened by desire to the colour of fine old brandy.

'Anywhere, so long as it's with you,' Hannah breathed and knew she meant every word.

'Leo?'

Hannah's voice was hesitant as she lay very still by his side, but she'd been lying here with her arms wrapped around him for a long time while she'd tried to compose her thoughts, and had finally found the courage to speak.

'Mmm?' The sound was a rumble in the depths of his chest under her ear, like the lazy purr of the lion he was named for, and for just a moment her arms tightened around him as she was overwhelmed by the realisation that today she'd come very close to losing him.

She'd sat beside him in the ambulance, perched on the edge of the trolley as they'd bumped and swayed towards St Augustine's, and when they'd reached the hospital he'd kept her by his side by the simple expedient of refusing to release her hand.

There had been an unmistakable gleam of approval in Wolff's eyes when he'd arrived to do the honours with Leo's scalp wound and had found the two of them together, Celia MacDonald's concern for an injured member of staff drawing her to prepare the suture tray herself.

'I expect superglue will be sufficient for the task, Sister,' he said with a grin as he drew her attention to their entwined hands. 'But I definitely think he'll need to take a couple of days off to recover from his injuries.'

Hannah looked up just in time to see the wink Wolff directed towards Big Mac.

'You think so, Doctor?' the senior sister said with an attempt at a frown that didn't manage to hide the twinkle in her eyes. 'In which case, do you think he ought to have someone with him to keep an eye on him? After all, he *has* suffered a head wound and he'll need someone to check up on him at intervals to make sure he isn't suffering from concussion. . .'

Hannah agreed to their suggestions with alacrity, and drove Leo home with every intention of persuading him to sleep for a while, promising to wake him up at intervals to check that his reactions were still normal.

In the event, Leo had been the one to entice *her* into

bed, seducing her shamelessly with words and caresses and the sort of kisses that made her forget her own name.

When he finally reached her last items of clothing she was unable to stop the reflex which brought her hands up to cover herself, but he was so gentle and matter-of-fact about her scars that she'd have dissolved into tears if he wasn't already arousing her beyond the point of embarrassment.

Their mutual pleasure in each other should have been proof enough that her disfigurement wasn't important to him but as she lay cradled in the warmth of his arms the doubts which she'd believed had been buried under an avalanche of ecstasy began to surface again and she knew she had to voice them.

'Leo, do...do you want me to have the implants done?'

Her stumbling question emerged in a rush, the words uncomfortable on her tongue, and when she felt the way silent tension suddenly filled his big body she almost wished she'd left well enough alone.

Had she spoiled everything by reminding him of all she could never be?

She'd once jokingly referred to the two of them as Beauty and the Beast and he'd pretended to bristle, not realising that she knew *he* was the beautiful one—her gorgeous tawny lion with the strangely compelling golden eyes—while she could never...

'No,' Leo said decisively, breaking into her fearful introspection with a jolt as he tightened his arm around her shoulders and tilted her face up so that she was forced to meet his eyes.

'I don't need you to have the implants done, Hannah, any more than I would want you to bleach your hair or wear coloured contact lenses—they wouldn't change the person you are inside. It's far more important to me to know that because of your bravery in having both breasts removed so quickly your cancer can't recur.'

'But?' she prompted when he paused. She'd heard the faint echo of pain in his voice and wondered if he was remembering when he'd lost Lisa. Her heart ached when she heard the unspoken reservation in his tone.

'But although you're still having check-ups you're passing with flying colours, and I think it would be a good idea for *your* sake if you had the implants done,' he continued softly, his sincerity clear in his eyes. 'I think it would give your self-confidence a boost—especially after the hatchet-job your ex-fiancé did on you.'

Hannah absorbed his words, revelling in the fact that his criteria were all based on her feelings until she remembered that some had wider implications. . .

'And. . .and what about children?' she questioned hesitantly. 'What if I can't—?'

'Lisa couldn't,' he reminded her bluntly. 'It didn't make a scrap of difference to me then, and it doesn't now. I love *you*, and whether we have children or not won't change that.'

Hannah gazed up into eyes that warmed her to her soul like clear golden sunlight and she thought for a moment. She sifted carefully through his words for the motives behind them and when she found only honesty and caring she was finally able to relax.

'Still. . .' he said, with a new huskiness creeping into his voice as his free hand slipped over the curve of her waist to caress her bottom and his fingers began a newly familiar path of exploration which took them closer and closer towards the liquid heat of her molten core.

'There's plenty of time to make decisions. . . There's no urgency about any of it,' he murmured distractedly as he teased her thighs into parting for him, his teeth closing gently on the softness of her lower lip before he soothed it with the tip of his tongue.

'No urgency?' she repeated as she felt the hard evidence of his own urgent desire against the curve of her hip and her breath caught in her throat.

'No urgency about anything except how soon you're going to marry me,' he muttered fiercely as he rolled over and pinned her underneath him in the middle of his enormous bed.

'And when you're going to stop talking and make love to me,' she murmured as she wrapped herself around him and welcomed him inside her body, revelling in the glorious completion.

She was still sprawled bonelessly across his body, her ragged breathing slowly returning to normal, when a stray memory floated to the surface to tease her.

'Leo. . .?' she began in a questioning tone, and he groaned dramatically as he flung his arms wide as if in abject surrender.

'Again. . .?' he exclaimed, as if in horror. 'Woman, you're going to kill me. . . Remember, I've been injured and I'm out of practice. . .'

Hannah chuckled at his nonsense.

'Not that I'm an expert, but it certainly doesn't show,' she commented cheekily as she ran teasing fingers over his broad muscled chest and followed the narrow curve of his waist towards his hip. 'I looked very carefully and I didn't see a sign of rust anywhere. . .'

He growled as he erupted and rolled her over to pin her beneath him again, his fingers tormenting her ribs mercilessly.

She shrieked with laughter as she retaliated, and they were both breathless when they finally declared a truce and retrieved the duvet from the floor at the foot of his enormous bed to wrap it cosily around them.

Hannah settled herself in his arms again, amazed that she felt as if she'd always belonged there—as if they'd been made especially for her—and suddenly she remembered what she'd wanted to ask.

'*Is* it just third time lucky for you, Leo?' she asked softly, her lips brushing against his neck as she voiced the tentative question. 'That's what the others were joking about when we went out for that meal with them. . .'

She felt his chuckle before she heard it, and her heart gave a silly leap when she heard the lazy indulgence in it.

'You can ask Polly and Laura about that, if you like, but you'll find that I've only ever been a friend to either of them,' he murmured, then paused long enough to hook one finger under her chin and raise her face for a tender kiss.

'I'd already met you,' he said quietly, his eyes intent as he scanned her face as if he wanted to be certain that she knew she had no need for jealousy. 'Met you, fallen in love with you and decided that I was going to wait for you to realise that you'd fallen in love with me too!'

'Such arrogance!' she exclaimed, laughing and loving him all the more for his patient constancy.

'But, then,' he added thoughtfully, 'I suppose some people could say that our love *is* third time lucky—after all, it'll be the third wedding in the A and E department in quick succession. . .'

Then, as she watched, his mouth curved in that familiar ladykiller grin, and her pulse leapt in response when she realised that she was going to be basking in that smile for the rest of her life.

'Ah, Hannah,' he murmured, his voice huskily intent. 'As far as I'm concerned, what we've found together is a once in a lifetime thing, and it's going to last a lifetime.'

'And beyond,' Hannah agreed as she gazed up into his loving eyes and her heart overflowed.

EPILOGUE

'Twins!' Hannah squeaked in delight when her friend passed on the news. 'Oh, Laura. I couldn't be more delighted for you. When did you find out?'

'About an hour ago,' Laura said with a happy smile as she reached for her husband's hand. 'Wolff was with me for the ultrasound scan, and he'd just made some wisecrack about looking for a litter of Wolff cubs when the technician said there were two in the litter!'

'I bet that shocked you.' Hannah laughed as she looked up into his lean dark face.

'Not as much as when she pointed out the fact that they were conveniently positioned so that we could see what sex they were,' he said.

'And?' Hannah prompted eagerly. 'Did you opt to find out or are you waiting until they arrive?'

'We couldn't help seeing, whether we wanted to or not,' Laura said with a chuckle of her own. 'It's one of each.'

'Perfect,' Hannah said, and hugged her friend over the pronounced bulge at her waist. She was already expanding visibly, even though she was barely four months pregnant.

'Especially if this is our only chance,' Laura said quietly. 'After all, I was told that the endometriosis could stop me having a family at all.'

'Well, all I can say is it couldn't have happened to a nicer couple. You and Wolff deserve them...both of them!'

'And the double lot of nappies and midnight feeds?'

Leo queried as he joined them in the staff lounge, obviously overhearing enough of the conversation to realise what was going on. He kissed Laura's cheek and slapped his friend on the shoulder. 'Congratulations to both of you—enjoy the peace and quiet while you can.'

'You're here early,' Hannah said as she claimed a kiss of her own, her hand lingering lovingly on Leo's cheek. 'I thought you weren't due on duty for several hours yet. Did you come in for the results of the scan?'

'Not specifically,' Leo said with a grin. 'I had a phone call from Nick asking me to cover for him—Polly's been in labour for about twelve hours and they'd just taken her into the delivery suite.'

'He was cutting it a bit fine, wasn't he?' Wolff commented, his dark brows meeting in a frown of concern. 'I'm surprised he didn't ask you to take over hours ago.'

'He would have done if he'd realised she was in labour. Polly only phoned him about an hour ago to tell him what was happening—said she didn't want him getting in a state when she wasn't sure if it was a false alarm.'

Hannah and Laura shared an understanding look.

Having lost one child, Nick had tended to treat Polly like a fragile flower while Polly's reaction to her own loss had been to make sure that she was kept as busy as possible. It was almost predictable that, without taking any silly risks, Polly would avoid going into hospital until the last moment.

'Anyway,' Leo continued, 'I phoned up a couple of minutes ago to find out how things were progressing. Apparently Nick arrived just in time to encourage her to push. Mother and daughter are doing well and father is delighted but still in shock.'

Amid exclamations of surprise and delight, there was one dissenting growl.

'If you try anything like that. . .' Wolff began, wagging a threatening finger at Laura.

'Don't worry, my love,' Laura said soothingly. 'By the time these two are ready to arrive I'll probably be only too pleased to put my feet up and let you do all the hard work. . .'

Leo wrapped his arms around Hannah's waist and she shivered deliciously as he tightened them until she was leaning against him, her head naturally falling back to rest on his shoulder.

'Shall we tell them?' Leo whispered in her ear, typically making the decision a joint one.

For just a second Hannah wanted to keep their secret to themselves for a little bit longer but then she nodded, turning her head to graze a kiss over his jaw.

'Actually,' he began, and had to pause to clear his throat. 'We've got a bit of news, too. Hannah's decided to postpone her surgery.'

There was a second's silence as Laura and Wolff took in the announcement, but they were obviously at a loss as to how they were supposed to react.

With Leo's encouragement, Hannah had finally told her friends about the traumas of the last couple of years, and had received nothing but support from them while she made her decision about having the implants done. For her to have changed her mind at such short notice was obviously puzzling them.

'What he hasn't told you,' Hannah added as she took pity on them, 'is that when I was having all my tests done before surgery they found out that I was pregnant so I decided—'

She didn't get a chance to finish before Laura and Wolff were swamping her with exclamations of pleasure and hugs of congratulations.

'So, what's it going to be?' Wolff asked when everything calmed down again. 'Are you going to go one better and manage triplets?'

'God, I hope not,' Leo said with a dramatic shudder, his arms tightening around Hannah again. 'It's enough of a shock to know there's *one* on the way.'

Hannah began to chuckle.

'I hate to think what the hospital grapevine is going to make of this when the news gets out—it was bad enough when one after the other of us paired up and got married, but now that we've all managed to get pregnant one after the other they're going to call us three of a kind!'

'I don't think that would be so bad,' Leo said, his voice slightly rough as he leaned his cheek against hers. 'All three couples have been lucky enough to find happiness within the last year so I say roll on the next year and here's to the future!'

'As long as it doesn't involve too many sets of twins,' Wolff added warily. 'We don't want an A and E department population explosion. . .'

Modern Romance™
...seduction and passion guaranteed

Tender Romance™
...love affairs that last a lifetime

Sensual Romance™
...sassy, sexy and seductive

Blaze
...sultry days and steamy nights

Medical Romance™
...medical drama on the pulse

Historical Romance™
...rich, vivid and passionate

27 new titles every month.

With all kinds of Romance for every kind of mood...

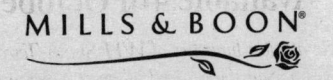

MILLS & BOON

Helen Brooks Kate Walker Sophie Weston

3 Full-length novels ONLY £4.99

MILLS & BOON

Blind-Date Brides

Marriages made...by matchmakers!

Available 4th October

Available at most branches of WH Smith, Tesco, Martins, Borders, Eason, Sainsbury's and all good paperback bookshops.

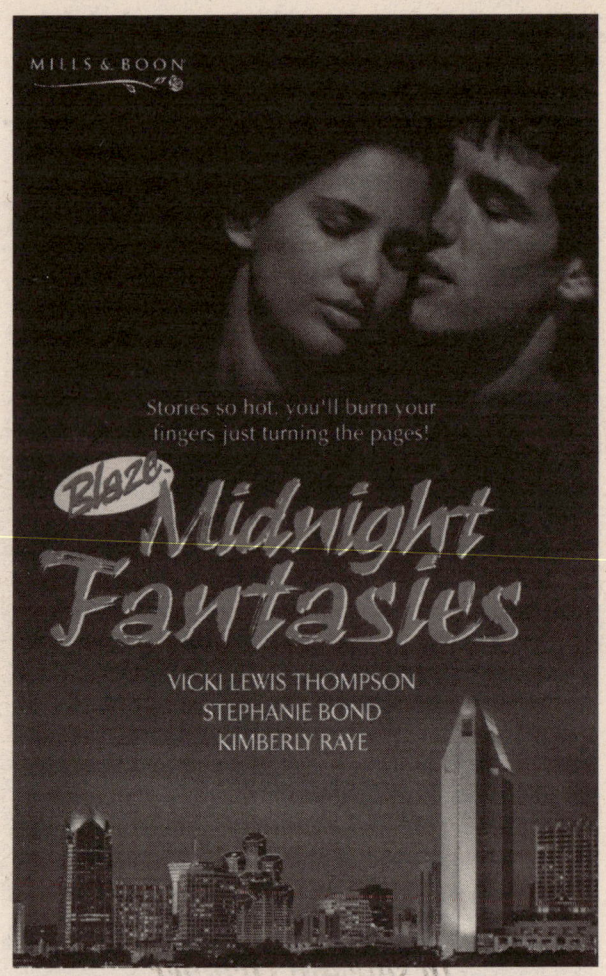

MILLS & BOON

Stories so hot, you'll burn your
fingers just turning the pages!

Blaze
Midnight Fantasies

VICKI LEWIS THOMPSON
STEPHANIE BOND
KIMBERLY RAYE

Available from 16th August 2002

*Available at most branches of WH Smith,
Tesco, Martins, Borders, Eason, Sainsbury's
and most good paperback bookshops.*

0802/24/MB47

Don't miss *Book Two* of this BRAND-NEW 12 book collection 'Bachelor Auction'.

Who says money can't buy love?

On sale 4th October

Available at most branches of WH Smith, Tesco, Martins, Borders, Eason, Sainsbury's, and all good paperback bookshops.

BA/RTL/2

MILLS & BOON

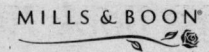

DON'T MISS...

MILLS & BOON

BETTY NEELS

ONLY BY CHANCE
& A HAPPY MEETING

THE ULTIMATE COLLECTION

VOLUME THREE

On sale 6th September 2002

*Available at most branches of WH Smith, Tesco, Martins, Borders,
Eason, Sainsbury's and all good paperback bookshops.*